Franz Ahn

A New Practica and Easy Method of Learning the German Language

1st course. 2d American, from the 8th London ed

Franz Ahn

A New Practica and Easy Method of Learning the German Language
1st course. 2d American, from the 8th London ed

ISBN/EAN: 9783337387624

Printed in Europe, USA, Canada, Australia, Japan

Cover: Foto ©Andreas Hilbeck / pixelio.de

More available books at **www.hansebooks.com**

A NEW

PRACTICAL AND EASY METHOD

OF LEARNING

THE

GERMAN LANGUAGE.

BY

F. AHN,

DOCTOR OF PHILOSOPHY AND PROFESSOR AT THE COLLEGE OF NEUSS.

———

FIRST COURSE.

SECOND AMERICAN FROM THE EIGHTH LONDON EDITION,

——— • ✦ • ———

NEW YORK:
D. APPLETON AND COMPANY
549 & 551 BROADWAY.
1872.

PREFACE.

Learn a foreign language as you learn your mother tongue: this is in a few words the method which I have adopted in this little work. It is the way that nature herself follows, it is the same which the mother points out in speaking to her child, repeating to it a hundred times the same words, combining them imperceptibly, and succeeding in this way to make it speak the same language she speaks. To learn in this manner is no longer a study, it is an amusement.

Supposing the pupil to have learned his own language by principles, I thought it proper to add a few rules, which will serve to shorten the course and render the progress more secure.

THE AUTHOR.

TABLE

OF THE GERMAN DECLENSIONS.

ARRANGED

By Dr. MARTIN WEISS,

FROM THE UNIVERSITY OF BERLIN, LATE FRENCH AND GERMAN MASTER, AT THE
ROYAL COLLEGE DUNGANNON.

———

Almost every German Grammar used in England states
a different number of Declensions. Dr. NŒHDEN whose
Grammar is in every respect unquestionably the best, has
attempted to reduce the number of Declensions to four, and
I think most successfully. But German Grammarians have
not adopted his system. WENDEBORN who tries to imitate
the Latin gives five Declensions, whilst Dr. RENDER in his
anxiety to smooth the way to the learner, has made appear
an absurd doctrine of one Declension. In Germany itself
Grammarians follow either ADELUNG or KLOPSTOCK. The
system of the former being the best and offering the least
confusion to the student. I have tried in the following
table to arrange the Declensions of all German Nouns upon
ADELUNG's plan.

I. The Genitive Singular being alike, and the Plural different.

	I. Der Hund.		II. Das Kind.		III. Der Engel.	
	Sing.	Plur.	Sing.	Plur.	Sing.	Plur.
N.	—	e.	—	er.	—	—
G.	es, s.	e.	es, s.	er.	s.	—
D.	e.	en.	e.	ern.	—	n.
A.	—	e.	—	er.	—	—

Column I — Der Hund.

Of this Declension are,

1. All derivatives in ling, and ing, as der Jüngling, Häring.
2. All Neuters in niß, as das Bildniß, Bekenntniß.
3. The Nouns collective beginning with ge, and not ending in e, l, or t, as das Gericht, Geschenk, Gebüsch.

Those collectives which end in e or r sion are of the third declension.

4. Foreign words in an, in, on, er, ier, an, and al, as Altar, Principal, &c. Several have the diphthong in the plural, as,

The Masculines,

Der Abt.........Aebte,
Ball............Bälle,
Rock...........Röcke.

The Neuters,

Das Arsenal......Arsenäle,
Chor............Chöre,
Floß............Flöße,
Boot...........Böte.

Column II — Das Kind.

Most Nouns of this Declension are of the Neuter Gender, as, das Amt, das Bild, &c. and those which have an a, o, or u, take the diphthong in the Plural, as, das Buch, die Bücher; das Blatt, die Blätter; das Dorf, die Dörfer.

The few Masculines of this declension are,

Der Bösewicht,	The Wicked man,
Geist,	Spirit,
Gott,	God,
Irrthum,	Error,
Leib,	Body,
Mann,	Man,
Ort,	Place,
Rand,	Border,
Reichthum,	Riches,
Dormund,	Guardian,
Wald,	Forest,
Wurm,	Worm.

Column III — Der Engel.

Of this Declension are all the Nouns.

1. In el, Masculine and Neuter.
2. In er, Masculine and Neuter.
3. In en, Masculine and Neuter.
4. The Diminutives in chen and lein, which are all of the Neuter Gender.
5. Neuters beginning with the syllable be and ge, and ending with e, as:

Das Gemälde, the Picture.
Das Gebirge, the Mountain.

6. Das Größe, the Inheritance.
Das Ende, the End.
and Der Käse, the Cheese.

II. The Plural being alike and the Genitive Singular different.

IV. Der Stiefel.	
Sing.	Plur.
—,	en, n.
en, n.	
en, n.	
en, n.	

The Substantives of this declension are mostly

1. Radical words ending in e, and consequently taking only n, as der Burge, der Affe.
2. The proper Names of Nations when they are of two syllables only, as der Baier, der Ungar, der Preuße, &c.
3. Masculines ending with two or three consonants, as Fürst, Herr, Mensch.
4. Foreign words in ant, at, aff, ent, et, iff, it, &c. with the accent upon the last syllable, as Abvokat, Client, Atheist, Christ.
5. The Names of Foreign Nations, with the accent upon the last syllable, as Polak, &c.
6. The Masculines,
Fels, Rock,
Rahm, Cream.

V. Der Friede.	
Sing.	Plur.
—	en.
ens.	en.
en.	en.
en.	en.

Of this Declension are the Masculines,
Funke, Spark,
Gedanke, Idea,
Glaube, Faith,
Haufe, Crowd,
Name, Name,
Saame, Seed,
Schade, Damage,
Wille, Will,
Buchstabe, Letter,
Eifer, Terror,
Schmerz, Pain.

The only Neuter of this declension is,

Das Herz, The Heart.

VI. Das Auge.	
Sing.	Plur.
—	en, n.
es, s.	en, n.
e.	en, n.
—	en, n.

Of this Declension are,
1. The radical words,
das Bett, the Bed,
der Daumen, the Thumb,
der Helm, the Helmet,
das Ohr, the Ear,
der See, the Lake,
der Sporn, the Spur,
der Staat, the State,
der Herrath, the Ornament.

2. Some Foreign words, as der Affe, Fett, Insekt, Thron.

3. Derivatives of the Masculine Gender,
Bauer, Peasant,
Ritter, Spangle,
Gevatter, Godfather,
Nachbar, Neighbor,
Pantoffel, Slipper,
Stachel, Thorn, Sting,
Stiefel, Boot,
Better, Uncle, Cousin,
Faber, Quarrel, Brawl,

which from their termination should follow the third declension, but are excepted.

III. The words remaining unchanged in the Singular.

VII.
Die Absicht.

Sing.	Plur.
--	en, n.
--	en, n.
--	en, n.
--	en, n.

Of this Declension are,

1. All Nouns Feminine in e, as die Amme, die Mumme.
2. Those in ee, and ie, die See, die Harmonie.
3. The Feminines in el, as die Gabel.
4. The Feminines in er, as die Feder.
5. Radical Feminines, as Thür, Uhr.
6. Derivatives with a particle in the beginning, as die Anbacht.
7. Those with an end-syllable, and particularly the words in ei, heit, in, keit, schaft, and ung.
8. Foreign words of the Feminine Gender which have the accent upon the last syllable, as: die Natur, Nature,
Figur, Figure,
Cur, Cure,
Diät, Regimen,
Facultät, Faculty,
Proving, Province,
Person, Person,
Musik, Music.

VIII.
Die Stadt.

Sing.	Plur.
--	e.
--	e.
--	en.
--	e.

Of this Declension are the following radical Nouns Feminine.

Angst, Fear,
Art, Axe,
Armbrust, Crossbow,
Aberlaß, Bloodletting,
Bank, Form, Bank,
Braut, Bride,
Brust, Breast,
Brunst, Conflagration,
Burg, Castle,
Faust, Fist,
Flucht, Flight,
Furcht, Fright,
Frucht, Fruit,
Gans, Goose,
Gruft, Pit, Grave,
Gunst, Favor,
Hand, Hand,
Kluft, Clift,
Kraft, Power,
Kunst, Art,
Kuh, Cow,
Laus, Louse,
Luft, Air,
Leinwand, Linen,
Lust, Lust,
Macht, Might,
Magd, Servant girl,
Maus, Mouse,
Nacht, Night,
Naht, Seam,
Noth, Necessity,
Nuß, Nut,
Sau, Sow,
Schnur, Lace, String,
Schwulst, Swelling,
Wand, Wall,
Wurst, Sausage,
Zunft, Society.

All those in a, o, u, take the diphthong in the Plural, except Leinwand.
All the Feminines in niß are also of this declension, as die Betrübniß, die Besorgniß, die Finsterniß, &c.

(1.)

(2.)

The Small Alphabet.

c	d	e	f	ff	g	h	i	j	k

n	o	p	q	r	s	s	st	sz

u	v	w	(x)	y	z	ue	oe	ae

CA. A. L. B. C. C. D. (E. F. F.

G. G. H. H. I. I. J. J. K. K. L. L.

M. M. N. O. O. P. P. Q. Q. R. R.

S. S. T. U. U. V. V. W. X. X.

Y. Y. Z. Z.

A. Davidson

A. Davidson

Double Letters and Combinations.

Ae Ae ä ae Oe Oe ö oe Ue Ue ü ue

ai ai au au äu aeu uei ui eu

ff ch gf ph ff th ß sz ff ss ff sch

tz tz ik ck.

I. THE ALPHABET.

The German Alphabet is composed of the following twenty-six letters:

𝔄, a, a.		𝔐, n, n.
𝔅, b, b.		𝔇, o, o.
ℭ, c, c.		𝔓, p, p.
𝔇, d, d.		𝔇, q, q.
𝔈, e, e.		𝔑, r, r.
𝔉, f, f.		𝔖, ſ, ß, s.
𝔊, g, g.		𝔗, t, t.
𝔥, h, h.		𝔘, u, u.
𝔍, i, i.		𝔙, v, v.
𝔍, j, j.		𝔚, w, w.
𝔎, k, k.		𝔛, x, x.
𝔏, l, l.		𝔜, y, y.
𝔐, m, m.		𝔷, z, z.

The vowels are: a, ä, e, i, o, ö, u, ü. The diphthongs or compound vowels are: ai, ei, au, äu, eu; all other letters are consonants.

II. SIMPLE VOWELS.

Every vowel, followed by two consonants, is pronounced short: followed by only one consonant, it is long.

𝔄, a, is pronounced like *a* in the English word *father*.

Alter,	banken,	Frage,
Vater,	laben,	Galle.

Ae, ä, is pronounced like *a* in the English word *care*.

Kälte,	Lärm,	Blätter,
Käſe,	Säbel,	Länder.

𝕰, 𝖊, is pronounced like *e* in the English word *letter*

Efel,   denfen,   Titel,
Efel,   trennen   Männer,
reden,   Ende,   Rebe.

𝕴, 𝖎, is pronounced like *e* in the English word *me*.

Iltis,   immer,   in,
finden,   Silber,   Kind.

𝕺, 𝖔, is pronounced like *o* in the English word *hope*.

Ofen,   sondern,   Koft,
rollen,   ober,   Wort.

𝕺𝖊, 𝖔̈, is pronounced like *u* in the English word *murder*.

Böse,   tönen,   Löffel,
Löwe,   können,   Dörfer.

𝖀, 𝖚, is pronounced like *oo* in the English word *roof*.

Blut,   Bruder,   Mund,
Blume,   Mutter,   Stunde.

𝖀𝖊, 𝖚̈, is pronounced like the French *u*. There is no corresponding sound in the English language.

üben,   müde,   Mütter,
trübe,   prüfen,   Nüffe.

𝖄, 𝖞, has the sound of the German *i*, by which it is generally replaced.

III. DOUBLE VOWELS.

The double vowels, aa, ee, oo, are no diphthongs, because only one letter is sounded, and the second only serves to indicate that the syllable is long.

Aar,   Meer,   Moos,
Saal,   Seele,   Boot.

𝕴𝖊, 𝖎𝖊, is pronounced like *ea* in the English word *meat*.

Biene,   Bier,   tief,
lieben,   Dieb,   Lied.

IV. DIPHTHONGS.

In the German diphthongs, the two vowels must be sounded one after the other, but so quickly as to form only one syllable.

𝖀𝖎 and 𝖊𝖎 are pronounced almost alike, and have the sound of the English *i* in the word *fire*.

| Salte, | Kaiſer, | leiben, |
| Seite, | reimen, | Wein. |

Au, is pronounced like *ou* in the English word *house.*

| Maus, | rauben, | blau, |
| Baum, | laufen, | kaum, |

Aeu and **eu,** are both pronounced like *oy* in the English word *joy.*

| Mäuſe, | Beutel, | Freund, |
| Bäume, | Feuer, | Treue. |

V. CONSONANTS.

The pronunciation of the consonants differ but little in the two languages; the scholar should remark the following peculiarities.

C, c, before ä, e, and i, is pronounced like *ts.*

| Cäſar, | Cedar, | Citrone. |

Before a, o, u, before a consonant and at the end of a syllable, it is pronounced like *k,* by which in most cases it may be replaced.

| Carl, | Curt, | Tombac, |
| Conrad, | Creole, | Claſſe. |

Ch, at the beginning of a word is pronounced like *k,* except in words derived from the French, when it preserves the French pronunciation.

| Chor, | Charlatan, |
| Chriſt, | Charivari. |

In the middle or at the end of a word ch has a pronunciation quite peculiar to the German language, and more or less gutteral, but for which no corresponding sound can be found in English; it is like the Scotch *ch* in the word *loch* after a, o, u, au, but softer after ä, e, i, ö, ü, äu, eu, and after a consonant.

Dach,	Rauch,	nichts,
Loch,	Küche,	rechnen,
Buch,	Kirche,	ſuchen,
Licht,	Tochter,	Bäumchen.

chs or **chſ** is pronounced like *x* when these consonants belong to the root or radical syllable.

| Wachs, | Fuchs, | wachſen, |
| Ochs, | ſechs, | Büchſe. |

1*

But the ch preserves its gutteral pronunciation, when it stands before the s or ſ by contraction or in a composed word.

nachsehen, wachsen, des Buchs instead of des Buches

G, g, at the beginning of a syllable is pronounced like the English *g* in the word *good;* but between two vowels, in the middle of a word, and at the end of a syllable, it has a sound like the ch, only much softened.

gehen,	groß,	Gabe,
Wagen,	Sieg,	artig,
Regen,	Krug,	richtig.

After n at the end of a word it is pronounced like a very soft *k*.

Gang,	Ring,	Sprung.

H, h, is always aspirated at the beginning of a syllable.

hier,	hart,	Hecht,
Haus,	Himmel,	Freiheit.

The aspiration becomes however almost imperceptible before an e in the end-syllables.

Reihe,	Ruhe,	ſehen.

After a vowel or a t, the h is not pronounced, but only indicates that the syllable is long.

Hahn,	Stroh,	Thier,
Mehl,	Reh,	Thür,
Uhr,	früh,	Rath.

J, j, only stands at the beginning of a syllable, and is pronounced like the English *y* in the word *yet.*

Jahr,	Joch,	Jugend.

ck replaces the double k, and is pronounced short.

Stock,	Brücke,	Acker.

Qu, qu, has the sound of *qu* in English.

Qual,	Quelle,	Quer.

S, ſ, s, at the beginning of a syllable is pronounced like the English *z*, at the end of a syllable, however, like the English *s*.

Sommer,	Reiſe,	Haus,
Sack,	Eiſen,	Reis.

The long ſ is placed at the beginning and in the middle, s only at the end of syllables. If in a non-

composed word there are two ſ, one after another, they
are written ſſ.

Waſſer, wiſſen, müſſen.

ß is only placed at the end or in the middle of syl·
lables; it is always preceded by a long vowel, and has
the sound of the English *ss*.

Straße, groß, fließen.

Sch, ſch is pronounced like the English *sh*.

Schatten, Schule, Peitſche,
ſchlafen, Schild, Tiſch.

ſt and ſp are pronounced like *st* and *sp* in English;
but in some parts of Germany they pronounce ſt at the
beginning of a word like *sht*, and ſp like *shp*.

Stuhl, ſtehlen, ſpielen,
Stern, ſprechen, ſtechen.

B, v has the sound of *f*.

Vater, Vogel, Vieh.

W, w is pronounced like the English *v*.

Welt, Wieſe, Wand.

Z, z is sounded like *ts*.

Zahl, Zorn, Holz,
Zeit, zwanzig, Herz.

ß replaces the double z and is pronounced very hard.

Blitz, Nutzen, ſetzen.

VI. SYLLABIC ACCENT.

The Germans never pronounce several successive syl·
lables one after the other with the same force; the principal syllables are pronounced with a louder, and the
others with a softer tone. The end-syllables in German
words are pronounced very softly.

The accent is always laid upon the radical syllable,
that is, upon the one which includes the principal idea;
thus in the word Gerechtigkeit (justice) which is derived
from recht (just), the second syllable is pronounced more
strongly than the rest.

In compound words, the first syllable always has the
accent, because it presents the principal idea and modifies the following one: Blumengarten, Gartenblume.

PART I.

1.

Singular. ich bin, I am;
bu bift, thou art;
er ift, he is;
fie ift, she is;
Plural. wir find, we are;
ihr feib, you are;
fie find, they are.

Gut, good; groß, great, large, big; flein, little, small; reich, rich; arm, poor; jung, young; alt, old; mübe, tired; frank, ill, sick.

Ich bin groß. Du bift flein. Er ift alt. Sie ift gut. Wir find jung. Ihr feib reich. Sie find arm. Bin ich groß? Bift bu mübe? Ift er frank? Ift fie jung? Sinb wir reich? Seib ihr arm? Sinb fie alt?

2.

I am little. Thou art young. We are tired. They are rich. Art thou sick? You are poor. Is she old? Are you sick? Are they good? He is tall (groß). Am I poor?

3.

Nicht, not.

Starf, strong; treu, faithful; faul, idle, lazy; fleißig, diligent; böfe, wicked, naughty; traurig, sad; glücflich, happy; höflich, polite.

Bift bu böfe? Ich bin nicht böfe. Er ift traurig. Wir find nicht ftarf. Sinb fie treu? Bift bu nicht glücflich? Ihr feib nicht fleißig. Sie ift nicht faul. Ift er nicht mübe? Wir find nicht arm. Sinb fie nicht höflich? Du bift nicht frank.

4.

I am not tall. They are idle. She is not ill. We are not happy. He is not short (flein). Are you not tired? They are not rich. Is he not diligent? Thou art not

12

strong. They are not happy. He is not polite. Are they not faithful? Is she not rich? He is not wicked.

5.

Masculine nouns : ber Bater, the father; ber Garten, the garden;
Feminine " : bie Mutter, the mother; bie Stabt, the town;
Neuter " : bas Kinb, the child; bas Haus, the house.
Schön, beautiful, fine; lang, long; hoch, high; neu, new; unb, and; sehr, very.

Der Bater ist gut. Die Mutter ist traurig. Das Kinb ist faul. Der Garten ist nicht sehr lang. Die Stabt ist groß unb reich. Das Haus ist nicht hoch. Ist ber Garten schön? Ist ber Bater krant? Ist bas Kinb nicht fleißig? Ist bas Haus neu? Der Bater unb bie Mutter sinb glücklich.

Observation. All German substantives begin with a capital letter. When two or more substantives follow each other, the article must be repeated before each, unless they are all of the same gender.

6.

The house is not new. The mother and (the) child are ill. The town is very beautiful. The child is not naughty. The father is very old. The house and (the) garden are very large. Is the mother not happy? The house is not very old. Is the garden not very fine? The house is very small.

7.

Masc. bieser Baum, this tree.
Fem. biese Frau, this woman.
Neut. bieses Pferb, this horse.

Der Mann, the man; ber Berg, the mountain; bie Blume, the flower; bas Fenster, the window; offen, open; zufrieben, contented, satisfied, pleased; ober, or.

Dieser Mann ist sehr arm. Dieses Fenster ist sehr hoch. Diese Blume ist schön. Dieses Pferb ist jung unb start. Ist biese Frau glücklich? Dieser Bater unb biese Mutter sinb nicht zufrieben. Dieser Baum ist sehr groß. Diese Frau ist arm unb krant. Dieses Kinb ist sehr böse. Dieser Mann ist nicht höflich. Bist bu traurig ober krant?

8.

This woman is tired. This mountain is not high. Is this child good or naughty? The man is not satisfied.

This child is not very diligent. Is this garden small or
large? Art thou not contented? This window is not open.
Is this house old or new? This tree is very fine. Is
this man rich or poor? This town is very dull (traurig).

9.

Masc.	Fem.	Neut.
Ein,	eine,	ein, a;
mein,	meine,	mein, my;
dein,	deine,	dein, thy;

Der Bruder, the brother; die Schwester, the sister; die Feder, the pen
das Buch, the book; der Freund, the friend; Karl, Charles; Louise,
Louisa; wo, where; hier, here; noch, still, yet; aber, but.

Mein Bruder ist traurig. Meine Schwester ist krank.
Mein Buch ist schön. Ist dein Garten groß? Ist deine
Feder gut? Ist dein Pferd klein? Karl ist noch ein Kind.
Berlin ist eine Stadt. Louise ist meine Schwester. Dein
Bruder ist mein Freund. Dein Vater ist nicht hier. Wo ist
mein Buch? Ist mein Buch nicht hier? Ist deine Mutter
noch krank? Ich bin noch nicht müde, aber dein Bruder und
deine Schwester sind sehr müde.

10.

Charles is my brother. This child is my sister. Thou
art my friend. Thy garden is very large. Where is thy
mother? A friend is faithful. Is this child thy brother?
This horse is still young. Where is my pen? Thy pen
is here. Louisa is still a child. Thy brother is idle.
My friend is very diligent.

11.

Masc.	Fem.	Neut.
Unser,	unsere,	unser, our;
euer,	euere,	euer, your;
ihr,	ihre,	ihr, their.

Der Sohn, the son; die Tochter, the daughter; die Thüre, the door;
immer, always.

Obs. In addressing any one, the third person plural is from politeness used instead of the second: Sie sind, instead of ihr seid. For the
same reason Ihr is used instead of euer. In this case the pronoun is
always written with a capital letter.

Unser Garten ist groß. Unsere Mutter ist krank. Unser
Pferd ist schön. Dieser Mann ist unser Vater. Diese Frau
ist unsere Mutter. Karl ist euer Bruder. Louise ist eure
Schwester. Ist Ihr Sohn fleißig? Ist Ihre Tochter zufrieden? Wo ist Ihr Buch? Unser Haus ist alt. Unsere

Thüre ist immer offen. Dieser Vater und diese Mutter sind sehr traurig; ihr Sohn ist immer krank.

12.

Our father is good. Our mother is little. Our child is ill. Is this man your brother? Is this woman your mother? Your son is not always diligent. Is your horse beautiful? This child is our brother. Is Charles not your friend? Louisa is not your sister.

13.

Klein, little, small; kleiner, smaller;
alt, old; älter, older;
groß, great.; größer, greater;
jung, young; jünger, younger;
fleißig, diligent; fleißiger, more diligent.

Nützlich, useful; unglücklich, unhappy; der Hund, the dog; die Katze, the cat; die Sonne, the sun; der Mond, the moon; als, than, as.

Obs. In forming the Comparative of an adjective, the radical vowel a generally changes into ä; o into ö; and u into ü.

Mein Bruder ist älter, als ich. Ich bin jünger, als mein Freund. Karl ist größer, als Louise. Dieser Mann ist größer, als wir. Der Hund ist treuer, als die Katze. Das Pferd ist schöner und nützlicher, als der Hund. Dieses Kind ist fleißiger, als du. Sie sind glücklicher, als Ihr Bruder. Karl ist stärker, als ich. Wir sind zufriedener, als ihr. Louise ist höflicher, als deine Schwester. Ist dein Bruder jünger, als du? Er ist älter, aber kleiner, als ich.

14

My brother is more diligent than thou. Thou art not younger than he. He is taller and stronger than I. Your son is younger than this child. The moon is smaller than the sun. Art thou older than I? This dog is finer than this cat. Your sister is politer than you. I am more contented than thou. You are richer than we. We are more unhappy than you.

15.

Gut, good; besser, better;
hoch, high; höher, higher;
dieser, diese, dieses, this, this one;
jener, jene, jenes, that, that one.

Das Eisen, the iron; das Blei, the lead; der Stahl, the steel; die Erde, the earth; schwer, heavy; hart, hard; theuer, dear; so, so, as; zu, too

Mein Buch ist schöner, als jenes. Meine Feder ist besser, als diese. Der Stahl ist härter, als das Eisen. Dieser Berg ist höher, als jener. Die Katze ist nicht so treu, als der Hund. Das Blei ist nicht so hart, als das Eisen. Ist Ihr Haus nicht größer, als jenes? Ist das Blei theurer, als das Eisen? Der Mond ist nicht so groß, als die Erde. Dieses Kind ist fleißiger, als jenes. Jene Frau ist ärmer, als diese. Unser Garten ist nicht so lang und schön, als dieser.

16.

(The) lead is heavier than (the) iron. This tree is not so high as that. Is this book not better than that? Our garden is smaller than this one. This house is higher than that one. (The) iron is more useful than (the) lead. I am not so old as he. (The) lead is not so dear as (the) steel. Our town is larger and finer than this one. We are not so rich as this man, but we are more contented than he.

17.

Singular.	ich habe, I have;
	du hast, thou hast;
	er, sie hat, he *or* she has;
Plural.	wir haben, we have;
	ihr habt, Sie haben, you have;
	sie haben, they have.

Die Uhr, the watch; das Messer, the knife; Recht, right; Unrecht, wrong; Heinrich, Henry; Ludwig, Lewis; für, for; auch, also; warum, why.

Obs. The Accusative of the fem. and neut. nouns is like the Nominative.—In German the verb *to have* is used with *right* and *wrong*, thus: ich habe Recht, er hat Unrecht.

Ich habe Recht. Du hast Unrecht. Ich habe ein Buch. Du hast eine Feder. Mein Bruder hat eine Uhr. Wir haben ein Haus. Ihr habt ein Pferd. Karl und Louise haben eine Katze. Hast du eine Schwester? Hat dieser Mann eine Tochter? Habt ihr ein Kind? Diese Uhr ist für meine Mutter? Diese Feder ist für Karl. Haben Sie noch Ihre Mutter? Warum hast du mein Messer? Ich habe dein Messer nicht.

18.

Charles, hast thou my pen? Louisa, hast thou my book? Henry has thy pen, and Lewis has thy book. Thou art right. My son is wrong. We have a book and a pen. Have you also a horse and a watch? This

knife is for Henry. Is this watch for thy mother? Has
your friend a knife? Charles and Lewis have a horse.
Has your father still a sister? Is this flower for my
daughter?

19.

Gefehen, seen; verloren, lost; gefunden, found; gefauft, bought; verfauft,
sold; genommen, taken.

Obs. The past participle is detached from the auxiliary and placed
at the end of the sentence.

Ich habe mein Buch verloren. Haft du mein Meffer ge=
funden? Ich habe dein Meffer nicht gefunden. Wo ist meine
Feder? Habt ihr meine Feder? Wir haben deine Feder
nicht. Mein Vater hat diefes Pferd gefauft. Wir haben
unfer Haus verfauft. Wo haft du meine Uhr gefunden?
Warum haben Sie meine Uhr genommen? Ich habe Ihre
Mutter und Ihre Schwefter gefehen. Warum hat Ihr Vater
diefes Haus nicht gefauft? Hat dein Bruder meine Feder
genommen? Er hat deine Feder nicht genommen.

20.

Where hast thou found this book? Have you lost
your pen? Has your father bought this horse? Why
have you sold your watch? Why have you not taken
my pen? My brother has found thy knife. We have seen
thy mother. I have not yet seen this woman. Charles
and Lewis have lost their mother; they are very sad.

21.

Nominative.	*Accusative.*	
Der Vater,	den Vater,	the father;
diefer Vater,	diefen Vater,	this father.

Der König, the king; der Hut, the hat, bonnet; der Stock, the stick,
cane; der Brief, the letter; geschrieben, written; erhalten, received, got;
oft, often; schon, already.

Obs. The subject is placed in the nominative case, and the object
in the accusative case.

Ich habe den König gefehen. Haft du den Brief erhalten?
Meine Schwefter hat den Brief nicht geschrieben. Heinrich
hat den Stock verloren. Mein Vater hat diefen Garten und
diefes Haus gefauft. Wo habt ihr diefen Hund und diefe
Katze gefunden? Ich habe diefen Mann schon oft gefehen.
Warum haben Sie diefen Hut genommen? Wir haben diefen
Brief gefunden. Hat dein Bruder diefen Stock verloren?

22.

We have sold the house and garden. Have you
bought this dog and this horse? I have seen the man
and woman, the son and daughter. I have not written
this letter. Where have you found this book and cane?
Has thy brother bought this tree? This letter is for
this man. Hast thou lost this hat? Hast thou not taken
this book and pen? Hast thou already seen the king?
I have not yet seen the king

23.

Nom. ein Garten, } a garden. *Nom.* mein Hund, } my dog.
Accus. einen Garten, *Acc.* meinen Hund,

Der Vogel, the bird; der Stuhl, the chair; der Tisch, the table; der
Bleistift, the pencil; der Nachbar, the neighbor.

Mein Bruder ist sehr zufrieden; er hat einen Vogel. Hast
du einen Brief erhalten? Ich habe meinen Hut verloren.
Haben Sie meinen Hund schon gesehen? Wir haben einen
Tisch und einen Stuhl gekauft. Mein Bruder hat deinen
Stock genommen. Wo hast du deinen Bleistift gekauft? Wir
haben unsern Vater und unsere Mutter verloren. Ich habe
Ihren Brief nicht erhalten. Hat dein Bruder unsern Garten
und unser Haus schon gesehen? Unser Nachbar hat den König
gesehen. Hast du diesen Vogel gekauft oder jenen?

24.

We have lost our dog. This man has lost a son and
a daughter. Where have you found my pencil? Have
you already seen my brother and mother? I have bought
a bonnet for my sister. Our neighbor has found thy
knife and cane. Where hast thou bought this table?
Thy brother has taken my chair. Have you written a
letter? We have found this stick and that one.

25.

Nom. sein, seine, sein, } his, its; ihr, ihre, ihr, } her.
Accus. seinen, seine, sein, ihren, ihre, ihr,

Gelesen, read; gekannt, known; der Onkel, the uncle; die Tante, the
aunt; der Fingerhut, the thimble; die Scheere, the scissors.

Mein Freund ist traurig; sein Vater und seine Mutter
sind krank. Meine Tante ist zufrieden; ihr Sohn und ihre
Tochter sind sehr fleißig. Heinrich hat seinen Stock, seine

Uhr und fein Meffer verloren. Louife hat ihren Fingerhut, ihre Feder und ihr Buch verloren. Euer Onkel hat fein Haus und feinen Garten verkauft. Diefe Frau hat ihren Mann und ihr Kind verloren. Diefe Tochter hat einen Brief für ihre Mutter gefchrieben. Karl hat feinen Vater nicht gekannt. Die Tante hat deinen und meinen Brief gelefen.

26.

The father has lost his son. This mother has lost her daughter. My uncle has sold his watch. Our aunt has sold her scissors. Henry has found his pencil. Louisa has found her thimble.. I have seen this man and his son, this woman and her daughter. My mother has lost her pen and her knife. My brother has taken his hat. I have seen your aunt; has she still her horse? This man is very sad; he has lost his wife (Frau). Charles has written a letter for his father. My aunt has bought this book for her son.

27.

Nom. die Mutter, the mother;   diefe Mutter, this mother;
Gen. der Mutter, of the mother;   diefer Mutter, of this mother.
Die Magd, the maid-servant; die Königin, the queen; die Nachbarin, the female neighbor; angekommen, arrived; abgereift, departed.

Die Mutter der Königin ift angekommen. Der Vater der Nachbarin ift abgereift. Ich habe den Garten der Tante gefehen. Haben Sie den Bleiftift der Schwefter gefunden? Diefe Frau ift die Schwefter der Nachbarin. Diefer Mann ift der Bruder der Magd. Das Kind diefer Frau ift immer krank.

28.

The bonnet of the mother is beautiful. The sister of the queen is not beautiful. Is the father of the servant arrived? Are you the brother of the (female) neighbor? I am the sister of this woman. Hast thou taken the chair of the sister? Have you seen the horse of the aunt? We have known the father of this servant.

29.

Nom. der Vater, the father;   diefer Vater, this father;
Gen. des Vaters, of the father;   diefes Vaters, of this father,
Nom. das Kind, the child;   diefes Kind, this child;
Gen. des Kindes, of the child;   diefes Kindes, of this child.

Der Schuhmacher, the shoemaker; der Schneider, the tailor; der Gärtner, the gardener; der Kaufmann, the merchant; der Arzt, the physician; das Zimmer, the room; das Volk, the people.

Obs. All neuter nouns and most masculine nouns take **s** or **es** in
the Genitive Singular.

Die Magd des Schneiders ist krank. Der Sohn des Nach=
bars ist noch sehr jung. Die Blume des Gärtners ist sehr
schön. Der Garten des Königs ist sehr groß. Der König
ist der Vater des Volkes. Die Frau des Arztes ist immer
zufrieden. Ich habe den Garten des Onkels gesehen. Wir
haben das Pferd des Kaufmanns gekauft. Hast du den Blei=
stift des Bruders genommen? Wo ist die Magd des Schuh=
machers? Die Thüre des Zimmers ist immer offen. Die
Tochter dieses Mannes ist abgereist. Wir haben die Mutter
dieses Kindes gekannt. Der Garten dieses Hauses ist klein.

30.

This man is the brother of the gardener. This woman
is the sister of the shoemaker. This child is the son
of the tailor. The door of the house is not open. I
have seen the son and daughter of the physician. We
have seen the horse of the merchant. The servant of
the neighbor is the sister of this gardener. Why is the
door of this room open? We have known the son of this
merchant. The dog of the neighbor is faithful. The
mother of this child is arrived.

31.

Nom. ein Vater, eine Mutter, ein Kind;
Gen. eines Vaters, einer Mutter, eines Kindes.

Der Regenschirm, the umbrella; das Federmesser, the penknife; gestern,
yesterday.

Obs. The pronouns mein, dein, sein, ihr, unser, euer, are declined
like 'ein, eine, ein.

Sind Sie der Sohn eines Arztes? Ich bin der Sohn
eines Kaufmanns. Haben Sie das Haus meines Nachbars
gekauft? Der Bruder deines Freundes ist gestern angekom=
men. Wo ist der Regenschirm deines Onkels? Hast du
das Zimmer meiner Schwester gesehen? Wir haben den
Brief deiner Mutter gelesen. Mein Onkel hat das Haus
Ihres Vaters gekauft. Ich habe den Stock Ihres Bruders
verloren. Der Garten unsers Nachbars ist sehr groß. Unsere
Magd ist die Tochter eures Gärtners. Wo ist der Regen=

ſchirm unſerer Mutter? Karl hat den Fingerhut ſeiner
Schweſter genommen. Louiſe hat das Federmeſſer ihrer Tant.
genommen.

32.

I have found the hat of a child. Are you the servant
of my uncle? I am the servant of your tailor. The
penknife of thy brother is very good. The pen of thy
sister is not good. The house of our aunt is large.
Henry has lost the letter of his father. Louisa has
found the pen of her brother. Is the garden of our
uncle as fine as this one? We have found the hat of
your neighbor's son (the hat of the son of your neighbor.) Lewis has read the letter of his friend. Louisa
has bought a flower for a child of her sister.

33.

Nom. der Bruder, the brother;
Dat. dem Bruder, to the brother;

Nom. das Buch, the book;   die Schweſter, the sister,
Dat. dem Buche, to the book;   der Schweſter, to the sister.

Gehört, belongs; geliehen, lent; gegeben, given; geſchickt, sent; verſprochen, promised; gezeigt, shown; der Freund, the friend; die Freundin, the female friend.

Obs. 1. If the Genitive terminates in es, the Dative takes e, Buches,
Buche. 2. The Dative generally precedes the Accusative. 3. In interrogative and negative sentences the English auxiliary verb *to do* is
not translated in German.

Dieſes Haus gehört dem Onkel meines Nachbars. Jener
Garten gehört der Tante meines Freundes. Ich habe dem
Vater einen Brief geſchrieben. Sie hat der Freundin ihrer
Schweſter eine Blume gegeben. Karl hat der Schweſter ſein
Federmeſſer geliehen. Haſt du dem Arzte mein Buch geſchickt?
Ich habe dieſem Kinde einen Vogel verſprochen. Heinrich hat
dieſer Frau unſern Regenſchirm geliehen. Louiſe hat dieſem
Manne unſern Garten gezeigt. Ich habe meine Feder dem
Freunde meines Bruders gegeben.

34.

This hat belongs to the gardener. This house belongs
to the mother of my friend. I have written to my uncle
and aunt. My sister has lent her thimble to the friend
(fem.) of your brother. My uncle has sent a watch to
the son of your neighbor (fem.) Have you given a

chair to this child? Have you lent an umbrella to this woman? Does this garden belong to the king? (belongs this garden, &c.) No, it belongs to the sister of the king. We have sold our horse to the friend of our uncle. Does this knife belong to this or to that servant?

35.

Nom. ein Buch, a book; eine Feder, a pen;
Dat. einem Buche, to a book; einer Feder, to a pen.
Der Vetter, the cousin; die Base, the female cousin; Amalie, Amelia; der Gärtner, the gardener; die Gärtnerin, the gardener's wife.

Dieser Garten gehört einem Schuhmacher. Dieses Messer gehört einer Magd. Louise hat meinem Vater einen Brief geschrieben. Heinrich hat meiner Mutter eine Blume gegeben. Ich habe Ihrem Onkel mein Pferd geliehen. Sie haben unserer Tante ihr Haus verkauft. Karl hat seinem Freunde ein Buch geschickt. Amalie hat ihrer Freundin einen Fingerhut geliehen. Dieser Mann hat eurer Nachbarin einen Vogel geschickt? Hast du meinem Vater diese Uhr gegeben? Habt ihr unserer Base einen Bleistift geliehen?

36.

I have lent my pen to a friend of my brother's. Hast thou given thy cat to a friend (fem.) of my sister's? We have given the letter to a servant of the physician's Have you sent this flower to our gardener? This garden belongs to my cousin (masc. and fem.) This umbrella does not belong (belongs not) to your brother. Does this pen belong (belongs this pen) to thy brother or to thy sister? Has Henry written to his father or to his mother? Has Louisa written to her uncle or aunt?

37.

Von, of, from, by.
Of the mother, der Mutter, or von der Mutter;
of the child, des Kindes, or von dem Kinde;
of the father, des Vaters, or von dem Vater;
of this garden, dieses Gartens, or von diesem Garten;
of my sister, meiner Schwester, or von meiner Schwester.

Ich spreche, I speak, *or* I am speaking; wir sprechen, we speak, we are speaking; wird geliebt, is loved.

Obs. Of is expressed by the Genitive, when *of* relates to a substantive, and by von followed by the Dative, when *of* relates to a verb

Ich habe das Buch des Arztes gesehen. Haben Sie dieses Buch von dem Arzte erhalten? Wir haben den Garten unsers Nachbars gekauft. Haben Sie diesen Garten von Ihrem Nachbar gekauft? Ich habe diese Uhr von meinem Onkel erhalten. Heinrich hat einen Brief von seinem Vater und (von) seiner Mutter erhalten. Ich spreche von dem Könige und der Königin. Wir sprechen von Ihrem Bruder und Ihrer Schwester, von diesem Manne und dieser Frau. Sprechen Sie von meinem Vetter oder meiner Base? Heinrich wird von seinem Vater und seiner Mutter geliebt.

38.

I have received this horse from my friend. I have bought this cat of thy sister. Louisa has got an umbrella from her uncle and a watch from her aunt. I speak of this dog and of this cat, of this bird and of this flower. We are speaking of your cousin (masc. and fem.) Amelia is loved by her uncle and aunt. Our gardener's wife has received a letter from her son and daughter. Henry is the son of this shoemaker and Louisa is the daughter of this tailor.

39.

Schön, beautiful; schöner, more beautiful; der. schönste, the most beautiful;

gut, good; besser, better; der beste, the best;

hoch, high: höher, higher; der höchste, the highest.

Das Thier, the animal; der Löwe, the lion; der Tiger, the tiger; das Metall, the metal; das Silber, the silver; das Gold, the gold.

Obs. The Superlative is formed by adding ste or ste, and softening the radical vowel.

Die Katze ist nicht so stark, als der Hund. Der Löwe ist stärker, als der Tiger. Der Löwe ist das stärkste Thier. Mein Nachbar ist reicher, als Sie; er ist der reichste Mann der Stadt. Das Gold ist schwerer, als das Silber. Das Eisen ist nützlicher, als das Silber. Das Eisen ist das nützlichste Metall. Louise ist schöner, als Amalie; aber Heinrich ist das schönste Kind. Ludwig ist jünger, als du; er ist der jüngste Sohn unsers Nachbars. Karl ist älter, als ich; er ist der älteste Sohn meines Onkels. Der Hund ist sehr treu. Der Hund ist das treueste Thier. Dieses Buch ist besser, als jenes. Du bist der beste Freund meines Bruders. Das Haus dieses Kaufmannes ist das höchste der Stadt.

It is, es ist; that is, das ist.

This bird is very little; it is the smallest bird. Louisa is very beautiful; she is more beautiful than her sister. (The) silver is not so useful as (the) iron. The tiger is not so strong as the lion. The tailor is the happiest man in the town. Henry is more diligent than Lewis, but Charles is the most diligent. Thy umbrella is very beautiful; the umbrella of my cousin is the most beautiful. You are not so poor as my cousin; he is the poorest man in the town. My chair is too high; this one is higher; but the chair of my mother is the highest. I have given my brother the best pencil and the best pen.

41.

Nom. wer, who?
Dat. wem, to whom?
Acc. wen, whom?

Was, what; etwas, something; nichts, nothing; Jemand, anybody, somebody; Niemand, nobody; hier, here; da, there.

Wer ist da? Es ist der Schneider; es ist Heinrich: ich bin es. Wer ist jener Mann? Es ist der Schuhmacher; es ist der Sohn des Arztes. Wer hat diesen Brief geschrieben? Wem gehört dieser Hund? Er gehört unserm Nachbar. Wem gehört diese Uhr? Sie gehört meiner Schwester. Wem haben Sie den Hut gegeben? Von wem haben Sie diese Blume erhalten? Wen haben Sie gesehen? Was haben Sie verloren? Ich habe nichts verloren. Haben Sie etwas gefunden? Wo ist Ihr Bruder? Er ist nicht hier. Ist Jemand da? Es ist Niemand da. Hat Jemand meine Feder genommen? Niemand hat ihre Feder genommen.

42.

Who is there? It is my tailor; it is Charles. Who is that woman? It is the wife of the shoemaker; it is the servant of the neighbor. To whom have you lent your knife? To the son of the gardener. To whom has your brother sold his dog? To the sister of my friend. From whom hast thou received this bird? From the father of this girl. What have you bought? I have bought an umbrella for my cousin (fem.) What have you taken? I have taken nothing. Of whom do you speak? (sprechen Sie). I am speaking of nobody. Has anybody read my letter? Nobody has read your letter.

43.

Nom. welcher, welche, welches, who *or* which;
Dat. welchem, welcher, welchem, to whom *or* to which;
Acc. welchen, welche, welches, whom *or* which.

Der Tischler, the joiner; gemacht, made; ausgegangen, gone out; ge‑
weint, cried, wept; in, in; mit, with; bei, with (at the house of).

Obs. The prepositions in, mit, bei govern the Dative.

Welcher Tischler hat diesen Tisch gemacht? Welche Magd
hat diesen Brief geschrieben? Welches Kind hat geweint?
Welchen Hund haben Sie gekauft? Welche Uhr hast du ver‑
loren? Welches Haus hat Ihr Vater verkauft? Von wel‑
chem Volke sprechen Sie? Mit welchem Freunde bist du aus‑
gegangen? In welchem Garten hat er den Vogel gefunden?
Welche Feder hast du da? Welcher Frau hast du dein Messer
gegeben? Welchem Mädchen hast du deinen Fingerhut gelie‑
hen? Bei welchem Kaufmann haben Sie diesen Bleistift ge‑
kauft? Mit welcher Feder haben Sie diesen Brief geschrie‑
ben? Mit wem sind Sie angekommen?

44.

Where is your sister? She is in her garden. Where
is your brother? He is with (at the house of) his friend.
Is your father gone out? He is gone out with the phy‑
sician. Which hat have you bought? Which book have
you read? Which pen have you taken? Which boy is
the most diligent? Which watch is the best? From
which gardener hast thou received this flower? At the
house of (bei) which woman hast thou bought this
bird? In which house have you lost your thimble?
With whom is your brother departed? To which man
have you lent your umbrella? Which stick have you
lost? Which joiner has made this table?

45.

Der Apfel, the apple; die Birne, the pear; gegessen, eaten.

Obs. In those sentences, which begin with a relative pronoun, the
verb is placed at the end.

Wir haben einen Bruder, welcher sehr groß ist. Ihr habt
eine Schwester, welche sehr klein ist. Mein Sohn hat ein
Buch, welches sehr nützlich ist. Der Garten, welchen dein
Onkel gekauft hat, ist sehr schön. Die Feder, welche mein
Vetter gefunden hat, ist sehr gut. Ich habe das Haus ge‑
sehen, welches Ihr Vater gekauft hat. Haben Sie den Fin‑

2

gerhut gefunden, welchen meine Schwester verloren hat? Haſt du den Apfel gegeſſen, welchen du gefunden haſt? Ich habe die Birne gegeſſen, welche ich gekauft habe. Hier iſt der Mann, welchem Sie Ihren Brief gegeben haben. Hier iſt die Frau, welcher wir unſern Hund verkauft haben. Hier iſt der Arzt, von welchem wir ſo oft ſprechen.

46.

Obs. Instead of welcher &c. may be used der, die das; for instance: der Garten, den *or* welchen wir gekauft haben.

I have a dog which is very little. We have a cat which is very fine. My father has bought a house which is very beautiful. Have you seen the umbrella which my mother has bought? Hast thou found the pear which thy brother has lost? We have seen the horse which your uncle has sold. Where is the thimble which you have found? I have taken the pencil which my cousin has bought. Henry has eaten the apple which his brother has received. Have you seen the woman of whom we speak? Have you read the letter which I have written? Have you found the boy to whom this penknife belongs?

47.

Derjenige welcher, he who; diejenige welche, she who; dasjenige welches, that which.

Obs. Instead of derjenige &c. may also be used der, die das; for instance: der, welcher.

Derjenige, welcher zufrieden iſt, iſt reich. Dieſer Fingerhut iſt beſſer, als derjenige meiner Schweſter. Dieſe Uhr iſt kleiner, als diejenige deines Bruders. Dieſes Haus iſt ſchöner, als dasjenige unſeres Nachbars. Ich habe meinen Hut verloren und den meines Vetters. Wir haben deine Feder gefunden und die deines Freundes. Heinrich hat mein Zimmer geſehen und das meines Onkels. Haſt du meinen Stock genommen oder den meines Bruders? Das iſt nicht deine Blume, das iſt die meiner Mutter. Haben Sie mein Meſſer oder das des Gärtners? Sprechen Sie von meinem Sohne oder von dem des Arztes? Das Pferd, welches wir gekauft haben, iſt jünger, als dasjenige Ihres Vaters.

48.

He who is rich, is not always contented. My dog is more faithful than that of my uncle. Our servant is stronger than that of our neighbor. My room is larger than that of my friend. This umbrella is finer than that which we have bought. Have you taken my pen or that of my sister? This is not your pencil; it is that of my brother. I speak of my book and of that of your friend. Louisa has lost her thimble and that of her mother. Thou hast eaten my apple and that of my cousin. My watch is better than that of my cousin (fem.) I have received your letter and that of your brother.

49.

Heinrich, Henry ;	Louise, Louisa ;
Heinrichs, Henry's ;	Louisens, Louisa's ;
dem Heinrich, to Henry ;	der Louise, to Louisa ;
von Heinrich, of *or* from Henry ;	von Louisen, of *or* from Louisa.
Wilhelm, William ;	Wien, Vienna ;
Johann, John ;	Köln, Cologne ;
Emilie, Emily ;	Aachen, Aix-la-Chapelle ;
heißt, is called ;	geht, goes ; wohnt, lives.

Er heißt Karl, his name is Charles.

The hat of Henry, der Hut Heinrichs; to Brussels, nach Brüssel; at Brussels, zu *or* in Brüssel.

Mein Bruder heißt Heinrich und meine Schwester heißt Louise. Der Vater Wilhelms ist angekommen. Die Mutter Louisens ist abgereist. Ludwigs Onkel ist sehr reich. Emiliens Hut ist sehr schön. Haben Sie diesen Hund von Heinrich oder von Ferdinand erhalten? Amalie hat dem Johann ihre Feder geliehen. Karl hat der Emilie eine Blume gegeben. Gehört dieser Garten dem Ludwig oder der Karoline? Wo ist Wilhelm? Er ist mit Karl und Joseph ausgegangen. Wohnt Ihr Onkel in Brüssel oder in Paris? Geht Ihr Vetter nach Wien oder nach Berlin? Ist Paris größer, als Lyon? Ist Ihr Freund von Köln oder von Aachen?

Obs. The proper names of persons are declined with or without an article. If declined with the article, they remain unchanged. Without the article, the feminine names ending in e add ns in the Genitive and n in the Dative.

50.

My cousin's name is John. The daughter of our gardener's wife is called Jane (Johanna). Art thou Charles's or Ferdinand's brother? Where are Henry and Lewis? They are in my father's room; they are gone out with William. Have you lent your pen to Henry? Who has given this flower to Louisa? We

have received a letter from Lewis; he is at Dussel-
dorf. The sister of Charles is very short. The bonnet
of Josephine is too large. My uncle lives in Vienna
and my cousin in Paris. My friend goes to Cologne.
William is arrived from Amsterdam. Have you seen
John and Lewis? My garden is larger than that of
Emily. Louisa is gone out with her mother. Henry
is departed with his friend Ferdinand.

PART II.

51.

Nom. bie Tiſche, the tables ;
Gen. ber Tiſche, of the tables ;
Dat. ben Tiſchen, to the tables ;
Acc. bie Tiſche, the tables.

Obs. Substantives of one syllable take *e* in the plural. Those
nouns the radical vowel of which is a, o, u, au, generally change
it into ä, ö, ü, äu. The Dative plural of all substantives terminates
in n.

Die Freunde meines Vaters ſind angekommen. Die
Söhne unſeres Nachbars ſind ſehr fleißig. Die Stühle,
welche wir gekauft haben, ſind ſehr ſchön. Haben Sie die
Städte Wien und Berlin geſehen? Karl hat die Hüte Wil-
helms und Ferdinands gefunden. Mein Vater hat die Briefe
Ihres Onkels nicht erhalten. Das Eiſen und das Silber
ſind Metalle. Die Pferde ſind nützlicher, als die Hunde.
Die Mägde eures Nachbars ſind ſehr fleißig. Die Aerzte
in dieſer Stadt ſind ſehr reich. Wem haben Sie die Stöcke
meines Bruders gegeben? Die Thiere, welche wir in Ihrem
Garten geſehen haben, ſind ſehr ſtark. Haben Sie den
Freunden Heinrichs geſchrieben? Gebet dieſen Hund den
Söhnen meines Bruders. Wir ſprechen von den Briefen
des Arztes.

52.

Thy brother has bought the dogs of my neighbor.
The friends of Charles are ill. Have you seen the
horses of our uncle? Who has written the letters of

my brother? Where are the hats that you have bought?
I have received this bird from the sons of the physician. I have given your umbrella to the maid-ser-
vants. (The) metals are very useful. (The) dogs are
very faithful. Your brother is gone out with the sons
of our neighbor (fem.). Cologne and Aix-la-Chapelle
are towns. I speak of Henry's and William's friends.

53.

Der Zahn, the tooth;	der Ring, the ring;
der Fuß, the foot;	die Nuß, the nut;
die Hand, the hand;	der Baum, the tree;
der Schuh, the shoe;	warm, warm; rein, clean;
der Strumpf, the stocking;	weiß, white.

Obs. The determinative words, as: dieſer, jener, mein, dein, welcher
&c. take in the plural the same terminations as the article.

Meine Zähne ſind ſehr weiß. Ich habe die Füße ſehr
warm. Ihre Hände ſind nicht rein. Hat der Schuhmacher
meine Schuhe gebracht? Wer hat meine Strümpfe genommen? Sind das Ihre Strümpfe? Das ſind nicht die meiner Schweſter. Wo haben Sie dieſe Nüſſe gekauft? Haben
Sie meine Bäume ſchon geſehen? Von welchen Bäumen ſprechen Sie? Von denjenigen, welche ich von dem Gärtner der
Königin gekauft habe. Unſere Freunde ſind ſchon abgereiſt.
Wer hat dieſe Briefe geſchrieben? Mein Vater hat ſeine
Pferde und Hunde verkauft. Mein Nachbar hat einen Brief
von ſeinen Söhnen erhalten, welche in Berlin ſind. Hat
Jemand meine Ringe gefunden? Niemand hat deine Ringe
geſehen. Karl wird von ſeinen Freunden geliebt.

54.

Their, ihr; those, diejenigen *or* die.

Charles and Henry have lost their sticks. The shoemaker has not made your shoes. Where have you
bought these tables and chairs? From whom have
you received these pencils? My feet are very small.
My sister has lost her thimbles. I have received these
letters from my friends. These trees are higher than
those. These animals are very fine. These servants
are very lazy. Have you already seen our hats and
our rings? Emily's stockings are whiter than those
of Louisa. Your teeth are not clean. My hands are very
warm. I have found these nuts in my uncle's garden.

55.

Alle, all.

Das Kind, the child ;	das Dorf, the village ;
das Buch, the book ;	das Blatt, the leaf ;
das Haus, the house ;	das Loch, the hole ;
das Volk, the people ;	das Huhn, the chicken ;
das Glas, the glass ;	das Kalb, the calf ;
das Band, the ribbon ;	der Wurm, the worm ;
das Kleid, the dress ;	der Wald, the forest ;
das Schloß, the castle ;	der Mann, the man, the husband.

Obs. All these monosyllabical nouns are exceptions from the general rule, and form their plural by adding er, and softening the radical vowel. Substantives ending in thum follow the same rule, as : Irrthum, Irrthümer (mistake).

Diese Häuser sind höher, als jene. Jene Bänder sind schöner, als diese. Deine Bücher sind nützlicher, als die Louisens. Diese Mutter hat ihre Kinder verloren. Der König hat seine Schlösser verkauft. Von wem haben Sie diese Gläser erhalten? Wer hat diese Kleider gemacht? Dieser Mann ist schon sehr alt; er hat alle seine Zähne verloren. Wo sind Ihre Freunde? Alle meine Freunde sind ausgegangen. Diese Völker sind sehr glücklich; sie haben einen König, welcher sehr gut ist. Die Könige sind nicht immer glücklich. Heinrich und Wilhelm haben alle ihre Bücher verloren. Alle eure Briefe sind angekommen. Wir haben alle diese Nüsse in dem Walde unseres Onkels gefunden. Der Vater ist mit allen seinen Kindern abgereist. Diese Dörfer sind sehr schön. Von welchen Dörfern sprechen Sie? Welche Städte haben Sie gesehen? Sind alle diese Strümpfe für Louisen oder für Emilien? Haben Sie den Kindern des Nachbars einen Vogel gegeben? Wer hat alle diese Löcher in meinem Tische gemacht?

56.

Not yet, noch nicht.

Where are your children? My children are gon out. Their friends are arrived. Have you not yet written your letters? Who has bought all these ribbons? Henrietta has lost all these books. We have seen all these houses. Have you also seen the castles of the king? Who has taken all my nuts? These children have lost their hats. Give these glasses to Henry and these rings to Louisa. This tree has lost all its leaves. My neighbor has sold all his chickens.

57.

German	English	German	English
Der Stiefel,	the boot;	der Kutscher,	the coachman;
der Spiegel,	the mirror	das Fenster,	the window;
der Löffel,	the spoon;	das Mädchen,	the girl;
die Nadel,	the needle	der Engländer,	the Englishman;
die Gabel,	the fork;	der Italiener,	the Italian.

Obs. Masc. and neuter substantives ending in er, el, en, do no change in the plural; the feminine nouns ending in er and el take n, except: die Mutter, the mothers; die Töchter, the daughters; der Vetter, the cousin, die Vettern.

Die Schneider und Schuhmacher in dieser Stadt sind alle reich. Diese Engländer sind sehr fleißig. Meine Brüder sind alle krank. Haben Sie meine Schwestern gesehen? Wo haben Sie diese Messer, Löffeln und Gabeln gekauft? Die Fenster Ihres Zimmers sind offen. Karl und Heinrich sind meine Vettern. Wir haben diese Vögel in dem Walde gefunden. Die Tiger sind sehr stark. Diese Mädchen sind sehr glücklich. Sind meine Töchter ausgegangen? Sind meine Zimmer nicht sehr schön? Hat Ihre Tante alle diese Spiegel gekauft? Wer hat die Bücher und Federn dieses Mädchens genommen? Wem gehören diese Gärten und Häuser? Louise und Henriette haben ihre Nadeln verloren. Der Schuhmacher hat Ihre Schuhe und Stiefel noch nicht gebracht. Wer sind jene Männer? Es sind Italiener; es sind die Onkel meines Freundes. Diese Mütter sind sehr traurig; sie haben alle ihre Kinder verloren.

58.

The shoemaker has brought your shoes and boots. The houses of this village are all very fine. Bring us (bringen Sie uns) the spoons, forks and knives. Where have you bought these needles? Your brothers and sisters are not come. Lewis and Ferdinand are cousins. Our mothers have seen the gardens of the king. My sons have bought the mirrors of my neighbor. (The) horses are bigger than (the) tigers. Are my stockings clean? Are your shoes new?

59.

Eins, (ein)	one;	vier,	four;
zwei,	two;	fünf,	five;
drei,	three;	sechs,	six

fteben, seven;
acht, eight;
neun, nine;
zehn, ten;
elf, eleven;
zwölf, twelve;
dreizehn, thirteen;
vierzehn, fourteen;
fünfzehn, fifteen;
sechszehn, sixteen;
siebenzehn, seventeen;
achtzehn, eighteen;

neunzehn, nineteen;
zwanzig, twenty;
die Aufgabe, the task; exercise
das Jahr, the year;
die Woche, the week;
der Monat, the month (pl. e)
der Tag, the day;
die Stunde, the hour,
der Knabe, the boy;
seit, since (Dat.);
es gibt, es ist, there is;
es gibt, es sind, there are;
gemacht, made, done.

Obs. Substantives ending in *e* take n in the plural.

In unserm Hause sind vierzehn Zimmer. In diesem Zimmer sind zwei Tische und zwölf Stühle. Unser Nachbar hat fünf Kinder: drei Söhne und zwei Töchter. Wir haben vier Katzen und drei Hunde. In eurem Garten sind fünfzehn Bäume. Das Jahr hat zwölf Monate; der Monat hat vier Wochen; die Woche hat sieben Tage. Ich habe von meinem Vater sechs Aepfel und acht Birnen erhalten. Mein Onkel hat meiner Schwester ein Federmesser und zwanzig Federn gegeben. Hast du schon alle deine Aufgaben gemacht? Johann hat noch nicht seine Aufgabe gemacht. Mein Bruder ist schon drei Jahre in Berlin. Haben Sie noch nicht gegessen? Ich habe schon seit drei Stunden gegessen. Ist Ihr Vater noch nicht angekommen? Er ist schon seit zwei Tagen angekommen. Mein Onkel ist seit vier Monaten krank; er hat seit acht Tagen nichts gegessen. Mein Bruder ist neun Jahre alt, aber meine Schwester ist noch nicht sieben Jahre alt.

60.

My father has three houses and two gardens. This man has five boys and four girls. My friend has seven sisters. We have received six letters. In this town there are twenty physicians. My cousins (fem.) have bought two cats. My cousin is seventeen years and two months old. My mother has bought six knives, twelve forks and eighteen spoons. Our joiner has made three tables and ten chairs. We have received this week fifteen chickens and three calves. William has eaten five apples, four pears and eleven nuts. Henry is arrived three days ago (since three days). My uncle is departed a twelvemonth ago (since a year). Charles and Ferdinand have made six exercises

There are two holes in this door. The gardener has
given three flowers to my children.

61.

Das Brod, the bread; Brod, some or any bread
Das Fleisch, the meat; Fleisch, some meat;
die Aepfel, the apples; Aepfel, some apples.
Der Wein, the wine; die Kirsche, the cherry;
das Bier, the beer; die Pflaume, the plum;
das Wasser, the water; die Dinte, the ink;
das Gemüse, the vegetables; die Suppe, the soup;
der Zucker, the sugar; man findet, one finds, they find;
der Kaffee, the coffee; getrunken, drunk;
geben Sie mir, give me; bringen Sie uns, bring us.

Ich habe Brod und Fleisch gegessen. Wir haben Kirschen
und Pflaumen gekauft. Mein Bruder hat Wein getrunken
und ihr habt Bier und Wasser getrunken. Der Schuhmacher
macht Schuhe und Stiefel. Der Tischler macht Tische und
Stühle. Bei diesem Kaufmann findet man Bücher, Federn,
Dinte und Bleistifte. Geben Sie mir Suppe und Gemüse.
Hier ist Wein und Wasser, und da ist Kaffee und Milch.
Haben Sie auch Zucker? Wir haben Messer und Gabeln,
Tassen und Gläser gekauft. Der Gärtner hat der Louise Kir-
schen und Blumen gegeben. Haben Sie schon Kaffee getrunken?
In jenem Hause findet man Spiegel, Regenschirme, Bänder,
Fingerhüte und Nadeln. Meine Freundin hat von ihrem
Onkel Birnen und Nüsse erhalten. Wir haben Löwen, Tiger,
Katzen und Hunde gesehen. In dieser Stadt gibt es Schnei-
der und Schuhmacher, welche sehr reich sind.

62.

Wollen Sie? will you (have); gefälligst, if you please.

Will you have some wine or some beer, some milk or
some water? Give me, if you please, some soup, vegetables, meat and bread. Where does one find (finds one)
ink and pens? Are you a father? Have you children?
Has your father bought any trees or flowers? My brother has books and friends. Here is coffee and sugar
My neighbor has birds, dogs and horses. We are speaking of towns and villages, of houses and gardens. Iron
and silver are metals. Vienna and Berlin are towns.
What have you made? We have done exercises (Aufgaben gemacht), we have written letters. We have eaten
apples and plums, and we have drunk some wine and beer

63.

wenig, little, few;	zu, too; wie? how?
viel, much;	das Obſt, die Frucht, the fruit;
viele, many;	das Geld, the money;
genug, enough;	der Pfeffer, the pepper;
mehr, more;	das Salz, the salt;
weniger, less, fewer;	der Senf, the mustard.

Heinrich hat viel Geld; er hat mehr Geld, als ich. Geben Sie mir ein wenig Fleiſch. Ich habe genug Brod. Du haſt zu viel Salz und Pfeffer. Wir haben weniger Obſt, als Ihr. Louiſe hat weniger Federn, als Henriette. Karl hat mehr Aufgaben gemacht, als Ludwig. Haſt du ſo viel Geld, als mein Bruder? Der Arme hat wenig Freunde. Es gibt wenig Menſchen, welche zufrieden ſind. Geben Sie der Henriette nicht zu viel Senf. Mein Bruder hat zu viel Wein getrunken. Dieſe Mutter hat viele Kinder. Dieſer Mann hat viele Blumen. Wie viele Hunde hat Ihr Vater? Es gibt dieſes Jahr wenig Kirſchen, aber viele Pflaumen. Mein Freund hat dieſe Woche mehr Briefe erhalten, als ich. Hat dein Vater ſo viele Bücher, als mein Onkel? Geben Sie mir gefälligſt ein wenig Dinte. Wollen Sie noch mehr? Ich habe genug.

64.

There is much fruit this year. Our gardener has many trees and flowers. Will you have a little meat or some vegetables? Have you mustard enough? I have salt and pepper enough. Our neighbor has much money; he is very rich. Give a little wine to this woman. This man has few friends, but he has many dogs and cats. There are many birds in this forest. How many physicians are there in your town? Have you as many apples and pears as we? We have not so many as you, but we have more plums and nuts than you. Charles has fewer friends than Henry. This tree has fewer leaves than that one. There are too many chairs in this room.

65.

Das Stück, the piece;	das Dutzend, the dozen;
die Flaſche, the bottle;	der Korb, the basket;
die Taſſe, the cup;	die Leinwand, the linen;
das Pfund, the pound;	das Taſchentuch, the pocket hand-
die Elle, the yard, ell;	kerchief;
das Paar, the pair;	der Handſchuh, the glove;

das Hemb, the shirt;   der Käfe, the cheese,
die Halsbinde, the cravat;   der Schinken, the ham.

Obs. The words Pfund, Paar and Dutzend are invariable when they are preceded by a number.—The English word *of* which follows the names of weights and measures is not expressed in German.

Meine Mutter hat der Henriette drei Paar Handschuhe, sechs Paar Strümpfe, zwei Dutzend Hemden und einen Korb Kirschen geschickt. In diesem Koffer sind zehn Ellen Leinwand, vier Taschentücher und sechs Halsbinden. Mein Bruder hat zwei Paar Schuhe und ein Paar Stiefel gekauft. Wir haben dem Freunde unsers Onkels zwanzig Pfund Zucker und zehn Flaschen Wein geschickt. Geben Sie mir ein Stück Käse, eine Flasche Bier und ein wenig Senf. Ich habe ein Glas Wein getrunken und ein Stück Schinken gegessen. Wir haben bei unserer Freundin eine Tasse Kaffee getrunken. Geben Sie mir ein Glas Wasser und ein Stück Zucker. Meine Schwester hat zwei Pfund Kirschen und ein Pfund Pflaumen gekauft. Wir haben ein Dutzend Stühle bei dem Tischler unsers Onkels gekauft. Ich habe von dem Gärtner einen Korb Blumen erhalten.

66.

The shoemaker has made a pair of shoes for Louisa and two pair of boots for William. We have drunk two glasses of wine and three glasses of beer. Give me a bottle of water and a little meat and bread. Will you have a piece of ham or cheese? My aunt has bought a dozen of cravats, two dozen of shirts and ten pair of gloves and stockings. How many shirts have you? I have three dozen. This linen is very fine; how many yards have you bought? I have bought twenty yards. That is not enough for ten shirts. My uncle has given to Henry a penknife, twenty pens, two cravats and a pair of gloves. Ferdinand has bought a pound of plums, six pounds of coffee and two yards of ribbon. Will you have a cup of coffee or a glass of wine? Give me, if you please, a glass of water.

67.

Sing. guter, gute, gutes; *Plur.* gute.

Schlecht, bad;   vortrefflich, excellent;
kalt, cold;   liebenswürdig, amiable;
hübsch, pretty;   das Papier, the paper;
tobt, dead;   das Geschäft, the affair, busines

Obs. If the Adjective is not preceded by an article or any othei determinative word, it takes the terminations of biefer, biefe, biefe*.

Hier ist guter ·Schinken, gute Suppe und gutes Brod Haben Sie gutes Papier und gute Dinte? Wir haben schlechten Wein und gutes Bier getrunken. Unser Gärtner hat vortreffliches Obst. Unsere Magd hat guten Senf, aber schlechten Pfeffer gekauft. Eduard hat gute Freunde und nützliche Bücher. Mein Onkel hat schöne Gärten und große Häuser. Euer Nachbar hat treue Hunde. Johann, geben Sie mir ein Glas Wasser! Wollen Sie kaltes oder warmes ·Wasser? Meine Schwester hat ein Paar hübsche Handschuhe gekauft. Euer Bruder spricht immer von gutem Wein und guter Suppe, aber nicht von nützlichen Büchern, von Aufgaben und Geschäften. Paris und London sind schöne Städte. Heinrich hat ein Paar neue Schuhe erhalten.

68.

Have you any good mustard? We have good bread and good meat. Your gardener has very fine flowers. These children have fine dresses. We have faithful friends, amiable brothers and useful books. Give me some better cheese and better beer. At (bei) this merchant's one finds pretty gloves, fine penknives, and good pens. Iron and silver are very useful metals. You always have excellent wine. My brother is not gone out, he has too many affairs. Henry has bought good paper and good ink. We speak of good coffee, of excellent fruit and new dresses.

69.

Ein guter, eine gute, ein gutes.

Golden, of gold, golden;   gesund, healthy, wholesome;
silbern, of silver;   kein, no, none.

Obs. If the adjective is preceded by the indefinite article, by kein or by a possessive pronoun, as: mein, dein, unser, &c., it takes in the Nominative Sing. the terminations er, e, es, and in all other cases en, except the Accusative fem. and neuter, which is the same as the Nominative.

Unser Gärtner ist ein guter Mann. Eure Gärtnerin ist eine gute Frau. Emilie ist ein gutes Kind. Wir haben einen guten Vater und eine gute Mutter. Heinrich hat ein schönes Pferd und einen schönen Hund. Louise hat große Zähne, aber eine kleine Hand und einen kleinen Fuß. Ferdinand ist mit meinem jüngern Bruder ausgegangen. Henriette

ift mit meiner älteren Schwefter abgereift. Geben Sie diefes
Brod einem armen Kinde. Diefes Federmeffer gehört einem
jungen Manne, der bei unferm Nachbar wohnt. Ludwig ift
der Sohn eines reichen Kaufmanns. Haben Sie guten Wein
oder gutes Bier? Wir haben keinen guten Wein und kein
gutes Bier. Wer hat meine filberne Uhr und meinen golde=
nen Ring genommen? Wir haben unfern beften Freund ver=
loren. Eure kleinen Kinder find fehr gefund. Es giebt keine
guten Kirfchen diefes Jahr. Mein Onkel hat feine fchönften
Pferde verkauft. Bift du mit deinen neuen Stiefeln zufrieden?
Haft du fchon von unfern guten Pflaumen gegeffen?

70.

Charles is a good boy. Henrietta is a pretty girl
That is a happy mother. That is an excellent wine.
Where is my little Henry, my good Louisa? We have
a very rich uncle. William has an old father. Iron
is a useful metal. The dog is a faithful animal. I
have received a new umbrella and a gold watch. My
neighbor has done much business this year. Give this
bottle of wine to a poor man or to a poor woman. I have
no friend in this town. Have you no good pens for this
child? Our best friends are dead. This joiner makes
no good chairs.

71.

Der gute, die gute, das gute.

Geftern, yesterday;	der Schüler, the pupil, schoolboy
heute, to-day;	die Schule, the school;
ich liebe, I love, I like;	das Leben, the life.

Obs. When the adjective is preceded by the definite article, or
any other determinative word, which has the same termination, as ·
diefer, jener, &c., it takes in the Nominative Sing. the final e, and in
all other cases en, except the Accusative Sing. fem. and neuter.

Der gute Heinrich ift krank. Die kleine Sophie ift fehr
liebenswürdig. Das arme Kind hat feine Mutter verloren
Das ift der höchfte Baum in unferm Garten. Lifette ift die
fleißigfte von unfern Mägden. Diefer reiche Engländer
wohnt bei meinem Onkel. Wo haben Sie diefe goldene
Nadel gefunden? Wem gehört diefes große Haus und jener
fchöne Garten? Franz ift mit dem kleinen Karl ausgegan=
gen. Wir haben geftern bei der guten Emilie Kirfchen ge=
geffen. Wer wohnt in diefem fchönen Schloffe? Wie heißt

dieſe hübſche Blume? Wo haben Sie dieſen ſchlechten Wein und dieſes ſchlechte Bier gekauft? Ich liebe die fleißigen Schüler und die treuen Freunde. Der Löwe und der Tiger ſind die ſtärkſten Thiere. Das ſind die glücklichſten Tage meines Lebens. Geben Sie dieſem armen Manne ein wenig Wein. Leihen Sie dieſem kleinen Mädchen Ihren Regenſchirm.

72.

Every one, Jedermann.

The diligent pupil is loved by every one. The idle child is loved by nobody. The good king is loved by his people. This poor woman has no bread for her children. This rich merchant has given much money to the poor. I like the pretty flowers and the pretty children. I do not like the fine dresses. This fruit is not wholesome. My brother has found this gold ring to-day. Lewis is gone out with his little brother. The father of this young man is a shoemaker. The daughter of this old woman is ill. Have you drunk of this excellent wine? Will you (have) some of these fine plums? Which hat have you taken? I have taken the white hat. Which watch have you sold? I have sold the silver watch.

73.

Der erſte, the first;	unartig, naughty;
der zweite, the second;	beſcheiden, modest;
der dritte, the third;	der Theil, the part;
der vierte, the fourth;	der Band, the volume;
der letzte, the last;	nur, only; die Klaſſe, the class.

Der wievielſte? what day of the month?

Obs. Of before the name of a month is not expressed in German.

Dieſer junge Mann iſt ſehr fleißig: er iſt der erſte in der Klaſſe. Karl iſt der zweite; der beſcheidene Heinrich der dritte; Johann iſt der vierte; der kleine Wilhelm iſt der fünfte; Paul iſt der ſechste; Franz iſt der achte; Guſtav iſt der neunte; der unartige Eduard iſt der elfte und der faule Ludwig iſt der letzte. Zwei iſt der fünfte Theil von zehn. Fünf iſt der vierte Theil von zwanzig. Ein Tag iſt der ſiebente Theil einer Woche. Den wievielſten des Monats haben wir heute? Wir haben heute den dreizehnten oder den vierzehnten. Iſt es nicht der zwanzigſte? Mein Vater iſt den dritten Mai abgereiſt. Mein Onkel iſt den zehnten Dezember angefommen. Haben Sie den erſten und zweiten Band? Ich habe nur den erſten.

74.

Louisa is the first in the class; Maria is the second; the good Josephine is the third; Henrietta is the fifth; the modest Sophia is the ninth; Matilda (Mathilde) is the fifteenth; the naughty Caroline is the last. Three is the sixth part of eighteen. A week is the fourth part of a month; and a month is the twelfth part of a year. What day of the month is it (have we)? It is to-day the eleventh or the twelfth. We departed on the second of May and arrived on the sixteenth. Which volume have you taken? Have you taken the third and the fourth? I have only taken the third.

75

Singular.   *Plural.*

Der meinige, die meinige, das meinige, mine;   die meinigen;
der deinige, thine;   der unſrige, ours;
der ſeinige, his;   der eurige, Ihrige, yours;
der ihrige, hers;   der ihrige, theirs;
    leicht, easy, light.

Obs. Instead of: der meinige, der deinige, &c. may be said, meiner meine, meines or meins, with the terminations of dieſer, dieſe, dieſes.— The declension of der meinige, derjenige, &c. is the same as that of the adjective, preceded by the definite article.

Dein Vater iſt größer, als der meinige. Meine Mutter iſt kleiner, als die deinige. Unſer Buch iſt nützlicher, als das Ihrige. Mein Sohn iſt nicht ſo alt, als der deinige. Euer Pferd iſt jünger, als das unſrige. Unſere Bücher ſind nützlicher, als die eurigen. Mein Vater hat ſeine Uhr verloren; Heinrich hat auch die ſeinige verloren. Meine Schweſter hat die ihrige verkauft. Mein Vater hat deinen Brief und den meinigen geleſen. Meine Tante hat ihren Garten und den unſrigen verkauft. Hat dein Bruder meinen Stock oder den ſeinigen genommen? Hat Louiſe meinen Fingerhut oder den ihrigen gefunden? Deine Aufgaben ſind leichter, als die meinigen. Dieſe Bäume ſind höher, als die unſrigen. In unſerer Stadt ſind mehr Aerzte, als in der eurigen.

76.

My thimble is as fine as yours. Your umbrella is not so large as mine. My son is more diligent than thine

My friend has sold his house and mine. My sister has
eaten her apple and thine. Has Louisa taken my pen
or hers; my pencil or hers? Henry has read my books
and yours. Your sisters are younger than ours. We
speak of our friend and of yours. Is my room smaller
than thine? I have promised a book to your son and to
mine, to your daughter and to mine. I speak of my
tasks and of thine. This castle belongs to my uncle and
to yours.

77.

Singular.		Plural.
Nom. er, he; fie, she; es it;		fie, they;
Acc. ihn, him; fie, her; es, it;		fie, them;
Gehabt, had;	gekannt, known;	ja, yes;
gelesen, read;	gebracht, brought;	nein, no.

Haben Sie meinen Stock? Ja, ich habe ihn. Haben
Sie meine Uhr? Nein, ich habe sie nicht. Haben Sie mein
Messer? Ich habe es nicht. Haben Sie meine Schuhe?
Ja, ich habe sie. Wo ist mein Hund? Ich habe ihn nicht
gesehen. Wer hat meine Feder genommen? Dein Bruder
hat sie genommen. Wo hast du dieses Taschentuch gefunden?
Ich habe es in ihrem Zimmer gefunden. Diese Vögel sind
sehr schön. Von wem hast du sie erhalten? Deine Schwester
ist sehr fleißig; meine Mutter liebt sie sehr. Haben Sie mei=
nen Oheim gekannt? Ich habe ihn nicht gekannt. Dies ist.
ein nützliches Buch; haben Sie es schon gelesen? Wo ist
mein Fingerhut? Ich habe ihn Ihrer Schwester gegeben;
sie hat ihn verloren. Hat Jemand meine Gabel genommen?
Karl hat sie genommen. Wem hat der Gärtner alle diese
Blumen geschickt? Er hat sie Ihrer Mutter geschickt. Hat
Heinrich deinen Bleistift gehabt? Nein, er hat ihn heute
nicht gehabt.

78.

Has the shoemaker brought my boot? Yes, he has
brought it. Hast thou already done thy task? I have
not yet done it. Have you seen my new room? No,
I have not yet seen it. Where hast thou bought these
pretty rings? I have bought them in Paris. Who has
had my penknife? I have not had it, your brother has
had it. I have received a letter from my aunt, have
you read it? Have you already seen the king? I have
not yet seen him. You have a good pen; lend it to

my sister. There is your brother; do you see him?
Do you not see him? Where are your gloves? Lend
them to your aunt. Where is your umbrella? Give
it to this child. My aunt is dead; did you know her?
Which books have you there? Have you read them?
Where is thy dog? My father has sold it.

79.

Ich bin gewesen, I have been;
du bist gewesen, thou hast been;
er ist gewesen, he has been;
wir sind gewesen, we have been;
ihr seid gewesen, you have been;
sie sind gewesen, they have been.

Herr, Mr.;	zusammen, together;
der Herr, gentleman;	lange, long, a long time;
Fräulein, Miss;	der Morgen, the morning;
das Fräulein, the young lady;	das Viertel, the quarter;
Madame, Madam, Mrs.;	ein halber, e, es, half a.
die Dame, the lady;	

Das erste Mal, the first time; das letzte Mal, the last time; ein Mal,
once; zwei Mal, twice.

Obs. The word Herr takes in all cases of the Singular n, and in
all cases of the Plural en. It is also used with the article in the sense
of Mr. In speaking politely, the words Herr, Frau and Fräulein are
used as a title, as in French, for instance: Ihr Herr Vater, your
father; Ihre Frau Mutter, your mother; Ihre Fräulein Schwestern,
your sisters.

Wer ist hier gewesen? Herr Moll ist hier gewesen; er
hat dieses Buch gebracht. Bist du bei dem Schuhmacher ge=
wesen? Ich bin heute bei deinem Schuhmacher gewesen; er
hat Ihre Stiefel schon gemacht. Wo seid ihr diesen Morgen
gewesen? Wir sind bei unserm Freunde Karl gewesen, welcher
sehr krank ist. Dieser Herr ist drei Jahre in Wien gewesen,
und seine Brüder sind sehr lange in Konstantinopel gewesen.
Du bist nicht fleißig gewesen, du hast deine Aufgaben noch
nicht gemacht. Ich bin gestern bei Madame Röder gewesen;
sie ist eine sehr liebenswürdige Frau. Ist Fräulein N. oft
in dieser Stadt gewesen? Sie ist schon drei Mal hier ge=
wesen. Haben Sie den Herrn Scholl gekannt? Ich habe
ihn in Berlin gekannt; wir sind oft zusammen ausgegangen.
Wie lange sind Sie in Madrid gewesen? Ich bin nur ein
halbes Jahr da gewesen, aber ich bin drei Viertel Jahr in
Lissabon gewesen. Haben Sie die Herren Rollet schon ge=
sehen? Ich habe sie gestern bei einem meiner Freunde gesehen

80.

Have they (has one) brought my shoes? Yes, they have brought them. Has the tailor been here?˙ No, he has not yet been here. Hast thou been at the joiner's? No, I have not yet been there. We have many flowers; we have been in the garden of (the) Mr. Nollet. Have you also been at Mr. Moll's? My brother has never been more contented than to-day; he has received from his uncle a beautiful gold watch, and half a dozen pocket-handkerchiefs. How long have you been in Paris? We have been there six months. These gentlemen have done much business; they have been very happy. Are Messrs. N. already departed for Cologne? They have departed this morning with their uncle; I have seen them at Mrs. Sicard's.

81.

Ich war, I was;
du warſt, thou wast;
er war, he was;
wir waren, we were;
ihr waret, you were;
ſie waren, they were.

Ehemals, formerly; warum, why; als, when.

Obs. When a sentence begins with **als**, when, the verb is placed at the end of the phrase.

Wo warſt du dieſen Morgen? Ich war bei meinem Vetter, welcher von Frankfurt angekommen iſt. Mein Bruder und ich, wir waren bei deinem Vater. Ihre Tante war ſchon abgereiſt. Herr Moll war ehemals ſehr reich; er hat ſeit zehn Jahren viel verloren. Waren Sie noch nicht bei Herrn Mably? Ich bin geſtern da geweſen, aber er war ausgegangen. Wie alt war Ihr Bruder, als er in Köln war? Er war zehn oder elf Jahre alt. Wir waren nicht zuſammen; er war in Köln und ich war in Düſſeldorf. Meine Schweſtern waren lange in Brüſſel bei Herrn Nollet. Warum ſind Sie geſtern nicht gekommen? Ich war geſtern krank. Waren dieſe Herrn immer ſo reich? Haben Sie immer ſo viele Freunde gehabt? Warſt du dieſen Morgen in der Schule? Ich bin heute nicht in der Schule geweſen.

82.

I was formerly much happier; I was young and strong. Wast thou always as contented as to-day? My father was formerly very rich. You were gone out, when I came (I

am come.) Where were you, when we (are) arrived?
My sisters were very ill yesterday. How old were you
when you were at N.? I was fifteen years and six
months old. Was my room open when you came (you
are come)? No, but the windows were open. This girl
was much prettier when she was young. John and William were always my brother's friends. Were you not
with my brother, when he (has) lost his handkerchief?

83.

Ich hatte, I had;
du hatteſt, thou hadst;
er hatte, he had;
wir hatten, we had;
ihr hattet, you had;
ſie hatten, they had.

Die Eltern, the parents; der Beſuch, the visit;
der Handel, the commerce; der andere, the other.

Wir hatten dieſe Woche den Beſuch der Herren Moll,
welche mit ihrer Schweſter angekommen ſind. Ihr hattet
viele Freunde, als ihr noch jung waret. Wir hatten mehr
Bücher, als ihr. Unſer Onkel hatte ehemals viele Pferde
und Hunde. Du warſt ſehr fleißig, als du noch deine Eltern hatteſt. Dieſe zwei Kaufleute waren ehemals ſehr reich;
ſie hatten einen großen Handel. Ich hatte zwei Brüder;
der eine war in Wien, der andere in Berlin. Haſt du meine
zwei Brüder gekannt? Ich habe denjenigen gekannt, welcher in Berlin war; der andere war jünger, als ich. Wo
iſt euer Vetter, der ſo viele Vögel hatte? Er iſt ſeit einem
Jahre in Brüſſel. Mein Federmeſſer war verloren; Ihr
Bruder hat es gefunden. Hattet ihr eure Briefe ſchon geſchrieben, als wir ausgegangen ſind? Wir hatten ſie noch
nicht geſchrieben; wir hatten keine guten Federn und kein gutes
Papier.

84.

Der Verſtand, the intellect; die Güte, the kindness.

Mr. Maury was formerly much happier, he had many
friends, much money, many horses and dogs. Henry
is dead; he was a good boy, he had so much intellect
and kindness, he was loved by everybody. We were
often in his garden; his sisters were very amiable and
they had many flowers and books. His parents were
not rich, but they had a great trade. I was ill yester-

day: I had eaten too much fruit. Hadst thou not yet done thy exercises when I came (I am come)? No, I had not yet done them. My brother had already done his, when thou camest (art come.)

85.

Mir, to me, me ;	ihm, to him, him ;
dir, to thee, thee ;	ihr, to her, her.

zu, to.

Kaufen, to buy ;	schreiben, to write ;
verkaufen, to sell ;	lesen, to read ;
geben, to give ;	sehen, to see ;
leihen, to lend ;	(die) Lust, a mind ;
thun, to do ;	die Zeit, the time ;
machen, to make, to do ;	das Vergnügen, the pleasure.

Ich kann, I can ; du kannst, thou canst ; er kann, he can ; wir können, we can ; ihr könnet, you can ; sie können, they can.

Obs. The infinitive is placed at the end of the sentence.

Kannst du mir dieses Buch leihen? Ich kann dir dieses Buch nicht leihen; es gehört meinem Vetter Heinrich. Wer kann diesen Brief lesen? Ich kann ihn lesen; er ist sehr gut geschrieben. Wir können diesen Morgen nicht schreiben. Warum könnet ihr nicht schreiben? Wir haben keine Dinte. Können Sie meinem Bruder Ihre Uhr leihen? Ich kann ihm meine Uhr nicht leihen, ich habe sie dem Herrn S. ver= kauft. Haben Sie meiner Schwester eine Feder gegeben? Ich habe ihr keine Feder gegeben. Haben Sie Lust, diesen Hund zu kaufen? Ich habe keine Lust, ihn zu kaufen; er ist nicht treu. Hat ihr Bruder heute nichts zu thun? Er hat drei Briefe zu schreiben. Wir haben noch zwei Aufgaben zu machen. Ich habe gestern das Vergnügen gehabt, Ihr Fräu= lein Schwester zu sehen. Haben Sie Zeit, diesen Brief zu lesen? Ich habe jetzt nicht Zeit, ihn zu lesen. Können Sie mir einen Regenschirm geben? Ich kann Ihnen keinen geben, ich habe nur einen. Ihr Herr Bruder hat die Güte, mir den seinigen zu leihen. Sind Sie gestern bei meiner Tante gewe= sen? Nein, ich war gestern nicht bei ihr; ich hatte zu viele Geschäfte.

86.

Can you do that? Yes, I can (it); but my brother cannot. Will you lend me your penknife? I cannot lend thee my penknife; my sister has taken it. Have you given a pen to my cousin? Yes, I have given him one. Hast thou sold thy dog to my sister? I have not sold her my dog. Canst thou not do thy exercise? I cannot do it to-day. We can read this book. These gentleman cannot write their letters; they have no paper. Hast thou a mind to buy a pair of boots? Has your brother a mind to sell his ring? Have you had the kindness to give a glass of water to this poor man? My friend has had the pleasure to see his parents. I have not had time to read all these letters. My father has had the kindness to buy me a gold watch. Hast thou seen it? I have not yet seen it. Have you been with Ferdinand to-day? I have been with him this morning.

87.

Uns, to us, us; euch, Ihnen, to you, you; ihnen, to them, them

Gehen, to go;	haben, to have;
kommen, to come;	sein, to be; wenn, if;
trinken, to drink;	unwohl, indisposed;
essen, to eat;	jetzt, now, at present.

Ich will, I will; du willst, thou wilt; er will, he will; wir wollen, we will; ihr wollet, you will; sie wollen, they will.

Willst du mit mir gehen? Ich kann nicht mit dir gehen, ich habe keine Zeit. Ich will dir ein schönes Buch leihen, wenn du fleißig bist. Kann dein Bruder heute nicht kommen? Er hat keine Lust zu kommen, er ist unwohl. Wir wollen jetzt unsere Aufgaben machen. Wollen Sie ein Glas Wein trinken? Ich habe schon ein Glas Bier getrunken. Ich will ein Stück Fleisch oder Käse essen. Wollen Sie ein wenig Senf und Salz? Können Sie uns diesen Stock leihen? Ich kann Ihnen diesen Stock nicht leihen, mein Bruder will ihn haben. Man kann nicht unglücklicher sein, als dieser junge Mann; er hat seine Eltern und seine Brüder und Schwestern verloren. Wer will diesen Apfel haben? Ich will ihn haben. Was willst du jetzt thun? Ich will ein paar Briefe schreiben. Ich will euch einen Korb Kirschen geben, wenn ihr fleißig sein wollet. Wollen Sie die Güte haben, mir eine Nadel zu geben? Ich habe jetzt keine, ich kann Ihnen keine geben. Haben Sie Zeit, mit uns zu gehen? Ich habe keine Zeit, mit Ihnen zu gehen. Haben Sie den Herren N. schon einen Besuch gemacht? Ich habe ihnen diesen Morgen einen Besuch gemacht.

88.

What hast thou to do? I have nothing to do. Wilt thou read this book? Yes, I will read it. How is thy

brother? He is indisposed, he cannot come. Where
can one buy these fine penknives? One can buy them
at the merchant's who lives at our neighbor's. Will you
give me a little ink? Can your sister lend me her penknife? What do these gentlemen want (what will, &c.)?
These ladies will buy an umbrella. One cannot be more
unhappy than I (am); one cannot have more misfortune
than I. Give us something to drink. What will you
(have)? Will you have wine or beer? I have lent you
my stick. Where are your brothers? I have sold them
my dog. This man is very rich; all these houses belong
to him.

89.

Mich, me, myself; dich, thee, thyself.
uns, us, ourselves; euch, you, yourselves;
sich, one's self, him- her- itself, themselves.

Loben, to praise;	gelobt, praised;
lieben, to love, like;	geliebt, loved;
besuchen, to visit;	besucht, visited;
schlagen, to beat;	geschlagen, beaten;
sich schlagen, to fight;	der Lehrer, the master;
waschen, to wash;	gewaschen, washed.

Der Lehrer hat dich gelobt, weil du fleißig gewesen bist.
Dein Bruder ist ein böser Knabe; er hat mich gestern ge=
schlagen. Hast du dich schon gewaschen? Ich habe mich
noch nicht gewaschen; aber Heinrich hat sich schon seit einer
Stunde gewaschen. Warum willst du meinen Hund schlagen?
Er hat mein Brod genommen. Unsere Eltern sind unsere
besten Freunde; wir wollen sie immer lieben. Karl, du bist
sehr unartig; man kann dich nicht lieben. Wie viele Gläser
Wein hast du getrunken? Ich habe nur eine halbe Flasche
getrunken. Wo bist du diesen Morgen gewesen? Ich bin mit
meinem Vater bei Herrn N. gewesen. Ist Herr N. noch immer
unwohl? Er ist seit gestern ein wenig besser; aber er kann
noch nicht essen, noch trinken. Der Arzt war heute zweimal
bei ihm. Ich will ihn morgen auch besuchen, oder ihm einen
kleinen Brief schreiben. Aber warum haben Sie uns noch nicht
besucht? Ich habe noch keine Zeit gehabt, Sie zu besuchen.

90.

Who has beaten thee? Your cousin has beaten me.
With whom wilt thou fight? I will not fight. I have no

mind to fight. Lewis will fight with Henry. The servant has not yet washed my shirts. She will wash
them now. I have sold you my penknife, but you have
not yet given me the money. Your children have been
very good (artig) to day; the master has praised them
very (much); he has given them a beautiful book, and
a basket of cherries. Why has the master not yet vi-
sited us? He has no time; he is always in his school.
He is an amiable man: he is loved by all his pupils.
There is Ferdinand; hast thou washed thyself, my
child? Yes, mamma, (Mama) I have already washed
myself.

91.

Sagen, to say, to tell; glauben, to believe;
schicken, to send; wissen, to know.

Müssen, must; ich muß, I must; du mußt, thou must; er muß, he
must; wir müssen, we must; ihr müsset, you must; sie müssen, they
must.

Obs. The Accusative of the personal pronoun is placed before the
Dative.

Können Sie mir sagen, wo Herr Moll wohnt? Ich kann
es Ihnen nicht sagen. Wollen Sie mir diese Feder leihen?
Ich kann sie Ihnen nicht leihen, sie gehört mir nicht. Ich
muß heute dem Fräulein S. einen Besuch machen, sie ist gestern mit ihrer Mutter angekommen. Mußt du jetzt schon
gehen? Wo sind meine Schuhe? Hat der Schuhmacher sie
noch nicht gebracht? Nein, er will sie dir in einer Stunde
schicken. Wie kannst du das wissen? Er hat es mir gesagt.
Ich kann es nicht glauben. Dein Bruder muß noch seine Aufgaben machen. Wir müssen Alles thun, was unsere Eltern
und Lehrer wollen. Ihr müsset meinen Vater einmal besuchen;
er ist seit drei Wochen krank. Heinrich und Wilhelm müssen
viele Bücher haben. Wer hat dir diesen Ring gegeben? Meine
Tante hat ihn mir gegeben. Louise, ich will dir etwas sagen;
du hast meine Scheere genommen. Ich habe es schon gesehen,
Mutter. Wollen Sie meiner Schwester diesen Fingerhut geben? Ich will ihn ihr jetzt geben. Wer hat Ihnen diesen
Brief geschrieben? Meine Base hat ihn mir geschrieben.

92.

My friend has had the kindness to send me a basket
of cherries. You have not yet sent me my book. I have
not yet had time, to send it you. Who has taken my

pen? I cannot tell (it) thee. Wilt thou not believe me? This penknife belongs to my brother; thou must give it him. Charles will not lend me his umbrella. Why will he not lend it thee? My uncle is arrived. Your brother has told (it) us. Who must do that? Your sisters must do it. You must tell it to Mr. Moll. This letter is not well written; I cannot read it. Hast thou my stick? No, I have it not. I have lent it to you. You have not lent it to me.

PART III.

93.

Ich lobe, I praise ; I am praising, I do praise ;
du lobest, du lobst, thou praisest, &c. ;
er lobet, er lobt, he praises ;
wir loben, we praise ;
ihr lobet, ihr lobt, you praise ;
sie loben, they praise ;

Finden, to find ;
wohnen, to live, to dwell ;
bringen, to bring ;
theuer, dear ;

das Tuch, the cloth ;
die Straße, the street ;
suchen, to seek, look for.

Was suchen Sie? Ich suche meine Feder. Mein Bruder sucht seinen Bleistift. Wir suchen unsern Hund. Diese Kinder suchen ihre Bücher. Wo kaufen Sie Ihr Papier? Wir kaufen unser Papier bei dem Buchhändler. Ich finde meinen Stock nicht. Wer hat meinen Stock genommen? Ich glaube, daß Ihr Bruder ihn genommen hat. Ich liebe diesen Knaben nicht, er ist immer unartig. Du liebst deinen Lehrer. Gott liebt die guten Menschen. Gute Kinder lieben ihre Eltern. Ist es wahr, daß Ihr Onkel sein Haus verkauft? Wie theuer verkaufen Sie die Elle von diesem Tuche? Ich verkaufe die Elle dieses Tuches zu vier Thaler. Das ist sehr theuer. Findest du nicht, Heinrich, daß das sehr theuer ist? Ja, ich finde es sehr theuer. Wir verkaufen aber viel von diesem Tuche. Jedermann findet es schön. Schicken Sie mir drei und eine halbe Elle. Wissen Sie, wo ich wohne? Ja, Sie wohnen in der Petersstraße. Meine Magd kann es Ihnen heute noch bringen.

49

94.

Tadeln, to blame;   Alles, all, every thing;
arbeiten, to work;   Alles was, all that.

What are you doing? I am reading the book, which
your brother has lent me. You read too much. Why
do you not write? I have already written three letters.
My cousins never write. You always blame your cousins; one must blame nobody. What art thou doing?
I am doing my exercise. What is thy sister doing?
She is working. What do you drink? I drink wine and
my brother drinks beer. We drink no wine. I eat
cherries. My brothers eat plums. You are always
eating, but you do not work. Can you tell me, where
Mr. N. lives? He lives in (the) William-street. Livest
thou with thy uncle? No, I do not live with him.
Dost thou go to Paris? No, I do not go to Paris. I do
not like this young man; he always blames his friends.
He will never lend me his penknife. I lend him all
that I have. We lend everything to our friends. You
always beat my brother; you are very naughty. These
boys beat everybody. Do you sell paper? I sell paper,
pens, and ink. What do you say? I say, that you have
taken my knife.

95.

Ich lobte, I praised, I did praise, was praising;
du lobtest, thou praisest, &c. ;
er lobte, he praised;
wir lobten, we praised;
ihr lobtet, you praised;
sie lobten, they praised.

Spielen, to play;   die Geschichte, the story;
lachen, to laugh;   der Abend, the evening;
tanzen, to dance;   so sehr, so much;
erzählen, to tell, relate;   ganz, quite, whole;
theilen, to share, divide;   bis, till, until;
erlauben, to allow, permit;   daß, that.

Obs. The adverb so, which connects two sentences, is not translated
in English.

Dein Bruder und ich, wir wohnten zu N. in dem nämlichen Hause. Wir waren den ganzen Tag zusammen. Wir
machten unsere Aufgaben zusammen, wir spielten zusammen
und hatten kein größeres Vergnügen, als wenn wir zusammen
waren. Er liebte mich und ich liebte ihn so sehr, daß wir wie

3

Brüder waren. Wenn sein Vater ihm etwas schickte, so theilten wir es. Ich arbeitete oft für ihn und er arbeitete für mich.
Der Lehrer lobte und liebte uns. Alle guten Schüler waren
unsere Freunde; sie besuchten uns jeden Tag; wir erzählten
uns schöne Geschichten und lachten und tanzten, bis es Abend
war. Du schicktest uns oft hübsche Bücher, welche uns viel
Vergnügen machten. Wir hatten sehr oft Zeit zu lesen. Wenn
wir unsere Aufgaben gemacht hatten, erlaubte der Lehrer uns
immer zu spielen oder ein nützliches Buch zu lesen.

96.

Wählen, to choose;   das Spiel, the play, the game;
weinen, to cry, to weep;   während, while, during.

Obs. The Nominative is always placed after its verb, in a sentence,
which serves to complete the preceding one; wenn er kommt, gehe ich
mit ihm.

When we were young, we lived in this house. Your
sister bought some ribbons and chose the finest for
you. Formerly I loved play, but at present I love
books. This people always loved their king. Thy cousin was still looking for his hat, when we (are) departed. The merchant, whom thou soughtest yesterday, has been here. Thy brother sold his penknife
this morning. While we were crying, you were laughing
and dancing. My father allowed me always to read
good books and to play with my friends. We often
worked together, when you were living with your
uncle. I danced better than you, but you did your
exercise better than I. Thou wast often idle, and
thou hadst not always a mind to read and to write. I
told thee pretty stories, but thou lovedst play too much,
thou didst play the whole day. The master blamed
thee often, and the good scholars did not love thee

97.

Ich werde loben, I shall *or* I will praise;
du wirst loben, thou wilt praise;
er wird loben, he will praise;
wir werden loben, we shall praise;
ihr werdet loben, you will praise;
sie werden loben, they will praise.

Obs. Werden, taken in an absolute sense, signifies *to become;* but
when constructed with another verb, it answers to the English auxiliary verb *shall* or *will.*

Ich werde diesen Abend das Vergnügen haben, meinen Onkel zu sehen. Ich werde dir diesen hübschen Ring geben, wenn du fleißig sein wirst. Heinrich wird mir heute ein Paar schöne Handschuhe kaufen. Deine Schwester wird zufrieden sein, wenn sie ihre Aufgabe gemacht hat. Wenn wir in N. sein werden, werden wir viel Vergnügen haben. Wann werden Sie mich besuchen? Ich glaube, wir werden Sie morgen besuchen. Meine Brüder werden auch heute oder morgen kommen. Es wird meinem Vater sehr viel Vergnügen machen, sie noch einmal zu sehen. Wann werden Sie Ihrem Freunde Karl schreiben? Ich schreibe ihm in acht bis vierzehn Tagen. Wollen Sie die Güte haben, mir das Buch zu schicken, welches Sie mir versprochen haben? Ich werde es Ihnen heute schicken, Fräulein. Mein Bedienter wird es Ihnen bringen. Ich hatte es einem Freunde geliehen, der es bis jetzt gehabt hat.

98

. Müde, tired, fatigued; das Wetter, the weather; hierher, hither.

Shall you go with us? I do not believe, that my father will allow me (allows it to me). Has the shoemaker brought my boots? No, he will bring them to you this evening. What shall we do now? We will drink a glass of wine. Will you have the kindness to lend me your horse? I shall lend it you with much pleasure. We shall play to-day in the garden of our uncle; he will allow (it) us. I shall tell you a beautiful story, if you are good and diligent. Wilt thou work to-day? I believe that I shall not work to-day. Come hither, my children; you will be very tired. If your cousins are departed, they will have fine weather. Thy exercise is badly done; the master will blame thee. All (the) scholars will go to N. to-day. Charles, thou must wash thyself, if thou wilt go with Henry. Yes, Mamma, I shall wash myself at present.

99.

Ich würde loben, I should or would praise;
du würdest loben, thou wouldst praise;
er würde loben, he would praise;
wir würden loben, we should praise;
ihr würdet loben, you would praise;
sie würden loben, they would praise.

Wenn ich hätte, if I had; wenn ich wäre, if I were; gern, willingly; ob, if.

Obs. After the conjunctions wenn and ob, if, the Subjunctive Mood is used in German, when the verb is in the Imperfect or in the Pluperfect tense.

Ich würde glücklicher sein, wenn ich Bücher und Freunde hätte. Ich würde mehr Vergnügen haben, wenn meine Vettern hier wären. Du würdest nicht so reich sein, wenn du nicht so viele Geschäfte gemacht hättest. Wenn Heinrich Geld hätte, würde er diese Messer kaufen. Ich würde deinen Bruder besuchen, wenn ich Zeit hätte. Du würdest diesen Hund nicht so sehr lieben, wenn er nicht so treu wäre. Wir würden dich nicht tadeln, wenn du fleißiger gewesen wärest. Dein Onkel sagte mir, du würdest morgen nicht kommen. Welchen von diesen Stöcken würdest du wählen? Wem würdet ihr eure Blumen geben? Was würdest du sagen, wenn ich meinen Hund verkaufte? Ich würde dir erlauben zu spielen, wenn du deine Aufgaben gemacht hättest. Diese Kinder würden sehr weinen, wenn ihre Mutter abgereist wäre. Dein Vater würde uns eine schöne Geschichte erzählen, wenn wir artiger gewesen wären. Wenn du Zeit zu lesen hättest, würde ich dir ein nützliches Buch leihen. Ich würde gern mit dir gehen, aber mein Lehrer will es nicht erlauben; ich muß heute noch drei Briefe schreiben.

100.

Louisa would be very (much) pleased, if she had all these flowers. Henry would not have so many friends, if he were not so kind (gut) and good (artig). We should not yet have (be) come, if we had not received a letter from our father. We should not have sold our house, if my father had done more business (pl.) The master would blame thee, if thou hadst not done thy exercise. I should not believe it, if thou hadst not seen it. If we had an apple, we would share it. We should go with you, if we were not so tired. If I had some money, I should buy a pound of cherries. If you loved me, I should love you also. If you told me, where Mr. N. lives, I would give you a glass of wine. Would you believe that I have done this? Would you do me this pleasure, if I allowed you to play this evening? I would do it willingly, if I had time.

101.

Ausgehen, to go out.
Ich gehe aus, I go out;

du gehſt aus, thou goest out
er geht aus, he goes out;
wir gehen aus, we go out;
ihr gehet aus, you go out;
ſie gehen aus, they go out.

· Aufmachen, to open ;   abſchreiben, to copy ;
zumachen, to shut ;   mittheilen, to communicate ;
zurückſchicken, to send back ;   anziehen, to put on ;
angenehm, pleasant ;   ſchwarz, black ;
die Nachricht, the news ;   früher, earlier, sooner.

Obs. The compound verbs are formed by the addition of a particle which modifies the sense of the simple verb, and which is detached from it in the Present and Imperfect tenses of the Indicative Mood, unless the sentence begins with a conjunction or a relative pronoun.

Ich gehe heute nicht aus ; das Wetter iſt zu ſchlecht. Mein Bruder will auch nicht ausgehen. Wenn das Wetter ſchöner wäre, würden wir gern ausgehen. Heinrich, du machſt nie die Thüre zu. Kannſt du dieſe Kommode aufmachen? Ich mache mein Zimmer zu, wenn ich ausgehe. Ich ſchicke Ihnen dieſen Abend das Buch zurück, welches Sie mir geliehen haben. Mein Vetter ſchickte mir geſtern den Stock zurück, den ich ihm geliehen hatte. Schreibſt du alle dieſe Briefe ab? Mußt du alles das abſchreiben? Ich ſchreibe nur ſo viel ab, als ich will. Ich würde dieſe Aufgabe noch abſchreiben, wenn mein Lehrer es mir erlaubte. Ich muß Ihnen etwas mittheilen. Was wollen Sie mir mittheilen? Ich theile Ihnen eine angenehme Nachricht mit. Warum theilten Sie mir das nicht früher mit? Welches Kleid ziehſt du heute an? Ich ziehe mein ſchwarzes Kleid an und meine Schweſter wird ihr weißes Kleid anziehen. Wo iſt das Kleid, welches Sie anziehen? Hier iſt es.

102.

Die Gewohnheit, the habit;   aufſtehen, to get up ;
Der Spaziergang, the walk;   weggehen, to go away ;
    einen Spaziergang machen, to take a walk.

Do you not yet get up? No, I am indisposed; I shall not get up to-day. You always get up very late, that is a bad habit. I go away; I have much to do. I shall also go away. The weather is so fine, that I have a mind to take a walk. Shut the door, if you please. Open the window. Your brother always opens the door and the windows. Do you not go out to-day? I shall not go out to-day. My father wishes (will) it not. My

brother goes out twice every day. I shall send you back
your umbrella to-morrow. Send me also back the cane,
which I have lent you. What is my son doing? He
copies the letters which you have written this morning.
My uncle is arrived; I shall communicate to him the
good news. Put on your new dress; Mr. N. comes to
see (visits) us to-day.

103.

Betrügen, to deceive;	zerreißen, to tear;
beleidigen, to offend;	warten, to wait;
verlieren, to lose;	anwenden, to employ;
verbessern, to correct;	zurückgeben, to give back;
verbieten, to forbid;	die Gesellschaft, the company;
erziehen, to bring up;	die Sorgfalt, the care;
erhalten, to receive;	sogleich, immediately, at once.

Obs. The syllables be, ge, ent, er, ver and zer serve to form the
derived verbs, and are not detached from the simple verb.

Dieser Kaufmann ist ein Betrüger, er betrügt Jedermann.
Man muß Niemand betrügen. Wir betrügen Niemand. Du
beleidigst mich immer. Dein Vetter beleidigte gestern die
ganze Gesellschaft. Warum beleidigen Sie diesen Mann?
Ich erhalte heute einen Brief von meinem Freunde in Köln.
Wir erhalten alle Tage Nachricht von unserm Vater. Ich
werde morgen Geld erhalten. Diese Mutter erzieht ihre
Kinder mit vieler Sorgfalt. Wenn wir wollen, daß unsere
Kinder gut werden, müssen wir sie mit Sorgfalt erziehen.
Was suchst du, Karl? Ich habe meinen Ring verloren. Du
verlierst immer etwas. Komm, wir müssen gehen, wir können
nicht länger warten; du kannst den Ring später suchen. Gehen
Sie nur, ich komme sogleich; ich werde den Ring finden.
Warum zerreißest du dieses Papier? Das Papier ist mein,
ich kann es zerreißen. Ich verbiete dir es, es zu zerreißen.
Willst du die Güte haben, mir meine Aufgaben zu verbessern?
Dein Bruder verbesserte mir immer meine Aufgaben, als er
noch hier war. Wann geben Sie mir meinen Bleistift zurück
Deine Brüder geben nie zurück, was man ihnen leiht. Wendet
eure Zeit gut an. Man muß seine Zeit immer gut anwenden.

104.

I will not wait (any) longer. I lose my time. Shall
you play to-day? No we shall not play, we always lose.
You would not lose, if you played better. We should
play better, if you played oftener If I receive my money

I shall play once more (noch einmal). Does your father
not forbid you to play? No, he does not forbid (it) us
This child is very naughty; he tears his dresses. My
neighbor brings up his children very badly. I do not
like this young man; he always offends me. Henry
corrects his exercise; he employs his time well. He
who employs well his money, is wise (weise). If you
give me back my pencil, I shall give you back your pen.
One must always give back, what is lent us (what one
lends us).

105.

Wohnen, to dwell;	gewohnt, dwelt, been dwelling;
beleidigen, to offend;	beleidigt, offended;
anwenden, to employ;	angewendet, employed.

Obs. The past Participle of simple verbs is formed by the addition
of the initial syllable ge, and the final syllable et or t. In compound
verbs ge is placed after the particle; the derived verbs take only the
final et or t.

Haben Sie Ihre Aufgabe schon verbessert? Ich habe sie
noch nicht verbessert; ich werde sie sogleich verbessern. Ihr
Bruder hat mich gestern beleidigt; ich will nichts mehr mit
ihm zu thun haben; von heute (an) ist er mein Freund nicht
mehr. Wir wollen einen Spaziergang zusammen machen.
Ich kann in diesem Augenblicke nicht ausgehen; ich habe diesen
Morgen schon einen Spaziergang gemacht. Warum haben
Sie mir mein Federmesser noch nicht zurückgegeben? Wer hat
die Thüre aufgemacht? Wer hat Ihnen diese Nachricht mit=
getheilt? Ihr Vater hat uns gestern eine artige Geschichte
erzählt. Meine Mutter hat mir erlaubt, diesen Abend nach
N. zu gehen. Sind Sie gestern bei meinem Vetter gewesen?
Ja, wir haben den ganzen Tag bei ihm gespielt, gelacht und
getanzt. Aber habt ihr auch gearbeitet? Ich glaube es nicht;
der Lehrer hat dich schon mehrere Male getadelt, deine Schwe=
ster hat es mir oft gesagt. Wer hat euch diesen Korb Kirschen
geschickt? Hast du deinen kranken Freund noch nicht besucht?
Mein Onkel hat ein neues Pferd gekauft; er hat das alte dem
Kutscher unsers Nachbars für zwanzig Thaler verkauft.

106.

Einzig, single, only; nicht mehr, no more; Sache, Ding, thing.

Thou hast employed thy time very badly, my dear
Henry. I see that thou hast not done a single exercise

I have always praised thee, but I shall praise thee no
more. Have you played together, my children? Yes,
mamma, we have been playing and working. That is
very well (gut); I shall give you some cherries and
plums. I will divide them. We have divided them
already. Why have you shut all (the) windows? The
weather is so fine; I shall open them. Who has copied
these letters? I believe that Henry has copied them.
Have you been waiting long? We have waited (for)
half an hour. Mr. N. has sent back the umbrella, which
you had lent him. I have received a letter from my aunt
which I have not yet opened. Your cousin is arrived;
he has told us (a) hundred things. One must not believe
all that he tells. I have not believed all.

107.

Um......ʒu, in order to, to;
um ʒu loben, in order to praise, to praise;
um anʒuwenden, in order to employ.

Wünſchen, to wish; abreiſen, to depart, set out; gefällig, obliging,
ſondern, but (after a negative phrase).

Obs. The preposition ʒu, which generally precedes the Infinitive,
is placed in the compound verbs between the particle and the verb.

Ich komme, um dir ʒu ſagen, daß ich morgen abreiſe. Ich
habe meinen Bedienten geſchickt, um mir ein Pfund Zucker ʒu
kaufen. Wir leben nicht, um ʒu eſſen, ſondern wir eſſen, um
ʒu leben. Um glücklich ʒu ſein, muß man ʒufrieden ſein. Um
Freunde ʒu haben, muß man gefällig ſein. Ich habe nicht
Zeit, auszugehen. Haben Sie die Güte, dieſe ʒwei Briefe
abʒuſchreiben. Wollen Sie ſo gut ſein, die Thüre aufʒu-
machen? Wir haben Luſt, einen kleinen Spaziergang ʒu
machen. Mein Nachbar hat ʒwei Pferde ʒu verkaufen. Wer
hat dir erlaubt, ſo früh wegʒugehen? Iſt es noch nicht Zeit,
aufʒuſtehen? Ich habe das Vergnügen gehabt, den Herrn
Moll ʒu ſehen. Wünſchen Sie mit meinem Vater ʒu ſprechen?
Ich wünſche mit Ihrer Frau Mutter ʒu ſprechen. Haben
Sie Geld, um dieſen Ring ʒu kaufen? Haſt du Zeit, mir
meine Aufgabe ʒu verbeſſern? Hat dein Vater dir dieſes
Geld gegeben, um es ſo ſchlecht anʒuwenden?

108.

Das Unglück, the misfortune; der Gegenſtand, the subject.

It is no subject for laughter (in order to laugh). It is
very difficult. I have had the pleasure to dance with Miss

N. Mr. Nollet has had the kindness to lend me his horse. Do you wish to go out with me? I have no time to go to N. We have much to do to-day. My brother has six letters to copy. I have good news to communicate to you. Have the kindness to send me back my book It is time to set out. Which dress do you wish to put on? Allow me to open the window, it is so warm. I am come to see, if you are well (wohl). I am very (much) indisposed; I have too much to do. You have the bad habit, to get up too late. A young man must get up earlier. My friend has had the misfortune to lose his parents. I come to bring you your boots. That is very well (gut). I had no mind to wait (any) longer.

109.

Ich werde geliebt, I am loved;	ich wurde geliebt, I was loved,
du wirst geliebt,	du wurdest geliebt,
er wird geliebt,	er wurde geliebt,
wir werden geliebt,	wir wurden geliebt,
ihr werdet geliebt,	ihr wurdet geliebt,
sie werden geliebt,	sie wurden geliebt.

Belohnen, to reward; strafen, to punish; achten, to esteem; verachten, to despise; geschickt, clever; unwissend, ignorant.

Obs. The verb werden constructed with the past participle forms the passive voice. Thus the verb *to be* is translated by werden, when the subject is sensible of a certain action; and by sein, when he finds himself in a certain condition. *I am paid* in the sense of: *they pay me,* is expressed by: ich werde bezahlt; but in the sense of: *they have paid me,* it is expressed by: ich bin bezahlt.

Ich werde von meinem Vater gelobt, wenn ich fleißig und artig bin. Du wirst von deinem Lehrer getadelt, weil du immer faul bist. Heinrich wird gestraft, weil er unartig ist. Welcher Mann wird gelobt und welcher wird getadelt? Der geschickte Mann wird gelobt und der unwissende getadelt. Welche Knaben werden belohnt und welche werden gestraft? Diejenigen, welche fleißig sind, werden belohnt, und die, welche faul sind, gestraft. Wir werden von unsern Eltern geliebt; ihr werdet von den eurigen getadelt. Meine Brüder werden von Jedermann geachtet. Wir werden von unsern Feinden verachtet. Wird dieses Kind nie gestraft? Von wem werdet ihr gelobt? Deine Schwester wird von ihrer Mutter getadelt, weil sie nicht arbeitet. Ich wurde immer von meinem Lehrer geliebt und gelobt, weil ich fleißig und artig war. Heinrich

3*

wurde immer von seinem Vater gestraft, wenn er nicht arbeitete.

110.

Ich bin geliebt worden, I have been loved;
du bist geliebt worden,
er ist geliebt worden,
wir sind geliebt worden,
ihr seid geliebt worden,
sie sind geliebt worden.

Tödten, to kill; erfunden, invented; entdeckt, discovered; die Mühe, the trouble, pains; das Pulver, gunpowder; mehrere, several.

Ich bin von meinem Vater gestraft worden, weil ich diese Briefe nicht abgeschrieben habe. Du bist von deinem Onkel belohnt worden, weil du seine Uhr gefunden hast. Heinrich ist für seine Mühe nicht belohnt worden. Diese Nachricht ist uns durch Herrn Moll mitgetheilt worden. Von wem ist diese Aufgabe verbessert worden? Wir sind von diesem Menschen mehrere Male beleidigt worden. Diese Herren sind gestern in der Gesellschaft sehr getadelt worden. Dieses Kind ist von seiner Mutter gewaschen worden. Es ist mir gesagt worden, daß Sie einen Bedienten suchten. Von wem sind diese Kinder geschickt worden? Diese Häuser sind gestern alle verkauft worden. Wir sind oft von unserm Lehrer gelobt worden, weil wir immer unsere Aufgaben machten. Gustav Adolph ist bei Lützen getödtet worden. Das Pulver ist von Berthold Schwarz erfunden worden. Amerika ist von Columbus entdeckt worden.

111.

Sich freuen, to rejoice.

Ich freue mich, I rejoice;   Ich habe mich gefreut, I have rejoiced;
du freust dich,   du hast dich gefreut,
er freut sich,   er hat sich gefreut,
wir freuen uns,   wir haben uns gefreut,
ihr freuet euch,   ihr habt euch gefreut,
sie freuen sich.   sie haben sich gefreut.

Sich irren, to be mistaken; sich befinden, to be, to do; sich wundern, to be astonished; sich ankleiden, to dress (one's-self); sich unterhalten, to be amused; danken, to thank; zweifeln, to doubt; wiedersehen, to see again; selten, seldom; auf, on, upon.

Guten Tag, lieber Heinrich. Ich freue mich, dich wiederzusehen. Wie geht es? Wie befindest du dich? Ich danke dir, ich befinde mich sehr wohl, seit ich auf dem Lande wohne. Was macht dein Bruder? Ist er wohl? Ja, er

befindet sich sehr wohl. Was thust du, Ludwig? Ich kleide
mich an. Kleidet Ihr euch noch nicht an? Wir werden uns
später ankleiden. Haben Sie sich schon gewaschen, Henriette?
Ich habe mich noch nicht gewaschen, aber meine Schwester hat
sich schon gewaschen. Ist das mein Bruder, der da mit dem
Herrn N. kommt? Sie irren sich, es ist nicht Ihr Bruder.
Ich glaube nicht, daß ich mich irre. Ich irre mich selten. Ich
habe mich noch nie geirrt. Wir gehen diesen Abend nach N.
Ich zweifle nicht, daß wir uns gut unterhalten werden. Wie
haben Sie sich gestern in dem Concert unterhalten? Sehr gut,
Herr N. hat sehr gut gespielt. Ich wundere mich, daß Sie
nicht da waren. Ich hatte noch Vieles zu thun; ich habe bis
zehn Uhr gearbeitet.

112.

Art thou not yet dressed, Charles? I shall dress myself at present. Why hast thou not yet dressed thyself? I had still two exercises to do. I rejoice to see,
that thou art so diligent. I love him, who rejoices
when his friend is praised. I saw your brother yesterday. You are mistaken; my brother is no longer here.
I am not mistaken, I have seen him with his friend Ferdinand. Why have you not washed yourself? I should
have washed myself, if I had had any water. We were
in the country yesterday; we have been very much
amused. How does your sister do? She is very well,
since she has been (is) with her uncle. And how have
you been, since I saw you? I have been very well. I
am astonished that you are not yet departed. I shall
set out this evening.

113.

Es regnet, it rains;	es freut mich, I am glad, happy;
es schneit, it snows;	es thut mir leid, I am sorry;
es hagelt, it hails;	es ist mir kalt, I am cold;
es blitzt, it lightens;	es ist mir warm, I am warm;
es donnert, it thunders;	es hungert mich, I am hungry;
es friert, it freezes;	es durstet mich, I am thirsty.

Befehlen, to command; bleiben, to stay; erwarten, to expect; zu
Mittag essen, to dine; leben Sie wohl, farewell, adieu.

Regnet es? Nein, es regnet nicht. Es regnete, als ich
gekommen bin. Es hat die ganze Nacht geregnet. Es wird
morgen gewiß regnen. Ich glaube, daß es schneit. Hat es
geschneit? Wenn es schneite, würde es nicht regnen. Es wird

dieſe Nacht frieren, denn es iſt ſehr kalt. Ich muß ausgehen, aber es hagelt, wie ich ſehe. Mir iſt ſehr warm; es blitzt, ſogleich wird es donnern. Wir wollen nach Haus gehen. Es freut mich, daß ich Sie finde; aber es thut mir leid, daß ich nicht mit Ihnen gehen kann. Mein Onkel iſt geſtern Abend angekommen und wünſcht, daß wir heute bei ihm zu Mittag eſſen. Haben Sie nichts zu trinken, mich durſtet ſehr. Wün- ſchen Sie ein Glas Bier oder Waſſer? Sie haben nur zu be- fehlen; hier iſt, was Sie wünſchen. Aber mich hungert auch; geben Sie mir ein Stück Schinken und ein wenig Brod. Sie haben da ſchöne Birnen und Pflaumen. Es giebt dieſes Jahr viel Obſt. Wollen Sie heute bei uns bleiben? Ich danke Ihnen, ich habe meinem Vetter verſprochen, heute mit ihm nach S. zu gehen; er wird mich gewiß ſchon erwarten. Leben Sie wohl.

114.

Was für Wetter iſt es? What kind of weather is it.

What sort of weather is it? It is bad weather; it is raining (it rains). It did not rain when you came. It will rain the whole day. It has been raining this morn- ing. Does is snow? No, it does not snow. It would snow, if it were colder. I believe that it freezes. The weather is finer to-day; it is warm. I am very warm. It has lightened; it will thunder later. I am sorry that you did not come sooner. Art thou hungry? Yes, I am hungry and thirsty. I have taken (made) a long walk. I shall drink a glass of wine, if you (will) allow it. My sister will be happy to see you again. She has often spoken of you to me. Will your nephew come also? I doubt whether he will come (comes). He has too much to do.

115.

Wie viel Uhr iſt es?	What o'clock is it?
es iſt ſechs Uhr;	it is six o'clock;
es iſt halb ſieben;	it is half past six;
es iſt ein Viertel auf ſieben;	it is a quarter past six.

Aufſtehen, to get up; ſchlafen gehen, to go to bed; ausruhen, to repose: ſpazieren, ſpazieren gehen, to go to walk; zu Abend eſſen, to sup.

Um wie viel Uhr ſtehen Sie gewöhnlich auf? Ich ſtehe jeden Morgen um ſechs Uhr auf und gehe um zehn Uhr ſchlafen. Sind Sie ſpazieren geweſen? Ja, ich habe eine Stunde in dem Walde ſpaziert. Ich bin ſehr müde, ich

will ein wenig ausruhen. Wie viel Uhr ist es? Es ist acht
Uhr; es ist noch nicht halb neun. Um wie viel Uhr sind Sie
angekommen? Ich bin um ein Viertel auf sechs angekommen.
Meine Schwester ist um drei Viertel auf acht abgereist. Wie
lange bleiben Sie hier? Ich werde nur zwei bis drei Tage
bleiben. Um wie viel Uhr essen wir zu Mittag? Ich glaube
um zwölf Uhr oder um halb eins. Um drei Uhr trinken wir
Kaffee und um sieben Uhr essen wir zu Abend.

116.

Zahlreich, numerous; vor, before; nach Hause, home.

Have the kindness to tell me what o'clock it is. It is
not yet eleven o'clock; it is half past ten. I must depart
at twelve o'clock, or at half past twelve. Have you already dined? No, I shall dine with my cousin; we dine
generally at two o'clock. At what o'clock do you sup?
I shall sup at nine o'clock. Have you a mind to walk
a little? If it does not rain, I will walk a little with you.
It is fine weather; we will go to N., we shall find there
a numerous party (Gesellschaft). Are you already tired?
I am very tired; it is too warm. If you allow (it) I will
repose a little. Get up; it is time to go home. I must
go to bed before ten o'clock, in order to get up to-morrow
at five o'clock.

117.

Acc.	Dat.	Dat. and Acc.
für, for;	aus, out of;	an, at, of;
durch, by, through;	mit, with;	auf, upon, on;
ohne, without;	nach, to, after;	in, in, into;
gegen, to, towards, against;	von, from;	unter, under.

Friedrich, Frederick; der Markt, the market; der Willen, the will; der
Keller, the cellar; die Küche, the kitchen; die Kirche, the church; legen,
to put, lay; sitzen, to sit; denken, to think; wo, where; wohin, where
to; woher, where from.

Obs. The propositions an, auf, in, unter, govern the Accusative,
when the verb of the phrase denotes a movement or a direction towards an object; and the Dative, when it does not express this
movement.

Für wen sind diese Bücher? Dieses ist für mich und jenes
ist für meine Schwester. Wo ist der junge Mann, für den
Sie alle diese Sachen gekauft haben? Durch welche Straße
müssen wir gehen, um auf den Markt zu kommen? Durch

die Friedrichsstraße oder die Wilhelmsstraße? Gehen Sie ohne Regenschirm aus? Es wird sogleich regnen. Was ist das Leben ohne einen Freund? Ich kann ohne dich nicht leben. Du bist gegen den Willen deines Vaters ausgegangen. Warum ist dein Bruder immer gegen mich? Woher kommst du? Ich komme vom Spaziergange, aus der Schule, aus der Kirche. Die Magd kommt aus dem Keller, aus dem Garten, aus der Küche. Mit wem seid ihr ausgegangen? Mit dem Onkel, mit der Tante, mit Ihnen. Nach dem Essen gehen wir aus. Wann kommen Sie zurück? Kommen Sie vor oder nach uns zurück? Wir werden nach Ihnen zurückkommen. Wo ist meine Schwester? Sie ist in der Kirche, in dem Garten, auf dem Markte. Wohin geht deine Mutter? Sie geht in die Küche, in den Keller, auf den Markt. Wohin hast du mein Buch gelegt? Ich habe es auf den Tisch, unter den Stuhl gelegt. Wo ist die kleine Louise? Sie sitzt auf dem Stuhle, unter dem Tische, an der Thüre. Schreiben Sie an Ihren Vetter oder an Ihre Base? An wen denken Sie? Ich denke an die arme Frau, welche ich gestern bei Ihnen gesehen habe.

118.

Der Schrank, the closet; undankbar, ungrateful.

This is for me, that is for you. He who is not for me, is against me. I cannot do this without him, without her, without you. I shall arrive before you; you will arrive after me. You are ungrateful towards us. I always think of you, but you never think of me. There is thy little sister; hast thou nothing for her? You do not love my brother, you are always against him. Where is your son? This fruit and these flowers are for him. Where have you been? We have been at (in the) church and at (in the) school. Where are you going? We are going into the garden, to (on the) market, into the kitchen. Where do these children come from? They come from the public walk (Spaziergang), from church, from the garden. Where have you put my stockings and shoes? I have put them on your chair, on the table, in the closet. Have you seen my brother? I have seen him at the public walk, in the garden, at the door. I write to my uncle and aunt. We often speak of him and of her.

119.

Im instead of in dem;   am instead of an dem;
ins .... in das;   ans .... an das;
zum .... zu dem;   vom .... von dem,
zur .... zu der;   unterm ...... unter dem.

Das Feuer, the fire; sich stellen, to place one's-self, to stand.

Obs. The quickness of the pronunciation has introduced the custom of contracting the definite article with certain prepositions.

Die Magd ist im Keller oder im Garten. Wir gehen diesen Abend ins Theater oder ins Concert. Schicken Sie den Bedienten zum Schuhmacher oder zum Schneider? Gehen wir heute zur Tante oder bleiben wir zu Hause? Waren Sie gestern bei dem Minister? Kommen Sie zu mir oder zu meinem Bruder? Warum sitzen Sie immer beim Feuer? Ist Ihnen so kalt? Was haben Sie am Auge, am Fuße? Warum tragen Sie eine Feder am Hute? Stellen Sie sich an die Thüre oder ans Fenster. Haben Sie diese Blume vom Gärtner erhalten? Sie arbeiten vom Morgen bis zum Abend. Was machen Sie unterm Tische? Ich suche meine Bleifeder. Karl hat sie ins Schreibzeug gelegt.

120.

Wovon, of what;   davon, of that, of it;
womit, with what;   damit, with that, with it
wozu, for what;   dazu, for that, for it;
woran, at what;   daran, at that, at it;
worin, in what;   darin, in that, in it;
wodurch, by what;   dadurch, by that, by it.

Herab, hinab, down;
herauf, hinauf, up;
herein, hinein, in.

Brauchen, to use; gesprochen, spoken; gedacht, thought; ging, went; fiel, fell; das Klavier, the piano.

Obs. 1. All these particles are formed of prepositions, combined with the adverbs wo, da, her and hin. If, in the formation of these words, two vowels meet, an r is inserted, to avoid the hiatus. 2. Her denotes a movement towards the person speaking; hin a movement from the speaker.

Wovon sprechen Sie? Ist dies das Buch, wovon Sie sprechen? Womit haben Sie das gemacht? Ist das die Feder, womit Sie diesen Brief geschrieben haben? Wozu brauchen Sie das? Woran denken Sie denn? Ist das das Haus, worin Ihr Onkel wohnt, die Stadt, wodurch Sie gekommen sind? Hat man von meinem Unglück gesprochen? Ja, man hat davon gesprochen. Haben Sie an meine Sache gebacht? Nein, ich habe nicht daran gedacht. Sind Sie mit Ihrem neuen Klavier zufrieden? Nein, ich bin nicht zufrieden damit. Ist noch Wein in der Flasche? Nein, es ist keiner mehr darin. Wie viel Ellen müssen Sie zu einem neuen Rocke haben? Ich muß drei und eine halbe Elle dazu haben. Kommen Sie herauf. Gehen Sie hinab, hinunter. Warum kommen Sie nicht herein? Warum gehen Sie nicht hinein? Der Knabe ging zu nah' ans Wasser und fiel hinein. Werden Sie diesen Abend ins Theater gehen? Wir werden nicht hin= gehen, aber Heinrich und Karl gehen hin.

121.

Bitten, to beg, to ask; der Krieg, the war; das Schauspiel, the play.

Do you know of what I speak, of what I think? That is not the same street, through which we came (are come) this morning, the same house where we were yesterday. Do you speak of (the) war? Yes, we speak of it. Do you think of the concert? We do not think of it. Are you pleased with this ring? I am very (much) pleased with it. Why do you not come up? Tell your brother that I am coming down directly. Come in, my friends. I beg you to come in. Do you go to the play this evening? We shall not go there. Do you know, where this gentleman lives, where he goes to, and where he is? We do not know it.

122.

Der Tisch, the table; das Tischchen, the little table.
Die Taube, the pigeon; pflanzen, to plant; eben, so eben, just now, just.

Obs. Diminutives are formed by adding the syllable chen, and softening the radical vowel. If the primitive word ends in e or en, this termination is omitted.

Amalie hat ihr Hütchen verloren. Wir haben drei hübsche Bäumchen gepflanzt. Wem gehört dieses artige Gärtchen? Wie viel hast du für dieses Täubchen bezahlt? Wohin gehen diese Herrchen? Komm, Louischen, wir wollen zu der Tante gehen, sie hat ein neues Kätzchen und ein neues Hündchen. Ich habe eben ein Briefchen von meiner Schwester erhalten, worin sie mich bittet, ihr ein Messerchen und ein Löffelchen zu kaufen. Ich will recht artig sein, Mütterchen, wenn du mir ein neues Kleidchen kaufst. Trage dieses Tischchen in den Garten, Henriette, wir wollen ein Stündchen darin arbeiten.

Welches Dörfchen sehe ich da unten im Walde? Welches
Kind hat diese Schühchen verloren? Friedrich hat ein artiges
Vögelchen vom Gärtner erhalten. Wem gehören alle diese
Blümchen? Wo ist dein Schwesterchen, Johann?

123.

Nöthig haben, to want; sich schämen, to be ashamed of; pflegen, to
use, to be in the habit of; schläfrig, sleepy; Durst haben, to be thirsty;
der Spaziergang, the walk, the public walk; scheinen, to shine; früh,
early; spät, late; ich möchte, I should like.

Heinrich, hast du Lust, einen Spaziergang mit mir zu machen? Ich habe keine Lust, jetzt auszugehen. Ich bin schläfrig. Schämst du dich nicht, so faul zu sein? Komm, wir
wollen in den Garten meines Onkels gehen. Wie viel Uhr
ist es? Es ist erst sechs Uhr, die Sonne scheint noch. Du
hast Recht, es ist noch früh, ich will mit dir gehen. Ich pflege
jeden Abend einen Spaziergang zu machen, ehe ich zu Bette
gehe. Das ist eine gute Gewohnheit. Es ist mir aber sehr
warm; wir gehen zu geschwinde. Ich habe großen Durst,
ich möchte einmal trinken. Wenn man warm ist, muß man
nicht trinken. Ich habe nöthig, ein wenig auszuruhen; ich bin
so müde, daß ich nicht mehr fort kann. Du mußt einen Augenblick Geduld haben. Komm, ich fürchte zu spät nach
Hause zu kommen.

124.

To have patience, Geduld haben; to fear, fürchten; to be hard-
hearted, hartherzig sein; to have the head-ache, Kopfweh haben; to
take pains, sich bemühen; the moment, der Augenblick; some pretext,
ein Vorwand, (masc.); directly, sogleich; the advice, der Rath.

How, you are still in bed? Are you not ashamed, to
sleep so long? I should be ashamed to get up so late.
I cannot get up to-day, I have the head-ache. You are
a little idler (Faulenzer). When you must go to school,
you always look for some pretext. You are in the
habit of going to bed early and getting up late. That
is a bad habit. I beg you, to have patience (for) a
moment. I shall get up directly. I have no mind, to
wait (any) longer. I fear to come to church too late.
You are very hard-hearted; you have no pity for a poor
patient (der Kranke). You are not ill; you have no mind
to go to school. You are right my friend; I shall take
pains to get rid of this fault (diesen Fehler abzulegen) and
to follow your good advice.

125.
Glauben, to believe.

I believe that it is already late. We do not believe it. Neither does my brother believe it. Do you believe it? I do not believe it. If I did believe it, you would laugh. I have never believed this. Who would have believed that? I should believe it, if you told me so (it me). It is an incredible thing. You would believe it indeed, if you saw it. These gentlemen do not believe it. How will you have me (that I should) believe it? Your brother believed every thing that was told him (all that one told him); he was too credulous. He would not believe it, if he knew you.

Neither, auch nicht; laugh, lachen; would have, hätte; incredible, unglaublich; indeed, wohl; saw, sehen; credulous, leichtgläubig; knew, könnte.

126.
Sagen, to say, to tell.

I have something to tell you. What have you to say to me? I tell you nothing. Tell (it) me only. I shall tell you another time. You will not tell my brother, what I have written to you? Do not tell him, that I am still in bed. What has he told you? Have I not told it you? You have not yet told (it) me. Do you wish (will you) me to (that I) tell it? One must not tell everything that one knows. He has told it me in a whisper. Your uncle told me yesterday, that he would sell his house. What do you say to that? I would tell you with pleasure, if I knew it. If I said otherwise, I should lie.

Only, nur; knows, weiß; in a whisper, ins Ohr; if I knew, wenn ich wüßte; otherwise, anders; lie, lügen.

127.
Wünschen, to wish; hoffen, to hope.

I wish, that your enterprise may succeed. We often wish (for) things, which are hurtful to us. I should wish to be able to serve you. I hope that our friend will obtain the situation that he wishes (to get). She did hope to win her law-suit, but she was mistaken. My cousin has nothing more to hope. We hope every-thing of Providence. My sister hopes, that you will do what you have promised her. Never wish (for) what

you cannot have. What do you wish? (For) what do
you hope? I believe that my father will arrive to-day
We must hope it. These gentlemen wish that we
should depart. Does your sister wish to go with us?

May succeed, gelingen; ·hurtful, ſchädlich; to be able, können; to
serve, bienen, nützlich ſein; obtain, erhalten; situation, Stelle (fem.);
win, gewinnen; law-suit, Prozeß; Providence, Vorſehung (fem.); for
what, worauf.

128.

Schreiben, to write; ich ſchrieb, I wrote; geſchrieben, written;
leſen, to read; ich las, I read; geleſen, read.

I am writing a letter to my brother. My mother
will write to him to-morrow. You wrote better formerly. What have you written to him? Have you not
yet written to him, that our friend Henry is dead?
Write that to him. If I had a good pen, I should
write also. You write too fast; write more slowly.
Show me what you have written. You must write
once more. What do you read? I read an amusing
book. What didst thou read yesterday, when thou wast
with thy uncle? I read the fables of Gellert, which
are very well written. We should read oftener if we
had more time. How must we (one) read this word?
Remember well, what you have read. Would you like
(will you) me to (that I should) read this letter to you?
I should like to know how to read like you.

Formerly, früher, ſonſt; fast, ſchnell; slowly, langſam; show, zeigen;
once more, noch einmal; amusing, unterhaltend; fable, Fabel (fem.);
remember, behalten; I should like to know how, ich möchte können;
like, wie.

129.

Sehen, to see; ich ſah, I saw; geſehen, seen;
kennen, to know; ich kannte, I knew; gekannt, known.

What do I see? Do you not see it? I see nothing.
But do look. It is well worth the trouble to see it. I
saw your cousin yesterday. Have you not seen him?
Do you see how I do this? Your cousin does not see
me. If I saw my friend, I should tell him that you are
here. Would you like (will you) me to (that I) bring
(a) light; or can you see still? I have seen Mr. N. to-
day. Does he know me? I believe that he knows you.
He has greeted me. Have you also known my uncle?
Have you not told me that you knew him? I should

know him again if I saw him. Your brother has recognized me by my˙voice. These children do not know me (any) more.

Do look, ſeḥen Sie boḍ einmal; well worth the trouble, woḥl ber Müḥe werth; to greet, grüßen; to know again, to recognize, wieber erfennen; by the voice, an ber Stimme.

130.

Geḥen, to go; iḍ ging, I went; gegangen, gone; weggeḥen, to go away; ausgeḥen, to go out.

Where are you going? I am going to my aunt, and my brother goes to school. Where did you go this morning with your cousin? We went to church. I should willingly go to walk, if you would go with me. I shall go with you, but do not go so fast. Where is your sister? She is gone to see her uncle. We should have gone together if I had had time. Shall you not go to N. to-morrow? My father does not wish (will not) me to (that) I should go there. I go away. Do you go away already? Henry does not yet go away. William is already gone away. Go away. I must go away. I believe that your friends are gone away already. At what o'clock do you go out? I go out every morning at seven o'clock. And at what o'clock dost thou go out? I went out yesterday at six o'clock. Is your brother already gone out? To-morrow I shall go out early. I must go out at half past one. My mother did not wish (would not) that I should go out (went out).

To go to walk, ſpazieren geḥen; to go to see any one, zu Semanbem geḥen.

131.

Kommen, to come; iḍ fam, I came; gefommen, come; zurüffommen, to come back; anfommen, to arrive.

Whence do you come so late? We come out of the garden. Eliza does not come to-day; she is gone into the country with her father. Come to see me this afternoon. It is possible that I may come. I should wish that you came early. Formerly you came every day. I should come oftener if I had not so much to do. My brother is not yet come back. He will come back this evening. My uncle does not come back (any) more. We saw your uncle, when we came back from the country. At what o'clock does the post arrive? I believe it arrives at three o'clock. Yesterday it came very late. Formerly it arrived at two o'clock. My sisters will arrive to-day from Liege.

Eliza, Glife; to come to see, befuchen; afternoon, Nachmittag; possible, möglich; evening, Abend; the post, die Poft; Liege, Lüttich.

132.

Trinken, to drink; ich trank, I drank; getrunken, drunk; austrinken, to finish (a glass, a cup, &c.); essen, to eat; ich aß, I ate; gegessen, aten; zu Mittag essen, to dine.

Have you nothing to drink. I drink no wine. We drink only water, and my brother drinks beer. You do not drink. I have the honor to drink your health. When I was young, I drank nothing but (only) milk. This gentleman has drank a little too much. He does not eat much, but he drinks much. Who has drunk out of my glass? I will drink no more. We will drink another glass. The wine which we drank yesterday was so good, that every one drank a bottle. Finish your glass. You have not yet finished your glass. Drink again. Have you no appetite? Eat a little ham. I have eaten enough, I have no more appetite. You will eat another piece of meat. This child eats the whole day. We ate some days ago (some) delicious fish. At what o'clock do you dine? I dine generally at two o'clock, but to-day I dine at four o'clock. After dinner I drink a cup of coffee and then I go out to walk.

To your health, auf ihre Gesundheit; the honor, die Ehre; another glass, noch ein Glas; every one, Jeder; again, noch einmal; the appetite, der Appetit; some days ago, vor einigen Tagen; delicious fish, töftliche Fifche; the dinner, das Mittageffen; then, dann.

133.

Können, to be able, to know; ich konnte, I could; gekonnt, been able; wiffen, to know; ich wußte, I knew; gewußt, known.

Can you tell me what o'clock it is? I cannot tell (it) you, I have not (got) my watch with me. If I had it with me, I could tell you exactly. I shall not be able to go out to-day; my father is ill. My brother will not be able to come. I should wish, however, that he could come. I should be able to lend you this book, if it belonged to me. Lewis can carry this letter to the post-office. I could not go out yesterday. My friend could not answer your letter, because he had too much to do. Do you know when my father will

come back? I do not know. Does your sister know it?
We know all, that we must die. Do you know (how) to
dance? I have known it, but I do not know it (any)
more. My father knew several languages. Henry can
speak German. These boys know neither how to read
nor how to write. The men do not know (how) to employ their time. I did not know that your brother was
departed. I shall soon know who has done that. How
can you suppose (will you) that I should know this?
I should wish that you knew it. (I would, &c.)

Exactly, genau; however, jedoch; I should wish, ich wollte; to belong, gehören; answer, antworten auf (Acc.); because, weil; to dance,
tanzen; to speak German, deutsch sprechen.

134.

Thun, to do; ich that, I did; gethan, done;
nehmen, to take; ich nahm, I took; genommen, taken.

What are you doing? I do what you have ordered
me (to do). What were you doing when I came in? I
was lighting the fire. What will you do this evening?
I shall do nothing this evening. Your brother does
nothing but run. These children do nothing but drink
and eat. When one has done one's duty, one has nothing to reproach one's self (with). You have done a good
action. Why are you in bad spirits? What have they
done to you? One must do the will of God. You will
write to him; in your place I should not do it. I
shall do my best to satisfy him. I take this for myself.
How many books do you take? Your brother always
takes my pen. Will you take my place? Take what
you wish. Take this child by the hand. Who has
taken my copy-book? Your cousin took my cane yesterday. I shall take one of these apples, if you allow
(it). I have taken the liberty to write to him. We
took some chairs and we sat down. If I took these
books, my father would scold me.

To order, befehlen; to come in, hereinkommen; to light, anzünden;
nothing but, nichts als; one's duty, seine Pflicht; to reproach one's
self, sich vorwerfen; action, Handlung, That; in bad spirits, übler
Laune; in your place, an Ihrer Stelle; to do one's best, sein Möglich-
stes thun; to satisfy, befriedigen; myself, mich; place, Platz (m.); by
the hand, bei der Hand; liberty, Freiheit; to sit down, sich setzen; to
scold any one, mit Jemandem schmälen.

135.

Schlafen, to sleep; ich schlief, I slept; geschlafen, slept; brechen, zerbrechen, to break; ich brach, I broke; gebrochen, broken.

We sleep too much; you sleep less than we. I sleep generally (for) seven hours. Formerly I slept longer. My brother slept yesterday till eight o'clock; but to-morrow he will not sleep so long, because he must depart for Cologne at four o'clock. Our mother does not allow us to sleep longer, than till six o'clock. I sleep soundly. You were very uneasy in your sleep last night. This child sleeps very peaceably. We have no knife to cut our bread; therefore we break it. You will break this stick, if you bend it so. I do not believe that it (will) break. I should not like it to (that it did) break. This boy has broken a pane. He broke two last week. This servant is very heedless; she breaks something every day. Yesterday she broke two glasses, and on Sunday half a dozen cups and saucers.

Less, weniger; soundly, sehr fest; to be uneasy in one's sleep, unruhig schlafen; last, vorig; peaceable, sanft; to cut, schneiden; therefore, beßhalb; to bend. beugen; I should not like, ich möchte nicht; pane, Scheibe; heedless, unbedacht; on Sunday, am Sonntag; cups and saucers, Tassen.

136.

Rathen, to advise; ich rieth, I advised; gerathen, advised; bringen, te bring; ich brachte, I brought; gebracht, brought; empfehlen, to re commend; ich empfahl, I recommended; empfohlen, recommended.

I do not know what to resolve; what do you advise me to do? One advises me this, the other that. They advised me yesterday, to give up a part of my rights. I should like you to (that you advised) me; in you I have the greatest confidence. Because you wish me to (that I advise) you, I tell you that the most unprofitable accommodation is better than the most favorable law-suit. I shall bring you the fruits which you desire (to have). I believe they have brought them to me already. They brought me yesterday some letters from Berlin. When you come back, bring your sister with (you). Mr. N. will bring his son with (him) to-morrow. They brought their aunt with (them) from Vienna. I should wish you to (that you brought) the young man with (you) of whom you have spoken. He recommends his son to me. You recommended your

business to him.   I have recommended him to watch
over him.

What to resolve, wozu id) mid) entfd)ließen foll; ore, they, man;
even, fogar; to give up, abtreten; the right, das Recht; I should like,
id) wollte; in you, zu Ihnen; the greatest confidence, das meiste Zu=
trauen; the most unprofitable accommodation, &c., ein magerer Ver=
gleid) ist beffer, als ein fetter Prozeß; to desire, wünfd)en; the business,
das Gefd)äft; to watch, wad)en; over, über.

EXERCISES FOR READING.

1. THE LITTLE DOG.

Ein Fräulein, mit Namen Karoline, ging einst an dem Ufer
eines Fluffes fpazieren.   Sie begegnete hier einigen böfen
Knaben, die ein Hündd)en ertränken wollten; fie hatte Mitleid
mit dem armen Thiere, kaufte es und nahm es mit fid) auf das
Sd)loß.

Das Hündd)en hatte bald mit feiner neuen Gebieterin Be=
kanntfd)aft gemad)t und verließ fie keinen Augenblick mehr.
Eines Abends, als fie fid) zu Bette legen wollte, fing das
Hündd)en plötzlid) an zu bellen.   Karoline nahm das Lid)t,
fah unter das Bett und erblickte einen Menfd)en, von fürd)ter=
lid)em Ausfehen, der fid) hier verborgen hatte.   Es war ein
Dieb.

Karoline rief um Hülfe und alle Bewohner des Sd)loffes
eilten auf ihr Gefd)rei herbei.   Sie ergriffen den Räuber und
überlieferten ihn der Gered)tigkeit.   Er geftand in feinem Ver=
höre, daß es feine Abfid)t gewefen wäre, das Fräulein zu er=
morden und das Sd)loß zu plündern.

Karoline dankte dem Himmel, daß er fie fo glücklid) geret=
tet habe, und fagte: Niemand hätte geglaubt, daß das arme
Thierd)en, dem id) das Leben gerettet habe, mir aud) das mei=
nige retten würde.

2. THE GOOD NEIGHBORS.

Der kleine Knabe eines Müllers näherte fid) zu fehr dem
Bad)e und fiel hinein.   Der Sd)mied, welcher jenfeit des Ba=
d)es wohnte, fah es, fprang in das Waffer, zog das Kind
heraus und brad)te es dem Vater.

Ein Jahr darauf brach während der Nacht Feuer in der Schmiede aus. Das Haus stand ganz in Flammen, ehe der Schmied es merkte. Er rettete sich mit Frau und Kindern. Nur sein kleinstes Töchterchen hatte man im ersten Schrecken vergessen.

Das Kind fing in dem brennenden Hause an zu schreien; allein kein Mensch wollte sich hineinwagen. Da kam plötzlich der Müller, sprang in die Flammen, brachte das Kind glücklich heraus, gab es dem Schmied in die Arme und sagte:

Gott sei gelobt, daß er mir Gelegenheit gab, Euch meine Dankbarkeit zu beweisen. Ihr habt meinen Sohn aus dem Wasser gezogen, und ich habe mit Gottes Hülfe Eure Tochter aus dem Feuer errettet.

3. THE BROKEN HORSE-SHOE.

Ein Bauer ging mit seinem Sohne, dem kleinen Thomas, in die Stadt. Sieh, sagte er unterwegs zu ihm, da liegt ein Stück von einem Hufeisen an der Erde, hebe es auf und stecke es in die Tasche. Bah, versetzte Thomas, das ist nicht der Mühe werth, daß man sich dafür bückt. Der Vater erwiederte nichts, nahm das Eisen, und steckte es in seine Tasche. Im nächsten Dorfe verkaufte er es dem Schmiede für drei Heller und kaufte dafür Kirschen.

Hierauf setzten sie ihren Weg fort. Die Sonne war brennend heiß. Man sah weit und breit weder Haus, noch Wald, noch Quelle. Thomas verging vor Durst und konnte seinem Vater nur mit Mühe folgen.

Da ließ dieser, wie durch Zufall, eine Kirsche fallen. Thomas hob sie so gierig auf, als wäre es Gold, und steckte sie schnell in den Mund. Einige Schritte weiter ließ der Vater eine zweite Kirsche fallen, welche Thomas mit derselben Gierigkeit ergriff. Dieß dauerte fort, bis er sie alle aufgehoben hatte.

Als er die letzte verzehrt hatte, wandte der Vater sich zu ihm hin und sagte: Sieh, wenn du dich ein einziges Mal hättest bücken wollen, um das Hufeisen aufzuheben, so würdest du nicht nöthig gehabt haben, es hundert Mal für die Kirschen zu thun.

4. THE HIDDEN TREASURE.

Kurz vor seinem Tode sagte ein Bauer zu seinen drei Söhnen: Liebe Kinder, ich kann euch nichts hinterlassen, als diese

4

Hütte und den Weinberg, der daran stößt. Allein in diesem Weinberge liegt ein Schatz verborgen. Grabet fleißig nach, so werdet ihr ihn finden.

Nach dem Tode des Vaters gruben die Söhne den ganzen Weinberg mit dem größten Fleiße um, aber sie fanden weder Gold noch Silber. Da sie aber den Boden noch nie mit so viel Sorgfalt bearbeitet hatten, so brachte er eine solche Menge Trauben hervor, daß sie darüber erstaunten.

Jetzt erriethen die Söhne, was ihr Vater mit dem Schatze gemeint hatte, und sie schrieben an die Thüre des Weinberges mit großen Buchstaben: Arbeitsamkeit ist der größte Schatz des Menschen.

5. THE OAK AND THE WILLOW.

Nach einer sehr stürmischen Nacht ging ein Vater mit seinem Sohne auf das Feld, um zu sehen, welchen Schaden der Sturm verursacht habe. Sieh doch, rief der Knabe, da liegt die große, starke Eiche auf dem Boden hingestreckt, während die schwache Weide am Bache noch aufrecht dasteht. Ich hätte geglaubt, der Sturmwind würde leichter die Weide als die Eiche niedergerissen haben.

Mein Sohn, sagte der Vater, die stolze Eiche, die sich nicht biegen kann, mußte brechen; allein die geschmeidige Weide hat dem Sturmwinde nachgegeben und ist daher verschont geblieben.

6. THE GRATEFUL LION.

Ein armer Sklave, der aus dem Hause seines Herrn entflohen war, wurde zum Tode verurtheilt. Man führte ihn auf einen großen Platz, welcher mit Mauern umgeben war, und ließ einen furchtbaren Löwen auf ihn los. Tausende von Menschen waren Zeugen dieses Schauspiels.

Der Löwe sprang grimmig auf den armen Menschen zu; allein plötzlich blieb er stehen, wedelte mit dem Schweife, hüpfte voll Freude um ihn herum und leckte ihm freundlich die Hände. Jedermann verwunderte sich, und fragte den Sklaven, wie das komme.

Der Sklave erzählte: Als ich meinem Herrn entlaufen war, verbarg ich mich in einer Höhle mitten in der Wüste. Da kam auf einmal dieser Löwe herein, winselte und zeigte mir seine Tatze, in der ein großer Dorn stak. Ich zog ihm den

Dorn heraus und von der Zeit an versah mich der Löwe mit Wildpret und wir lebten in der Höhle friedlich zusammen. Bei der letzten Jagd wurden wir gefangen und von einander getrennt. Nun freut sich das gute Thier, mich wieder gefunden zu haben.

Alles Volk war über die Dankbarkeit dieses wilden Thieres entzückt, und bat laut um Gnade für den Sklaven und den Löwen. Der Sklave wurde frei gelassen und reichlich beschenkt. Der Löwe folgte ihm wie ein Hündchen und blieb stets bei ihm, ohne Jemand ein Leid zu thun.

COLLECTION OF WORDS.

1. THE TOWN.

Die Stadt, the town;
die Vorstadt, the suburb;
das Thor, the gate;
der Platz, the square;
der Markt, the market-place;
die Straße, the street;
das Pflaster, the pavement;
das Haus, the house;
das Gebäude, the building;
die Kirche, the church;
der Thurm, the tower, spire;
die Domkirche, the cathedral;
die Post, the post-office;

das Zollhaus, the custom house;
das Theater, the theatre;
die Börse, the exchange;
das Spital, the hospital;
das Wirthshaus, the inn;
das Kaffeehaus, the coffee-house;
der Palast, the palace;
die Mauer, the wall;
die Festung, the fortress;
der Hafen, the harbor;
die Umgegend, the environs.

2. THE HOUSE.

Das Haus, the house;
die Thür, the door;
das Thor, the gate;
das Schloß, the lock;
der Schlüssel, the key;
die Klingel, the bell;
die Treppe, the staircase;
eine Stufe, a step;
ein Zimmer, a room;
der Saal, the saloon;
das Fenster, the window;
die Laden, the shutters;

die Decke, the ceiling;
der Fußboden, the floor;
die Wand, the wall;
der Kamin, the chimney;
die Küche, the kitchen;
der Keller, the cellar;
der Speicher, the garret, loft;
das Dach, the roof;
der Hof, the court-yard;
der Garten, the garden;
der Stall, the stable;
der Brunnen, the well.

3. THE FURNITURE.

Der Tisch, the table;
der Stuhl, the chair;
der Spiegel, the looking-glass;
der Schrank, the wardrobe;

die Kommode, the chest of drawers;
das Kanapee, the couch;
das Gemälde, the picture;

die Staubuhr, the clock;
das Bett, the bed;
die Matratze, the matress;
die Decke, the bed-cloth;
der Ofen, the stove;
der Leuchter, the candlestick;
der Löffel, the spoon;
die Gabel, the fork;
das Messer, the knife;
die Tasse, the cup and saucer;

das Tischtuch, the table-cloth,
das Tellertuch, the napkin;
das Handtuch, the towel;
die Lichtscheere, the snuffers;
der Teller, the plate;
das Kissen, the pillow;
das Bettuch, the sheet;
die Vorhänge, the curtains;
das Glas, the glass;
die Flasche, the bottle;
der Korb, the basket.

4. THE PROFESSIONS.

Das Handwerk, the profession;
der Handwerker, the artisan;
der Metzger, the butcher;
der Bäcker, the baker;
der Müller, the miller;
der Hutmacher, the hatter;
der Schneider, the tailor;
der Schuster, the shoemaker;
der Barbier, the barber;
der Schreiner, the joiner;
der Zimmermann, the carpenter;
der Glaser, the glazier;

der Schlosser, the lock-smith;
der Schmied, the smith;
der Hufschmied, the farrier;
der Sattler, the saddler;
der Böttcher, the cooper;
der Gerber, the tanner;
der Kaufmann, the merchant;
der Buchhändler, the bookseller;
der Buchbinder, the bookbinder;
der Maurer, the mason;
die Nähterin, the seamstress;
die Wäscherin, the laundress.

5. THE VICTUALS.

Das Brod, the bread;
das Mehl, the meal, flour;
das Fleisch, the meat;
der Braten, the roast-meat;
Kalbfleisch, veal;
Rindfleisch, beef;
Hammelfleisch, mutton;
der Fisch, the fish;
das Ei, the egg;
der Salat, the salad;
der Senf, the mustard;

das Salz, the salt;
das Oel, the oil;
der Essig, the vinegar;
Schweinefleisch, pork;
der Schinken, the ham;
das Gemüse, the vegetable;
die Suppe, the soup;
der Kohl, the cabbage;
die Kartoffel, the potato;
die Erbse, the pea;
die Bohne, the bean;

der Kuchen, the cake;
das Obst, the fruit;
der Pfeffer, the pepper;
die Butter, the butter;
der Käse, the cheese;
die Milch, the milk;
der Wein, the wine;

das Bier, the beer;
das Frühstück, the breakfast;
das Mittagsessen, the dinner;
das Vesperbrod, the afternoon's luncheon;
das Abendessen, the supper.

6. THE CLOTHING.

Der Rock, the coat;
das Kleid, the gown;
der Mantel, the cloak;
die Weste, the waistcoat;
die Jacke, the jacket;
der Schuh, the shoe;
der Strumpf, the stocking;
der Stiefel, the boot;
der Pantoffel, the slipper;
das Hemd, the shirt, shift;
die Schürze, the apron;
der Handschuh, the glove;
der Ring, the ring;

das Taschentuch, the handkerchief;
der Hut, the hat;
die Mütze, the cap;
die Uhr, the watch;
der Regenschirm, the umbrella;
der Sonnenschirm, the parasol;
der Fächer, the fan;
der Schleier, the veil;
der Stock, the cane;
der Beutel, the purse;
die Brille, the spectacles.

7. THE HUMAN BODY.

Der Mensch, the man;
der Körper, the body;
der Kopf, the head;
das Haar, the hair;
das Gesicht, the face;
die Stirne, the forehead;
das Auge, the eye;
die Nase, the nose;
das Ohr, the ear;
der Mund, the mouth;
das Kinn, the chin;
der Bart, the beard;
die Lippe, the lip;
der Zahn, the tooth;
die Zunge, the tongue;

der Hals, the neck;
die Schulter, the shoulder;
der Rücken, the back;
der Arm, the arm;
die Hand, the hand;
der Finger, the finger;
der Nagel, the nail;
die Brust, the breast;
das Herz, the heart;
der Magen, the stomach;
das Bein, the leg;
der Fuß, the foot;
das Knie, the knee;
die Zehe, the toe;
das Gehirn, the brain

8. THE QUADRUPEDS.

Das Thier, the animal;
das Pferd, the horse;
der Esel, the donkey;
der Hund, the dog;
die Katze, the cat;
die Ratte, the rat;
die Maus, the mouse;
der Maulwurf, the mole;
das Schwein, the hog;
die Ziege, the goat;
die Gemse, the chamois;
der Hase, the hare;
das Eichhorn, the squirrel;
der Affe, the monkey;

der Hirsch, the stag;
das Reh, the roe;
der Ochse, the ox;
der Stier, the bull;
die Kuh, the cow;
das Kalb, the calf;
das Schaf, the sheep;
das Lamm, the lamb;
der Fuchs, the fox;
der Wolf, the wolf;
der Bär, the bear;
der Löwe, the lion;
das Kameel, the camel;
der Elephant, the elephant.

9. THE BIRDS.

Der Vogel, the bird;
der Hahn, the cock;
das Huhn, the hen;
das Hühnchen, the chicken;
der Schwan, the swan;
die Gans, the goose;
die Ente, the duck;
die Taube, the pigeon;
der Pfau, the peacock;
die Wachtel, the quail;
die Schnepfe, the snipe;

das Rebhuhn, the partridge;
der Krammetsvogel, the field
fare.
die Amsel, the black-bird;
die Lerche, the lark;
die Nachtigall, the nightingale;
die Schwalbe, the swallow;
der Zeisig, the green-finch;
der Fink, the finch;
der Sperling, the sparrow.

10. THE FISHES AND INSECTS.

Der Fisch, the fish;
der Hecht, the pike;
der Lachs, the salmon;
der Karpfen, the carp;
die Schleie, the tench;
der Aal, the eel;
die Forelle, the trout;
die Kröte, the toad;
der Frosch, the frog;

der Wurm, the worm;
die Raupe, the caterpillar;
die Ameise, the ant;
die Spinne, the spider;
der Häring, the herring;
die Auster, the oyster;
die Muschel, the muscle-fish;
der Krebs, the craw-fish;
die Schlange, the snake;

die Fliege, the fly;   die Wespe, the wasp;

die Biene, the bee;   der Schmetterling, the butterfly

11. THE TREES AND FLOWERS.

Der Baum, the tree;   die Rose, the rose;

der Apfelbaum, the apple-tree;   die Nelke, the pink;

der Birnbaum, the pear-tree;   die Tulpe, the tulip;

der Pflaumenbaum, the plum-tree;   die Lilie, the lily;

die Levkoje, the stock;

der Kirschbaum, the cherry-tree;   das Veilchen, the violet;

die Maiblume, the lily of the valley;

der Nußbaum, the nut-tree;

die Eiche, the oak-tree;   die Kornblume, the corn-flower;

die Fichte, the pine-tree;   der Flieder, the lilac;

die Tanne, the fir-tree;   die Sonnenblume, the sun-flower;

die Buche, the beech;

die Ulme, the elm;   das Geißblatt, the honey-suckle.

die Pappel, the poplar;

die Blume, the flower;

12. THE COUNTRY.

Das Land, the country, land;   die Hütte, the cottage;

das Feld, the field;   das Dorf, the village;

die Gegend, the country;   der Flecken, the borough;

die Ebene, the plain;   das Schloß, the castle;

der Berg, the mountain;   der Meierhof, the farm;

das Thal, the valley;   die Mühle, the mill;

der Wald, the forest;   das Korn, the corn;

der Busch, the copse;   der Weizen, the wheat;

der Weg, the road;   die Gerste, the barley;

der Bach, the brook;   der Hafer, the oats;

die Wiese, the meadow;   das Stroh, the straw;

die Haide, the heath;   das Heu, the hay;

der Hügel, the hill;   die Traube, the bunch of grapes;

EASY DIALOGUES.

1. EATING AND DRINKING.

Are you hungry?	Sind Sie hungrig?
I have a good appetite.	Ich habe guten Appetit.
I am very hungry?	Ich bin sehr hungrig.
Eat something.	Essen Sie etwas.
What will you eat?	Was wollen Sie essen?
What do you wish to eat?	Was wünschen Sie zu essen?
You do not eat.	Sie essen nicht.
I beg your pardon; I eat very heartily.	Ich bitte um Verzeihung, ich esse sehr viel.
I have eaten very heartily.	Ich habe sehr viel gegessen.
I have dined with a good appetite.	Ich habe mit gutem Appetit zu Mittag gegessen.
Eat another piece.	Essen Sie noch ein Stückchen.
I can eat no more.	Ich kann nichts mehr genießen.
Are you thirsty.	Sind Sie durstig?
Are you not thirsty?	Haben Sie keinen Durst?
I am very thirsty?	Ich bin sehr durstig.
I am dying of thirst.	Ich vergehe vor Durst.
Let us drink.	Lassen Sie uns trinken.
Give me something to drink.	Geben Sie mir zu trinken.
Will you drink a glass of wine?	Wollen Sie ein Glas Wein trinken?
Drink a glass of beer.	Trinken Sie ein Glas Bier.
Drink another glass of wine.	Trinken Sie noch ein Glas Wein
Sir, I drink to your health.	Mein Herr, ich trinke auf ihr Gesundheit.
I have the honor, to drink to your health.	Ich habe die Ehre, auf ihre Gesundheit zu trinken.

4*

2. GOING AND COMING.

Where are you going?	Wohin gehen Sie?
I am going home.	Ich gehe nach Hause.
I was going to your house.	Ich wollte zu Ihnen.
Where do you come from?	Woher kommen Sie?
I come from my brother's.	Ich komme von meinem Bruder.
I am coming from church.	Ich komme aus der Kirche.
I just left the school.	Ich komme so eben aus der Schule.
Will you go with me?	Wollen Sie mit mir gehen?
Whither do you wish to go?	Wohin wollen Sie gehen?
We will go for a walk.	Wir wollen spazieren gehen.
We will take a walk.	Wir wollen einen Spaziergang machen.
With all my heart, most willingly.	Sehr gern, mit Vergnügen.
What way shall we take?	Welchen Weg wollen wir nehmen?
Any way you like.	Welchen Weg Sie wollen.
Let us go into the park.	Lassen Sie uns in den Park gehen.
Let us take your friend along on our way.	Lassen Sie uns im Vorbeigehen ihren Freund abholen.
As you please.	Wie es Ihnen gefällig ist.
Is Mr. B. at home?	Ist Herr B. zu Hause?
He is gone out.	Er ist ausgegangen.
He is not at home.	Er ist nicht zu Hause.
Can you tell us, where he is gone?	Können Sie uns sagen, wohin er gegangen ist?
I cannot tell you, precisely.	Ich kann es ihnen nicht gewiß sagen.
I think he is gone to see his sister.	Ich glaube, daß er zu seiner Schwester gegangen ist.
Do you know when he will come back?	Wissen Sie, wann er zurückkommt?
No, he said nothing about it, when he went out.	Nein; er hat nichts davon gesagt, als er ging.
Then we must go without him.	Dann müssen wir ohne ihn gehen.

3. QUESTIONS AND ANSWERS.

Come nearer; I have something to tell you.	Treten Sie näher, ich habe Ihnen etwas zu sagen.
I have a word to say to you.	Ich habe Ihnen ein Wörtchen zu sagen.
Listen to me.	Hören Sie mich an.
I want to speak to you.	Ich möchte mit Ihnen sprechen.
What is your wish?	Was steht zu Ihren Diensten?
I am speaking to you.	Ich spreche mit Ihnen.
I am not speaking to you.	Ich spreche nicht mit Ihnen.
What do you say?	Was sagen Sie?
What did you say?	Was haben Sie gesagt?
I say nothing.	Ich sage nichts.
Do you hear?	Hören Sie?
Do you hear what I say?	Verstehen Sie, was ich sage?
Do you understand me?	Verstehen Sie mich?
Will you be so kind, as to repeat....?	Wollen Sie so gut sein, zu wiederholen....?
I understand you well.	Ich verstehe Sie wohl.
Why do you not answer me?	Warum antworten Sie mir nicht?
Do you not speak French?	Sprechen Sie nicht französisch?
Very little, Sir.	Sehr wenig, mein Herr.
I understand it a little, but I do not speak it.	Ich verstehe es ein wenig, aber ich spreche es nicht.
Speak louder.	Sprechen Sie lauter.
Do not speak so loud.	Sprechen Sie nicht so laut.
Do not make so much noise.	Machen Sie nicht so viel Lärm.
Hold your tongue.	Schweigen Sie.
Did you not tell me, that...?	Sagten Sie mir nicht, daß....?
Who told you that?	Wer hat Ihnen das gesagt?
They have told me so.	Man hat es mir gesagt.
Somebody has told it to me.	Es hat mir's Jemand gesagt.
I have heard it.	Ich habe es gehört.
What do you wish to say?	Was wollen Sie sagen?
What is that good for?	Wozu soll das dienen?
How do you call that?	Wie nennen Sie das?
That is called....	Das heißt....

May I ask you....?	Darf ich Sie fragen....?
What do you wish?	Was wünschen Sie?
Do you know Mr. G.?	Kennen Sie Herrn G.?
I know him by sight.	Ich kenne ihn von Ansehen.
I know him by name.	Ich kenne ihn dem Namen nach

4. THE AGE.

How old are you?	Wie alt sind Sie?
How old is your brother?	Wie alt ist Ihr Herr Bruder?
I am twelve years old.	Ich bin zwölf Jahre alt.
I am ten years and six months old.	Ich bin zehn und ein halbes Jahr alt.
Next month I shall be sixteen years old.	Im nächsten Monat werde ich sechzehn Jahre alt.
I was eighteen years old last week.	Vergangene Woche bin ich achtzehn Jahre alt geworden.
You do not look so old	Sie sehen nicht so alt aus.
You look older.	Sie sehen älter aus.
I thought you were older.	Ich hielt Sie für älter.
I did not think you were so old.	Ich hielt Sie nicht für so alt.
How old may your uncle be?	Wie alt mag ihr Oheim sein?
He may be sixty years old.	Er kann etwa sechzig Jahre haben
He is about sixty years old.	Er ist ungefähr sechzig Jahre alt
He is more than fifty years old.	Er ist über fünfzig Jahre alt.
He is a man of fifty and upwards.	Er ist ein Mann von fünfzig und einigen Jahren.
He may be sixty or thereabouts.	Er kann etwa sechzig Jahre zählen.
He is above eighty.	Er ist über achtzig Jahre alt.
That is a great age.	Das ist ein hohes Alter.
Is he so old?	Ist er so alt?
He begins to grow old.	Er fängt an zu altern.

5. THE TIME.

What o'clock is it?	Wie viel Uhr ist es?
Pray, tell me what time it is?	Ich bitte, sagen Sie mir, welch Zeit es ist.
It is one o'clock.	Es ist ein Uhr.

It is past one.	Es ist ein Uhr vorbei.
It has struck one.	Es hat eins geschlagen.
It is a quarter past one.	Es ist ein Viertel auf zwei.
It is half past one.	Es ist halb zwei.
It wants ten minutes to two.	Es fehlen zehn Minuten an zwei
It is not yet two o'clock.	Es ist noch nicht zwei Uhr.
It is only twelve o'clock.	Es ist erst zwölf.
It is almost three o'clock.	Es ist beinahe drei.
It is on the stroke of three.	Es ist gegen drei.
It is going to strike three.	Es wird gleich drei Uhr schlagen
It is ten minutes past three.	Es ist zehn Minuten nach drei.
The clock is going to strike.	Die Uhr wird sogleich schlagen.
There the clock strikes!	Da schlägt die Uhr!
It is not late.	Es ist nicht spät.
It is later than I thought.	Es ist später, als ich dachte.
I did not think it was so late.	Ich dachte nicht, daß es so spät wäre.

6. THE WEATHER.

What kind of weather is it?	Was ist es für Wetter?
It is bad weather.	Es ist schlechtes Wetter.
It is very cloudy.	Es ist trübe.
It is dreadful weather.	Es ist ein abscheuliches Wetter.
It is fine weather.	Es ist schönes Wetter.
We are going to have a fine day.	Wir werden einen schönen Tag haben.
It is dewy.	Es thaut.
It is foggy.	Es ist nebelig.
It is rainy weather.	Es ist regnerisches Wetter.
It threatens to rain.	Es droht zu regnen.
The sky becomes very cloudy.	Der Himmel umzieht sich.
The sky is getting very dark.	Der Himmel wird dunkel.
The sun is coming out.	Die Sonne fängt an sich zu zeigen.
The weather is clearing up again.	Das Wetter klärt sich wieder auf
It is very hot.	Es ist sehr heiß.
It is sultry.	Es ist eine erstickende Hitze.

It is very mild.	Es ist sehr mild.
It is cold.	Es ist kalt.
It is excessively cold.	Es ist eine übermäßige Kälte.
It is raw weather	Es ist rauhes Wetter.
It rains.	Es regnet.
It has been raining.	Es hat geregnet.
It is going to rain.	Es wird gleich regnen.
I feel some drops of rain.	Ich fühle Regentropfen.
There are some drops of rain falling.	Es fallen Regentropfen.
It hails.	Es hagelt.
It snows; it is snowing	Es schneit; es fällt Schnee.
It has been snowing.	Es hat geschneit; es ist Schnee gefallen.
It snows in large flakes.	Es schneit in großen Flocken.
It freezes.	Es friert.
It has frozen.	Es hat gefroren.
It begins to moderate.	Es fängt an gelinder zu werden.
It thaws.	Es thaut auf.
It is very windy.	Es ist sehr windig.
The wind is very high.	Der Wind weht stark.
There is no air stirring.	Es weht kein Lüftchen.
It lightens.	Es blitzt.
It has lightened all night.	Es hat die ganze Nacht geblitzt.
It thunders.	Es donnert.
The thunder roars.	Der Donner rollt.
The thunderbolt has fallen.	Es hat eingeschlagen.
It is stormy weather.	Es ist stürmisches Wetter.
We shall have a thunderstorm.	Wir werden ein Gewitter bekommen.
The sky begins to clear up.	Der Himmel fängt an, sich aufzuheitern.
The weather is very unsettled.	Das Wetter ist sehr unbeständig.
It is very muddy.	Es ist sehr schmutzig.
It is very dusty.	Es ist sehr staubig.
It is very slippery.	Es ist sehr glatt.
It is bad walking.	Es ist schlechtes Gehen.

It is day-light.	Es ist Tag.
It is dark.	Es ist dunkel.
It is night.	Es ist Nacht.
It is moon-light.	Der Mond scheint.
Do you think it will be fine weather.	Glauben Sie, daß es gutes Wetter geben wird?
I do not think that it will rain.	Ich glaube nicht, daß es regnen wird.
I am afraid it will rain.	Ich fürchte, es wird regnen.
I fear so.	Ich fürchte es.

7. THE SALUTATION.

Good morning, Sir!	Guten Morgen, mein Herr!
I wish you a good morning.	Ich wünsche Ihnen guten Morgen.
How do you do?	Wie befinden Sie sich?
How is your health?	Wie geht es mit Ihrer Gesundheit?
Do you continue in good health?	Befinden Sie sich immer wohl?
Pretty good; and how is yours?	Ziemlich wohl, und Sie?
Are you well?	Sind Sie wohl?
Very well, and you?	Sehr wohl, und Sie auch?
I am perfectly well.	Ich befinde mich sehr wohl.
And how is it with you?	Und wie geht es mit Ihnen?
As usual.	Wie gewöhnlich.
Pretty well, thank God.	Ziemlich gut, Gott sei Dank.
I am very happy to see you well.	Es freut mich sehr Sie wohl zu sehen.

8. THE VISIT.

There is a knock.	Es klopft.
Somebody knocks.	Es klopft Jemand.
Go and see who it is.	Geh' und sieh, wer da ist.
Go and open the door.	Geh' und öffne die Thür.
It is Mrs. B.	Es ist Madame B.

I wish you a good morning.	Ich wünsche Ihnen guten Morgen.
I am happy to see you.	Es freut mich, Sie zu sehen.
I have not seen you this age.	Es ist ein Jahrhundert, seit ich Sie nicht sah.
It is a novelty to see you.	Es ist eine Seltenheit, Sie zu sehen.
Pray, sit down.	Setzen Sie sich, ich bitte.
Sit down, if you please.	Setzen Sie sich gefälligst.
Take a seat.	Nehmen Sie Platz.
Give a chair to the lady.	Gib Madame einen Stuhl.
Will you stay and take some dinner with us?	Wollen Sie zum Mittagsessen bei uns bleiben?
I cannot stay.	Ich kann nicht bleiben.
I only came in to see how you are.	Ich bin nur gekommen, um zu erfahren, wie Sie sich befinden.
I must go.	Ich muß gehen.
You are in a great hurry.	Sie sind sehr eilig.
Why are you in such a hurry?	Weshalb sind Sie so eilig?
I have a great many things to do.	Ich habe viel zu thun.
Surely you can stay a little longer.	Sie können wohl noch einen Augenblick bleiben.
I will stay longer another time.	Ein ander Mal will ich länger bleiben.
I thank you for your visit.	Ich danke Ihnen für Ihren Besuch.
I hope to see you soon again.	Ich hoffe Sie bald wieder zu sehen.

9. THE BREAKFAST.

Have you breakfasted?	Haben Sie gefrühstückt?
Not yet.	Noch nicht.
You are come just in time.	Sie kommen gerade zu rechter Zeit.
You will breakfast with us.	Sie werden mit uns frühstücken.
Breakfast is ready.	Das Frühstück ist bereit.

Do you drink tea or coffee?	Trinken Sie Thee oder Kaffee?
Would you prefer chocolate?	Wollen Sie vielleicht lieber Chocolade?
I prefer coffee.	Ich ziehe den Kaffee vor.
What can I offer you?	Was kann ich Ihnen anbieten?
Here are rolls and toast.	Hier sind Milchbröbchen und geröstete Brodschnittchen.
What do you like best?	Was mögen Sie am liebsten?
I shall take a roll.	Ich werde ein Bröbchen nehmen.
How do you like the coffee?	Wie finden Sie den Kaffee?
Is the coffee strong enough?	Ist der Kaffee stark genug?
It is excellent.	Er ist vortrefflich.
Is there enough sugar in it?	Ist genug Zucker darin?
If there is not, do not make any ceremony.	Ist es nicht, so machen Sie keine Komplimente.
Do as if you were at home.	Thun Sie, als ob Sie zu Hause wären.

10. BEFORE DINNER.

At what time do we dine to-day?	Um welche Zeit essen wir heute zu Mittag?
We shall dine at two o'clock.	Wir werden um zwei Uhr essen.
We shall not dine before three o'clock.	Wir werden nicht vor drei Uhr essen.
Shall we have anybody at dinner to-day?	Werden wir heute zum Essen Jemanden bei uns haben?
Do you expect company?	Erwarten Sie Gesellschaft?
I expect Mr. B.	Ich erwarte Herrn B.
Mr. D. has promised to come if the weather permits it.	Herr D. hat versprochen zu kommen, wenn es das Wetter erlaubt.
Have you given orders for dinner?	Haben Sie die Befehle zum Mittagsessen gegeben?
What have you ordered for dinner?	Was haben Sie zum Essen bestellt?
Have you sent for fish?	Haben Sie Fisch besorgen lassen?
I could not get any fish.	Ich habe keinen Fisch bekommen können.

I fear, we shall have a very indifferent dinner.	Ich beforge, baß wir kein fon= berliches Mittagseffen haben werden.
We must do as we can.	Wir müffen uns behelfen.

11. DINNER.

What shall I help you to?	Was soll ich Ihnen vorlegen?
Will you take a little soup?	Wollen Sie etwas Suppe?
No, I thank you. I will trou- ble you for a little beef.	Ich banke. Ich werde Sie um etwas Rindfleisch bitten.
It looks so very nice.	Es sieht so gut aus.
Which piece do you like best?	Welches Stück haben Sie am liebsten?
I hope this piece is to your liking.	Ich hoffe, baß dies Stück nach Ihrem Geschmacke ist.
Gentlemen, you have dishes near you.	Meine Herren, die Schüffeln stehen vor Ihnen.
Help yourselves.	Bedienen Sie sich.
Take without ceremony what you like best.	Nehmen Sie ohne Umstände, was Ihnen beliebt.
Would you like a little of this roast-meat?	Wollen Sie ein wenig von die= fem Braten?
Do you choose some fat?	Wollen Sie Fettes?
Give me some of the lean, if you please.	Geben Sie mir Mageres, wenn es Ihnen gefällig ist.
How do you like the roast-meat?	Wie finden Sie den Braten?
It is excellent, delicious.	Es ist vortrefflich, köstlich.
What will you take with your meat?	Was wünschen Sie zum Fleisch?
May I help you to some ve-getables?	Darf ich Ihnen Gemüfe geben?
Will you take peas or cauli-flower?	Wünschen Sie Erbsen oder Blu= menkohl?
It is quite indifferent to me.	Es ist mir ganz gleich.
I shall send you a piece of this fowl.	Ich will Ihnen ein Stückchen von diesem Geflügel reichen.

No, thank you, I can eat no more.	Ich danke, ich kann nichts mehr essen.
You are a poor eater.	Sie sind ein schwacher Esser.
You eat nothing.	Sie essen gar nichts.
I beg your pardon, I do honor to your dinner.	Ich bitte um Verzeihung, ich mache Ihrem Essen Ehre.
You may take away.	Ihr könnt alsdann abdecken.

12. TEA.

Have you carried in the tea-things?	Hast du Alles gebracht, was zum Thee gehört?
Everything is on the table.	Es ist Alles auf dem Tische.
Does the water boil?	Kocht das Wasser?
Tea is ready.	Der Thee ist fertig.
They are waiting for you.	Sie werden erwartet.
Here I am.	Hier bin ich.
We have not cups enough.	Wir haben nicht Tassen genug.
We want two more cups and saucers.	Wir müssen noch zwei Tassen haben.
Bring another tea-spoon and a saucer.	Bringe noch einen Theelöffel und eine Untertasse.
You have not brought in the sugar-tongs.	Du hast die Zuckerzange nicht gebracht.
Do you take cream?	Nehmen Sie Rahm?
The tea is so strong.	Der Thee ist so stark.
I shall thank you for a little more milk.	Ich werde noch um etwas Milch bitten.
Here are cakes and muffins.	Hier ist Kuchen und Brodkuchen.
Do you prefer some bread and butter?	Essen Sie lieber Butterbrod?
I shall take a slice of bread and butter.	Ich werde ein Butterbrod nehmen.
Pass the plate this way.	Schieb den Teller hierher.
Ring the bell, if you please.	Schellen Sie gefälligst.
Will you kindly ring the bell?	Wollen Sie gütigst die Klingel ziehen?
We want some more water.	Wir brauchen noch mehr Wasser.

Bring it as quickly as possible.	Bringe es so schnell als möglich.
Make haste.	Beeile dich.
Take the plate with you.	Nimm den Teller mit.
Is your tea sweet enough?	Ist der Thee süß genug?
Have I put sugar enough in your tea?	Habe ich genug Zucker in Ihren Thee gethan?
It is excellent.	Er ist vortrefflich.
I do not like it quite so sweet.	Ich habe ihn nicht gern so süß.
Your tea is very good.	Ihr Thee ist sehr gut.
Where do you buy it?	Wo kaufen Sie ihn?
I buy it at....	Ich kaufe ihn bei
Have you already done?	Sind Sie schon fertig?
You will take another cup?	Sie werden noch eine Tasse nehmen?
I shall pour you out half a cup.	Ich werde Ihnen noch eine halbe Tasse einschenken.
You will not refuse me.	Sie werden es mir nicht abschlagen.
I have already drunk three cups, and I never drink more.	Ich habe schon drei Tassen getrunken, und mehr trinke ich nie.

A NEW

PRACTICAL AND EASY METHOD

OF LEARNING

THE ·

GERMAN LANGUAGE.

BY

F. AHN,

DOCTOR OF PHILOSOPHY AND PROFESSOR AT THE COLLEGE OF NEUSS.

———

SECOND COURSE.

FIRST AMERICAN FROM THE EIGHTH LONDON EDITION

NEW YORK:

D. APPLETON AND COMPANY,

549 & 551 BROADWAY

1872.

INDEX.

THEORETICAL PART.

CHAPTER I.

§ 1. The German Language is composed of eight kinds of words, called the *parts of speech*. They are: the Article, the Substantive, the Adjective, the Pronoun, the Verb, the Adverb, the Preposition, and the Conjunction.

§ 2. There are in German two *numbers:* the Singular and the Plural; three *genders:* the masculine, the feminine, and the neuter; four *cases:* the Nominative, the Genitive, the Dative, and the Accusative.*

OF THE ARTICLE.

§ 3. We distinguish in German two kinds of Articles: the definite Article der, die, das, and the indefinite Article ein, eine, ein.

1. DECLENSION OF THE DEFINITE ARTICLE.

	Singular.			*Plural*	
	Masc.	*Fem.*	*Neut.*	*for all genders.*	
Nom.	der,	die,	das,	die,	the,
Gen.	des,	der,	des,	der,	of the,
Dat.	dem,	der,	dem,	den,	to the,
Acc.	den,	die,	das,	die,	the.

2. DECLENSION OF THE INDEFINITE ARTICLE.

Nom.	ein,	eine,	ein,	a,
Gen.	eines,	einer,	eines,	of a,
Dat.	einem,	einer,	einem,	to a,
Acc.	einen,	eine,	ein,	a.

* The Nominative answers to the English nominative case, the Accusative to the objective case, and the Genitive to the possessive case.

It is to be observed that almost all declinable words, excepting the Substantives, take the same terminations as the definite article, viz. ·

	Masc.	*Fem.*	*Neut.*
Nom.	er,	e,	es,
Gen.	es,	er,	es,
Dat.	em,	er,	em,
Acc.	en,	e,	es.

The neuter Gender differs from the masculine only in the Nominative and Accusative. The Accusative of the feminine and neuter genders is always the same as the Nominative.

CHAPTER II.

OF THE SUBSTANTIVE.

I. OF THE GENDER OF SUBSTANTIVES.

§ 4. Of the masculine gender are:

1. The substantives, which denote a male being as well by nature as by condition or occupation. Ex.:

der Sohn, the son;   der Schneider, the tailor;
der Hirt, the herdsman,   der Stier, the bull.

2. The names of the seasons, months and days. Ex.:

der Winter, the winter;   der Mai, May;
der Herbst, the autumn;   der Sonntag, Sunday.

3. The Substantives ending in all, el, er, en and ing. Ex.:

Der Ball, the ball;   der Kutscher, the coachman;
der Stall, the stable;   der Degen, the sword;
der Löffel, the spoon;   der Ofen, the stove;
der Schlüssel, the key;   der Sperling, the sparrow; —
der Hammer, the hammer;   der Häring, the herring.

Exceptions from the preceding rules:

die Gabel, the fork;   die Schüssel, the dish;
die Kartoffel, the potato;   die Feier, the festival;
die Leiter, the ladder;   die Leier, the lyre;
das Ruder, the oar;   das Kissen, the cushion;
das Alter, the age;   das Zeichen, the mark;
das Fenster, the window;   das Eisen, iron;
das Fieber, the fever;   das Messing, brass.

§ 5. Of the feminine gender are:

1. The Substantives which denote a female being, as well by nature as by condition or occupation. Ex.:

Die Tochter, the daughter; die Magd, the maid-servant;
die Wirthin, the hostess; die Ziege, the she-goat.

2. The Substantives ending in ei, heit, keit, schaft ng, in and niß. Ex.:

Die Druckerei, the printing-office; die Hoffnung, hope;
die Abtei, the abbey; die Königin, the queen;
die Gesundheit, health; die Herrin, the mistress;
die Sauberkeit, neatness; die Kenntniß, knowledge;
die Freundschaft, friendship; die Erlaubniß, the permission.

Exceptions:

Das Weib, the woman; das Bündniß, the alliance;
das Frauenzimmer, the woman; das Bekenntniß, the confession,
das Bildniß, the image; das Zeugniß, the testimony;
das Verhältniß, the proportion; das Hinderniß, the obstacle;
das Bedürfniß, the want; das Ereigniß, the event;
das Gleichniß, the similitude; das Begräbniß, the burial.

§ 6. Of the neuter gender are:

1. The names of metals, countries, towns, and letters. Ex.:

Das Eisen, the iron; Petersburg, Petersburgh;
das Gold, the gold; Preußen, Prussia;
das A, das B, the A, the B; Holland, Holland.

2. The Substantives ending in thum, sal and sel. Ex.:

Das Ritterthum, chivalry; das Schicksal, fate;
das Alterthum, antiquity; das Räthsel, the riddle.

3. The diminutives in chen and lein. Ex.:

Das Stühlchen, the little chair; das Bächlein, the little brook;
das Söhnchen, the little son; das Fräulein, the young lady;
das Mädchen, the girl; das Knäblein, the little boy.

4. The Substantives beginning with the syllable ge. Ex.:

Das Geschrei, the clamor; das Gewölk, the clouds;
das Gebet, the prayer; das Gedächtniß, memory.

5. All kinds of words taken substantively. Ex.:

Das Warum, the why; das Trinken, drinking;
das Nein, the no; das Nützliche, the useful.

Exceptions:

Der Stahl, the steel; der Gedanke, the thought;
der Tomback, tombac; der Geruch, the odor, smell;
der Zink, zinc; der Geschmack, the taste;
die Platina, platina; der Gebrauch, the use:

der Gehorsam, obedience ; die Türkei, Turkey ;
der Gewinn, the gain ; die Pfalz, Palatinate ;
der Gesang, the song ; die Moldau, Moldavia ;
die Gestalt, the shape ; die Schweiz, Switzerland ;
die Gefahr, the danger ; der Irrthum, the error ;
die Geduld, patience ; der Reichthum, wealth.

§ 7. Compound Substantives take the gender of their last component. Ex.:

Der Hausherr, the master of the house ;
die Hausfrau, the mistress of the house ;
— das Rathhaus, the town-house.

Exceptions. The following words, although terminated by the masculine Substantive, der Muth, the courage, are of the feminine gender:

Die Anmuth, gracefulness ; die Sanftmuth, meekness ;
die Demuth, humility ; die Wehmuth, sadness ;
die Großmuth, generosity ; die Schwermuth, melancholy.

The other words compounded with Muth, are masculine. Ex.: der Hochmuth, haughtiness.

§ 8. There are some Substantives which have two genders, but with different meanings:

Der Band, the volume ; das Band, the ribbon ;
der Erbe, the heir ; das Erbe, the inheritance ;
der Schild, the shield ; das Schild, the sign (of an inn) ;
der Thor, the fool ; das Thor, the gate ;
der Verdienst, the gain ; das Verdienst, merit ;
der See, the lake ; die See, the sea ;
der Leiter, the guide ; die Leiter, the ladder ;
der Heide, the heathen ; die Heide, the heath.

II. OF THE DECLENSION OF SUBSTANTIVES.

§ 9. In general there are three declensions admitted for the German Substantives:
The first forms the Genitive in S.
The second forms the Genitive in n.
The third is in the Genitive like the Nominative.

First Declension.

§ 10. The first declension comprehends:
1. All neuter Substantives without exception.
2. All masculine Substantives, which do not follow the second declension.

1. *Genitive in* **ŝ.**

Nom. der Spiegel, the mirror;
Gen. des Spiegels, of the mirror;
Dat. dem Spiegel, to the mirror;
Acc. den Spiegel, the mirror.

To be declined in the same way:

Der Himmel, the sky;   das Fenster, the window;
der Vater, the father;   das Auge, the eye;
der Degen, the sword;   das Mädchen, the girl.

2. *Genitive in* **eŝ.**

When euphony demands it, the ŝ of the Genitive may
be preceded by an e, and this e must be preserved in the
Dative. In familiar style this softening is almost always
neglected, but it is necessary in the Genitive of all those
Substantives the terminations of which would be too hard
without this half-mute e. Ex.:

Nom. der Tisch, the table;   das Kind, the child;
Gen. des Tisches,   des Kindes,
Dat. dem Tische,   dem Kinde,
Acc. den Tisch.   das Kind.

To be declined the same way:

Der Fuß, the foot;   das Dorf, the village;
der Hut, the hat;   das Land, the country;
der Arzt, the physician;   das Haus, the house.

3. *Genitive in* **nŝ.** ·

The following masculine Substantives:

der Name, the name;   der Wille, the will;
der Gedanke, the thought;   der Glaube, the belief;
der Funke, the spark;   der Schade, the damage;
der Friede, the peace;   der Buchstabe, the letter;

were formerly terminated in e n in the Nominative (der
Namen, der Willen) and are even now often met with in
this obsolete form, from which they derive their other
cases: der Name, des Namens, dem Namen, den Namen.

The two words: der Schmerz, the pain, and das Herz,
the heart, are in the Genitive des Schmerzens, or Schmer-
zes; des Herzens; in the Dative dem Schmerze, dem Herzen
or Herze, and in the Accusative den Schmerz, das Herz.

Second Declension.

§ 11. The second declension comprehends only mas
culine nouns. The Genitive is in n or en. The other
cases of the Singular preserve the termination of the
Genitive. Ex.:

1. *Genitive in* n.

Nom. der Löwe, the lion
Gen. des Löwen,
Dat. dem Löwen,
Acc. den Löwen.

2. *Genitive in* en.

In most Substantives of this declension, which end in the Nominative by a consonant, the n of the Genitive is preceded by an e. Ex.:

Nom. der Graf, the count;
Gen. des Grafen,
Dat. dem Grafen,
Acc. den Grafen.

§ 12. The second declension comprehends:

1. All masculine nouns of men and animals, terminating in e, as:

Der Knabe, the boy;   der Bürge, the bail;
der Erbe, the heir;   der Affe, the monkey;
der Bote, the messenger; der Hase, the hare.

2. The names of nations ending in e:

Der Deutsche, the German;   der Sachse, the Saxon;
Der Franzose, the Frenchman; der Schwede, the Swede.

Those ending in er follow the first declension: der Spanier, des Spaniers.

3. The following nouns of men and animals:

Der Held, the hero;   der Gesell, the partner;
der Graf, the count;   der Geck, the dotard;
der Fürst, the prince;   der Thor, the fool;
der Hirt, the herdsman;   der Narr, the fool;
der Mensch, the man;   der Bär, the bear;
der Herr, the gentleman;   der Ochs, the ox.

4. Most nouns of persons derived from foreign languages, and terminated by a long syllable:

Der Soldat, the soldier;   der Katholik, the catholic;
der Jesuit, the jesuit;   der Theolog, the theologian;
der Adjutant, the adjutant; der Philosoph, the philosopher;
der Student, the student;   der Astronom, the astronomer.

Third Declension.

§ 13. The third declension comprehends all feminine Substantives. It is distinguished from the two former ones, by not taking any inflexion in the Singular. Ex.:

Nom. die Hand, the hand;
Gen. der Hand,
Dat. der Hand,
Acc. die Hand.

To be declined in the same manner:

Die Frau, the woman;   die Kirſche, the cherry;
die Stadt, the town;   die Gabel, the fork;
die Luft, the air;   die Tugend, the virtue.

III. OF THE FORMATIONS OF THE PLURAL.

§ 14. In order to form the Plural of German Substantives, e, er, en or n is added to the Singular; sometimes also the Nominative Plural is the same as the
Nominative Singular.

1. *Plural in* e.

1. All monosyllables, save a few exceptions:

Der Hund, the dog;   die Hunde, the dogs;
die Hand, the hand;   die Hände, the hands;
das Bein, the leg;   die Beine, the legs.

2. The Substantives ending in niß, ſal and ing, as
well as those beginning by ge and ending by the radical
syllable:

Die Kenntniß, knowledge;   die Kenntniſſe, knowledge;
das Scheuſal, the monster;   die Scheuſale, the monsters;
der Fremdling, the stranger;   die Fremdlinge, the strangers;
das Gebet, the prayer;   die Gebete, the prayers;
das Geſchenk, the present;   die Geſchenke, the presents.

2. *Plural in* er:

1. The Substantives ending in thum:

Der Reichthum, wealth;   die Reichthümer, the riches;
der Irrthum, the error;   die Irrthümer, the errors.

2. The following monosyllables:

Der Geiſt, the mind;   der Rand, the border;
Der Leib, the body;   der Wald, the forest;
Der Gott, the god;   der Wurm, the worm:
der Mann, the man.   der Ort, the place

Das Amt, the office;   das Faß, the cask;
das Band, the ribbon;   das Feld, the field;
das Bild, the image;   das Glas, the glass;
das Brett, the board;   das Glied, the limb;
das Buch, the book;   das Grab, the grave;
das Dach, the roof;   das Haus, the house;
das Dorf, the village;   das Huhn, the chicken;
das Blatt, the leaf;   das Kalb, the calf;
das Kind, the child;   das Schloß, the castle;
das Kleid, the dress;   das Thal, the valley;
das Lied, the song;   das Volk, the people;
das Loch, the hole;   das Weib, the woman.

5*

3. *Plural in* n:

8. All Substantives of the second declension, which take n in the Genitive of the Singular:

Der Knabe, the boy;   die Knaben, the boys;
der Deutfche, the German;   die Deutfchen, the Germans.

2. The feminine Substantives in e, el and er:

die Biene, the bee;   die Bienen, the bees;
die Schwefter, the sister;   die Schweftern, the sisters;
die Gabel, the fork;   die Gabeln, the forks.

4. *Plural in* en:

1. All Substantives of the second declension, which take en in the Genitive Singular:

Der Fürft, the prince;   die Fürften, the princes;
der Solbat, the soldier;   die Solbaten, the soldiers.

2. The Substantives ending in heit, keit, fchaft, in and ung:

die Freiheit, liberty;   die Freiheiten;
die Artigkeit, politeness;   die Artigkeiten;
die Freundfchaft, friendship;   die Freundfchaften;
die Wirthin,* the hostess;   die Wirthinnen;
die Meinung, the opinion;   die Meinungen.

3. The following Substantives:

Das Bett, the bed;   die Frau, the woman;
das Hemb, the shirt,   die Schlacht, the battle;
das Herz, the heart;   die Welt, the world;
das Ohr, the ear;   die That, the deed;
die Art, the kind;   die Schrift, the writing;
die Pflicht, the duty;   die Schulb, the debt;
die Uhr, the watch;   die Zeit, time;
die Zahl, the number;   die Qual, the torment

5. *Plural like the Singular.*

1. The masculine and neuter Substantives in er, el and en:

Der Spiegel, the mirror;   die Spiegel, the mirrors;
der Abler, the eagle;   die Abler, the eagles;
das Mädchen, the girl;   die Mädchen, the girls.

2. The two feminine nouns, die Mutter, the mother, die Tochter, the daughter, which make their Plural: die Mütter, die Töchter.

---

* Words ending in in double their final consonant in the Plural.

§ 15. When the Nominative Plural terminates in n, all other cases have the same termination; but when it does not terminate in n, only the Dative takes this letter, and the Genitive and Accusative are like the Nominative. Ex.:

Nom. bie Grafen, the counts ;   bie Hänbe, the hanas ,
Gen. ber Grafen, of the counts;   ber Hänbe, of the hands :
Dat. ben Grafen, to the counts;   ben Hänben, to the hands ·
Acc. bie Grafen, the counts;   bie Hänbe, the hands.

Nom. bie Häufer, the houses ;
Gen. ber Häufer, of the houses ;
Dat. ben Häufern, to the houses ;
Acc. bie Häufer, the houses.

In this way are declined the Plurals of

Der Schuh, the shoe ;   ber Helb, the hero ;
ber Tisch, the table ;   bie Schulb, the debt;
bas Kinb, the child ;   bas Ohr, the ear.

§ 16. Most Substantives change in the Plural the radical vowel a into ä, o into ö, u into ü and a u into äu. Of this number are :

1. All Substantives which take the ending er :

Der Mann, the man ;   bie Männer, the men ;
ber Irrthum, the error;   bie Irrthümer, the errors ;
bas Loch, the hole;   bie Löcher, the holes ;
bas Haus, the house ;   bie Häufer, the houses.

2. The masculine and feminine Substantives, which take the termination e :

Die Hanb, the hand :   bie Hänbe, the hands,
ber Sohn, the son ;   bie Söhne, the sons ;
ber Hut, the hat;   bie Hüte, the hats.

The following masculine Substantives are exceptions :

Der Arm, the arm ;   ber Stoff, the stuff;
ber Laut, the sound ;   ber Schuh, the shoe ;
ber Dolch, the dagger ,   ber Punkt, the point ;
ber Hunb, the dog ;   ber Tag, the day.

3. The following Substantives, which do not change in the Plural :

Der Apfel, the apple ;   ber Vater, the father ;
ber Mangel, the want ;   ber Bruber, the brother ;
ber Nagel, the nail ;   ber Garten, the garden ;
ber Sattel, the saddle ;   ber Faben, the thread ;
ber Mantel, the cloak ;   ber Ofen, the stove ;
ber Vogel, the bird ;   bie Mutter, the mother ;
ber Hammer, the hammer ;   bie Tochter, the daughter.

TABLE
of the different inflexions of German Substantives.

I. *Singular.*

	1.	2.	3.
Nom.	—	—	—
Gen.	ŝ or eŝ	n or en	—
Dat.	— or e	n or en	—
Acc.	—	n or en	—

II. *Plural.*

	1.	2.	3.	4.
Nom.	e	er	n or en	—
Gen.	e	er	n or en	—
Dat.	en	rn	n or en	n
Acc.	e	er	n or en	—

IV. OF PROPER NAMES.

§. 117. The proper names of persons arc declined with or without the article. If declined with the article they do not change in the Singular. Ex.:

Nom. ber Karl, Charles ;   ber Schiller, Schiller ;
Gen. beŝ Karlŝ, of Charles ;   beŝ Schiller, of Schiller ;
Dat. bem Karl, to Charles ;   bem Schiller, to Schiller ;
Acc. ben Karl, Charles ;   ben Schiller, Schiller.

Used without the article, proper names take no other inflexion than an ŝ in the Genitive. Ex.:

Nom. Karl, Charles ;   Schiller, Schiller ;
Gen. Karlŝ,   Schillerŝ,
Dat. Karl,   Schiller,
Acc. Karl,   Schiller.

The proper names of women are declined like those of men, except those ending in e, which take in the Genitive nŝ, and in the Dative n. Ex.:

Nom. Sophie, Sophia :   Karoline, Caroline .
Gen. Sophienŝ,   Karolinenŝ,
Dat. Sophien,   Karolinen,
Acc. Sophie,   Karoline.

When proper names are used in the Plural, the masculine ones take the termination e, and the feminine the termination n or en. Ex. :

Ludwig, Lewis ;   bie Ludwige,
Abelheib, Alice ;   bie Abelheiben.

The names of towns and countries are always declined without the article, and only take ŝ in the Genitive. Ex.:

Rom, Rome ;   Romŝ, of Rome ;
Neapel, Naples ;   Neapelŝ, of Naples.

V. OF THE FORMATION OF FEMININE NOUNS.

§ 18. In order to form the feminine-of a masculine noun, the syllable i n is added to the latter. Ex.:

Ein König, a king;   eine Königin, a queen;
ein Schauspieler, an actor;   eine Schauspielerin, an actress.

If the masculine ends in e, this termination is omitted in forming the feminine. Ex.:

Der Gatte, the husband;   die Gattin, the wife;
der Löwe, the lion;   die Löwin, the lioness.

Mostly, in adding in the vowels a, o, u arc changed into ä, ö, ü.

Der Graf, the count;   die Gräfin, the countess;
der Bauer, the peasant;   die Bäuerin, the peasant-wife;
der Thor, the fool;   die Thörin, the fool.

From this rule arc excepted all Substantives derived from foreign languages. Ex.:

Der General,   die Generalin,
·der Professor,   die Professorin.

There are in German, as in English, some feminine nouns, which are not derived from their masculines. Ex.:

Der Mann, the man;   die Frau, the woman;
der Vetter, the cousin;   die Base, the cousin;
der Neffe, the nephew;   die Nichte, the niece.

VI. OF THE DIMINUTIVES.

§ 19. The German language is very fond of diminutives, and particularly in familiar conversation they arc frequently used. They are formed by adding the syllable chen or lein, to the primitive word. Ex.:

Der Tisch, the table;   das Tischchen, the little table;
der Mann, the man;   das Männchen, the little man;
die Feder, the feather;   das Federchen, the little feather;
das Kind, the child;   das Kindlein, the little child,

If the primitive word ends in e or e n, this termination is suppressed in forming the diminutive:

Die Taube, the pigeon;   das Täubchen, the little pigeon;
der Garten, the garden;   das Gärtchen, the small garden.

Almost all diminutives change a, o, u into ä, ö ü.

CHAPTER III.
OF THE ADJECTIVE.

I. DECLENSION OF THE ADJECTIVES.

§ 20. The Adjective is employed either as an attri-bute or as an epithet. In this phrase: My father is good, the adjective *good* is an attribute; in this other one: A good father loves his children, it is an epithet.

The Adjective employed as an attribute is invariable in all genders and numbers. Ex.:

Der Vater ist gut,   the father is good:
die Mutter ist gut,   the mother is good;
die Kinder sind gut,   the children are good.

The Adjective employed as an epithet always pre-cedes its Substantive, and is declined in three different ways, according to its being combined with the definite article, with the indefinite article, or as it is without any article.

1. If the Adjective is preceded by the definite article, it takes in the Nominative Singular the ending e and in all other cases, Singular and Plural, en. The Accusa-tive Singular of the feminine and neuter genders, however, is the same as the Nominative. Ex.:

SINGULAR.
Masculine.

N. der gute Mann, the good man;
G. des guten Mannes, of the good man;
D. dem guten Manne, to the good man:
A. den guten Mann, the good man.

Feminine.

N. die gute Frau, the good woman;
G. der guten Frau, of the good woman;
D. der guten Frau, to the good woman;
A. die gute Frau, the good woman.

Neuter.

N. das gute Kind, the good child;
G. des guten Kindes, of the good child;
D. dem guten Kinde, to the good child;
A. das gute Kind, the good child.

PLURAL FOR ALL GENDERS.

N. die guten Männer, Frauen, Kinder;
G. der guten Männer, Frauen, Kinder;
D. den guten Männern, Frauen, Kindern;
A. die guten Männer, Frauen, Kinder.

The Adjective is declined in the same manner, if it is preceded by any determinative word which has the terminations of the definite article, as: biefer, jener this, that; jeber, every; welcher, which.

2. If the Adjective is preceded by the indefinite article, it takes in the Nominative of the Singular the ending e r for the masculine, e for the feminine, and 8 for the neuter. All other cases take e n, except the Accusative feminine and neuter, which is like the Nominative. Ex.:

Masculine.

N. ein ganzer Tag, a whole day;
G. eines ganzen Tages, of a whole day;
D. einem ganzen Tage, to a whole day;
A. einen ganzen Tag, a whole day.

Feminine.

N. eine ganze Nacht, a whole night;
G. einer ganzen Nacht, of a whole night;
D. einer ganzen Nacht, to a whole night;
A. eine ganze Nacht, a whole night.

Neuter.

N. ein ganzes Jahr, a whole year;
G. eines ganzen Jahres, of a whole year;
D. einem ganzen Jahre, to a whole year:
A. ein ganzes Jahr, a whole year.

The Adjective is declined in the same way, when preceded by the determinative word fein, no, or by one of the possessive pronouns mein, bein, fein, unfer, euer, ihr, my, thy, his, our, your, their. If preceded by any of these words in the plural, it takes the termination e n in all cases. Ex.:

PLURAL FOR ALL GENDERS.

N. feine guten Männer, Frauen, Kinder;
G. feiner guten Männer, Frauen, Kinder;
D. feinen guten Männern, Frauen, Kindern;
A. feine guten Männer, Frauen, Kinder.

3. If the Adjective is preceded by neither an article nor by any other determinative word, it adopts the terminations of the definite article and is declined in the following manner:

SINGULAR.

Masculine.

N   guter Wein, good wine *or* some good wine ; *
G.   guten Weines, of good wine ; †
D.   gutem Weine, to good wine ;
A.   guten Wein, good wine.

Feminine.

N.   frische Milch, fresh milk ;
G.   frischer Milch, of fresh milk ;
D.   frischer Milch, to fresh milk ;
A.   frische Milch, fresh milk.

Neuter.

N.   schwarzes Tuch, black cloth ;
G.   schwarzes Tuches, of black cloth ;
D.   schwarzem Tuche, to black cloth ;
A.   schwarzes Tuch, black cloth.

PLURAL FOR ALL GENDERS.

N.   schöne Blumen, fine flowers ;
G.   schöner Blumen, of fine flowers ;
D.   schönen Blumen, to fine flowers ;.
A.   schöne Blumen, fine flowers,

Participles, used adjectively, are declined like adjectives.

II. DEGREES OF COMPARISON OF THE ADJECTIVES.

§ 21. The Comparative of an adjective is formed by adding the termination e r, and the Superlative by adding the termination st e. Ex.:

Reich, rich ;   reicher, richer ;   der reichste, the richest ;
schön, fine ;   schöner, finer ;   der schönste, the finest ;
mild, mild ;   milder, milder ;   der mildeste,‡ the mildest.

The radical vowel of the Positive is softened in the Comparative and Superlative: a changes into ä, o into ö, u into ü. Ex.:

Alt, old ;   älter, older ;   der älteste, the oldest ;
groß, great ;   größer, greater ;   der größte, the greatest ;
jung, young ;   jünger, younger ;   der jüngste, the youngest.

---

* The word *some* before a Substantive, is never translated in German.

† In the Genitive masculine and neuter they employ at present more frequently the termination e n, guten Weines, schwarzen Tuches.

‡ Instead of st e, we add e st e, when euphony demands it.

The following Adjectives are exceptions:

Wahr, true; — ſachte, soft, slow;
ſchlank, slender; farg, stingy;
ſchlaff, lax; rund, round;
ſanft, soft; bunt, motley;
matt, faint; ſtumpf, blunt;
flach, flat; froh, joyful;
falſch, false; hold, gracious;
blaß, pale; — roh, raw;
glatt, slippery; toll, mad;
gerade, straight; voll, full;

as well as the Adjectives ending in b a r, h a f t and ſ a m. Ex.: dankbar, grateful; dankbarer, more grateful; boshaft, malicious; boshafter, more malicious; ſparſam, economical; ſparſamer, more economical.

§ 22. The following Adjectives are irregular.

gut, good; beſſer, better; der beſte, the best;
nah, near; näher, nearer; der nächſte, the next;
hoch, high; höher, higher; der höchſte, the highest;
viel, much; mehr, more; der meiſte, the most.

§ 23. Comparatives and Superlatives are declined according to the same rules as the Adjectives in the Positive. Ex.: der kleine Tiſch, the small table; der kleinere Tiſch, the smaller table; der kleinſte Tiſch, the smallest table; ein kleiner Tiſch, a little table; ein kleinerer Tiſch, a smaller table; ein ſchönes Buch, a beautiful book; ein ſchöneres Buch, a more beautiful book.

CHAPTER IV.

OF THE NUMBERS.

§ 24. The cardinal numbers are;

1	eins,	11	elf,
2	zwei,	12	zwölf,
3	drei,	13	dreizehn,
4	vier,	14	vierzehn,
5	fünf,	15	fünfzehn,
6	ſechs,	16	ſechszehn,
7	ſieben,	17	ſiebenzehn,
8	acht,	18	achtzehn,
9	neun,	19	neunzehn,
10	zehn,	20	zwanzig,

21 ein und zwanzig,	80 achtzig,
22 zwei und zwanzig,	90 neunzig,
23 drei und zwanzig,	100 hundert,
24 vier und zwanzig,	101 hundert eins,
25 fünf und zwanzig,	102 hundert zwei,
30 dreißig,	103 hundert drei,
40 vierzig,	200 zweihundert,
50 fünfzig,	1000 tausend,
60 sechzig,	2000 zweitausend,
70 siebenzig,	10,000 zehntausend.

1850 tausend achthundert neun und fünfzig, or achtzehn hundert neun und fünfzig; a million, eine Million.

Eins is the neuter of ein, and is only used when no object of determinate masculine or feminine gender is understood. Zwei and drei, if not preceded by any determinative word, take in the Genitive the termination e r. Ex.: die Aussage zweier Zeugen, the deposition of two witnesses. The other cardinal numbers remain unaltered, except in the Dative, where they sometimes take the termination e n.

§ 25. The ordinal numbers are adjectives, and are derived from the cardinal numbers by the addition of the syllable t e or ste. From two to nineteen is added t e, the rest take ste.

Der erste, the first;	der zwanzigste, the twentieth;
der zweite, the second;	der ein und zwanzigste, the twenty-first;
der dritte, the third;	
der vierte, the fourth;	der dreißigste, the thirtieth;
der fünfte, the fifth;	der fünfzigste, the fiftieth;
der achte, the eighth;	der hundertste, the hundredth;
der zwölfte, the twelfth;	der tausendste, the thousandth.

From these are derived, by the addition of n s, the ordinal adverbs:

Erstens, firstly, in the first place;
Zweitens, secondly, in the second place;
Drittens, thirdly, in the third place;
Viertens, fourthly, in the fourth place.

§ 26. The other numbers are:

1. *Multiplicative Numbers.*

Einfach, single;	zehnfach, tenfold;
zweifach, double; *	hundertfach, a hundredfold;
dreifach, treble;	tausendfach, a thousandfold.

---

* Instead of zweifach etc. may be said: zweifältig, tausendfältig etc.

We may add to these the adverbs which are formed by the substantive Mal, time:

Einmal, once; viermal, four times;
zweimal, twice; hundertmal, a hundred times;
dreimal, thrice; tausendmal, a thousand times.

2. *Distributive Numbers.*

Halb, half; einzeln, one by one;
die Hälfte, the half; paarweise, by pairs;
das Drittel, the third part; je drei und drei, by threes;
das Viertel, the fourth part; dutzendweise, by the dozen.

Add to these the adverbs, formed by the old word [ei] which signifies sort or kind:

Einerlei, of one kind; mancherlei, of several kinds,
zweierlei, of two kinds; vielerlei, of many kinds;
dreierlei, of three kinds; allerlei, of all kinds.

Observe also the following ways of speaking of the Germans:

Anderthalb, one and a half; halb eins, half past twelve;
britthalb, two and a half; halb zwei, half past one;
vierthalb, three and a half; halb drei, half past two.

§ 27. The ordinal numbers are used as in English, after the names of sovereigns, and in dates:

Der vierte April, the fourth of April;
der achte Mai, May the eighth;
Ludwig der elfte, Lewis the eleventh;
Heinrich der vierte, Henry the fourth.

CHAPTER V.

OF PRONOUNS.

---

1. DETERMINATE PERSONAL PRONOUNS.

§ 28. The first person is expressed by ich, I; Plural, wir, we; the second person by du, thou; Plural, ihr, you; the third person by er, he; sie, she; es, it; and sie, they; Plural for all genders. They are declined in the following manner.

SINGULAR.

First person.	Second person.
N. ich, I;	du, thou;
G. meiner, of me;	deiner, of thee;
D. mir, to me;	dir, to thee;
A. mich, me;	dich, thee.

PLURAL.

N. wir, we;   ihr, you;
G. unfer, of us   euer, of you;
D. uns, to us;   euch, to you;
A. uns, us;   euch, you.

Third person.
SINGULAR.

	Masculine.	Feminine.	Neuter.
N.	er, he;	fie, she;	es, it;
G.	feiner, of him;	ihrer, of her;	feiner, of it;
D.	ihm, to him;	ihr, to her;	ihm, to it;
A.	ihn, him.	fie, her.	es, it.

PLURAL FOR ALL GENDERS.

N. fie, they;
G. ihrer, of them;
D. ihnen, to them;
A. fie, them.

§ 29. The reflective pronoun of the third person fich, himself, herself, itself, has no Nominative, and is declined thus:

	Masculine and Neuter.	Feminine.	Plural.
G.	feiner, of himself;	ihrer, of herself;	ihrer, of themselves;
D.	fich, to himself;	fich, to herself;	fich, to themselves;
A.	fich, himself.	fich, herself.	fich, themselves.

Sometimes the word felbft, self, is joined to the personal pronouns. Ex.: ich felbft, myself; bu felbft, thyself; er felbft, himself; fich felbft, one's self; wir felbft, ourselves.

In joining the word felbft to a verb, the pronouns are not repeated as in English. Ex.: Er hat es felbft gefagt, he said so himself; fie hat es mir felbft gefagt, she told it to me herself.

§ 30. The pronoun bu is used in intimacy or contempt. When the Germans speak to a person who deserves respect, they employ Sie and Ihnen, that is to say, the plural of the pronoun in the third person. Ex.

Sie haben es mir gefagt, you told me so;
ich kenne Sie nicht, I do not know you;
ich will es Ihnen geben, I will give it to you.

2. INDETERMINATE PERSONAL PRONOUNS.

31. The indeterminate personal pronouns are:

Man, one, they;   Sebermann, every one;
Semand, somebody;   Einer, some one;
Niemand, nobody;   Keiner, no one.

Man is indeclinable; Jedermann takes in the Genitive an ß; Jemand and Niemand are either invariable or take the endings of the definite article. Ex.:

Wenn man reich ist, hat man Freunde. When one is rich one has friends.
Jedermann wird es ihnen sagen. Every one will tell you.
Es hat Jemand nach Ihnen gefragt. Somebody has asked for you.
Man muß Niemanden hassen. We must hate nobody.
Keiner weiß, ob er morgen noch leben No one knows if he will live till
wird. to-morrow.

§ 32.   Add to these pronouns the following words:

Etwas, something, anything;
nichts, nothing;
jeder, jede, jedes, every, each, every one;
aller, alle, alles, all, everything;
solcher, solche, solches, such;
mancher, manche, manches, many a, many a one;
mehrere, several;
irgend ein, any, some
einige, some;
die meisten, the most.

Examples.

Ich habe etwas Neues vernommen. I have heard something new.
Ich habe nichts gehört. I have heard nothing.
Jeder muß seine Pflichten erfüllen. Every one must fulfil his duties.
Jedes Land hat seine Gebräuche. Every country has its customs.
Alle Menschen sind sterblich. All men are mortal.
Alles ist verloren. Every thing is lost.
Ein solcher Verlust ist unersetzlich. Such a loss is irreparable.
Mancher säet, der nicht erndtet. Many a one sows, who does not reap.

Ich habe manchen Tag verloren. I have lost many a day.
Geben Sie mir einige Federn. Give me some pens.
Leihen Sie mir irgend ein Buch. Lend me some book.
Mein Bruder hat mehrere Freunde. My brother has several friends.
Die meisten Menschen urtheilen nach Most men judge according to ap-
dem Schein. pearances.

CHAPTER VI.
OF ADJECTIVE AND RELATIVE PRONOUNS.

1. DEMONSTRATIVE PRONOUNS.

§ 33.   The demonstrative pronouns are:

For near objects:
dieser, diese, dieses, this, this one.
For distant objects:
jener, jene, jenes, that, that one.

Ex. Dieser Mann, this man; diese Frau, this woman; dieses Kind, this child; jener Tisch, that table; jene Feder, that pen; jenes Buch, that book. Dieſer iſt glücklich, Jener iſt unglücklich, this one is happy that one is unhappy.

The demonstrative Pronouns have the same termina-tions as the definite article, and are declined in the same manner.

	Masculine.	Feminine.	Neuter.	Plural.
N.	dieſer,	dieſe,	dieſes,	dieſe,
G.	dieſes,	dieſer,	dieſes,	dieſer,
D.	dieſem,	dieſer,	dieſem,	dieſen,
A.	dieſen,	dieſe,	dieſes,	dieſe.

Instead of dieſes, one may say dieß in the Nominative and Accusative Neuter: dieß Buch, this book.

§ 34. Instead of dieſer and jener the article der, die, das, is very often employed, on which in that case a greater stress is placed. Ex.:

Der Mann, this man; die Frau, this woman ; das Kind, this child.

When der, die, das, taking the place of dieſes or jenes, does not accompany a substantive, it is declined as fol-lows :

	Masculine.	Feminine.	Neuter.	Plural.
N.	der,	die,	das,	die,
G.	deſſen,	deren,	deſſen,	derer,
D.	dem,	der,	dem,	denen,
A.	den,	die,	das,	die.

§ 35. With the adjective pronouns are also numbered :

Derjenige, diejenige, dasjenige, the one ; derſelbe, dieſelbe, daſſelbe, the same.

These words are compound of the definite article which is declined in all cases, and of jenige and ſelbe, which are declined like adjectives. Ex.:

	SINGULAR.			PLURAL.	
	Masculine.	Feminine.	Neuter.		
N.	derſelbe,	dieſelbe,	daſſelbe,	dieſelben,	the same ;
G.	desſelben,	derſelben,	desſelben,	derſelben,	of the same ;
D.	demſelben,	derſelben,	demſelben,	denſelben,	to the same ;
A.	denſelben,	dieſelbe,	dasſelbe,	dieſelben,	the same.

§ 36. Derjenige, &c. is always construed with the re-lative pronoun welcher, welche, &c. and answers in this construction to the English; he who, that which, the one who or which. Ex.:

Derjenige, welcher kommt, he who comes ; diejenige, welche ſpricht, she who speaks ; dasjenige, welches ich meine, that which I mean ; diejenigen, welche bereit ſind, those who are ready.

2. POSSESSIVE PRONOUNS.

§ 37. The possessive pronouns are either joined to a substantive or they stand alone; or in other words they are either conjoined or disjoined.
The conjoined possessive pronouns are the following:

Masculine.	Feminine.	Neuter.	
mein,	meine,	mein,	my;
dein,	deine,	dein,	thy;
sein,	seine,	sein,	his;
ihr,	ihre,	ihr,	her;
sein,	seine,	sein,	its;
unser,	unsere,	unser,	our;
euer,	euere,	euer,	your;
ihr,	ihre,	ihr,	their.

§ 38. The conjoined possessive pronouns take the same inflexions as the article ein, eine, ein. Ex.:

	Singular.	Plural.
N.	mein Bruder, my brother;	meine Brüder, my brothers;
G.	meines Bruders,	meiner Brüder,
D.	meinem Bruder,	meinen Brüdern,
A.	meinen Bruder,	meine Brüder.

§ 39. The disjoined possessive pronouns are derived from the conjoined ones, by adding the syllable ig.

der meinige,	die meinige,	das meinige,	mine;
der deinige,	die deinige,	das deinige,	thine;
der seinige,	die seinige,	das seinige,	his;
der ihrige,	die ihrige,	das ihrige,	hers;
der seinige,	die seinige,	das seinige,	its;
der unsrige,	die unsrige,	das unsrige,	ours;
der eurige,	die eurige,	das eurige,	yours;
der ihrige,	die ihrige,	das ihrige,	theirs.

Instead of der meinige, der deinige, &c. they say very frequently der meine, der deine; or without the article, meiner, meine, meines; deiner, deine, deines or deins.

3. RELATIVE PRONOUNS.

§ 40. Relative pronouns always refer to a preceding substantive. There are two of them in German:

welcher, der, } who; welche, die, } who; welches, das, } which or that.

Welcher, welche, welches are declined like the definite article; der, die, das are declined like the demonstrative pronouns, ber, bic, bas, with the only difference that in the Genitive Plural it has always beren.   Ex.:

Der Mann, welcher arbeitet,	the man who works;
die Frau, welche weint,	the woman who is crying;
bas Kind, welches spielt,	the child that is playing.

Der Knabe, ben Sie loben,	the boy whom you praise;
ber Garten, welchen Sie sehen,	the garden which you see;
bie Häuser, welche Sie kaufen,	the houses which you buy.

Der Bebiente, bem Sie es ge= geben haben,	the man-servant to whom you gave it;
bie Magb, welcher Sie es ge= sagt haben,	the maid-servant to whom you said it;
bie Freunbe, benen wir schreiben,	the friends to whom we write.

§ 41.   One may use indifferently welcher or ber, except in the Genitive, for which welcher is not used. *Whose of whom* and *of which* are always expressed by bessen and beren.   Ex.:

Der Mann, bessen Sohn krank ist,	the man whose son is ill;
bie Frau, beren Kinder gestorben sind,	the woman whose children have died;
bie Kinder, beren Mutter angekom= men ist,	the children whose mother is arrived.

4. INTERROGATIVE PRONOUNS.

§ 42.   The interrogative pronouns are;

wer, who; was, what;
welcher, welche, welches, which.

Wer and was are never accompanied by a substantive; wer is declined like the demonstrative pronoun ber; and was is ordinarily indeclinable.

Wer ist ba?	Who is there?
Wer ist bieser Mann?	Who is this man?
Wer ist biese Frau?	Who is this woman?
Wessen Haus ist bies?	Whose house is this?
Wem schreiben Sie?	To whom do you write?
Wen suchen Sie?	Whom do you look for?
Was sind wir?	What are we?
Was sagen Sie?	What do you say?

The interrogative pronoun welcher, which is usually accompanied by a substantive and is declined like the definite article.   Ex.:

Welcher Arzt ist angekommen?	Which physician is arrived?
Welche Feder ist die meinige?	Which pen is mine?
Welches Haus ist zu verkaufen?	Which house is to be sold?
Welchen Hut wählen Sie?	Which hat do you choose?
Welcher Blume geben Sie den Vorzug?	To which flower do you give the preference?
Welcher von diesen Gärten gehört Ihnen?	Which of these gardens belongs to you?
Welches von diesen Häusern wollen Sie kaufen?	Which of this houses do you wish to buy?
Welchem von diesen Knaben hast du dein Brod gegeben?	To which of these boys hast thou given thy bread?
Ich habe dein Federmesser einer deiner Schwestern gegeben? Welcher?	I have given thy penknife to one of thy sisters. To which (of them)?

§ 43. The pronoun was, accompanied by the indefinite article ein, and the preposition für, may equally be employed as an interrogative, and answers to the English: *what kind of*. Ex.:

Was für ein Buch liesest du?	What or what kind of book do you read?
Was für ein Mann war Sokrates?	What sort of man was Socrates?
Was für eine Feder suchst du?	What pen do you look for?
Was für einen Hund verkaufst du?	What dog do you sell?

In the Plural the indefinite article disappears: Was für Männer? What kind of men?

§ 44. The interrogative Pronoun wer is often used instead of derjenige welcher, he who, and was instead of dasjenige welches, that which. Ex.:

Wer zufrieden ist, ist glücklich.	He who is contented, is happy.
Was schön ist, ist nicht immer nützlich.	That which is beautiful is not always useful.

CHAPTER VII.

OF THE VERB.

I. PRELIMINARY NOTIONS.

§ 45. German verbs have only three moods: the Indicative, the Subjunctive, and the Imperative.

The Indicative Mood has but two simple tenses, viz.:

The Present Tense: ich schreibe, I write;
The Imperfect Tense: ich schrieb, I wrote.

6

All other tenses are formed by means of the auxiliary
verbs. Ex.:

Perfect Tense: idj babe gefdjrieben, I have written.
Pluperfect Tense: idj batte gefdjrieben, I had written.
1st Future Tense: idj werbe fdjreiben, I shall write.
2d Future Tense: idj werbe gefdjrieben baben, I shall have written.

The Subjunctive Mood has the same tenses as the
Indicative Mood. The Potential or Conditional Mood
is expressed either by the Imperfect tense of the Subjunctive mood or by a circumlocution.

§ 46. The Infinitive of all German verbs terminates
in en; by taking off this termination we find the *root* of
the verb. Ex.: Sdjreib is the root of the verb fdjreiben,
to write; fag the root of the verb fagen, to say.

§ 47. The regular German verbs are divided into
assonant and *dissonant* verbs.

We call assonant those verbs, in which the modi-
fications of tenses, persons, &c. are marked by *terminations* or *initials* added to the root, without this root's
suffering any alteration.

We call dissonant those verbs, whose Imperfect and
often also the Imperative and Past participle are formed
by changing the vowel of the root.

2. OF THE CONJUGATION OF ASSONANT VERBS.

§ 48. The Present tense of the Indicative Mood of
assonant verbs is formed by the following terminations:

Sing. 1.—e
2.—ft
3.—t
Plur. 1.—en
2.—t
3.—en.

The Present tense of the Subjunctive Mood is like
that of the Indicative Mood, with the exeption that the
third person Singular is like the first, and that the terminations ft and t are always preceded by an e. Ex.:

Sing. 1.—e
2.—eft
3.—e
Plur. 1.—en
2.—et
3.—en.

The Imperfect tense of the Indicative as well as of the Subjunctive Mood is formed by adding the following terminations:

> Sing. 1.—te
> 2.—teſt
> 3.—te
> Plur. 1.—ten
> 2.—tet
> 3.—ten.

The Imperative Mood is formed by adding to the root of the verb an e for the Singular and et for the Plural.

The present participle is formed by adding enb to the root. The past participle is formed by placing the initials ge before, and the termination t after the root.

MODEL OF CONJUGATION.

Loben, to praise.

Present Tense.

Indicative Mood.	Subjunctive Mood.
idy lob—e, I praise, I do praise, [am praising.	idy lob—e, (if) I praise.
bu lob—ſt	bu lob—eſt
er lob—t	er lob—e
wir lob—en	wir lob—en
ihr lob—et	ihr lob—et
ſie lob—en	ſie lob—en.

Imperfect Tense.

idy lob—te, I praised, I did praise, [was praising.	idy lob—te, (if) I praised.
bu lob—teſt	bu lob—teſt
er lob—te	er lob—te
wir lob—ten	wir lob—ten
ihr lob—tet	ihr lob—tet
ſie lob—ten	ſie lob—ten.

Imperative Mood: lob—e, praise (thou); lob—et, praise (ye).
Present Participle: lob—enb, praising.
Perfect Participle: ge—lob—t, praised.

Observation. When the euphony demands it, the terminations of the Imperfect, as well as those of the Present Tense in t and ſt, are preceded by an e. Ex.: Idy rebe, I speak; bu rebeſt, thou speakest; er rebet, he speaks; ihr rebet, you speak. Idy rebete, I spoke; bu rebeteſt, thou spokest; er rebete, he spoke; wir rebeten, we spoke; ihr rebetet, you spoke; ſie rebeten, they spoke. In those verbs, the root of which ends in b or t this softening always takes place.

§ 49. There are assonant as well as dissonant verbs, which do not take the initials g e in the Perfect Participle. Of this class are:

1. The verbs, which have the foreign termination iren or ieren. Ex.:

regieren, to govern	regiert, governed
ſpaȝieren, to walk	ſpaȝiert, walked
abbiren, to add	abbirt, added.

2. Those derived verbs, which begin by one of the particles be, ge, ent, emp, er, ver, ȝer.* Ex.:

beſuchen, to visit	beſucht, visited
erlangen, to attain	erlangt, attained
verweilen, to stay	verweilt, staid
ȝerſtören, to destroy	ȝerſtört, destroyed.

3. The verbs, which are compounded with an inseparable preposition or adverb. Ex.:

unterrichten, to instruct	unterrichtet, instructed
widerlegen, to refute	widerlegt, refuted
vollenden, to complete	vollendet, completed.

In verbs, which are compounded with a separable preposition or adverb, the syllable g e is placed between the verb and the preposition or adverb. Ex.:

abkürȝen, to shorten	abgekürȝt, shortened
anklagen, to accuse	angeklagt, accused
fortjagen, to send away	fortgejagt, sent away.

§ 50. Conjugate the following verbs:

ſagen, to say	weinen, to weep
lieben, to love	lachen, to laugh
glauben, to believe	fühlen, to feel
wünſchen, to wish	hören, to hear
hoffen, to hope	ſpielen, to play.

3. OF THE CONJUGATION OF THE DISSONANT VERBS.

§ 51. The number of dissonant verbs is about 150 and they take in the Present Tense of the Indicative and Subjunctive Moods the same terminations as the assonant verbs.

The Imperfect Tense of the Indicative Mood in dissonant verbs is formed by changing the radical vowel or diphthong. The first and third person Singular

---

* See the Chapter on derived and compound verbs.

take no inflexion, the other persons take the same as in the Present tense of the Indicative Mood.

The Imperfect tense of the Subjunctive Mood is formed by softening the vowel of the Indicative (a into ä, o into ö, u into ü), and adding the terminations of the Present tense (Subjunct. Mood.)

The Imperative Mood takes commonly the same terminations as in the assonant verbs; sometimes also it is formed by changing the radical vowel.

The Present Participle is always the same as in the assonant verbs; but the Perfect Participle terminates in c n instead of c t and very often undergoes also an alteration of the radical vowel.

MODEL OF CONJUGATION.

Trinken, to drink.

Present Tense.

Indicative Mood.	Subjunctive Mood.
ich trinf—e, I drink, am drinking.	ich trinf—e, (if) I drink.
bu trinf—ft	bu trinf—eft
er trinf—t	er trinf—e
wir trinf—en	wir trinf—en
ihr trinf—t	ihr trinf—et
fie trinf—en	fie trinf—en.

Imperfect Tense.

ich tranf, I drank, did drink, was [drinking.	ich tränf—e, (if) I drank.
bu tranf—ft	bu tränf—eft
er tranf	er tränf—e
wir tranf—en	wir tränf—en
ihr tranf—t	ihr tränf—et
fie tranf—en	fie tränf—en.

Imperative Mood: trinf—e, drink (thou); trinf—et, drink (ye).
Present Participle: trinf—enb, drinking.
Perfect Participle: ge—trunf—en, drunk.

Observation. The e of the Imperative may be suppressed: trinf, trinft; lob', lobt.

§ 52. The Singular of the Imperative Mood is sometimes formed by changing the radical vowel (§ 51), but the Plural always keeps the form of the assonant verbs: geben, to give; gib, give (thou); gebet, give (ye).

Every time the Imperative Mood is formed by changing the radical vowel, the 2d and 3d Persons of Present Tense, Indicative Mood, undergoes the same change: geben, to give; gib, give (thou); bu gibſt, thou givest; er gibt, he gives. Ex.:

Sterben, to die.

Present Tense.

Indicative Mood.	*Subjunctive Mood.*
ich ſterb—e, I die.	ich ſterb—e, (if) I die.
bu ſtirb—ſt	bu ſterb—eſt
er ſtirb—t	er ſterb—e
wir ſterb—en	wir ſterb—en
ihr ſterb—t	ihr ſterb—et
ſie ſterb—en	ſie ſterb—en.

Imperative Mood: ſtirb, die (thou); ſterb—et, die (ye).

§ 53. The dissonant verbs change, in the Imperfect Tense of the Indicative as well as the Subjunctive Mood, their radical vowel either into o, i, a or u. Hence we have four different classes of dissonant verbs. The Perfect Participle either keeps the vowel of the Imperfect Tense, or takes back that of the root, or differs from both, as is shown in the following table.

Class.	Imperf.	Perf. Part.
1.	o	o
2.	i	i
3.	a	u or o
4.	u, a, i.	radical vowel.

FIRST CLASS.

The first class comprehends those dissonant verbs, which change their radical vowel into a long or short o:

1. o long.

Infinitive.	*Imperfect.*	*Perfect Part*
ſchieben, to push	ſchob	geſchoben
biegen, to bend	bog	gebogen
fliegen, to fly	flog	geflogen
wiegen, to weigh	wog	gewogen
frieren, to freeze	fror	gefroren
verlieren, to lose	verlor	verloren
bieten, to offer	bot	geboten
fliehen, to flee	floh	geflohen
ziehen, to draw	zog	gezogen

ſdjeren, to shear	ſdjor	geſdjoren
ſdjwören, to swear	ſdjwor	geſdjworen
ſaugen, to suck	ſog	geſogen
lügen, to lie (speak an untruth)	log	gelogen
betrügen, to deceive	betrog	betrogen

2. o short.

ſdjießen, to shoot	ſdjoß	geſdjoſſen
gießen, to pour	goß	gegoſſen
• genießen, to enjoy	genoß	genoſſen
ſdjließen, to shut	ſdjloß	geſdjloſſen
— verdrießen, to grieve	verdroß	verdroſſen
ſprießen, to germinate	ſproß	geſproſſen
kriedjen, to crawl	krodj	gekrodjen
riedjen, to smell	rodj	gerodjen
triefen, to drip	troff	getroffen
— ſieben, to boil	ſott	geſotten
fedjten, to fight	fodjt	gefodjten
— fledjten, to plait, to braid	flodjt	gefledjten
quellen, to spring	quoll	gequollen
ſdjwellen, to swell	ſdjwoll	geſdjwollen
ſaufen, to drink (to animals)	ſoff	geſoffen.

Observation. Most verbs of the first class have i e for their radical vowel. The verb ȝieben changes in the Imperf. Tense and in the Perfect Part. ḥ into g; triefen, ſieben and ſaufen double the end-consonant of the root, in order to make the o short.

SECOND CLASS.

The second class comprehends those verbs, which change their radical vowel into i (i short) or into ie (i long).

1. i short.

Infinitive.	*Imperfect.*	*Perfect Part.*
pfeifen, to whistle	pfiff	gepfiffen
— greifen, to seize	griff	gegriffen
— kneifen, to pinch	kniff	gekniffen
— ſdjleifen, to grind	ſdjliff	geſdjliffen
beißen, to bite	biß	gebiſſen
reißen, to tear	riß	geriſſen
— ſdjleißen, to split	ſdjliß	geſdjliſſen
ſdjmeißen, to throw	ſdjmiß	geſdjmiſſen
gleidjen, to resemble	glidj	geglidjen
ſdjleidjen, to sneak	ſdjlidj	geſdjleidjen
ſtreidjen, to stroke	ſtridj	geſtridjen
weidjen, to yield	widj	gewidjen
gleiten, to glide	glitt	geglitten
reiten, to ride on horseback	ritt	geritten
— ſdjreiten, to stride	ſdjritt	geſdjritten
ſtreiten, to dispute	ſtritt	geſtritten
leiden, to suffer	litt	gelitten
ſdjneiden, to cut	ſdjnitt	geſdjnitten

2. ie long.

Infinitive.	Imperfect.	Perfect Part.
bleiben, to stay	blieb	geblieben
reiben, to rub	rieb	gerieben
schreiben, to write	schrieb	geschrieben
treiben, to drive	trieb	getrieben
meiden, to avoid	mied	gemieden
scheiden, to part	schied	geschieden
steigen, to ascend	stieg	gestiegen
schweigen, to be silent	schwieg	geschwiegen
leihen, to lend	lieh	geliehen
zeihen, to accuse	zieh	geziehen
gedeihen, to thrive	gedieh	gediehen
scheinen, to shine	schien	geschienen
weisen, to show	wies	gewiesen
preisen, to praise	pries	gepriesen
schreien, to cry	schrie	geschrieen
speien, to spit	spie	gespieen.

Observation. All verbs of the second class have e i for their radical vowel. those which change it into i short double the end-consonant of their root; except ch and ß.

THIRD CLASS.

The third class comprehends those verbs, which change their radical vowel in the Imperfect Tense into a, and in the Perfect Participle into u or o:

1. a and u.

Infinitive.	Imperfect.	Perfect Part.
binden, to tie	band	gebunden
finden, to find	fand	gefunden
schwinden, to vanish	schwand	geschwunden
winden, to wind	wand	gewunden
bringen, to press	drang	gedrungen
gelingen, to succeed	gelang	gelungen
klingen, to sound	klang	geklungen
ringen, to wrestle	rang	gerungen
schlingen, to sling	schlang	geschlungen
schwingen, to swing	schwang	geschwungen
singen, to sing	sang	gesungen
springen, to spring	sprang	gesprungen
zwingen, to force	zwang	gezwungen
sinken, to sink	sank	gesunken
stinken, to stink	stank	gestunken
trinken, to drink	trank	getrunken

2. a and o.

Infinitive.	Imperfect.	Perfect Part.	Imperative.
brechen, to break	brach	gebrochen	brich
stechen, to sting	stach	gestochen	stich
sprechen, to speak	sprach	gesprochen	sprich

helfen, to help	half	geholfen	hilf
gelten, to be worth	galt	gegolten	gilt
—ſchelten, to chide	ſchalt	geſcholten	ſchilt
ſterben, to die	ſtarb	geſtorben	ſtirb
—werben, to enlist	warb	geworben	wirb
verderben, to spoil	verbarb	verdorben	verdirb
werfen, to throw	warf	geworfen	wirf
bergen, to hide	barg	geborgen	birg
treffen, to meet	traf	getroffen	triff
nehmen, to take	nahm	genommen	nimm
ſtehlen, to steal	ſtahl	geſtohlen	ſtiehl
befehlen, to command	befahl	befohlen	befiehl.
beginnen, to begin	begann	begonnen	
rinnen, to flow	rann	geronnen	
ſpinnen, to spin	ſpann	geſponnen	
ſinnen, to meditate	ſann	geſonnen	
gewinnen, to gain	gewann	gewonnen	
ſchwimmen, to swim	ſchwamm	geſchwommen.	

Observation. All verbs of the third class have i or e for their radical vowel; those which have e change it in the Imperative Mood into i, and this i is preserved in the second and third persons of the Present Tense of the Indicative Mood (§ 52): nimm, du nimmſt, er nimmt; ſtiehl, du ſtiehlſt, er ſtiehlt.

FOURTH CLASS.

The fourth class comprehends all those verbs, which have in the Imperfect Tense u, a or ie, and which take back their radical vowel in the Perfect Participle:

Infinitive.	*Imperfect.*	*Perfect Part.*	
fahren, to ride in carriage	fuhr	gefahren	
graben, to dig	grub	gegraben	
ſchlagen, to beat	ſchlug	geſchlagen	
tragen, to carry	trug	getragen	
laden, to load	lud	geladen	
waſchen, to wash	wuſch	gewaſchen	
wachſen, to grow	wuchs	gewachſen	
backen, to bake	buk	gebacken.	

			Imperative.
geben, to give	gab	gegeben	gib
treten, to step	trat	getreten	tritt
leſen, to read	las	geleſen	lies
ſehen, to see	ſah	geſehen	ſieh
geſchehen, to happen	geſchah	geſchehen	—
eſſen, to eat	aß	gegeſſen	iß
freſſen, to eat (of animals)	fraß	gefreſſen	friß
meſſen, to measure	maß	gemeſſen	miß.
bitten, to beg	bat	gebeten	
ſitzen, to sit	ſaß	geſeſſen	
liegen, to lie down	lag	gelegen	
kommen, to come.	kam	gekommen.	

blafen, to blow	blies	geblafen
fallen, to fall	fiel	gefallen
braten, to roast	briet	gebraten
rathen, to advise	rieth	gerathen
halten, to hold	hielt	gehalten
schlafen, to sleep	schlief	geschlafen
laffen, to let	ließ	gelaffen
hangen, to hang	hing	gehangen
fangen, to catch	fing	gefangen
laufen, to run	lief	gelaufen
rufen, to call	rief	gerufen
heißen, to be called	hieß	geheißen
stoßen, to push	stieß	gestoßen
hauen, to hew	hieb	gehauen.

Observation. The verbs of the fourth class which have a for their radical vowel, soften this letter in the second and third person Sing. of the Present Tense Ind. Mood; bu fährst, er fährt; bu fällst, er fällt. The same thing is to be observed in the verbs laufen and stoßen, which make: bu läufst, er läuft; bu stößest, er stößt. The verb hauen takes a b in the two Imperfect Tenses.

§ 54. There are still six verbs which, though changing their radical vowel, take the terminations of the assonant verbs:

fenben, to send	fanbte	gefanbt
wenben, to turn	wanbte	gewanbt
rennen, to run	rannte	gerannt
nennen, to name	nannte	genannt
brennen, to burn	brannte	gebrannt
fennen, to know	fannte	gefannt.

The Imperfect Tense of the Subjunctive Mood is formed without altering the radical vowel, fenbete, wenbete, nennte, brennte, &c.

4. OF THE CONJUGATION OF THE IRREGULAR VERBS.

§ 55. There are in the German language but fifteen irregular verbs:

1. Müffen, must, to be obliged; bürfen, may, to be allowed; fönnen, can, to be able; mögen, to wish, to like; are conjugated in the following manner:

Present Tense (Indicative Mood).

I must	I may	I can	I like
ich muß	ich barf	ich fann	ich mag
bu mußt	bu barfst	bu fannst	bu magst
er muß	er barf	er fann	er mag
wir müffen	wir bürfen	wir fönnen	wir mögen
ihr müßt	ihr bürft	ihr fönnt	ihr mögt
fie müffen	fie bürfen	fie fönnen	fie mögen

Present Tense (Subjunct. Mood).

(if) I must	(if) I may	(if) I can	(if) I like
ich müſſe	ich bürfe	ich fönne	ich möge
bu müſſeſt	bu bürfeſt	bu fönneſt	bu mögeſt
er müſſe	er bürfe	er fönne	er möge
wir müſſen	wir bürfen	wir fönnen	wir mögen
ihr müſſet	ihr bürfet	ihr fönnet	ihr möget
ſie müſſen	ſie bürfen	ſie fönnen	ſie mögen.

Imperfect Tense (Ind. Mood).

ich muſte	ich burfte	ich fonnte	ich mochte.

Imperfect Tense (Subj. Mood).

ich müſte	ich bürfte	ich fönnte	ich möchte.

The Imperative Mood is wanting.
The Present Participle is regular.
Perfect Participle; gemuſt, geburſt, gefonnt, gemocht.

2. **Wiſſen**, to know, is conjugated as follows:

Present Tense.

Indicative Mood.	*Subjunctive Mood.*
ich weiß, I know	ich wiſſe (if) I know
bu weißt	bu wiſſeſt
er weiß	er wiſſe
wir wiſſen	wir wiſſen
ihr wißt	ihr wiſſet
ſie wiſſen	ſie wiſſen.

Imperfect Tense.

ich wuſte, I knew.	ich wüſte, (if) I knew.

Imperative Mood: wiſſe, know (thou); wiſſet, know (ye).
Present Part.: wiſſenb, knowing.
Past Participle: gewuſt, known.

3. **Wollen**, will, to be willing; **ſollen**, shall, ought; *b6e* are irregular only in the Pres. Tense, Ind. Mood.

ich will, I will	ich ſoll, I ought
bu willſt	bu ſollſt
er will	er ſoll
wir wollen	wir ſollen
ihr wollt	ihr ſollt
ſie wollen	ſie ſollen.

The Imperf. Tense of the Subj. Mood is like that or the Indic. Mood: ich wollte, I would, (if) I would; ich ſollte, I should, (if) I should.

4. **Bringen**, to bring; **benfen**, to think; **gehen**, to go; **ſtehen**, to stand, and **thun** (contraction of thuen), to do; are only irregular in the Imperf. Tense and in the Perfect Participle:

bringen	brachte	gebracht
benken	bachte	gebacht
gehen	ging	gegangen
stehen	stand	gestanden
thun	that	gethan.

The verb thun has in the Present Tense of the Ind.
Mood: ich thue, bu thust, er thut, wir thun, ihr thut, sie
thun. In the Present Tense Subj. Mood the contraction
does not take place: ich thue, bu thueft, er thue.

5. Sein, to be, is conjugated as follows:

Present Tense.

Indicative Mood.	Subjunctive Mood.
ich bin, I am	ich sei, (if) I be
bu bist	bu seist
er ist	er sei
wir sind	wir seien
ihr seid	ihr seiet
sie sind	sie seien

Imperfect Tense.

ich war, I was	ich wäre, (if) I were
bu warst	bu wärest
er war	er wäre
wir waren	wir wären
ihr waret	ihr wäret
sie waren	sie wären.

Imperative Mood: sei, be (thou); seid, be (ye).
Present Participle: seiend, being.
Past Participle: gewesen, been.

6. Haben, to have, is conjugated thus:

Present Tense.

Indicative Mood.	Subjunctive Mood.
ich habe, I have	ich habe, (if) I have
bu hast	bu habest
er hat	er habe
wir haben	wir haben
ihr habt	ihr habet
sie haben	sie haben.

Imperfect Tense.

| ich hatte, I had | ich hätte, (if) I had. |

The Imperative Mood and the two Participles are irregular.

7. Werden, to be, to become, is conjugated thus:

Present Tense.

Indicative Mood.	Subjunctive Mood.
ich werde, I become	ich werde, (if) I become
bu wirst	bu werdest
er wird	er werde

wir werden   wir werden
ihr werdet   ihr werdet
fie werden   fie werden.

Imperfect Tense.

ich wurbe, I became.   ich würbe, (if) I became.

The Imperative Mood and Present Part. are regular, the Past Participle is geworden, become, and worden, been.

In order to facilitate the researches, we have added at the end of this part of the Grammar, an alphabetical list of the Imperfect and Present Tenses, the Imperative Moods and Past Participles of the dissonant and irregular verbs, indicating also the Infinitives to which these Tenses belong.

5. OF THE FORMATION OF THE COMPOUND TENSES.

§ 56. The Germans have three auxiliary verbs: fein, to be; haben, to have; werden, to become, shall or will. The verb fein serves to form the Perfect Tenses of most neuter verbs; haben to form those of the active and reflected verbs; and werden serves to form the Future tenses and the Conditional Mood*\of all verbs without distinction. Ex.:

1. Trinken, to drink.

Perfect Tense.

Ind. Mood.   *Subj. Mood.*

Ich habe getrunken, I have drunk.   ich habe getrunken, (if) I have drunk.
du haft getrunken, 2c.   du habeft getrunken, 2c.

Pluperfect Tense.

ich hatte getrunken, I had drunk.   ich hätte getrunken, (if) I had drunk.
du hatteft getrunken, 2c.   du hätteft getrunken, 2c.

First Future Tense.

ich werde trinken, I shall or will drink.   ich werde trinken, (if) I shall or will drink.
du wirft trinken, 2c.   du werdeft trinken, 2c.

Second Future Tense.

ich werde getrunken haben, I shall or will have drunk.   ich werde getrunken haben, (if) I shall or will have drunk.
du wirft getrunken haben, 2c.   du werdeft getrunken haben, 2c.

---

* The *Conditional Mood* is, properly speaking, only another way of expressing the Imperfect and Pluperfect Tenses of the Subjunct. Mood; inasmuch as it is quite the same if we say: ich hätte or ich würde haben; ich hätte gehabt, or ich würde gehabt haben.

First Conditional Tense.
id̨ würbe trinfen, I should or would drink.
bu würbeſt trinfen ꝛc.

Second Conditional Tense.
id̨ würbe getrunfen ħaben, I should or would have drunk.
bu würbeſt getrunfen ħaben, ꝛc.

2. Ŕommen, to come.
Perfect Tense.

Indic. Mood.	*Subj. Mood.*
Id̨ bin gefommen, I am come.	id̨ fei gefommen, (if) I be come.
bu biſt gefommen, ꝛc.	bu feiſt gefommen, ꝛc.

Pluperfect Tense.
id̨ war gefommen, I was come.	id̨ wäre gefommen, (if) I were come.
bu warſt gefommen, ꝛc.	bu wäreſt gefommen, ꝛc.

First Future Tense.
id̨ werbe fommen, I shall or will come.	id̨ werbe fommen, (if) I shall or will come.
bu wirſt fommen, ꝛc.	bu werbeſt fommen, ꝛc.

Second Future Tense.
id̨ werbe gefommen fein, I shall or will be come.	id̨ werbe gefommen fein, (if) I shall or will be come.
bu wirſt gefommen fein, ꝛc.	bu werbeſt gefommen fein, ꝛc.

First Conditional Tense.
id̨ würbe fommen, I should or would come.
bu würbeſt fommen, ꝛc.

Second Conditional Tense.
id̨ würbe gefommen fein, I should or would be come.
bu würbeſt gefommen fein, ꝛc.

By the two preceding models we see:

1. That the Perfect Tense is composed of the Present Tense of ħaben or fein and of the Perfect Part. of the verb;

2. That the Pluperfect Tense is composed of the Imperfect Tense of ħaben or fein and of the Perfect Participle of the verb;

3. That the first Future Tense is composed of the Present Tense of werben, and of the Present of the Infinitive of the verb;

4. That the second Future Tense is composed of the Present Tense of werben and the Perfect of the Infinitive of the verb;

5. That the first Conditional Tense is formed of the Imperfect Tense, Subj. Mood, of werben and the Present of the Infinitive of the verb;

6. That the second Conditional Tense is formed of the same Tense of werben, and of the Perfect of the Infinitive of the verb.

§ 57. As to the formation of the composed Tenses of the auxiliary verbs, haben and fein form their Perfect Tenses of themselves, and werben forms them by the auxiliary fein. Ex.:

1. Haben, to have.

Perfect Tense.
Ich habe gehabt, I have had;
ich habe gehabt, (if) I have had.

Pluperfect Tense.
ich hatte gehabt, I had had;
ich hätte gehabt, (if) I had had.

2. Sein, to be.

Perfect Tense.
Ich bin gewesen, I have been;
ich sei gewesen, (if) I have been.

Pluperfect Tense.
ich war gewesen, I had been;
ich wäre gewesen, (if) I had been.

3. Werben, to become.

Perfect Tense.
Ich bin geworden, I have become;*
ich sei geworden, (if) I have become.

Pluperfect Tense.
ich war geworden, I had become;
ich wäre geworden, (if) I had become.

The two Future and the two Conditional Tenses are formed like those of the other verbs by the auxiliary werben. Ex.:

First Future Tense.	*Second Future Tense.*
Ich werde haben, I shall have;	ich werde gehabt haben, I shall have had;
ich werde fein, I shall be;	ich werde gewesen fein, I shall have been;
ich werde werben, I shall become;	ich werde geworben fein, I shall have become.

---

* Instead of geworden we say simply worden, when the verb werben is constructed with an other verb and only has the function of an auxiliary.

First Conditional Tense.	*Second Conditional Tense.*
idy würde haben, I should have ;	idy würde gehabt haben, I should have had ;
idy würde fein, I should be ;	idy würde gewesen fein, I should have been ;
idy würde werden, I should become	idy würde geworden fein, I should have become.

§ 58. Besides the verbs haben, fein and werden, the Germans employ also, like the English, wollen, will; laffen, let; mögen, may; follen, shall, and müffen, must, as auxiliary verbs, in order to express different respects of Moods and Tenses.

Laßt uns gehen, let us go ;
wir wollen gehen, we will go ;
du follst sterben, thou shalt die ;
du mußt sterben, thou must die ;
idy wünsche, daß er es erhalten möge, I wish that he may receive it ;
möge er glücklich ankommen, may he arrive safely.

§ 59. Conjugate the following verbs in all their Moods and Tenses :

Assonant.	*Dissonant.*
Zahlen, to pay	leiben, to suffer
leben, to live	singen, to sing
kaufen, to buy	werfen, to throw
arbeiten, to work	fallen, to fall
lernen, to learn	kommen, to come

6. OF THE CONJUGATION OF PASSIVE VERBS.

§ 60. Transitive verbs have two forms: the active form and the passive form. It is in the active form, when the subject does the action which the Verb expresses, it is in the passive form when the subject suffers the action expressed by the verb. In the sentences: idy liebe, I love, and idy werde geliebt, I am loved, the verb lieben is presented in those two forms.

§ 61. We have already in the preceding paragraphs shown the conjugation of the active form of verbs; it is therefore only left to represent their passive form. The verb in the passive voice has but composed Tenses, which are all formed by means of the auxiliary werden, and the Perfect Part. of the verb.

MODE OF THE CONJUGATION OF A PASSIVE VERB.

Geliebt werden, to be loved.

Present Tense.

Indicative Mood.	Subjunctive Mood.
Ich werde geliebt, I am loved;	ich werbe geliebt, (if) I be loved;
du wirst geliebt	du werbest geliebt
er wird geliebt	er werde geliebt
wir werden geliebt	wir werden geliebt
ihr werdet geliebt	ihr werdet geliebt
sie werden geliebt	sie werden geliebt.

Imperfect Tense.

ich wurde geliebt, I was loved;	ich würde geliebt, (if) I were loved
du wurdest geliebt	du würdest geliebt
er wurde geliebt	er würde geliebt
wir wurden geliebt	wir würden geliebt
ihr wurdet geliebt	ihr würdet geliebt
sie wurden geliebt.	sie würden geliebt.

Perfect Tense.

ich bin geliebt worden, I have been loved;	ich sei geliebt worden, (if) I have been loved;
du bist geliebt worden	du seist geliebt worden
er ist geliebt worden	er sei geliebt worden
wir sind geliebt worden	wir seien geliebt worden
ihr seid geliebt worden	ihr seiet geliebt worden
sie sind geliebt worden.	sie seien geliebt worden.

Pluperfect Tense.

ich war geliebt worden, I had been loved;	ich wäre geliebt worden, (if) I had been loved;
du warst geliebt worden	du wärest geliebt worden
er war geliebt worden	er wäre geliebt worden
wir waren geliebt worden	wir wären geliebt worden
ihr waret geliebt worden	ihr wäret geliebt worden
sie waren geliebt worden.	sie wären geliebt worden.

First Future Tense.

ich werde geliebt werden, I shall be loved;	ich werde geliebt werden, (if) I shall be loved;
du wirst geliebt werden	du werdest geliebt werden
er wird geliebt werden	er werde geliebt werden
wir werden geliebt werden	wir werden geliebt werden
ihr werdet geliebt werden	ihr werdet geliebt werden
sie werden geliebt werden.	sie werden geliebt werden.

Second Future Tense.

ich werde geliebt worden sein, I shall have been loved;	ich werde geliebt worden sein, (if) I shall have been loved,
du wirst geliebt worden sein	du werdest geliebt worden sein
er wird geliebt worden sein	er werde geliebt worden sein

wir werden geliebt worden sein
ihr werdet geliebt worden sein
sie werden geliebt worden sein.

wir werden geliebt worden sein
ihr werdet geliebt worden sein
sie werden geliebt worden sein.

Conditional Mood.

First Tense.	Second Tense.
ich würde geliebt werden, I should be loved;	ich würde geliebt worden sein, I should have been loved;
du würdest geliebt werden	du würdest geliebt worden sein
er würde geliebt werden	er würde geliebt worden sein
wir würden geliebt werden	wir würden geliebt worden sein
ihr würdet geliebt werden	ihr würdet geliebt worden sein
sie würden geliebt werden.	sie würden geliebt worden sein.

Imperative Mood.

werde geliebt, be (thou) loved.
werdet geliebt, be (ye) loved.

Participles.

Present: geliebt werdend, being loved.
Perfect: geliebt worden, been loved.

7. OF REFLECTIVE VERBS.

§ 62. When a transitive verb expresses an action which falls back directly or indirectly upon the person who performs it, we call it a *reflective verb*. The reflective verbs like the transitive verbs take haben for their auxiliary and the second pronoun, which is the Accusative of the first, is placed now before and now after the verb.

CONJUGATION OF THE REFLECTIVE VERB.

Sich freuen, to rejoice.

Present Tense.

Indic. Mood.	Subj. Mood.
Ich freue mich, I rejoice.	ich freue mich, (if) I rejoice.
du freust dich	du freuest dich
er freut sich	er freue sich
wir freuen uns	wir freuen uns
ihr freut euch	ihr freuet euch
sie freuen sich.	sie freuen sich.

Imperfect Tense.

ich freute mich, I rejoiced.	ich freute mich, (if) I rejoiced.
du freutest dich	du freutest dich
er freute sich	er freute sich
wir freuten uns	wir freuten uns
ihr freutet euch	ihr freutet euch
sie freuten sich.	sie freuten sich.

Perfect Tense.

Indic. Mood.	Subj. Mood.
ich habe mich gefreut, I have re-joiced;	ich habe mich gefreut, (if) I have rejoiced;
du haft dich gefreut	du habeft dich gefreut
er hat fich gefreut	er habe fich gefreut
wir haben uns gefreut	wir haben uns gefreut
ihr habt euch gefreut	ihr habet euch gefreut
fie haben fich gefreut.	fie haben fich gefreut.

Pluperfect Tense.

ich hatte mich gefreut, I had re-joiced;	ich hätte mich gefreut, (if) I had rejoiced;
du hatteft dich gefreut	du hätteft dich gefreut
er hatte fich gefreut	er hätte fich gefreut
wir hatten uns gefreut	wir hätten uns gefreut
ihr hattet euch gefreut	ihr hättet euch gefreut
fie hatten fich gefreut.	fie hätten fich gefreut.

First Future Tense.

ich werde mich freuen, I shall re-joice;	ich werde mich freuen, (if) I shall rejoice;
du wirft dich freuen	du werdeft dich freuen
er wird fich freuen	er werde fich freuen
wir werden uns freuen	wir werden uns freuen
ihr werdet euch freuen	ihr werdet euch freuen
fie werden fich freuen.	fie werden fich freuen.

Second Future Tense.

ich werde mich gefreut haben, I shall have rejoiced;	ich werde mich gefreut haben, (if) I shall have rejoiced;
du wirft dich gefreut haben	du werdeft dich gefreut haben
er wird fich gefreut haben	er werde fich gefreut haben
wir werden uns gefreut haben	wir werden uns gefreut haben
ihr werdet euch gefreut haben	ihr werdet euch gefreut haben
fie werden fich gefreut haben.	fie werden fich gefreut haben.

Conditional Mood.

First Tense.	Second Tense.
ch würde mich freuen, I should re-joice;	ich würde mich gefreut haben, I should have rejoiced;
du würdeft dich freuen	du würdeft dich gefreut haben
er würde fich freuen	er würde fich gefreut haben
wir würden uns freuen	wir würden uns gefreut haben
ihr würdet euch freuen	ihr würdet euch gefreut haben
fie würden fich freuen.	fie würden fich gefreut haben.

Imperative Mood.

freue dich, rejoice (thou).
freuen wir uns, let us rejoice.
freuet euch, rejoice (ye).

48

Participles.

ſich freuenb, rejoicing.
ſich gefreut haben, having rejoiced.

Conjugate in this manner:

ſich beflagen, to complain.

§ 63. There are some reflective verbs, whose second pronouns are in the Dative, as ſich ſchmeicheln, to flatter one's self. Ex.:

ich ſchmeichle mir, I flatter myself;
bu ſchmeichelſt bir
er ſchmeichelt ſich
wir ſchmeicheln uns
ihr ſchmeichelt euch
ſie ſchmeicheln ſich.

8. OF IMPERSONAL VERBS.

§ 64. Impersonal verbs are those, which can only be used in the third person Singular and with the neuter pronoun es, it. Their composed Tenses are formed by means of the auxiliary haben. Ex.:

	Indic. Mood.	Subj. Mood.
Pres. T.	es regnet, it rains ;	es regne, (if) it rain ;
Imp. T.	es regnete, it did rain ;	es regnete, (if) it rained ;
Perf. T.	es hat geregnet, it has been raining ;	es habe geregnet, (if) it have been raining ;
Plup. T.	es hatte geregnet, it had been raining ;	es hätte geregnet, (if) it had been raining ;
1st Fut. T.	es wird regnen, it will rain ;	es werbe regnen, (if) it will rain ;
2d Fut. T.	es wird geregnet haben, it will have been raining.	es werbe geregnet haben, (if) it will have been raining.

1st Cond. T. es würbe regnen, it would rain ;
2d Cond. T. es würbe geregnet haben, it would have been raining ;
Imperat. T. es regne, may it rain ;
Perfect Part. geregnet, rained.

§ 64. There are verbs which are impersonal by their nature, as :

regnen, to rain.	ſchneien, to snow.
bonnern, to thunder.	nebeln, to be foggy.
bliſzen, to lighten.	hageln, to hail.

There are also others, which are employed impersonally but in certain ways of speaking :

geben, to give; es gibt, there is, there are; es gab, there was, there were.

fein, to be; es ist, it is, there is; es ist warm, it is warm; es war kalt, it was cold.

Some verbs are employed impersonally in German, which are not in English:

es ist mir warm, I am warm.
es friert mich, I am cold.
es schläfert mich, I am sleepy.
mich hungert, I am hungry.*
mich dürstet, I am thirsty.
mir ist bange, I am afraid.

es ist mir lieb, I am glad.
es thut mir leid, I am sorry.
es freut mich, I am glad.
es wundert mich, I am astonished.
mir wird übel, I feel sick.
es reut mich, I repent.

es gelingt mir, I succeed.

All these verbs can express the three persons of Plural as well as of the Singular. Ex.:

es freut mich, I am glad.
es freut dich, thou art glad.
es freut ihn, he is glad.
es freut uns, we are glad.
es freut euch, you are glad.
es freut sie, they are glad.

es gelingt mir, I succeed.
es gelingt dir.
es gelingt ihm.
es gelingt uns.
es gelingt euch.
es gelingt ihnen.

---

9. OF COMPOUND VERBS.

§ 66. A simple verb becomes a compound one by the addition of certain ~~particles~~ which are joined to it and precede it.

There are two kinds of compound verbs:

1. Those, the joined ~~particle~~ of which remains always attached to them in all Tenses and Moods: these verbs form their Perfect Participle without adding the syllable ge, and are called *inseparable verbs.*

2. Those whose ~~particle~~ is not always joined to the verb, but is detached from it in certain Tenses: those ones are called *separable verbs.*

§ 67. Inseparable verbs are those, whose accent rests on the verb and not on the ~~particle~~. There are but very few of them, and they begin either by the prepositions hinter and wider, or by the adverbs offen and voll. Ex.:

---

* When an impersonal verb is constructed with a personal pronoun, the word es may be omitted.

widerſprechen, to contradict; ich widerſpreche, ich habe widerſprochen; hinterbringen, to inform; ich hinterbringe, ich habe hinterbracht; vollenden, to complete; ich vollende, ich habe vollendet; offenbaren, to reveal; ich offenbare, ich habe offenbart.

The *compound verbs* must not be confounded with the *derived verbs;* the latter are formed of a verb and a prefixed syllable, that is never detached from it. Ex.:

achten, to esteem; verachten, to despise; ich verachte, I despise; ſagen, to say; entſagen, to renounce; ich entſage, I renounce.

§ 68. Separable verbs are those, whose accent rests on the particle and not on the verb. Their number is very great, and they begin either by one of the prepositions ab, an, auf, aus, bei, ein, mit, nach, vor, zu, or by one of the adverbs dar, fort, weg, hin, fehl, los, and nieder. Ex.:

abſchreiben, to copy.	vorſtellen, to represent.
anfangen, to begin.	zuſchreiben, to ascribe.
aufſtehen, to get up.	darbieten, to offer.
auslegen, to explain.	fortſchicken, to send away.
beifügen, to add.	weggehen, to go away.
einführen, to introduce.	fehlſchlagen, to fail.
mittheilen, to communicate.	losmachen, to detach.
nachſehen, to revise.	niederwerfen, to throw down.

§ 69. The compound verbs, which are formed by the prepositions durch, hinter, über, um, unter, are sometimes separable, sometimes inseparable, according to their having the accent on the verb or on the particle. Ex.:

über ſe tz en, to translate; ich überſetze, ich habe überſetzt; ü b e r ſetzen, to cross (a river); ich ſetze über, ich habe übergeſetzt.

Practice only can make up this rule.

CONJUGATION OF A COMPOUND SEPARABLE VERB.

Abſchreiben, to copy.

Present Tense.

Indic. Mood.	Subj. Mood.
Ich ſchreibe ab, I copy;	ich ſchreibe ab, (if) I copy;
du ſchreibſt ab	du ſchreibeſt ab
er ſchreibt ab	er ſchreibe ab
wir ſchreiben ab	wir ſchreiben ab
ihr ſchreibt ab	ihr ſchreibet ab
ſie ſchreiben ab.	ſie ſchreiben ab.

Imperfect Tense.

ich ſchrieb ab, I copied	ich ſchriebe ab, (if) I copied
du ſchriebſt ab, ꝛc.	du ſchriebeſt ab, ꝛc.

ich habe abgeschrieben, I have co- ich habe abgeschrieben, (if) I have
    pied;   copied;
ich hatte abgeschrieben, I had co- ich hätte abgeschrieben, (if) I had
    pied.   copied.

First and Second Future Tenses.

ich werde abschreiben, I shall copy; ich werde abschreiben, (if) I shall
                                          copy;
ich werde abgeschrieben haben, I shall ich werde abgeschrieben haben, (if).
    have copied.   I shall have copied.

First and Second Conditional Tenses.

ich würde abschreiben, I should ich würde abgeschrieben haben, I
    copy.   should have copied.

Imperative Mood.

schreibe ab, copy (thou); laßt uns abschreiben, let us copy;
    schreibt ab, copy (ye).

Participles.

abschreibend, copying; abgeschrieben, copied.

If the compound verb is reflective, the particle is
always placed at the end. Ex.:

sich einbilden, to imagine.

Present Tense.

ich bilde mir ein, I imagine;
bu bildest dir ein
er bildet sich ein
wir bilden uns ein
ihr bildet euch ein
sie bilden sich ein.

CHAPTER VIII.

OF PREPOSITIONS.

§ 70. The prepositions are invariable words which
are placed before the nouns or pronouns in order to
express the relations which would not be sufficiently
pointed out by the cases. They are:

1. Either primitive words, as an, at, to; auf, upon
in, in; für, for; mit, with;

2. Or derived or compound words, as außer, out of;
zwischen, between; oberhalb, above; anstatt, instead of;

3. Or words taken from other parts of speech, like
fraft, by virtue of; troß, notwithstanding; zufolge, in consequence of.

§ 71. Nouns or pronouns, whose relations are defined
by a preposition, are always placed either in the Genitive, or in the Dative, or in the Accusative. Some prepositions govern but one case, others govern two, according
to the kind of relation we wish to express.

1. PREPOSITIONS GOVERNING THE GENITIVE.

Unweit, während,
mittels, fraft,
laut, vermöge,
innerhalb, außerhalb,
oberhalb, unterhalb,
diesseit, jenseit,
halben, wegen,
ungeachtet, statt.

Unweit, not far from: unweit des Schlosses, not far from the castle ;
unweit der Stadt, not far from the town.

Während, during: während des Sommers, during the summer; während der Nacht, during the night.

Mittels, mittelst or vermittelst, by means of: mittels Ihres Beiftandes,
Ihrer Hilfe, by means of your assistance.

Kraft or vermöge, by virtue of: kraft des Gesetzes, by virtue of the law ;
vermöge seines Befehls, by virtue of his order.

Laut, according to : laut meines Schreibens, according to my letter.

Oberhalb, above ; unterhalb, below; innerhalb, on the inside; außerhalb, on the outside: außerhalb des Hauses, on the outside of the
house.

Diesseit, on this side of; jenseit, on that side of: diesseit des Flusses,
on this side of the river.

Halben, halber or wegen, on account of, by reason of; precede or follow their substantive : der Armuth halben, by reason of poverty ;
wegen seines Alters or seines Alters wegen, on account of his age.
When halben or wegen are preceded by a personal pronoun, the
final r of the pronoun is changed into t and the two words drawn
together : meinethalben, deinetwegen, seinethalben, Ihretwegen, for
my sake, on my account, &c. Unser and euer keep their final r before the t: unserthalben, euertwegen or euretwegen, for the sake of us,
of you.

Ungeachtet, notwithstanding, is placed before and after its substantive
or pronoun: ungeachtet seiner Unschuld, notwithstanding his innocence;
alles dessen ungeachtet, notwithstanding all this.

Statt or anstatt, instead of: statt or anstatt meines Bruders, instead of
my brother; an meiner Schwester Statt, in my sister's stead.

⟩ There are three more prepositions, which govern the Genitive or Dative indiscriminately; längš, along; zu= folge, in consequense of, and trotz, in spite of: längš bem Fluſſe or längš beš Fluſſeš, along the river; zufolge beš Vertrageš or zufolge bem Vertrage, in consequence of the treaty; trotz ſeinen Vorſtellungen or trotz ſeiner Vorſtellun= gen, in spite of his remonstrances.

2. PREPOSITIONS GOVERNING THE DATIVE.

Mit, nebſt, ſammt,
bei, ſeit, von, nach,
auš, außer, zu, zuwiber,
entgegen, gegenüber.

Mit, with: er iſt mit meinem Bruber angekommen, he is arrived with my brother; ich gehe mit bir, I go with thee.

Nebſt or ſammt, with, together with: er, nebſt ſeiner Schweſter, he and his sister; bie Mutter nebſt or ſammt ihren Kindern, the mother with her children.

Bei, near, at, with: er war bei mir, he was with me, at my house; bei ben Römern, with the Romans; bei Berlin, near Berlin.

Seit, since: ſeit ſeiner Zurückfunft, since his arrival; ſeit zwei Jahren, for two years; ſeitbem, since then.

Von, of, from: ich habe eš von bem Grafen erhalten, I have received it from the count; ein Kind von brei Jahren, a child of three years; ich komme von Berlin, I come from Berlin.

Nach, after, to, according to: er kam nach mir, he came after me; nach bem Eſſen, after dinner; nach bem Geſetze, according to law; ich gehe nach Berlin, I go to Berlin.

Auš, out of, from: wir kommen auš ber Schule, we come from school; auš bem Schranke nehmen, to take out of the cupboard; auš allen Kräften, with all (one's) power.

Außer, out of, besides: er wohnt außer ber Stadt, he lives out of town; ich habe keinen Freund außer Ihnen, I have no other friend but you.

Zu, to, at: kommen Sie zu mir, come to me; ſetzen Sie ſich zu mei= nem Bruber, sit down by my brother; wohnen Sie zu Lüttich? do you live at Liege? Iſt Ihr Vater zu Hauſe? is your father at home?

Zuwiber, against, follows always its regimen; ber Verorbnung zuwiber, against the ordinance; ber Wein iſt mir zuwiber, I dislike wine.

Entgegen, against, to meet; gegenüber, opposite, follow generally their regimen; er kam mir entgegen, he came to meet me; er wohnt mir gegenüber, he lives opposite me.

7

3. PREPOSITIONS GOVERNING THE ACCUSATIVE

Durch, für, um,
ohne, fonder,
gegen, wider.

Durch, through, by means of: burch bas Dorf gehen, to go through the village; burch bich ist er reich geworden, by means of you (by your help) has he become rich; bas ganze Jahr burch or hinburch, the whole year through.

Für, for: biefes Buch ist für mich, this book is for me; für biefes Gelt will ich mir Bücher kaufen, for this money will I buy books.

Um, round, about, at: um bie Kirche, um bie Stabt gehen, to go round the church, round the town; um Neujahr, um Oftern, about New-year's-day, about Easter; um wieviel Uhr? at what o'clock? um fünf Uhr, um Mitternacht, at five o'clock, at midnight; um bie Zeit ber Ernbte, at harvest-time.

Ohne, fonder, without: ich kann nicht leben ohne bich, I cannot live without you; was ist bas Leben ohne einen Freund? what is life without a friend? Sonder is no more used except in poetry; fonder Zweifel, fonder Mühe, without doubt, without trouble.

Gegen, wider, to, towards, against: bie Pflichten gegen bie Eltern, the duties towards parents; milbthätig gegen bie Armen, charitable to the poor; gegen Abenb, towards evening; wider bie Mauer, against the wall; wider bie Gefetze, against the laws.

4. PREPOSITIONS GOVERNING THE DATIVE AND ACCUSATIVE.

An, auf, in,
über, unter, vor,
hinter, neben, zwischen.

These prepositions govern the Accusative, when the verb of the sentence denotes either a movement or a direction towards an object, and the Dative, when it does not denote this movement.

An, at, on: with the Dative: er steht an ber Thür, he stands at the door; biefe Stabt liegt am Rhein, this town is situated on the Rhine; an bir habe ich einen Freund, in thee I have a friend. With the Accusative: fetze ben Topf an bas Feuer, put the pot by the fire; ich bachte an bich, I thought of thee; er wenbete sich an ben König, he addressed himself to the king.

Auf, on, upon: with the Dative: sie sitzt auf bem Stuhle, she is sitting on the chair; bas Buch liegt auf bem Tifche, the book lies on the table; mein Bruber ist auf ber Jagb, my brother is out hunting. With the Accusative: fetzen Sie sich auf biefen Stuhl, sit down upon this chair; legen Sie bas Buch auf ben Tifch, put the book on the table; wir gehen heute auf bie Jagb, we go out hunting to-day.

Jn, in, into; *with the Dative:* er wohnt in der Stadt, he lives in the town; er wohnt in der Mitte seiner Kinder, he lives surrounded by his children; sie ist noch im Bette, she is still in bed. *With the Accusative:* ich gehe in die Schule, in den Garten, I go to school, into the garden; das Kind fiel in den Fluß, the child fell into the river; er sagte es mir in's Ohr, he whispered it into my ear.

Ueber, above, over; *with the Dative.* das Gemälde hängt über der Thür, über dem Spiegel, the picture hangs above the door, above the window; über mir wohnt ein Künstler, an artist lives above me. *With the Accusative:* hängen Sie den Käfig über die Thür; hang the cage over the door; wir gehen über diese Brücke, we shall pass this bridge; die Ehre geht über den Reichthum, honor is better than riches.

Unter, under, beneath, among; *with the Dative:* unter dem Tische liegen, to lie under the table; Sie wohnen unter mir, you lodge beneath me; unter der Regierung Ludwig's, in the reign of Louis; unter Freunden, among friends. *With the Accusative:* stelle dich unter den Baum, place yourself under the tree; Wasser unter den Wein thun, to put water with the wine.

Vor, before; *with the Dative:* vor dem Hause steht ein Baum, before the house stands a tree; vor dem Kriege war er sehr arm, before the war he was very poor; ich bin vor dir angekommen, I am arrived before you; dieses ist vor meinen Augen geschehen, that has happened before my eyes. *With the Accusative:* er trat vor den Spiegel, he stepped before the looking-glass; vor den Richter rufen, to summon before the judge.

Hinter, behind; *with the Dative:* wir wohnen hinter der Kirche, we live behind the church; er kam hinter mir, he came after me. *With the Accusative:* er stellt sich hinter die Thür, hinter mich, he places himself behind the door, behind me.

Neben, by the side of; *with the Dative:* er saß neben mir, neben meiner Schwester, he sat by the side of me, beside my sister *With the Accusative:* er setzte sich neben mich, he sat down beside me

Zwischen, between, among; *with the Dative:* zwischen dem Hause und dem Garten ist der Hof, between the house and the garden is the yard; es entstand zwischen dem Manne und der Frau ein Streit, there arose a quarrel between the man and the woman. *With the Accusative:* er setzte den Stuhl zwischen die beiden Tische, he put the chair between the two tables; der Ring fiel zwischen die Steine, the ring dropt among the stones.

§ 72. Frequently the prepositions are united in one word with the Dative or Accusative of the Article Ex.:

am instead of an dem	vom instead of von dem
ans — — an das	fürs — — für das
zum — — zu dem	beim — — bei dem
zur — — zu der	durchs — — durch das

CHAPTER IX.

OF ADVERBS.

§ 78. The Adverbs are divided into three principal classes; Adverbs of *place*, of *time*, and of *quality*.

1. ADVERBS OF PLACE.

Wo, where
hier, here
ba, bort, there
weit, fern, far
nahe, near
hinten, behind
vorn, before
oben, above
unten, below

irgenbwo, anywhere, somewhere
nirgenbwo, nowhere
überall, everywhere
zurück, backward
vorwärts, forward
seitwärts, sideways
rückwärts, backwards
links, on the left
rechts, on the right, &c.

2. ADVERBS OF TIME.

Wann, when
heute, to-day
morgen, to-morrow
übermorgen, the day after to-morrow
gestern, yesterday
vorgestern, the day before yesterday
jetzt, now
ehemals, formerly

bamals, then, at the time
oft, often
nie, never
zuweilen, sometimes
immer, always
zuvor, before
schon, already
früh, early
spät, late
gleich, sogleich, directly, &c.

3. ADVERBS OF QUALITY OR KIND.

Wie, how
so, thus
gern, willingly
gut, well
schlecht, badly

warum, why
beinahe, almost
zwar, indeed, although
gewiß, certainly
vielleicht, perhaps, &c.

This last class of adverbs is the most numerous; it comprehends all adjectives, which can be employed adverbially, and which in English take the termination *ly*. Ex.:

Dieses Haus ist neu, this house is new;
dieses Haus ist neu angestrichen, this house has been newly painted.

§ 74. The two adverbs ĥer, here, ĥin, there, are very often combined with other adverbs or with prepositions, and serve to form a great number of adverbs of place. Ĥer denotes a movement towards the place, where the speaker is; ĥin a movement from that place. Ex.:

ĥerab, ĥinab, down	ĥierĥer, ĥierĥin, this way
ĥerauf, ĥinauf, up	daĥer, daĥin, there
ĥerein, ĥinein, in	dortĥer, dortĥin, from there, there
ĥeraus, ĥinaus, out	woĥer, woĥin, whence, where
ĥerunter, ĥinunter, down	obenĥer, obenĥin, at the surface.

The adverbs ĥier, here, da, there, combined with prepositions and adverbs, serve likewise to form compound adverbs. Ex.:

ĥieran, by this	daran, by that*
ĥierauf, hereupon	darauf, thereupon
ĥierbei, hereby	dabei, thereby
ĥierburĉ, hereby	daburĉ, by that
ĥieraus, out of this	daraus, out of that
ĥierin, in this	darin, therein
ĥierfür, for this	dafür, therefore
ĥiergegen, against this	dagegen, against it.

The adverb wo, where, is combined in the same manner:

woran, at which	woburĉ, whereby
worauf, upon which	womit, wherewith
woraus, out of which	woran, wherefrom
worin, in which	woʒu, for what
wobei, whereby	wonaĉ, after which.†

§ 75. Some adverbs, and especially adjectives used adverbially, are susceptible of being compared, and form their degrees·of comparison in the same manner as the adjectives:

fpät, late ;	fpäter, later ;	fpäteſt, latest ;
oft, often ;	öfter, oftener ;	öfteſt, oftenest.

The simple form of the Superlative in eſt is little used; we more frequently have recourse to circumlocutions, in which the adverb is replaced by the neuter of the adjective, preceded by the prepositions an or auſ Ex.:

---

* The primitive form of da is dar, and is used every time when, in the formation of these words, two vowels meet.

† When wo is combined with a word beginning by a vowel, an r is inserted, to avoid the hiatus.

am fpäteften, latest;　　auf baß genauefte, most minutely;
am öfteften, oftenest;　　auf baß gefdywinbefte, most quickly.

The Superlative sometimes also takes the ending en ß, Ex.:

früheftenß, at the soonest;　höchftenß, at the most.

The following adverbs form their degrees of comparison irregularly:

gut, well;　　　　beffer, better;　　am beften, best,
biel, much;　　　mehr, more;　　　am meiften, most;
balb, soon;　　　eher, sooner;　　am eheften, soonest;
gern, willingly;　lieber, more willingly;　am liebften, most willingly.

_/1_

CHAPTER X.

OF CONJUNCTIONS.

§ 76. The following is a list of the principal conjunctions.

1. SIMPLE CONJUNCTIONS.

Unb, and; ober, or;　　　　wenn, when, if; ob, if, whether;
aber, allein, but;　　　　wann, when; bann, then;
fonbern, but (after a negation);　baß, that;
alß, when, than;　　　　boch, yet;
benn, for; ba, as;　　　ehe, before;
weil, because;　　　　alfo, thus, consequently.

2. COMPOUND CONJUNCTIONS.

Damit, auf baß, in order that;　entweber...ober, either...or,
obgleich, obfchon, although;　weber...noch, neither...nor;
nachbem, after;　　　　fowohl...alß, as well...as;
inbem, while;　　　　wie...fo, as...as;
mithin, consequently;　　je...befto, the...the.

The conjunctions are followed now by the Subjunctive and now by the Indicative Mood; some of them change the construction of the sentence, others do not change it. (See the following Chapters.)

CHAPTER XI.

OF THE USE OF THE MOODS.

1. INDICATIVE MOOD.

§ 77. The Germans generally employ the Indicative Mood, where in English, for the sake of brevity, the Infinitive and Present participle are used. Ex.:

Ich glaube, daß er ein rechtschaffener Mann ist. — I believe him to be an honest man.

Wir haben immer gefunden, daß er die Wahrheit sprach. — We have ever found him to speak the truth.

Ich weiß nicht, was ich thun soll. — I do not know what to do.

Jemand, der in Deutschland reiste, fand — Some one, travelling in Germany, found

Weil ich nicht reich bin, habe ich keine Freunde. — Not being rich, I have no friends

Ich habe es gesehen, als ich vorbeiging. — I saw it in passing.

Man macht sich oft verhaßt, indem man die Wahrheit sagt. — We often make ourselves hated by speaking the truth.

(It will be remarked, that sentences of this kind are formed by circumscribing the English and adding either a relative pronoun, or one of the conjunctions, daß, da, weil, als, indem, wenn.)

Wenn man lange krank gewesen ist, fühlt man den Werth der Gesundheit besto mehr. — After having been ill for a long time, we feel the value of health the more.

Ehe man redet, muß man denken. — Before speaking, you must think.

Sometimes the Imperative is replaced by the Indicative Mood. Ex.:

Du bleibst! — Stay!

Ihr kommt her! — Come here!

2. SUBJUNCTIVE MOOD.

1. When relating or quoting what has been said or done, the Subjunctive Mood must be used in German. Ex.:

Er sagte mir, daß er krank gewesen wäre. — He told me that he had been ill.

Man fragte uns, welches unser Vaterland wäre. — They asked us, which was our country.

Ich glaubte, daß er krank wäre.   I thought he was ill.*
Wir hörten, der Zug sei abgegangen.   We heard the train had started.

2. After the conjunctions wenn and ob, if, when the verb is in the Imperfect or Pluperfect tense. Ex.:

Wenn Sie eher gekommen wären.   If you had come sooner.
Wenn ich viele Freunde hätte.   If I had many friends.
Ich fragte ihn, ob er es wüßte.   I asked him, if he knew it.

3. In exclamations and wishes, where the conjunction is understood. Ex.:

Hätte ich Geld!   If I had money!
Ach, wäre ich gesund!   Ah! if I were well!

4. Instead of the Conditional Mood. Ex.:

Ich könnte reich sein.   I might be rich.
Ich wäre glücklicher.   I should be happier.
Ich hätte mehr Freunde.   I should have more friends.

In general the Subjunctive Mood is used to express a thing of which we are not quite sure, and sometimes by using either the Subjunctive or Indicative Mood we show our belief or disbelief of an event or a circumstance. Ex.:

Ich habe gehört, daß der König an-   ⎫
 gekommen ist.   ⎬ I have heard, that the king has
Ich habe gehört, daß der König an-   ⎭ arrived.
 gekommen sei.

Man hat uns gesagt, daß der Friede   ⎫
 geschlossen ist.   ⎬ They have told us, that the peace
Man hat uns gesagt, der Friede sei   ⎭ is concluded.
 geschlossen.

In the first case we express our belief of the news, in the second we merely mention it, without believing it yet ourselves.

3. IMPERATIVE MOOD.

§ 78. The Imperative Mood, as we have seen, has only the second person of the Singular and of the Plural. When we wish to express a command to a third person, we make use of the present tense of the Subjunctive Mood, or of the verbs sollen, shall, and mögen, may. Ex.:

---

* The Subjunctive Mood is likewise used in expressing the opinion we had of ourselves, but which we have no more at the time we are speaking.

Er komme,
Er soll kommen. } He may or shall come.
Sie mögen kommen. They may come—let them come.

In the first person of the Imperative Mood we employ the verb laſſen. Ex.:

Sing. Laß uns gehen. } Let us go.
Plur. Laßt uns gehen. }

We may also say: gehen wir; or: wir wollen gehen, we will go.

4. INFINITIVE MOOD.

§ 79. The German Infinitive is used with or without the preposition zu. It is used without zu:

1. When it is the subject of a preposition. Ex.:

Viel trinken iſt ungeſund.   To trink much is unwholesome.

2. After the verbs dürfen, können, laſſen, mögen, müſſen, ſollen, werden, wollen, helfen, hören, lehren, lernen ſehen, fühlen. Ex.:

Ich darf hoffen.   I may hope.
Du kannſt ſchreiben.   Thou canst write.
Er muß arbeiten.   He must work.
Wir hören ihn reden.   We hear him speak.
Wir ſahen ſie tanzen.   We saw her dancing.
Mein Bruder lernt zeichnen.   My brother learns drawing.

In all other cases the Infinitive is preceded by the preposition zu. Ex.:

Er wünſcht mit Ihnen zu ſprechen.   He wishes to speak to you.
Wir hoffen morgen einen Brief zu erhalten.   We hope to receive a letter to morrow.
Ich bitte Sie, einen Augenblick aufzuſtehen.   I beg you to get up for a moment.
Ich fürchte es ihm zu ſagen.   I fear to tell it him.
Es iſt traurig, keine Freunde zu haben.   It is sad to have no friends.
Wir haben noch drei Meilen zu machen.   We have still three miles to go.

If we wish to indicate precisely the object, the motive of an action, um is added to the prep. zu. Ex.:

Ich komme, um mit Ihnen zu ſprechen.   I come in order to speak to you.
Wir leben nicht, um zu eſſen, ſondern wir eſſen, um zu leben.   We do not live in order to eat but we eat in order to live.

Every German Infinitive may be taken substantively, and be preceded by the article. Ex.:

bas Trinfen, drinking;   bas Tanzen, dancing.

5. PARTICIPLES.

§ 80. The present participle is mostly employed as an adjective. Ex.:

Der sterbende Greis;   the dying old man.
Die leidende Menschheit;   suffering humanity.
Das lesende Kind;   the reading child.

There are, however, cases, where the present Participle is also used in German to unite two sentences into one; which, however, can only take place, when the two sentences have the same subject. Ex.:

Zitternd sagte er mir......   He told me trembling
Erröthend vor Scham entfernte er   Blushing with shame he with-
sich.   drew.

§ 81. The past participle serves not only to form the compound tenses of verbs, but it is also very often used as an adjective.

Ein gekröntes Haupt;   a crowned head.
Das geliebte Kind;   the beloved child.
Der angefangene Brief;   the commenced letter.

The past participle replaces sometimes the Imperative, the Infinitive, and even the present participle. Ex.:

Getrunken, gespielt!   Let us drink, play!
Das heißt gearbeitet (instead of: That is called working.
arbeiten).
Er kam gelaufen, gesprungen.   He came on running, jumping.

Sometimes also the past participle of those verbs the Infinitive of which is used without zu (§ 79), is replaced by their Infinitive. Ex.:

Ich habe ihn ankommen sehen   I have seen him arrive.
(gesehen).
Er hat bezahlen müssen (gemußt).   He has been obliged to pay.
Wir haben ihn singen hören (ge-   We have heard him sing.
hört).
Sie hat es ihm nicht sagen dürfen   She dared not tell him.
(gedurft).

In rhetoric style, the past participle also serves to connect two sentences and to render the expression more concise and distinct. Ex.:

63

Von seinen Freunden verrathen, von seinen Feinden verfolgt, entfloh Themistokles nach Persien.
Die Unschuld ist der Seele Glück; Einmal verscherzt und aufgegeben, Verläßt sie uns· im ganzen Leben, Und keine Reu' bringt sie zurück.

Betrayed by his friends, persecuted by his enemies, Themistocles escaped to Persia.
Innocence is the happiness of the soul ; once forfeited and lost, it will leave us for ever, and no repentance can recall it.

CHAPTER XII.

OF THE USE OF THE TENSES.

1. PRESENT TENSE.

§ 82. The Present Tense is used in German as in English, and in addition in the following case, where the Perfect is substituted in English ; viz., when speaking of any length of time past, up to the present moment, and including it. Ex.:

Wir wohnen seit fünf Jahren in diesem Hause.
We have been living in this house for five years.

Ihr Oheim ist schon elf Jahre todt.
Their uncle has been dead these eleven years.

Ich habe es schon seit meiner Kindheit.
I have had it from my childhood.

Seit wann sind Sie hier?
How long have you been here ?

Ich warte bereits seit einer Stunde auf Sie.
I have been waiting for you this hour.

2. IMPERFECT TENSE.

§ 83. The Imperfect Tense is used in German,

1. In historical narrative. Ex.:

Friederich der Große war ein großer Feldherr, aber er liebte und beschützte auch die Wissenschaften.
Frederick the great was a great general, but he also loved and protected the sciences.

2. To express a time with relation to another. Ex.:

Ich schrieb, als du kamst.
I was writing when you came.

Als sie mich sah, fing sie an zu weinen.
When she saw me, she began to cry.

Während der Sturm tobte, schlief er ganz fest.
During the noise of the storm he slept quite soundly.

3. To narrate events, of which the narrator was an eye-witness. Ex.:

Geſtern ereignete ſich ein ſonderbarer Vorfall unter meinem Fenſter.
Der Profeſſor hielt eine lange Rede, und wir begleiteten ihn nach Hauſe zurück.

Yesterday a strange accident happened under my window.
The professor made a long speech, and we accompanied him home.

3. PERFECT TENSE. *AL 73*

§ 84. The Perfect Tense is used

1. In relating events of which the narrator was not an eye-witness. Ex.: *usw. ...*

Es hat ſich ein ſonderbarer Vorfall ereignet.
A strange accident has happened.

Der Profeſſor hat eine lange Rede gehalten und ſeine Zuhörer werden ſie drucken laſſen.
The professor has made a long speech, and his auditors will have it printed.

Der Herzog iſt geſtern in B. angekommen.
The duke arrived at B. yesterday.

2. In expressing any definite past time, without reference to another (when in English the Imperfect Tense is used). Ex.:

Ich bin heute in der Kirche geweſen.
I was at church to-day.

Wir ſind geſtern angekommen.
We arrived yesterday.

Ich habe dieſen Morgen meine Brieftaſche verloren.
I lost my pocket-book this morning.

Mein Freund hat voriges Jahr eine große Reiſe gemacht.
My friend performed a long journey last year.

Sind Sie geſtern im Konzert geweſen?
Were you at the concert yesterday?

§ 85. The Pluperfect and Future Tenses are employed in German as in English. *...*

Observation. In English there are three forms for the Present and Imperfect, and two forms for the Perfect and Pluperfect Tenses; viz.: I work, I am working, I do work, I worked, was working, did work; I have worked; I have been working; I had been working;—but in German they are all supplied by the simple form: ich arbeite, ich arbeitete, ich habe gearbeitet, ich hatte gearbeitet.

CHAPTER XIII.

OF THE CONSTRUCTION.

§ 86. The German construction differs in several points from the English. There are two principal rules to be observed: 1. that the word, expressing the principal idea, is always placed after those words which express only accessory ideas; 2. that the expression which is, so to say, the key of the sentence, and without which the sense could not be well understood, is always placed at the end of the sentence.

PARTICULAR RULES.

1. The adjective is always placed before its substantive, and preceded by all those words which depend on it. Ex.:

Ein gegen Jedermann höflicher Mensch.	A man, polite to everybody.
Die Ihnen vorgestern zugeschickten Waaren.	The goods sent to you the day before yesterday.

2. The Dative generally precedes the Accusative, except when both are personal pronouns, in which case the English construction is used. Ex.:

Geben Sie dem Herrn einen Stuhl.	Give a chair to the gentleman.
Ich habe Ihrem Bruder ein Buch geliehen.	I have lent a book to your brother.

But:

Ich schenke sie Ihnen.	I give them to you.
Man sagte es uns.	They told us so.
Er schrieb es mir.	He wrote it to me.

If one of the cases is a pronoun, it is placed before the noun. Ex.:

Ich kann es meinem Freunde nicht abschlagen.	I cannot refuse it to my friend.
Ich leihe dir meine Feder.	I lend thee my pen.

3. The Nominative case is placed after the verb, or after the auxiliary, when there is a compound tense, whenever the sentence begins with any other word than the Nominative. Ex.:

Morgen komme ich nicht.	To-morrow I shall not come.
Dort haben wir lange gewohnt.	We have lived there for a long time.
Reich ist er nicht, aber ehrlich.	He is not rich, but honest.
Für meine Freunde habe ich viele Gefälligkeit.	For my friends I have much courteousness.
Die Faulen kann ich nicht ausstehen.	I cannot bear idle folks.
Den Mädchen steht die Sittsamkeit an.	Modesty is becoming to girls.

There are, however, some conjunctions which do not cause the transposition of the Nominative, such as unb, benn, aber, allein, ba, and in general all those words which cause the verb to be placed at the end of the sentence. (§ 90.)

4. The Nominative is also placed after its verb, in a sentence which serves as complement to the one preceding it. Ex.:

Wenn er kommt, gehe ich fort.	When he comes, I go away.
Wenn Sie es befehlen, fo muß er es thun.	If you command, he must do it.
Je mehr ich trinke, besto burstiger bin ich.	The more I drink, the more thirsty I am.
Wenn die Einen gewinnen, so verlieren die Andern.	When one party gains, the others lose.

5. The Nominative is placed after its verb, when the conditional particle wenn is suppressed. Ex.:

Arbeitet ihr nicht, fo bekommt ihr auch fein Geld.	If you do not work, you do not get any money.
Bist bu nicht fleißig, fo machst bu keine Fortschritte.	If thou art not diligent, thou wilt make no progress.

6. Interrogative sentences are formed without the help of any auxiliary verb, by merely placing the verb before its Nominative. Ex.:

Gehen Sie heute aus?	Do you go out to-day?
Billigen Sie es nicht?	Do you not approve of it?
Kommt der Mann nicht wieder?	Does the man not come back again?

Negative sentences are likewise formed without the help of auxiliary verbs. Ex.:

Ich weiß es nicht.	I do not know it.
Er kommt nicht.	He does not come.

7. The Nominative is placed not only after the verb, but also after the adverb and other words depending on the verb, if the sentence begins with the neuter personal pronoun es. Ex.:

Es kam gestern Jemand.	Somebody came yesterday.
Es ereignet sich nicht alle Tage eine solche Gelegenheit.	Such an opportunity does not happen every day.

§ 87. The Germans place certain words at the end of the sentence, which are its *key*, and without which the sense would not be understood. These words are:

1. The attribute of the subject.
2. The adverb referring to the verb of the subject.
3. The preposition with its regimen or in its place the relative particles daran, darum, &c.
4. The prepositions and separable particles with which the verbs are compounded.
5. The Past Participle and the Infinitive.
6. Lastly the verb of the subject.

1) When the sentence begins with one of the conjunctions wenn, if; weil, because; obschon, although; daß, that; damit, in order that; bevor, ehe, before; als, da, when; während, while; nachdem, after; bis, until; 2) when the sentence begins with a relative pronoun; and 3) when it begins with an interrogative pronoun or adverb, provided that the interrogation be indirect.

Examples.

1	Ich bin meinen Freunden getreu.	I am true to my friends.
	Seid gegen Jedermann höflich.	Be polite to every one.
2.	Diese Frau liebt ihre Kinder nicht.	This woman does not love her children.
	Der Kranke befindet sich besser.	The patient is better.
	Sie singt dieses Lied schön.	She sings this song beautifully.
3.	Wir sprechen von unsern Geschäften.	We speak of our affairs.
	Was machen Sie damit?	What are you doing with it?
	Wollen Sie davon?	Do you wish some of it?
	Ich bekümmere mich nicht darum.	I do not trouble myself about it.
4.	Machet die Thüre zu.	Shut the door.
	Schreiben Sie diese Briefe ab.	Copy these letters.
	Ich stehe alle Morgen früh auf.	I get up early every morning.
5.	Ich habe heute noch nichts gegessen.	I have not yet eaten anything to-day.
	Er hatte mich um Erlaubniß gefragt.	He had asked my permission.
	Ich habe die Ehre, mich Ihnen zu empfehlen.	I have the honor to wish you good morning.
6.	Wenn ich Bücher und Freunde hätte.	If I had books and friends.
	Ich weiß nicht, ob er glücklich ist.	I do not know if he is happy.
	Als ich ihn zum ersten Male sah.	When I saw him for the first time.

Während er auf dem Lande war.	While he was in the country.
Ich glaube, daß er sehr zufrieden ist.	I believe that he is very happy
Derjenige, welcher zufrieden ist, ist glücklich.	He who is contented, is happy.
Wissen Sie, wer diesen Brief geschrieben hat?	Do you know who wrote this letter?

TABLE

OF ALL IRREGULAR FORMS OF DISSONANT AND IRREGULAR VERBS.

The first column contains the irregular form, the second the tense to which it belongs, and the third the Infinitive of the verb.)

aß, äße	Imp. Ind. and Subj.	effen, to eat
bäckſt, bäckt	Pres. Ind. 2d and 3d pers.	backen, to bake
band, bände	Imp. Ind. and Subj.	binden, to tie
barg, bärge	do.	bergen, to hide
bat, bäte,	do.	bitten, to beg
befahl, beföhle	do.	befehlen, to command
befiehlſt, befiehlt	Pres. Ind. 2d and 3d pers.	do.
befliß, befliſſe	Imp. Ind. and Subj.	ſich befleißen, to apply one's self.
befliſſen	Past part.	do.
befohlen	do.	befehlen, to command
begann	Imp. Ind.	beginnen, to begin.
begonn, begönne	Imp. Ind. and Subj.	do.
begonnen	Past Part.	do.
bewog, bewöge	Imp. Ind. and Subj.	bewegen, to move
bewogen	Past Part.	do.
bin, biſt	Pres. Ind. 1st and 2d pers.	ſein, to be
birg	Imperative	bergen, to hide
birgſt, birgt	Pres. Ind. 2d and 3d pers.	do.
biß, biſſe	Imp. Ind. and Subj.	beißen, to bite
bläſeſt, bläſt.	Pres. Ind. 2d and 3d pers.	blaſen, to blow
blieb, bliebe	Imp. Ind. and Subj.	bleiben, to remain
blies, blieſe	do.	blaſen, to blow
bog, böge	do.	biegen, to bend
borſt, börſte	do.	berſten, to burst
bot, böte	do.	bieten, to offer
brach, bräche	do.	brechen, to break
brachte, brächte	do.	bringen, to bring
brannte	Imp. Ind.	brennen, to burn
brätſt, brät	Pres. Ind. 2d and 3d pers.	braten, to roast

brid)	Imperative	bred)en, to break
brid)ft, brid)t	Pres. Ind. 2d and 3d pers.	do.
briet, briete	Imp. Ind. and Subj.	braten, to roast
bad)te, bäd)te	do.	benfen, to think
barf, barfft	Pres. Ind. 1st and 2d pers.	bürfen, to dare
brang, bränge	Imp. Ind. and Subj.	bringen, to press
brifd)	Imperative	brefd)en, to thrash
brifd)eft, brifd)t	Pres. Ind. 2d and 3d pers.	do.
brofd), bröfd)e	Imp. Ind. and Subj.	do.
burfte, bürfte	do.	bürfen, to dare
empfahl	Imp. Ind.	empfehlen, to recommend
empfiehl	Imperative	do.
empfiehlft, empfiehlt	Pres. Ind. 2d and 3d pers.	do.
empfohl, empföhle	Imp. Ind. and Subj.	do.
empfehlen	Past Part.	do.
erblid), erblid)e	Imp. Ind. and Subj.	erbleid)en, to grow pale
erblid)en	Past Part.	do.
erlifd)	Imperative	erlöfd)en, to extinguish
erlifd)eft, erlifd)t	Pres. Ind. 2d and 3d pers.	do.
erlofd), erlöfd)e	Imp. Ind. and Subj.	do.
erlofd)en	Past Part.	do.
erfd)oll, erfd)ölle	Imp. Ind. and Subj.	erfd)allen, to sound
erfd)ollen	Past Part.	do.
erfd)raf, erfd)räfe	Imp. Ind. and Subj.	erfd)recfen, to be frightened
erfd)rid	Imperative	do.
erfd)ridft, erfd)ridt	Pres. Ind. 2d and 3d pers.	do.
erfd)roden	Past Part.	do.
erwog, erwöge	Imp. Ind. and Subj.	erwägen, to consider
erwogen	Past Part.	do.
fährft, fährt	Pres. Ind. 2d and 3d pers.	fahren, to drive (in a carriage)
fällft, fällt	do.	fallen, to fall
fanb, fänbe	Imp. Ind. and Subj.	finben, to find
fängft, fängt	Pres. Ind. 2d and 3d pers.	fangen, to catch
fid)tft, fid)t	do.	fed)ten, to fight
fiel, fiele	Imp. Ind. and Subj.	fallen, to fall
fing, finge	do.	fangen, to catch
flid)tft, flid)t	Pres. Ind. 2d and 3d pers.	fled)ten, to braid
flod)t, flöd)te	Imp. Ind. and Subj.	do.
flog, flöge	do.	fliegen, to fly
floh, flöhe	do.	fliehen, to flee
floß, flöffe	do.	fließen, to flow
fod)t, föd)te	do.	fed)ten, to fight
fraß, fräße	do.	freffen, to eat(of animals
fror, fröre	do.	frieren, to freeze
friß	Imperative	freffen, to eat
friffeft, frißt	Pres. Ind. 2d and 3d pers.	do.
fuhr, führe	Imp. Ind. and Subj.	fahren, to drive (in a carriage)
gab, gäbe	do.	geben, to give
galt, gälte	do.	gelten, to be worth

gebacfen	Past Part.	bacfen, to bake
gebar, gebäre	Imp. Ind. and Subj.	gebären, to bear
gebetet	Past Part.	beten, to pray
gebier	Imperative	gebären
gebierft, gebiert	Pres. Ind. 2d and 3d pers.	gebären, to bear
gebiffen	Past Part.	beißen, to bite
geblafer.	do.	blafen, to blow
geblieben	do.	bleiben, to remain
gebogen	do.	biegen, to bend
geboren	do.	gebären, to bear
geborgen	do.	bergen, to hide
geborften	do.	berften, to burst
geboten	do.	bieten, to offer
gebradyt	do.	bringen, to bring
gebrannt	do.	brennen, to burn
gebraten	do.	braten, to roast
gebrochen	do.	brechen, to break
gebunden	do.	binden, to tie
gebadyt	do.	benfen, to think
gedieh, gediehe	Imp. Ind. and Subj.	gedeihen, to prosper
gediehen	Past Part.	do.
gedrofchen	do.	drefchen, to thrash
gedrungen	do.	bringen, to press
gedungen	do.	bingen, to bargain
geburft	do.	dürfen, to dare
gefahren	do.	fahren, to drive (in a
	do.	carriage.)
gefallen	do.	fallen, to fall
gefangen	do.	fangen, to catch
geflodyten	do.	flechten, to braid
geflogen	do.	fliegen, to fly
geflohen	do.	fliehen, to flee
gefloffen	do.	fließen, to flow
gefochten	do.	fechten, to fight
gefreffen	do.	freffen, to eat(of animals
gefroren	do.	frieren, to freeze
gefunden	do.	finden, to find
gegangen	do.	gehen, to go
gegeben	do.	geben, to give
gegeffen	do.	effen, to eat
geglichen	do.	gleichen, to resemble
geglitten	do.	gleiten, to glide
geglommen	do.	glimmen, to glow
gegohren	do.	gähren, to ferment
gegolten	do.	gelten, to be worth
gegoffen	do.	gießen, to pour
gegraben	do.	graben, to dig
gegriffen	do.	greifen, to seize
gehalten	do.	halten, to hold
gehauen	do.	hauen, to hew
geheißen	do.	heißen, to be called
gehoben	do.	heben, to lift
geholfen	do.	helfen, to help

gefannt	Past 1 art.	fennen, to know
geflommen	do.	flimmen, to climb
geflungen	do.	flingen, to sound
gefniffen	do.	fneifen, to pinch
gefommen	do.	fommen, to come
gefonnt	do.	fönnen, to be able
gefrochen	do.	friechen, to creep
gelaben	do.	laben, to load
gelang, gelänge	Imp. ind. and Subj.	gelingen, to succeed
gelaffen	Past Part.	laffen, to leave
gelaufen	do.	laufen, to run
gelegen	do.	liegen, to lie (down)
gelefen	do.	lefen, to read
geliehen	do.	leihen, to lend
gelitten	do.	leiben, to suffer
gelogen	do.	lügen, to lie (speak an untruth)
gelungen	do.	gelingen, to succeed
gemahlen	do	mahlen, to grind
gemeffen	do.	meffen, to measure
gemieben	do.	meiben, to avoid
gemocht	do.	mögen, to like
gemolfen	do.	melfen, to milk
gemußt	do.	müffen, to be obliged
genannt	do.	nennen, to name
genas, genäfe	Imp. Ind. and Subj.	genefen, to recover
genefen	Past Part.	do.
genommen	do.	nehmen, to take
genoffen	do.	genießen, to enjoy
genoß, genöffe	Imp. Ind. and Subj	do.
gepfiffen	Past Part.	pfeifen, to whistle
gepflogen	do.	pflegen (Rath ꝛc.), to consult
gepriefen	do.	preifen, to praise
gequollen	do.	quellen, to spring
gerannt	do.	rennen, to run
gerathen	do.	rathen, to advise
gerieben	do.	reiben, to rub
geriffen	do.	reißen, to snatch
geritten	do.	reiten, to ride (on horseback)
gerochen	do.	riechen, to smell
geronnen	do.	rinnen, to flow
gerufen	do.	rufen, to call
gerungen	do.	ringen, to wrestle
gefandt	do.	fenben, to send
gefchaffen	do.	fchaffen, to create
gefchah, gefchähe	Imp. Ind. and Subj	gefchehen, to happen
gefchehen	Past Part.	do.
gefchieben	do.	fcheiben, to part
gefchieht	Pres. Ind. 3d pers.	gefchehen, to happen
gefchienen	Past Part.	fcheinen, to seem
gefchlafen	do.	fchlafen, to sleep

geſchlagen	Past Part.	ſchlagen, to beat
geſchlichen	do.	ſchleichen, to sneak
geſchliffen	do.	ſchleifen, to whet
geſchliſſen	do.	ſchleißen, to split
geſchloſſen	do.	ſchließen, to shut
geſchlungen	do.	ſchlingen, to devour
geſchmiſſen	do.	ſchmeißen, to throw
geſchmolzen	do.	ſchmelzen, to melt
geſchnitten	do.	ſchneiden, to cut
geſchnoben	do.	ſchnauben, to snort
geſchoben	do.	ſchieben, to push
geſcholten	do.	ſchelten, to scold
geſchoren	do.	ſcheren, to shear
geſchoſſen	do.	ſchießen, to shoot
geſchrieben	do.	ſchreiben, to write
geſchrieen	do.	ſchreien, to cry
geſchritten	do.	ſchreiten, to step
geſchunden	do.	ſchinden, to flay
geſchwiegen	do.	ſchweigen, to be silent
geſchwollen	do.	ſchwellen, to swell
geſchwommen	do.	ſchwimmen, to swim
geſchworen	do.	ſchwören, to swear
geſchwunden	do.	ſchwinden, to vanish
geſchwungen	do.	ſchwingen, to swing
geſehen	do.	ſehen, to see
geſeſſen	do.	ſitzen, to sit
geſoffen.	do.	ſaufen, to drink (of ani mals)
geſonnen	do.	ſinnen, to meditate
geſotten	do.	ſieden, to seethe
geſpieen	do.	ſpeien, to spit
geſpliſſen	do.	ſpleißen, to split
geſponnen	do.	ſpinnen, to spin
geſprochen	do.	ſprechen, to speak
geſproſſen	do.	ſprießen, to germinate
geſprungen	do.	ſpringen, to jump
geſtanden	do.	ſtehen, to stand
geſtiegen	do.	ſteigen, to ascend
geſtochen	do.	ſtechen, to sting
geſtohlen	do.	ſtehlen, to steal
geſtorben	do.	ſterben, to die
geſtoßen	do.	ſtoßen, to push
geſtrichen	do.	ſtreichen, to stroke
geſtritten	do.	ſtreiten, to contend
geſtunken	do.	ſtinken, to stink
geſungen ‑	do.	ſingen, to sing
geſunken	do.	ſinken, to sink
gethan	do.	thun, to do
getragen	do.	tragen, to carry
getreten	do.	treten, to tread
getrieben	do.	treiben, to drive
getroffen	do.	treffen, to hit

getrogen	Past Part.	triegen, trügen, to deceive.
getrunken	do.	trinken, to drink
gewaschen	do.	waschen, to wash
gewandt	do.	wenden, to turn
gewann, gewänne	Imp. Ind. and Subj.	gewinnen, to win
gewachsen	Past Part.	wachsen, to grow
gewesen	do.	sein, to be
gewichen	do.	weichen, to yield
gewiesen	do.	weisen, to show
gewogen	do.	wiegen, to weigh
gewonnen	do.	gewinnen, to win
geworben	do.	werben, to enlist
geworden	do.	werden, to become
geworfen	do.	werfen, to throw
geworren	do.	wirren, to entangle
gewunden	do.	winden, to wind
gewußt	do.	wissen, to know
geziehen	do.	zeihen, to accuse.
gezogen	do.	ziehen, to draw
gezwungen	do.	zwingen, to compel
gib, gieb	Imperative	geben, to give
gibst, gibt	Pres.Ind. 2d and 3d pers.	do.
giltst, gilt	do.	gelten, to be worth
ging, ginge	Imp. Ind. and Subj.	gehen, to go
glich, gliche	do.	gleichen, to resemble
glit, glitte	do.	gleiten, to glide
glomm, glömme	do.	glimmen, to glimmer
gohr, göhre	do.	gähren, to ferment
golt, gölte	do.	gelten, to be worth
goß, göße	do.	gießen, to pour
gräbst, gräbt	Pres.Ind.2d and 3d pers.	graben, to dig
griff, griffe	Imp. Ind. and Subj.	greifen, to seize
grub, grübe	do.	graben, to dig
half, hülfe	do.	helfen, to help
hältst, hält	Pres.Ind.2d and 3d pers.	halten, to hold
hast, hat	do.	haben, to have
hatte, hätte	Imp Ind. and Subj.	do.
hieb, hiebe	do.	hauen, to hew
hielt, hielte	do.	halten, to hold
hieß, hieße	do.	heißen, to be called
hilfst, hilft	Pres.Ind.2d and 3d pers.	helfen, to help
hilf	Imperative	do.
hob, höbe	Imp. Ind. and Subj.	heben, to lift
iß	Imperative	essen, to eat
issest, ißt	Pres.Ind.2d and 3d pers.	do.
kam, käme	Imp. Ind. and Subj.	kommen, to come
kann, kannst	Pres.Ind.1st and 2d pers	können, to be able
kannte, könnte	Imp. Ind. and Subj.	kennen, to know
klang, klänge	do.	klingen, to sound
klomm, klömme	do.	klimmen, to climb
kniff, kniffe	do.	kneifen, to pinch
kömmst, kömmt	Pres.Ind. 2d and 3d pers.	kommen, to come

konnte, könnte	Imp. Ind. and Subj.	können, to be able
kroch, kröche	do.	kriechen, to creep
lag, läge	do.	liegen, to lie (down)
las, läse	do.	lesen, to read
lässest, lässt	Pres. Ind. 2d and 3d pers.	lassen, to leave
läufst, läuft	do.	laufen, to run
lief, liefe	Imp. Ind. and Subj.	do.
lies	Imperative	lesen, to read
liesest, liest	Pres. Ind. 2d and 3d pers.	do.
ließ, ließe	Imp. Ind. and Subj.	lassen, to let
litt, litte	do.	leiden, to suffer
log, löge	do.	lügen, to lie (speak an untruth)
lud, lüd	do.	laden, to load
mag, magst	Pres. Ind. 1st and 2d pers.	mögen, to like
maß, mäße	Imp. Ind. and Subj.	messen, to measure
mied, miede	do.	meiden, to avoid
miß	Imperative	messen, to measure
missest, mißt	Pres. Ind. 2d and 3d pers.	do.
mochte, möchte	Imp. Ind. and Subj.	mögen, to like
muß, mußt	Pres. Ind. 1st and 2d pers.	müssen, to be obliged
mußte, müßte	Imp. Ind. and Subj.	do.
nahm, nähme	do.	nehmen, to take
nannte	Imp. Ind.	nennen, to name
nimm	Imperative	nehmen, to take
nimmst, nimmt	Pres. Ind. 2d and 3d pers.	do.
pfiff, pfiffe	Imp. Ind. and Subj.	pfeifen, to whistle
pflog, pflöge	do.	pflegen (Rath ꝛc.), to consult
pries, priese	do.	preisen, to praise
quill	Imperative	quellen, to spring
quillst, quillt	Pres. Ind. 2d and 3d pers.	do.
quoll, quölle	Imp. Ind. and Subj.	do.
rang, ränge	do.	ringen, to wrestle
rann, ränne	do.	rinnen, to flow
rannte	Imp. Ind.	rennen, to run
räthst, räth	Pres. Ind. 2d and 3d pers.	rathen, to advise
rieb, riebe	Imp. Ind. and Subj.	reiben, to rub
rief, riefe	do.	rufen, to call
rieth, riethe	do.	rathen, to advise
riß, risse	do.	reißen, to snatch
ritt, ritte	do.	reiten, to ride (on horse back)
roch, röche	do.	riechen, to smell
sah, sähe	do.	sehen, to see
sandte	Imp. Ind.	senden, to send
sang, sänge	Imp. Ind. Subj.	singen, to sing
sank, sänke	do.	sinken, to sink
sann, sänne	do.	sinnen, to meditate
saß, säße	do.	sitzen, to sit
säufst, säuft	Pres. Ind. 2d and 3d pers.	saufen, to drink (of animals)
schalt, schälte	Imp. Ind. and Subj.	schelten, to scold

ſchieb, ſchiebe	Imp. Ind. and Subj.	ſcheiden, to part
ſchien, ſchiene	do.	ſcheinen, to seem
ſchiltſt, ſchilt	Pres. Ind. 2d and 3d pers.	ſchelten, to scold
ſchläfſt, ſchläft	do.	ſchlafen, to sleep
ſchlägſt, ſchlägt	do.	ſchlagen, to beat
ſchlang, ſchlänge	Imp. Ind. and Subj.	ſchlingen, to devour
ſchlich, ſchliche	do.	ſchleichen, to sneak
ſchlief, ſchliefe	do.	ſchlafen, to sleep
ſchliff, ſchliffe	do.	ſchleifen, to whet
ſchliß, ſchliſſe	do.	ſchleißen, to split
ſchloß, ſchlöſſe	do.	ſchließen, to shut
ſchlug, ſchlüge	do.	ſchlagen, to beat
ſchmilz	Imperative	ſchmelzen, to melt
ſchmilzeſt, ſchmilzt	Pres. Ind. 2d and 3d pers.	do.
ſchmiß, ſchmiſſe	Imp. Ind. and Subj.	ſchmeißen, to throw
ſchmolz, ſchmölze	do.	ſchmelzen, to melt
ſchnitt, ſchnitte	do.	ſchneiden, to cut
ſchnob, ſchnöbe	do.	ſchnauben, to snort
ſchob, ſchöbe	do.	ſchieben, to push
ſchalt, ſchölte	do.	ſchelten, to scold
ſchor, ſchöre	do.	ſcheren, to shear
ſchoß, ſchöſſe	do.	ſchießen, to shoot
ſchrieb, ſchriebe	do.	ſchreiben, to write
ſchrie, ſchriee	do.	ſchreien, to cry
ſchritt, ſchritte	do.	ſchreiten, to step
ſchuf, ſchufe	do.	ſchaffen, to create
ſchwamm, ſchwämme	do.	ſchwimmen, to swim
ſchwand, ſchwände	do.	ſchwinden, to vanish
ſchwieg, ſchwiege	do.	ſchweigen, to be silent
ſchwillſt, ſchwillt	Pres. Ind. 2d and 3d pers.	ſchwellen, to swell
ſchwill	Imperative	do.
ſchwoll, ſchwölle	Imp. Ind. and Subj.	do.
ſchwor, ſchwöre	do.	ſchwären, to fester
ſchwor, ſchwöre	do.	ſchwören, to swear
ſchwang, ſchwänge	do.	ſchwingen, to swing
ſchwur, ſchwüre	do.	ſchwören, to swear
ſieh	Imperative	ſehen, to see
ſiehſt, ſieht	Pres. Ind. 2d and 3d pers.	do.
ſoff, ſöffe	Imp. Ind. and Subj.	ſaufen, to drink (of animals)
ſog, ſöge	do.	ſaugen, to suck
ſott, ſötte	do.	ſieden, to seethe
ſpann, ſpänne	do	ſpinnen, to spin
ſpie, ſpiee	do	ſpeien, to spit
ſpliß, ſpliſſe	do.	ſpleißen, to split
ſprach, ſpräche	do.	ſprechen, to speak
ſprang, ſpränge	do.	ſpringen, to jump
ſprichſt, ſpricht	Pres. Ind. 2d and 3d pers.	ſprechen, to speak
ſprich,	Imperative	do.
ſproß, ſpröſſe	Imp. Ind. and Subj.	ſprießen, to germinate
ſtach, ſtäche	do.	ſtechen, to sting
ſtaf, ſtäfe	do.	ſtecken, to stick
ſtahl, ſtähle	do.	ſtehlen, to steal

stand, stände	Imp. Ind. and Subj.	stehen, to stand
stank, stänke	do.	stinken, to stink
starb, stürbe	do.	sterben, to die
stich	Imperative	stechen, to sting
stichst, sticht	Pres. Ind. 2d and 3d pers.	do.
stieg, stiege	Imp. Ind. and Subj.	steigen, to ascend
stiehl	Imperative	stehlen, to steal
stiehlst, stiehlt	Pres. Ind. 2d and 3d pers.	do.
stieß, stieße	Imp. Ind. and Subj.	stoßen, to push
stirbst, stirbt	Pres. Ind. 2d and 3d pers.	sterben, to die
stirb	Imperative	do.
stahl, stähle	Imp. Ind. and Subj.	stehlen, to steal
stößest, stößt	Pres. Ind. 2d and 3d pers.	stoßen, to push
strich, striche	Imp. Ind. and Subj.	streichen, to stroke
stritt, stritte	do.	streiten, to contend
starb, stürbe	do.	sterben, to die
that, thäte	do.	thun, to do
thu (e)	Imperative	do.
thust, thut	Pres. Ind. 2d and 3d pers.	do.
traf, träfe	Imp. Ind. and Subj.	treffen, to hit
trägst, trägt	Pres. Ind. 2d and 3d pers.	tragen, to carry
trank, tränke	Imp. Ind. and Subj.	trinken, to drink
trat, träte	do.	treten, to tread
trieb, triebe	do.	treiben, to drive
triff	Imperative	treffen, to hit
triffst, trifft	Pres. Ind. 2d and 3d pers.	do.
trittst, tritt		treten, to tread
tritt	Imperative	do.
trog, tröge	Imp. Ind. and Subj.	trügen, to deceive
trug, truge	do.	tragen, to carry
verdarb, verdürbe	do.	verderben, to spoil
verdirb	Imperative	do.
verdirbst, verdirbt	Pres. Ind. 2d and 3d pers.	do.
verdorben	Past Part.	do.
verdrossen	do.	verdrießen, to vex
verdroß, verdrösse	Imp. Ind. and Subj.	do.
verdarb, verdürbe	do.	verderben, to spoil
vergaß, vergäße	do.	vergessen, to forget
vergessen	Past Part.	do.
vergissest, vergißt	Pres. Ind. 2d and 3d pers.	do.
vergiß	Imperative	do.
verhohlen	Past Part.	verhehlen, to conceal
verloren	do.	verlieren, to lose
verlor, verlöre	Imp. Ind. and Subj.	do.
wächsest, wächst	Pres. Ind. 2d and 3d pers.	wachsen, to grow
wand, wände	Imp. Ind. and Subj.	winden, to wind
wandte	Imp. Ind.	wenden, to turn
war, wäre	Imp. Ind. and Subj.	sein, to be
warb	Imp. Ind.	werben, to enlist
ward	do.	werden, to become
warf, würfe	Imp. Ind. and Subj.	werfen, to throw
wäschest, wäscht	Pres. Ind. 2d and 3d pers.	waschen, to wash
weiß, weißt	Pres. Ind. 1st and 2d pers.	wissen, to know

wid), wid)e	Imp. Ind. and Subj.	weid)en, to yield
wies, wiefe	do.	weifen, to show
will, willft	Pres. Ind. 1st and 2d pers.	wollen, to be willing
wirbft, wirbt	Pres. Ind. 2d and 3d pers.	werben, to enlist
wirb .	Imperative	do.
wirf	do.	werfen, to throw
wirfft, wirft	Pres. Ind. 2d and 3d pers.	do.
wirft, wirb	do.	werben, to become
wog, wöge	Imp. Ind. and Subj.	wiegen, to weigh
wud)s, wüd)fe	do.	wad)fen, to grow
warb, würbe	do.	werben, to enlist
wurbe, würbe	do.	werben, to become
wufd), wüfd)e	do.	wafd)en, to wash
wußte, wüßte	do.	wiffen, to know
zieh, ziehe	do.	zeihen, to accuse
zog, zöge	do.	ziehen, to draw
zwang, zwänge	do.	zwingen, to compel

PRACTICAL PART.

ALPHABETICAL LIST

OF ALL THOSE WORDS WHICH ARE MET WITH IN THE 136 EXERCISES
OF THE FIRST COURSE, AND WITH WHICH THE PUPIL IS SUPPOSED
TO BE QUITE FAMILIAR.

1. SUBSTANTIVES

Aachen	Feuer	Italiener	Messer
Abend	Fingerhut	Kaffee	Metall
Amalie	Flasche	Kalb	Mittag
Apfel	Fleisch	Karl	Mond
Arzt	Fräulein	Käse	Monat
Aufgabe	Freund	Katze	Morgen
Augenblick	Freundin	Kaufmann	Mutter
Band	Freiheit	Keller	Mühe
Base	Friedrich	Kind	Nachbar
Baum	Frucht	Kirche	Nachbarin
Berg	Fuß	Kirsche	Nachricht
Besuch	Gabel	Klavier	Nadel
Bier	Garten	Kleid	Nuß
Birne	Gärtner	Köln	Obst
Blatt	Geld	König	Onkel
Blei	Gemüse	Königin	Paar
Bleistift	Geschäft	Kopfweh	Papier
Blume	Geschichte	Korb	Pflaume
Brief	Gesellschaft	Krieg	Pfeffer
Brod	Gewohnheit	Kutscher	Pflicht
Bruder	Glas	Küche	Pfund
Brüssel	Gold	Leben	Platz
Buch	Güte	Lehrer	Post
Ding	Halsbinde	Leinwand	Pulver
Dinte	Hand	Loch	Rath
Dorf	Handel	Löffel	Recht
Durst	Handschuh	Löwe	Regenschirm
Dutzend	Haus	Ludwig	Ring
Eisen	Heinrich	Louise	Sache
Elle	Hemd	Luft	Salz
Eltern	Herr	Lüttich	Schwester
Emilie	Huhn	Mädchen	Schuster
Engländer	Hund	Magd	Schneider
Feder	Hut	Mal	Schreiner
Federmesser	Jahr	Mann	Schuh
Fenster	Johann	Markt	Schloß

Schinken	Stimme	Thier	Vorwand
Schule	Stock	Thüre	Wald
Schüler	Straße	Tochter	Wasser
Schrank	Strumpf	Tuch	Wetter
Senf	Stuhl	Uhr	Wein
Silber	Stunde	Unglück	Wien
Sohn	Stück	Unrecht	Wilhelm
Sonne	Suppe	Vater	Willen
Sorgfalt	Tag	Vetter	Woche
Spaziergang	Tante	Vergnügen	Wurm
Spiegel	Taschentuch	Verstand	Zahn
Spiel	Taube	Viertel	Zeit
Stahl	Tiger	Vogel	Zimmer
Stelle	Tisch	Volk	Zucker
Stiefel	Theil	Vorsehung	

2. ADJECTIVES.

alt	hart	nöthig	treu
angenehm	hoch	nützlich	theurer
arm	höflich	offen	unartig
bescheiden	hübsch	reich	undankbar
böse	jung	rein	unglaublich
deutsch	kalt	schädlich	unglücklich
faul	klein	schläfrig	unwissend
fleißig	krank	schlecht	unwohl
gefällig	lang	schnell	vortrefflich
geschickt	langsam	schön	warm
gesund	leicht	schwarz	weiß
glücklich	leichtgläubig	schwer	zahlreich
golden	liebenswürdig	silbern	zufrieden
groß	müde	stark	
gut	neu	traurig	

3. VERBS.

abreisen	beleidigen	erfinden	grüßen
abschreiben	belohnen	erhalten	haben
achten	bemühen, sich	erlauben	hageln
ankleiden	besuchen	erzählen	heißen
ankommen	betrügen	erziehen	hungern
antworten	bitten	erwarten	irren, sich
anziehen	bleiben	essen	kaufen
anzünden	blitzen	fallen	kennen
anwenden	brauchen	finden	kommen
arbeiten	brechen	freuen, sich	können
aufmachen	bringen	frieren	lachen
aufstehen	danken	fürchten	legen
ausgehen	denken	geben	leihen
ausruhen	donnern	gehen	lesen
befehlen	dursten	gehören	lieben
befinden, sich	empfehlen	gewinnen	loben
behalten	entdecken	glauben	lügen

machen	schreiben	trinken	wiedersehen
mittheilen	sehen	unterhalten, sich	wissen
müssen	sein	verachten	wohnen
nehmen	setzen	verbessern	wollen
pflanzen	sitzen	verbieten	wundern, sich
pflegen	spazieren	verkaufen	wünschen
rathen	spielen	verlieren	zeigen
regnen	sprechen	versprechen	zerbrechen
sagen	stellen	warten	zerreißen
schämen, sich	strafen	waschen	zumachen
scheinen	tadeln	wählen	zurückgeben
schicken	tanzen	weggehen	zurückkommen
schlagen	theilen	weinen	zurückschicken
schneiden	tödten	werden	zweifeln
schneien			

4. DETERMINATIVE ADJECTIVES AND PRONOUNS.

der, die, das	mir, mich, dir, dich	andere, alle
dieser, jener	uns, euch, ihnen	ein, einzig
mein, dein, sein, &c.	wer, was	zwei, drei, &c.
deinige, meinige, &c.	welcher, welche, welches	erste, zweite, &c.
derjenige, diejenige, &c.	man, niemand	ganz, halb
ich, du, er	kein, nichts	
ihn, sie, es	jemand, mehre	

5. PARTICLES.

aber, sondern	gefälligst, lange	und, unter
als, für	hier, dort	viel, zu viel
auf, aus, an	herab, herein, &c.	wieviel, soviel
bei, bis	hinab, hinaus, &c.	wenig, weniger
eben, soeben	in, darin, worin	von, vor
da, davon, damit, &c.	mit, damit, &c.	wie, warum, weil
durch, dadurch	ja, nein	wo, wohin, woher
ehemals	noch, nicht	wovon, womit
gestern, heute	ob, oder, nur	woran, wozu, &c.
oft, immer	ohne, nach	wann, wenn
selten, spät	sehr, so sehr	zu, zusammen
früh, früher	schon, seit	
gern, genug	sogleich.	

EXERCISES.

1.

Die Rose, the rose, der Knabe, the boy; die Großmutter, the grand-mother; die Nacht, the night; vorig, last; besitzen, to possess.

Die Rose ist eine schöne Blume. Johann ist ein fauler Knabe. Louise ist ein fleißiges Mädchen. Unsere Großmutter ist eine alte Frau. Der Hund ist ein nützliches Thier. Dieser arme Mann ist sehr krank. Die vorige Nacht war sehr kalt. Heinrich ist mein alter Freund. Therese ist meine jüngste Schwester. Der Graf hat einen blinden Sohn und eine blinde Tochter. Ihr Nachbar besitzt ein schönes Haus und einen großen Garten.

2.

Der Bediente, the man-servant; der Geruch, the smell; die Sprache, the language; englisch, English; französisch, French; bewohnen, to inhabit; lernen, to learn; wiederfinden, to find again.

You have a bad pen. Henry has a good father and a good mother. We have a faithful (man-) servant. Our neighbor inhabits a very small house. This flower has an agreeable smell. We learn the German language. My son has read a French book. My uncle has received an English letter. My sister has lost her black cat. Louis has found again his little dog. The (maid-) servant has made a good fire.

3.

Kein, no, none, not any, not a.

Mein Bruder trinkt kein Bier und keinen Wein. Wir essen heute keine Suppe und kein Fleisch. Haben wir kein Brod und keinen Zucker? Ich esse kein schwarzes Brod. Dieser Herr ist kein Franzose. Diese Dame ist keine Engländerin. Mein Onkel hat keine Kinder. Ich habe keine Lust spazieren zu gehen. Ich habe kein Geld bei mir. Mein

Bruder hat auch keinen Pfennig. Meine Söhne haben keine
Tauben mehr. Karl hat keinen Freund mehr. Wir lesen
keine deutschen Bücher mehr. Ich bin kein Kind mehr. Ich
spreche kein Deutsch.

4.
Das Werk, the work.

I have no pen and ink. My cousin has no gloves.
The birds have no teeth. This boy eats no fruit. This
woman drinks no beer. This gentleman does not speak
English. What are you drinking? We drink good
beer and good wine. I have no more ink and paper
This young girl has fine teeth. This poor mother has
no more children. This man is not a shoemaker
My son reads no more English works.

5.
Die Börse, the purse, the exchange; die Schublade, the drawer; das
Land, the country; schenken, to give (as a present).

Wo ist dein Bruder? Ich glaube, daß er im Garten oder
in der Küche ist. Sind Sie heute in der Schule gewesen?
Meine Schwester ist seit drei Tagen auf dem Lande; sie befindet sich nicht wohl. Wohin gehen Sie jetzt? Ich gehe
mit meinem Bruder in die Kirche, und von da werden wir zur
Börse gehen. Tragen Sie diesen Brief auf die Post, ehe Sie
ins Theater gehen. Wohin haben Sie mein Federmesser
gelegt? Ich habe es in die Schublade gelegt. Woher kommen
diese Knaben? Ich glaube, sie kommen aus dem Walde.
Wenn Karl aus der Schule kommt, so schicken Sie ihn zu mir,
ich will ihm ein schönes Buch schenken.

6.
Der Stall, the stable; der Ball, the ball; das Konzert, the concert
das Schauspiel, the play; das Wirthshaus, the inn, the tavern; das
Tellertuch, the napkin; das Tischtuch, the table-cloth; der Neffe, th
nephew; gehen, to go, to walk.

Where have you been, my children? We have been
at school and at church. Is the coachman in the sta
ble? Is the (maid-) servant in the cellar? My mother
has been at the market, and my father at the post-
office. We shall go to the ball this evening. My brothers will go to the concert or to the play. My cousins

have been in the country these two months.* This man goes every day to the tavern. Where do you come from at present? We come from a walk. My aunt comes from church, and my uncle comes from the exchange. Your nephew comes out of the garden. Put these napkins into the drawer and this table-cloth into the cup-board. Do not go out of the room.

7.

Der **Fleiß**, application, assiduity; die **Bescheidenheit**, modesty; die **Kenntniß**, knowledge; der **Verwandte**, the relation; der **Bauer**, the peasant; der **Palast**, the palace; das **Gut**, the estate; das **Land**, the land; **prächtig**, magnificent; **herrlich**, splendid; **arbeitsam**, industrious.

Haben Sie Vergnügen auf dem Lande gehabt? Haben Sie Verwandte in Köln? Wir haben dort keine Verwandten, aber viele Freunde. Mein Nachbar hat Geld und Krebit, und er ist doch nicht zufrieden. Dieser junge Mann hat vielen Verstand und viele Kenntnisse; er ist sehr bescheiden. Ich habe Unglück gehabt; ich habe schlechte Geschäfte gemacht. Ihre Kinder haben Fleiß und Bescheidenheit; sie werden von Jedermann geliebt und gelobt. Mein Oheim besitzt große Güter, prächtige Paläste und herrliche Gärten. In unserm Lande gibt es große Städte, schöne Dörfer, reiche Kaufleute, arbeitsame Bauern und vortrefflichen Wein.

8.

Das **Glück**, (good) luck, happiness; der **Verdruß**, vexation, trouble, **munter**, gay; **verfolgen**, to persecute; **bei**, with, at the house of; das **Unglück**, bad luck; **es ist möglich**, it may be.

You have been playing to-day; have you had good luck? We have had bad luck; we have lost everything. If we had money, we should also have friends. If you were in (bad) trouble, you would not be so gay. We should have had pleasure, if you had been with us. It may be that you have knowledge, but you are not modest. If this man had had good luck, he would not be so poor. It is sad to have enemies, who persecute us.

9.

Das **Holz**, the wood; von **Holz**, **hölzern**, of wood, wooden; das **Gold**, the gold; von **Gold**, **golden**, of gold, golden; der **Griff**, the handle; die **Brücke**, the bridge; die **Treppe**, the staircase; der **Stoff**, the stuff;

---

* See § 82.

die Seide, silk; die Baumwolle, cotton; die Leinwand, linen; das Leder, leather; der Stein, the stone; der Marmor, the marble; das Elfenbein, ivory; die Zeitung, the newspaper; die Dose, the box; der Gesandte, the ambassador; der Kaiser, the emperor; Schlesien, Silesia; Oestreich, Austria; russisch, Russian; verwahren, to preserve.

Heinrich hat seine goldene Uhr verloren. Louise hat ihren silbernen Löffel zerbrochen. Die seidenen Stoffe sind theurer als die baumwollenen. Dieses Messer hat einen hölzernen Griff. Wir haben eine steinerne Brücke und eine marmorne Treppe gesehen. Geben Sie mir meine leinenen Strümpfe und meine ledernen Schuhe. Der Tabak verwahrt sich am besten in einer bleiernen Dose. Haben Sie die gestrige Zeitung gelesen? Die heutige ist noch nicht angekommen. Meine Schwester hat einen elfenbeinernen Fingerhut. Mein Vater hat dreißig Ellen schlesische Leinwand gekauft. Der österreich- ische Kaiser wird von seinem Volke geliebt. Der russische Gesandte ist abgereist.

10.

Die Wolle, wool; der Saal, the saloon, hall; die Bildsäule, the statue; die Kette, the chain; die Bank, the bench, the bank; der Knopf, the button; das Stück, the piece; das Werkzeug, the tool; Spanien, Spain; glänzend, bright, splendid; stolz, proud; dauerhaft, durable, solid; holländisch, Dutch; schmücken, to adorn; gefallen, to please; vorziehen, to prefer; morgen, to-morrow.

I do not like (the) woolen stockings; I prefer cotton (ones). This hall is adorned with marble statues. My uncle has given me a gold chain. I am tired; I will rest a little on this stone bench. Do you prefer silk or metal buttons? Iron tools are more solid than wooden (ones). Our servant has lost two silver spoons. I like to-day's play better than yesterday's. (To-day's play pleases me more than yesterday's.) To-morrow's ball will be very splendid. We like the French wines and the Dutch cheese. The Spanish ambassador is prouder than the English.

11.

Wer, who; welcher, who, which; die Brieftasche, the pocket-book.

Wer ist dieser Herr? Wer ist diese Dame? Wer hat Ihnen diesen Ring gegeben? Wem haben Sie Ihren Re- genschirm geliehen? Von wem haben Sie diese hübsche Brief- tasche erhalten? Wen suchen Sie? Für wen ist diese schöne Uhr? Wessen Kind ist krank? Wessen Buch ist dies? Wel-

her von biefen Stöcken ist der Ihrige? Welche von biesen
Federn ist die beste? Welches von diesen Kindern ist Ihr
Neffe? Von welchem dieser Offiziere haben Sie das Pferd
gekauft? Was haben Sie dafür bezahlt? Wovon spricht Ihr
Bruder? Woran denken Sie? Womit haben Sie dieses
gemacht? Woburch ist der Mann so unglücklich geworden?

12.

Die Vernunft, reason; das Gefecht, the battle; der Zeichnenlehrer,
the drawing-master; erfahren, to hear; verwunden, to wound; über=
geben, to deliver; kommen durch, to pass by; es ist die Rede, they are
talking.

Who is that man? Who are these ladies? Of whom
do you speak? To whom do you write? Of what are
you talking? Who has done that? To whom have you
given my cane? For whom do you work? What do
you seek? What did he answer you? What have
you taken? What is man without reason? Where is
Louisa? Does she not know that the drawing-master
will come? What would he say, if she were not here?
Who has been in my room? To whom have you told it?
From whom have you heard it? By which towns have
you passed? In which battle has your brother been
wounded? Which of your brothers is arrived? With
which of these gentlemen have you been in Paris? To
which of these servants have you delivered the letter?

13.

Der or welcher, who; dessen, deren, whose; die Tapferkeit, valor,
bravery; der Werth, the value; die Spitze, the point; der Edelstein, the
precious-stone; der Weinhändler, the wine-merchant; der Schwieger=
sohn, the son-in-law; breit, broad, wide; geräumig, spacious; retten,
to save; rühmen, to boast; sterben, to die; anvertrauen, to confide;
zubringen, to spend; abbrechen, to break down; da unten, down there.

Hier ist der junge Mann, der das Kind unsers Nachbars
gerettet hat. Das Haus, welches Sie da unten sehen, gehört
meiner Tante. Die Zimmer, welche ich bewohne, sind sehr
geräumig. Kennen Sie die Dame, von der wir sprechen?
Wo ist der arme Knabe, dem Sie das Brod gegeben haben?
Der Bediente, dem ich meine Briefe anvertraut hatte, ist nicht
zurückgekommen. Haben Sie den Soldaten gesehen, dessen
Mutter gestorben ist? Der junge Offizier, dessen Tapferkeit
man so sehr rühmt, ist der Schwiegersohn meines Nachbars.

Der Weinhändler, den Sie bei mir gesehen haben, hat mir
zwölf Flaschen Bordeaux geschickt. Die Bänder, die Sie mir
geschickt haben, sind zu breit. Die Tage, welche ich mit Ihnen
zugebracht habe, sind die angenehmsten meines Lebens gewesen.
Da ist der Baum, unter dem wir so oft ausgeruht haben.
Das sind Edelsteine, deren Werth ich nicht kenne. Hier ist
das Messer, dessen Spitze Karl abgebrochen hat. Das sind
die Herren, denen wir die Nachricht mitgetheilt haben.

14.

Die Leichtigkeit, facility, ease; die Rechtlichkeit, honesty.

There is the little boy who writes so well. This is
a young lady who speaks with much facility. I do not
like (the) children who speak too much. This is the
physician that I have seen, the lady whom you know.
These are the books which you look for. Where is the
letter of which you speak? This is a man whose
honesty I know. This is not the merchant of whom we
have bought our ribbons. Tell me, to whom you have
given my cane. Do you know to whom this beautiful
garden belongs? I do not know of which garden you
speak. Are these the children whose father is dead?

15.

Das was, that which, what; der Kummer, grief; die Gesundheit,
health; begegnen, to happen; verlangen, to ask, demand; hören, to
hear; begreifen, to conceive, to understand; vermeiden, to avoid; sehr
leid thun, to give great pain.

Sagen Sie mir, was Ihnen am besten gefällt. Erzählen
Sie mir, was er Ihnen gesagt hat. Ich weiß nicht, was
Sie wollen. Wissen Sie, was Ihm begegnet ist? Geben
Sie mir, was Sie mir versprochen haben. Sagen Sie uns,
was Sie davon denken. Glauben Sie nicht Alles, was er
sagt. Er hat mir seinen Kummer nicht anvertrauen wollen,
was mir sehr leid thut. Hier ist, was Sie verlangen. Neh=
men Sie, was Sie wollen. Er spricht von Allem, was er
hört. Das ist es, worüber ich mich freue. Das ist es nicht,
woran ich denke. Haben Sie gehört, was er gesagt hat?
Begreifen Sie, was er damit sagen will? Vermeiden Sie
immer das, was der Gesundheit schädlich ist. Sprechen Sie
nie von dem, was Sie nicht verstehen.

16.

Betrübt über, grieved at; ſich beklagen über, to complain of.

I have understood what you have told me. I shall
give you what I have promised you. Do you know what
he wants (will)? Has he told you what has happened
to him? We do not speak of everything that we hear.
We do not always say what we think. That is all
which I can tell you. Do you know of what I think,
of what I speak? This it is, about which we rejoice.
This it is, at which I am grieved and of which I complain. That which is beautiful is not always useful.

17.

Ganz, quite, all, whole; Alles, everything; all, alle, all; die Möbel,
the furniture; der Wohlthäter, the benefactor; der Anweſende, the
person present; der Gedanke, the thought, the idea; angelegt, arranged; ſich wenden, to apply; alle Tage, every day.

Ich habe Alles geſehen. Alle dieſe Möbel ſind ſehr ſchön.
Alle meine Kinder ſind ausgegangen. Der ganze Garten iſt
gut angelegt. Wir haben den ganzen Tag und die ganze
Nacht gearbeitet. Herr N. iſt der Wohlthäter aller Unglück-
lichen. Wir haben es allen Anweſenden mitgetheilt. Alle
unſere Verwandte ſind abgereiſt. Alle diejenigen, welche hier
waren, haben es gehört. Es iſt derſelbe Herr, den wir geſtern
geſehen haben. Es iſt immer dieſelbe Antwort. Er ſagt
immer daſſelbe. Ich hatte den nämlichen Gedanken, ich wollte
das Nämliche thun. Geben Sie mir von demſelben Tuche,
von der nämlichen Leinwand. Wir haben es demſelben Kaufmann geſchickt, derſelben Frau es geſagt. Er hat ſich an den-
ſelben Advokaten gewendet. Ich habe es ſelbſt gehört. Wir
werden es Ihnen ſelbſt bringen. Sagen Sie es ihm ſelbſt.

18.

Die Familie, the family; ſterblich, mortal; überſchwemmt, inundated,
overflowed.

All is lost. The whole country is inundated. The
whole family are (is) in the country. All men are mortal. All my friends are arrived. I see you every day. We
have seen it ourselves. The king himself has spoken of
it. It is the same man and the same woman. They are
the same children. We inhabit the same house. You are

always the same. I have bought of the same ink, of the same paper. I have given it to the same servant. My sisters will come themselves. One must not always speak of one's self.

19.

Nicht so, not so; eben so, so, as, just as; mehr als, more than; weniger als, less than; der Kupferstich, the engraving; die Landkarte, the map; die Belohnung, the reward; die Geduld, patience; der Thaler, the crown, dollar; erfreut, delighted; verdienen, to deserve; ausgeben, to spend (money).

Du bist größer, als ich; aber dein Bruder ist nicht so groß, als ich. Mein Oheim ist eben so reich, als dein Vater. Wir haben eben so viele Bücher, als Sie; aber wir haben nicht so viele Kupferstiche und Landkarten. Mein Sohn, du bist so fleißig gewesen, daß du eine Belohnung verdienst. Ich habe nicht so viel ausgegeben, als Sie glauben. Ich bin darüber eben so erfreut, als Sie. Ihre Schwester hat eben so schöne Kleider, als die meinige. Meine Söhne arbeiten nicht so viel, als die Ihrigen. Herr N. hat mehr Kinder, als wir; ich glaube, er hat deren mehr als neun. Louise hat weniger Freundinnen, als Henriette. Wir sind heute fleißiger gewesen, als gestern; wir haben zwei Aufgaben mehr gemacht. Ich habe viel Geduld, aber Sie haben deren noch mehr. Heinrich hat heute mehr als zehn Briefe abgeschrieben. Sie können ihm nicht weniger als zwei Thaler geben.

20.

Der Arbeiter, the workman; beschäftigt, occupied, busy; geschickt, clever; schlafen, to sleep.

Is your brother as tall as I? He is not so tall as you. Has he as many books as I? He has not so many books as you. The young man has as beautiful engravings as you. I love him as much as you love him. You do not love me as much as I love you. Your cousin was so busy, that he did not see me. Your physician is more lucky, but not so clever, as ours. This physician is very rich, he has more than thirty houses. This workman asks no less than six dollars. The child has slept more than two hours. Our gardener has many children, I believe that he has more than nine. We have done to-day three exercises more.

21.

Je mehr…desto mehr, the more…the more; je weniger…desto weniger, the less…the less; die Freude, the joy; die Behandlung, the treatment; nachsichtig, indulgent; streng, strict, severe; vernünftig, reasonable; leiden, to suffer; erleiden, to endure; nachdenken, to reflect; zuziehen, to incur; ermuntern, to encourage; beobachten, to observe; ansehen, to look at; sich betrüben, to give up one's self to… fehlen, to fail; etwas haben wider…, to have a grudge against; nun now; sonst, formerly.

Ich weiß nicht, was dir fehlen mag, liebe Julie; je mehr man hier lacht, desto mehr weinst du; je mehr man dich ermuntert, dich der Freude zu überlassen, desto mehr betrübst du dich. Nun ist es eine Viertelstunde, daß ich dich beobachte, und je mehr ich dich ansehe, desto weniger begreife ich, was dich so sehr weinen macht.—Ach, lieber Onkel, Sie wissen nicht Alles, was ich zu leiden habe. Jedermann hat etwas wider mich, und je mehr ich über die Behandlung nachdenke, die ich erleide, desto weniger kann ich begreifen, was sie mir zugezogen haben mag. So glücklich ich auf dem Lande war, so unglücklich bin ich in der Stadt. So nachsichtig Sie sonst waren, so streng sind Sie jetzt.—Du bist nie zufrieden, mein Kind; je mehr du hast, desto mehr verlangst du. Je weniger man wünscht, desto zufriedener ist man. Je älter man ist, desto vernünftiger muß man sein.

22.

Der Wunsch, the wish; geizig, avaricious, stingy; verschwenderisch. prodigal, extravagant; sparsam, economical; lehrreich, instructive; schädlich, hurtful, noxious; weich, soft; gelehrt, learned.

As happy as we were in the country, so unhappy are we in the town. As diligent as this young man is, so idle is his brother. As instructive as are good books, so hurtful are bad (ones). As extravagant as is Mr. N., so avaricious is his uncle. The more money one has, the more friends one has. The more he drinks, the more he is thirsty. The softer (the) pens are, the worse they are. The less desires one has, the more happy one is. The more one begs him, the less he does it. The less money he has, the more economical he is. The more learned we are, the more modest we ought to (must) be.

23.

Jeder, every, every one; einige, some; das Alter, the age; die

Pflanze, the plant; der Fehler, the fault; das Böse, the evil; kosten, to cost; erfüllen, to fulfil; stehen bleiben, to stop.

Jedes Alter hat seine Pflichten. Jeder hat seine Pflicht erfüllt. Jeder Baum, jede Pflanze, jedes Thier ist nützlich. Man muß jeden Tag gut anwenden. Dieser Knabe bleibt bei jedem Hause stehen. Jeder hat seine Fehler. Ich habe Jedem ein Buch geschenkt. Kennen Sie eine von diesen Damen? Ich kenne einige von diesen Herren, aber ich kenne keine von diesen Damen. Essen Sie einige Birnen. Da sind schöne Aepfel; geben Sie mir einige. Jemand hat mir gesagt, daß Sie morgen abreisten. Man muß von Niemand(em) Böses reden. Ich kann es dir nicht geben, denn ich habe es Jemand(em) versprochen. Niemand weiß, daß Sie hier sind. Wir haben es Niemand(em) gesagt. Ich habe keins von meinen Büchern verloren. Ich habe nichts zu thun. Wir haben von nichts gesprochen.

24.

Der Stand, the station, the state; der Fürst, the prince; der Unterthan, the subject; der Student, the student; das Geräusch, the noise; erschrecken, to frighten, terrify; einmal, once, some day.

Every station has its pleasures. Every noise terrifies him. I have told it to every boy and every girl. Every one must die some day. The prince speaks to every one of his subjects. Lend me some pens. We have seen some students. Some of our friends will come this evening. I shall take some of your books. Nobody knows it. I know nobody. I shall tell it to nobody. None of my friends will come. Do you know some of these ladies? I do not know any of them. I have spoken to none of the gentlemen. I speak of some one, whom you have not yet seen. I have lent my umbrella to somebody who will return it to me to-morrow.

25.

Der Eine, the one; der Andere, the other; Beide, both; einander, one another; mehrere, several; gewiß, certain; jeder der, any one who; weder...noch, neither...nor; der Vorwurf, the reproach; der Abschied, the leave; das Gesetz, the law; das Bein, the leg; selten, seldom, rare; geboren, born · trennen, to separate; beneiden, to envy; vertheidigen, to defend; angreifen, to attack.

Er gibt dem Einen, was er dem Andern nimmt. Beide haben Unrecht. Er hat Beiden Vorwürfe gemacht; aber weder der Eine noch der Andere hat sie verdient. Ich habe von Beiden Abschied genommen. Dieser Soldat hat beide Beine verloren. Diese beiden Brüder lieben sich sehr, sie gehen nie ohne einander aus. Sie können sich nicht von einander trennen. Geben Sie mir einen andern Hut und andere Handschuhe. Beneidet nicht das Glück Anderer. Sprechen Sie mir von etwas Anderm. Ich weiß darüber nichts Gewisses. Ein gewisser Herr und eine gewisse Dame haben es mir erzählt. Ich habe es von Mehreren gehört. Es ist selten, daß man mehrere Freunde hat. Ich würde dir eine Feder leihen, wenn ich mehrere hätte. Wir haben mehrere Tage in dieser Stadt zugebracht. Ich sage es einem Jeden, der es hören will. Wir werden uns gegen Jeden vertheidigen, der uns angreifen wird. Das Gesetz wird Jeden bestrafen, der es nicht beobachtet.

26.

Die Person, the person; die Langeweile, weariness, ennui; wohlthä-tig, charitable.

The thing is not yet certain. A certain boy has told me so (it me). I have given your book to a certain school-boy. My father knew nothing certain of it yet. Several of my friends know it. I have received to-day several letters. I have heard it of several persons. Give me another shirt and other stockings. One says this, the other says that. Have you no other ink, no other pens? These two boys love one another; they are both diligent. Men must love one another. These two friends think often of one another. Every one who is rich ought to be charitable. Whoever is industrious has no ennui.

27.

Die Gelegenheit, the opportunity; gewöhnt, accustomed; dick, thick, fat; gießen, to pour; benutzen, to profit by, to make use of; sich auf halten, to stay.

Ich gehe morgen nach Aachen. Mein Vater ist schon gestern hingegangen. Ich war noch nicht da. Sie haben nichts dabei gewonnen. Ich werde mich drei Tage dort aufhalten. Wir haben die Nacht dort zugebracht. Ich habe es ihm versprochen, und ich werde daran denken. Die Dinte war etwas zu dick; ich habe ein wenig Wasser dazu gegossen. Ich bin nicht daran gewöhnt. Wollen Sie sich auf diese Bank

ſetzen? Ja, ich will mich darauf ſetzen. Iſt Ihr Herr Vater
im Zimmer? Nein, er iſt nicht darin. Was haben Sie neben Ihre Blumen gepflanzt? Ich habe Gemüſe hingepflanzt.
Karl hat zehn Fehler gemacht, und ich habe deren neun gemacht.
Sind Sie mit meinem Sohne zufrieden? Ja, ich bin ſehr
zufrieden mit ihm. Haben Sie mit dem Fürſten über mein
Unglück geſprochen? Ich habe noch nicht mit ihm darüber geſprochen. Haben Sie Briefe erhalten? Ja, ich habe welche
erhalten. Wollen Sie ein Glas Wein? Ich danke Ihnen,
ich habe ſchon welchen getrunken. Haben Sie Geld? Nein,
ich habe keins. Das iſt eine gute Gelegenheit, ich werde ſie
benutzen.

28.

Have you some wine? I have some, I have none.
Has your brother any ink? He has some, he has none.
Hast thou any paper? I have some, I have not any.
Have these gentlemen any horses? They have some,
they have none. Has your aunt any sisters? She has
two. Has thy cousin been to the ball? She has not been
there. Is your uncle gone into the country? He is gone
there this morning. Will you think of my affair? I
shall think of it. We shall gain much by it. The
wine is too strong; pour a little water into it. How
many faults have you made? I have made six. Have
they spoken of the war? Yes, they have spoken of it.

29.

Der Dienſt, the service; der Undank, ingratitude; das Beiſpiel, the
example; die Verleumbung, calumny, slander; das Elend, the misery;
wichtig, important; lächerlich, ridiculous; achtungswerth, respectable;
abgeſchmackt, absurd; ſchrecklich, frightful; boshaft, malicious; rechtlich,
honest; ſich beſchweren, to complain; erweiſen, to do; läſtern, to back-
bite, to slander; vergeſſen, to forget; reißen, to pull, to snatch; vermuthen, to suppose, to presume; ſich überlaſſen, to give one's self up
to; einen Gefallen finden, to take pleasure in; ziemlich, rather, pretty;
bisweilen, sometimes.

Sie beſchweren ſich über den Undank der Menſchen; ja,
man belohnt bisweilen ſehr ſchlecht die wichtigſten Dienſte,
und es geſchieht ziemlich oft, daß diejenigen, denen man am
meiſten Gutes erwieſen hat, die Undankbarſten ſind. Ihr
Nachbar Robert zum Beiſpiel iſt der undankbarſte Menſch
von der Welt. Er findet einen Gefallen daran, ſeine Wohl-

thäter zu läſtern. Er hat mich dieſer Tage von den lächerlich-
ſten Dingen unterhalten; er hat von den achtungswertheſten
Perſonen Böſes geſagt und ſich den abgeſchmackteſten Ver-
leumdungen überlaſſen. Er vergißt, daß wir ihn aus dem
ſchrecklichſten Elende geriſſen haben. Das betrübt mich mehr,
als Sie glauben. Herr Robert ſpricht anders, als er denkt.
Er iſt nicht ſo boshaft, als Sie vermuthen. Der rechtliche
Mann ſpricht nicht anders, als er denkt.

30.

Das Verbrechen, the crime; das Verſprechen, the promise; der Weg,
the road; der Umſtand, the circumstance; die Lage, the situation; kurz,
short; beſtimmt, positive; merkwürdig, remarkable; ſingen, to sing;
verdienen, to deserve; entreißen, to snatch away; beſchuldigen, to ac
cuse; ſich erinnern, to remember; gewöhnlich, usually, generally.

My sister sings better than she plays. You are happier than you deserve. The ladies speak generally
more than they write. You have come sooner than I
thought. Mr. N. is the cleverest physician (that) I know.
We speak of the cleverest physician of the town. They
accuse him of the most frightful crime. He has given me
the most positive promise to write to me. We shall
take the shortest road to go to S. I remember still
the most important circumstances. I have been at N.
yesterday; it is one of the most remarkable towns of
Europe. We have rescued our friends from the most
unhappy situation.

31.

Die Weintraube, the bunch of grapes; reif, ripe; ordnen, to arrange;
verzeihen, to pardon; laufen, to run.

Setzen Sie ſich neben mich. Leſen Sie mir, was Sie geſchrieben haben. Betrüben Sie ſich nicht mehr darüber. Lernen Sie denken, bevor Sie ſchreiben. Ordnen Sie dieſe
Briefe, bevor Sie weggehen. Eſſen Sie keine Weintrauben
mehr; ſie ſind noch nicht reif. Kommen Sie hierher, mein
Freund. Gehen Sie dorthin, meine Liebe. Sprechen wir
nicht mehr davon. Wir wollen uns zu Tiſche ſetzen. Wir
wollen ein wenig ſpazieren gehen. Laßt uns unſeren Feinden
verzeihen. Laßt uns nach Hauſe gehen. Wir wollen nicht
länger bleiben. Gehen wir lieber in die Stadt zurück. Kommt
Kinder, es iſt ſchon ſpät. Lauf nicht ſo ſehr, Heinrich. Du
gehſt nicht mehr mit, wenn du nicht artiger biſt.

32.

Die Tugend, virtue; das Laster, vice; gerecht, just; rufen, to call · haſſen, to hate; plaudern, to chatter; heruntergehen, to go down, descend; näher treten, to approach; vorher, before, beforehand.

Let us give a piece of bread to this poor little boy. They call us, let us go down. Madam, take another (one more) cup of coffee. Let us read the newspaper before. Let us be just to every one. Let us love virtue and hate vice. Let us approach a little, come a little nearer. Look here, Sir. Let us hope always. Let us yet wait a moment. Do not go away yet. Wash yourselves before you go out. Go to bed. Do not get up. Let us work at present. We will not chatter any more.

33.

Die Lüge, the lie; der Lügner, the liar; der Müſſiggang, idleness; der Schmeichler, the flatterer; der Nächſte, the neighbor; der Umgang, the intercourse; ergeben, addicted; allgemein, universal; fliehen, to flee, to shun·; verachten, to despise; ſich hingeben, to give one's self up to....

Ich haſſe dieſen Menſchen; er iſt ein Lügner. Wir haſſen den Müſſiggang. Wir werden immer diejenigen haſſen, die dem Laſter ergeben ſind. Ich haſſe Niemanden. Gott will nicht, daß wir Jemanden haſſen. Haſſet die Lüge, aber haſſet euren Nächſten nicht. Fliehe die Böſen und ſuche den Umgang derjenigen, welche tugendhaft ſind. Dieſer Menſch wird allgemein verachtet; Jedermann flieht ihn. Wir fliehen alle diejenigen, welche ſich dem Müſſiggange hingeben. Mein Onkel hat mir gerathen, die Geſellſchaft dieſer jungen Leute zu fliehen. Laßt uns die Schmeichler fliehen. Die Zeit flieht, man muß ſie benutzen.

34.

Why do you hate me? I do not hate you. We must hate nobody. I have always hated (the) flatterers. Shun the evil and do (the) good. I shun (the) bad company. Shun the wicked. Let us all shun vice. Your sister must shun the intercourse with these ladies. Stay; do not flee. You have nothing to fear. Everybody shuns (the) liars. We must profit by our time. We despise those who do not fulfil their duty. He who is despised, is unhappy. Virtuous people are loved and esteemed.

35.

Die Ankunft, the arrival; die Gefahr, the danger; der Uebermuth, haughtiness; der Wind, the wind; unbekannt, unknown; sich beschäftigen, to be busy; sich vornehmen, to determine upon, to intend; sich hüten, to beware; sich bessern, to improve, to mend; sich·verirren, to lose one's way; sich aussetzen, to expose one's self; sich zuziehen, to incur.

Ich habe mich den ganzen Abend beschäftigt. Ich werde mich jetzt ankleiden. Wirst du heute spazieren gehen? Ich freue mich über die Ankunft meines Vaters. Die Langeweile ist demjenigen unbekannt, der sich zu beschäftigen weiß. Karl hat sich vorgenommen, diesen Nachmittag nach N. zu gehen. Wir werden uns dort viel Vergnügen machen. Man ist glücklich, wenn man sich wohl befindet. Lobe dich nicht selbst; hüte dich vor dem Uebermuth. Der Wind legt sich; wir bekommen gutes Wetter. Ruhen Sie ein wenig aus. Dieser Schüler hat sich gebessert. Wir haben uns verirrt. Ihr habt euch einer großen Gefahr ausgesetzt. Wir würden uns Vorwürfe zugezogen haben, wenn wir das gethan hätten.

36.

Wash yourself. You are not yet washed. I have washed myself this morning. Will you not wash yourself? At what do you rejoice? I rejoice at seeing you. We rejoice at your happiness. I cannot rejoice more. My sisters intend to go to the ball. This dog has lost his way. I shall not expose myself to this danger. At what are you busy? I am busy reading. You will incur reproaches if you do not go there. Beware of doing that. My cousin will never mend. We have been very much amused yesterday. Louisa is not yet dressed. You are mistaken, she is already gone to church.

37.

Der Ofen, the stove; das Bett, the bed; das Gras, the grass; verlangen, to desire; sich setzen, to sit down; stehen, to stand; liegen, to lie; sitzen, to sit.

Setze dich, mein Kind. Ich bin nicht müde; ich setze mich selten. Setzen Sie sich, ich werde mich auch setzen. Setzen Sie sich nicht auf jenen Stuhl, er ist zerbrochen. Wir wollen uns auf diese Bank setzen. Louise und Henriette, kommt und setzt euch neben mich. Warum sitzen Sie nicht? Ich habe zu lange gesessen, ich kann nicht mehr sitzen. Es ist mir unmög-

lich, den ganzen Tag zu sitzen. Wo ist dein Bruder? Er
sitzt vor der Thür. Die ganze Familie saß um den Tisch
herum. Mein Vater verlangt, daß ich immer sitze. Warum
stehen Sie, meine Herren? Setzen Sie sich. Ich kann nicht
lange stehen, ich bin sogleich müde. Ich habe über eine Stunde
hier gestanden, um auf dich zu warten. Wo ist dein Hund, Karl?
Er liegt hinter dem Ofen. Mein Vetter lag gestern um zehn
Uhr noch im Bette. Wir haben bis jetzt im Grase gelegen.

38.

Der **Chor**, the choir, the quire; **zwischen**, between; der **Platz**, tho
room.

Sit down, if you please. I beg you to sit down. I am
sitting already. I sit down where I find room. Will you
not sit down? I shall sit down by your side. Make
room, that this gentleman may (can) sit down. You do
not sit comfortably, (well,) Miss. I did not sit comfortably there; I have been sitting between your two sisters. Where were you sitting at church? We were
sitting in the choir. These gentlemen are always
standing; ask them to sit down. I have been standing (for) a whole hour.

39.

Geboren werden, to be born; **gefallen,** to please; **mißfallen,** to dis-
please; **es gefällt mir hier,** I like it here, I like this place; **gefälligst,**
if you please; **schweigen,** to be silent.

Wissen Sie, wann Sie geboren sind? Ich bin im Monat
Mai geboren. Jeder Mensch wird geboren, um zu sterben.
Dieser Knabe wurde nach dem Tode seines Vaters geboren.
Dieses Buch gefällt mir. Dieser Garten würde mir besser
gefallen, wenn er größer wäre. Mein Hut wird Ihnen gefallen. Wie gefällt es Ihnen hier? Es gefällt mir hier sehr
gut. Es würde mir aber noch besser gefallen, wenn ich einige
Freunde bei mir hätte; allein meine Freunde gefallen sich auf
dem Lande nicht. Es hat mir immer besser auf dem Lande
als in der Stadt gefallen. Warum schweigen Sie? Ich kann
nicht schweigen, wenn ich etwas sehe, was mir mißfällt. Ein
junger Mensch muß immer schweigen, wenn ältere Leute mit
einander reden. Schweigt, ich will nichts mehr davon hören

40.

When were you born? I was born in the month of

September. Corneille was born at Rouen. We are
all born, in order to die. I am born to be unhappy
I like this lady very much. I do not like it in the
country. I liked it much better in the town. Do you
like this place? We like it better here than at our
house. Come here, if you please. That has not pleased
me. Be silent. My aunt cannot be silent. We are silent
when ladies speak. I shall not be silent. I have
been silent too long. Why have you been silent? If I
had been silent, I should have done better.

41.
Nach, after.

Nach und nach, by degrees; nach wie vor, always the same; erst,
only, but; die Seite, the side; das Bild, the picture, the portrait; die
Meinung, the opinion; der Takt, the time, measure; der Anschein, the
appearances; sparen, to economize.

Deine Eltern sind nach Gott deine größten Wohlthäter.
Ich reise morgen nach London, und werde erst nach drei
Wochen wiederkommen. Nach welcher Seite muß man gehen,
um nach dem Schlosse zu kommen? Ich werde nach dem
Abendessen zu Ihnen kommen. Dieses Bild ist nach der Natur
gemalt. Herr N. war hier und hat nach Ihnen gefragt.
Allem Anscheine nach wirst du deinen Prozeß verlieren. Meiner
Meinung nach werde ich ihn gewinnen. Diese Waare wird
nach der Elle verkauft. Ihr Bruder kleidet sich immer nach
der Mode. Sie tanzen nicht nach dem Takte. Ich habe dir
gerathen zu sparen, damit du nach und nach reich werdest;
allein du lebst nach wie vor. Ich bewohne eine Stube, die
nach dem Garten geht. Nach dem, was Ihr Bruder mir
gesagt hat, sind Sie mit Ihrem Lehrer sehr zufrieden. Nach=
dem wir eine Stunde gewartet hatten, gingen wir fort.

42.
Bei, with, at.

Die Laune, the humor; die Angelegenheit, the affair; der Stiel, the
handle; die Klinge, the blade; die Ehre, honor; die Schlacht, the
battle; ein Römer, a Roman; das Geburtsfest, the birthday; versichern,
to assure; sich erkundigen, to inquire; annehmen, to accept; begegnen,
to meet; holen, to fetch; umkommen, to perish; in Thränen ausbre=
chen, to burst into tears; wichtig, important.

Ich war diesen Morgen bei dem preußischen Gesandten.
Er war bei sehr guter Laune, nahm mich bei der Hand und
versicherte mich, daß er sich heute noch bei dem Minister nach

meiner Angelegenheit erkundigen werde. Ich fand ihn bei
Tische, und dachte bei mir selbst, daß er meinen Besuch nicht
annehmen werde. Ich hatte einen wichtigen Brief bei mir,
den ich ihm übergeben habe. Haben Sie Geld bei sich? Bei
wem wohnen Sie? Ich wohne nahe bei der Kirche, nicht
weit von der Post. Nehmen Sie das Messer bei dem Stiel
und nicht bei der Klinge. Der Eine nahm ihn bei dem Kopfe,
der Andere bei den Beinen. Ich versichere Sie bei meiner
Ehre. Ich begegnete ihm beim Herausgehen aus dem Theater. Wir werden es ihm bei Gelegenheit sagen. Warum
sitzen Sie beim Feuer, sind Sie nicht wohl? Legen Sie mir
die Waaren bei Seite; ich werde sie holen lassen. Mein Bruder ist in der Schlacht bei Leipzig umgekommen. Bei diesen
Worten brach er in Thränen aus. Wir waren immer zusammen, bei Tag und bei Nacht. Es war eine alte Gewohnheit bei den Römern, seinen Freunden an ihrem Geburtstage
Geschenke zu schicken.

43.
Mit, with.

Die Klugheit, prudence; der Muth, courage; die Flinte, the gun; die
Kugel, the ball; die Landschaft, the landscape; das Gewissen, conscience;
die Stimme, the voice; das Hauptwort, the substantive; der Anfangs-
buchstabe, the initial letter; handeln, to act; laden, to load, to charge;
vorgehen, to pass; beehren, to honor.

Mit wem sind Sie spazieren gegangen? Mit welcher
Dame haben Sie getanzt? Handeln Sie stets mit Klugheit,
vertheidigen Sie sich mit Muth? Die Schönheit vergeht
mit den Jahren. Ist Ihre Flinte mit einer Kugel geladen?
Ihr Freund hat mich mit einem Besuche beehrt. Man ist
sehr zufrieden mit ihm. Er ist gestern mit der Post angekommen. Er trägt einen braunen Rock mit goldenen Knöpfen.
Der junge Mann mit den langen Haaren ist der Sohn des
Hauses. Haben Sie den Mann mit der großen Nase und
den schwarzen Augen gesehen? Mein Kind, du mußt dein
Fleisch mit der Gabel und nicht mit der Hand essen. Meine
Base hat mir mit Thränen in den Augen erzählt, daß sie
morgen abreisen muß. Diese Landschaft ist mit dem Bleistift, und nicht mit der Feder gezeichnet. Ich kann dieses
Geschenk nicht mit gutem Gewissen annehmen. Er trat mit
einer Pistole in der Hand herein, und schrie mit lauter
Stimme. Im Deutschen wird jedes Hauptwort mit einem
großen Anfangsbuchstaben geschrieben.

44.

Die Erfahrung, experience; die Absicht, the intention; der Neid, envy; die Uebung, the exercise; die Strafe, the punishment; das Licht, the light; der Tod, death; die Furcht, fear; der Hals, the throat; sonst, otherwise; übersetzen, to translate; Jahr aus, Jahr ein, from year to year.

Was machen Sie? Ich übersetze aus dem Deutschen in's Französische. Woher kommen Sie? Wir kommen aus der Schule, aus dem Garten. Woher sind Sie? Ich bin aus Berlin, und mein Freund ist aus Lyon. Wer hat aus diesem Glase getrunken? Ich weiß es aus Erfahrung. Ich habe es aus guter Absicht, aus Liebe zu ihm gethan. Ich ersehe aus Ihrem Briefe, daß Sie noch immer unwohl sind. Die Cholera kommt aus Asien. Diese Bildsäule ist aus Marmor. Diese Hüte sind aus der Mode. Er schreit aus vollem Halse. Ich liebe ihn aus ganzem Herzen. Mein Bruder kommt seit acht Tagen nicht aus dem Zimmer. Geht mir aus den Augen, der Neid spricht aus Ihnen. Ich habe lange nicht mehr Klavier gespielt, ich komme ganz aus der Uebung. Das Licht ist aus. Mit dem Tode ist Alles aus. Der Schüler muß aus gutem Willen und nicht aus Furcht vor Strafe arbeiten; sonst wird er Jahr aus Jahr ein in die Schule gehen, ohne große Fortschritte zu machen.

45.

Die Welt, the world; das Wort, the word; die Jagd, the chase; die Leiter, the ladder; der Lärm, the noise; der Fall, the case; das Gesicht, the face; steigen, to mount, ascend; zwingen, to compel; folgen, to follow; ertappen, to catch; rechnen, to reckon.

Auf Wiedersehen! Ja wohl, auf dem Balle werden wir uns wiedersehen. Nichts auf der Welt gefällt mir besser als ein Ball. Ich glaube dir auf dein Wort. Doch freue dich nicht zu sehr darauf, er kann leicht auf vierzehn Tage aufgeschoben werden. Meine Brüder gehen morgen auf die Jagd, und ich werde auf's Land gehen. Setzen Sie sich auf einen Stuhl, und steigen Sie nicht auf die Leiter. Wir haben ihm diese Summe auf sein gutes Gesicht geliehen. Er kam auf mich los, und wollte mich zwingen, ihm zu folgen. Ich höre Lärm auf der Straße; man hat einen Dieb auf frischer That ertappt. Meine Mutter ist drei Viertel auf sieben Uhr abgereist. Wie heißt diese Blume auf deutsch? Sind Sie böse

auf mich? Wie viele Groschen gehen auf einen Thaler? Ich
werde auf kurze Zeit verreisen. Auf alle Fälle bin ich aber
bis zum fünfzehnten dieses Monats wieder zurück. Auf's
Längste werde ich bis zum zwanzigsten bleiben. Sie können
es auf meine Gefahr thun. Ich habe auf immer Abschied
von ihm genommen. Er hofft zwar noch immer auf mich,
allein ich habe ihm erklärt, daß er auf mich nicht mehr zu
rechnen braucht.

46.

Ueber, over, above.

Das Gewitter, the thunder-storm; das Schwerdt, the sword; der
Schweiß, the perspiration; die Stirn, the forehead; die Kraft, the
force; das Gelingen, success; naß, wet; beständig, constantly; anfänglich, in the beginning; schuldig sein, to owe; in Schulden stecken,
to be in debt.

Es steht ein Gewitter über der Stadt. Das Schwerdt hing
über seinem Kopfe. Dein Vetter sitzt beständig über seinen
Büchern. Die Haare hängen ihm über die Augen. Der
Schweiß lief ihm über die Stirne. Er steckt bis über die
Ohren in Schulden. Das ist über seine Kräfte, über seinen
Verstand. Diese jungen Leute schlafen immer über dem Lesen
ein. Meine Frau ist über fünfzig und ich bin über sechzig
Jahre alt. Dieses Tuch ist über zwei Ellen breit. Wir
müssen über diesen Fluß, über jene Brücke. Ich werde über
Frankfurt nach Leipzig reisen. Die Ehre geht über den Reichthum. Heute über acht Tage kommt mein Vater an. Er ist
über ein halbes Jahr verreist gewesen. Dein Vetter ist mir
über hundert Thaler schuldig. Freue dich nicht zu früh über
das Gelingen deiner Unternehmung; du bist noch nicht über
den Berg. Es regnet sehr stark, wir sind über und über naß
geworden. Dein Freund schreibt uns nicht mehr; anfänglich
erhielten wir Briefe über Briefe von ihm.

47.

Gegen, against, to.

Die Waffe, the weapon; das Gesetz, the law; die Quittung, the
receipt; der Dienst, the service; wohlthätig, charitable; tragen, to
carry; bewundern, to admire; wetten, to bet; leisten, to do; betreten,
to set foot upon; freilassen, to set at liberty.

Dieser General trägt die Waffen gegen sein Vaterland.
Wer gegen sein Gewissen handelt, handelt gegen Gott und
das Gesetz. Ich bewundere seine Liebe gegen seine Familie
und seine Treue gegen seine Freunde. Unsere Fürstin ist wohl-

thätig gegen die Armen. Coriolan war undankbar gegen sein Vaterland. Er ist freigelassen worden gegen sein Versprechen, das Land nicht wieder zu betreten. Ich habe ihn gegen Quittung bezahlt. Ich wette zehn gegen eins, daß er nicht wiederkommt. Dieser Dienst ist nichts gegen denjenigen, den Sie mir geleistet haben. Dieses Dorf liegt gegen Norden. Er schlief gegen zwei Uhr ein, und stand gegen neun Uhr wieder auf. Mein Enkel wird gegen Ende des Winters ankommen.

48.

Wenn, if, when ; ob, if, whether ; wann, when.
Weil, because ; während, while, during ; der Rath, the advice ; klug, wise ; unterhaltend, amusing ; verbieten, to forbid.

Ich werde ihn gewiß belohnen, wenn ich mit ihm zufrieden bin. Ich werde es Ihnen sagen, wenn Sie zu mir kommen. Lassen Sie mich wissen, wann Sie kommen werden. Wenn ihr glücklich seid, so erinnert euch der Dienste, die wir euch geleistet haben. Wenn ich wüßte, wann er zurückkäme, so würde ich es Ihnen sagen. Wenn meine Schwester klug ist, so wird sie meinen Rath befolgen. Wenn sie älter sein wird und etwas mehr Erfahrung wird erlangt haben, so wird sie finden, daß ich Recht habe. Ich weiß nicht ob das wahr ist. Er fragt, ob Sie morgen abreisen werden. Ich kann nicht ausgehen, weil der Arzt es mir verboten hat. Ich will Ihnen ein unterhaltendes Buch leihen, weil Sie nicht ausgehen können. Er arbeitet fleißig, während sein Bruder spazieren geht. Er wird täglich von seinen Lehrern gelobt, während sein Bruder stets von ihnen getadelt wird.

49.

Da, as, because ; als, when.
Der Staat, the state ; annehmen, to accept ; einladen, to invite ; vorwerfen, to reproach ; aufwecken, to awake, to rouse ; trennen, to separate ; hinterlassen, to leave ; vorbeigehen, to pass ; ungerathen, illbred ; künftig, in future ; leise, low, soft.

Da ich heute seinen Besuch nicht annehmen kann, so will ich ihn auf künftigen Sonntag einladen. Da ich morgen abreisen muß, so bin ich gekommen, um Abschied von Ihnen zu nehmen. Da mein Vater krank ist, so kann ich nicht spazieren gehen. Weil wir fürchteten, Sie aufzuwecken, so haben wir leise gesprochen. Da wir gewohnt waren, mit einander zu leben, so hatten wir viele Mühe, uns zu trennen. Als

Pelopidas dem Epaminondas vorwarf, daß er dem Staate
keine Kinder hinterlasse, antwortete dieser: Du thust noch
weniger für das Vaterland, da du ihm nur einen ungerathenen
Sohn hinterlassen wirst. Als Titus einen Tag hatte vorbei=
gehen lassen, ohne Jemandem etwas Gutes zu erweisen, sagte
er: Ich habe einen Tag verloren.

50.

Wollen, to be willing; können, to be able, to know; lassen, to let,
to allow, to have (done).

Der Befehl, the order; die Reise, the journey; die Aufmerksamkeit,
the attention; die Lust, the mind, the wish; der Boden, the soil;
eigensinnig, obstinate; feucht, moist; besonders, particular; vorgerückt,
advanced; unternehmen, to undertake; sich wärmen, to warm one's
self; Schlittschuh laufen, to skate.

Die Kinder meines Nachbars sind so eigensinnig, daß sie
nie die Befehle ihrer Eltern erfüllen wollen. Will der Vater
sie auf den Spaziergang mitnehmen, so wollen sie zu Hause
bleiben; will die Mutter, daß sie arbeiten, so wollen sie aus=
gehen. Es ist kalt, wir wollen in's Haus gehen, oder wir
wollen ein wenig spielen, um uns zu erwärmen. Die Reli=
gion will, daß wir keinem Andern thun, was wir nicht wollen,
daß man es uns thue. Diese Pflanzen wollen einen feuchten
Boden und eine besondere Aufmerksamkeit. Wir können viel
thun, wenn wir nur wollen. Wir werden diese Reise nicht
mehr unternehmen können, weil die Jahreszeit schon zu weit
vorgerückt ist. Wer mit Nutzen reisen will, muß die Sprache
des Landes kennen, in welchem er reiset. Können Sie Schlitt=
schuh laufen? Ich konnte es ehedem wohl; aber seitdem ich
das Bein gebrochen habe, kann ich es nicht mehr. Ich habe
mir ein paar neue Stiefel machen lassen. Dieser Lehrer läßt
seine Schüler hinausgehen, so oft sie Lust haben.

DIVERSE EXERCISES.

1.

THE CANE-PIPE.

(The vocabulary is to be found at the end of the exercises.)

Ein König hatte einen Schatzmeister, der sich vom Hirten⸗
stabe zu diesem wichtigen Amte emporgeschwungen hatte. Der
Schatzmeister wurde aber bei dem Könige verklagt, daß er den
königlichen Schatz beraube und die geraubten Kostbarkeiten in
einem Gewölbe verberge, das mit einer eisernen Thür ver⸗
sehen sei.

Der König besuchte den Schatzmeister, besah seinen Palast,
und als er an die eiserne Thür kam, befahl er, sie zu öffnen.
Als der König hineintrat, war er ganz erstaunt. Er sah
nichts als die vier Wände, einen ländlichen Tisch und einen
Strohsessel. Auf dem Tisch lag eine Hirtenflöte, ein Hirten⸗
stab und eine Hirtentasche.

Der Schatzmeister aber sprach: In meiner Jugend hütete
ich die Schafe. Du, o König, zogst mich an deinen Hof.
Hier in diesem Gewölbe brachte ich seit der Zeit täglich eine
Stunde zu, erinnerte mich mit Freuden meines vorigen Stan⸗
des, und wiederholte die Lieder, die ich ehemals zum Lobe des
Schöpfers sang, als ich friedlich meine Heerde hütete. Ach,
laß mich wieder zurückkehren auf meine väterlichen Fluren, wo
ich glücklicher war, als an deinem Hofe!

Der König war sehr erzürnt über diejenigen, welche den
edlen Mann verleumdet hatten; er umarmte ihn und bat ihn
bei ihm zu bleiben.

2.

THE THREE ROBBERS.

Drei Räuber mordeten und plünderten einen Kaufmann,
der mit einer Menge Geld und Kostbarkeiten durch einen
Wald reiste. Sie brachten den geraubten Schatz in ihre

Höhle, und schickten den jüngsten von ihnen in die Stadt um Lebensmittel einzukaufen.

Als er fort war, sagten die beiden anderen: Warum sollen wir diese großen Reichthümer mit diesem Burschen theilen? Wenn er zurückkommt, wollen wir ihn tödten.

Der junge Räuber dachte unterwegs bei sich: Wie glücklich wäre ich), wenn all dieses Geld mir gehörte! Ich will meine zwei Gefährten vergiften, so behalte ich es für mich allein. —Als er in der Stadt angekommen war, kaufte er Lebensmittel ein, that Gift in den Wein und kehrte in den Wald zurück.

Kaum war er in die Höhle getreten, als die beiden anderen auf ihn zusprangen und ihn mit ihren Dolchen durchbohrten. Hierauf setzten sie sich, aßen und tranken den vergifteten Wein. Sie starben unter heftigen Schmerzen, und man fand ihre Leichname mitten unter den Schätzen, welche sie aufgehäuft hatten.

3.
THE PILGRIM.

In einem prächtigen Schlosse, von dem schon längst jede Spur verschwunden ist, lebte einst ein sehr reicher Ritter. Er verwandte viel Geld, um es zu verschönern, aber er that wenig für die Armen.

Da kam einmal ein armer Pilger, der um eine Nachtherberge bat. Der Ritter wies ihn trotzig ab und sagte: Dieses Schloß ist kein Gasthof. — Erlaubt mir nur drei Fragen, sagte der Pilger, so will ich weiter gehen. — Das gebe ich zu, versetzte der Ritter.

Wer bewohnte vor Euch dieses Schloß? fragte der Pilger. — Mein Vater. — Wer war vor ihm der Bewohner dieses Schlosses? — Mein Großvater. — Und wer wird nach Euch darin wohnen? — Mein Sohn, wenn es Gott will.

Nun, sprach der Pilger, wenn Jeder nur eine gewisse Zeit in diesem Schlosse wohnt, und wenn immer Einer dem Andern Platz darin macht, so seid Ihr nur Gäste hier und das Schloß ist wirklich ein Gasthaus. Verwendet daher nicht so viel, um dieses Haus so sehr zu verschönern, welches Ihr nur für so kurze Zeit besitzt. Thut lieber den Armen Gutes, so werdet Ihr im Himmel eine ewige Wohnung erlangen. — Der Ritter nahm diese Worte zu Herzen, gewährte dem Pilger seine Bitte und wurde für die Folge wohlthätiger gegen die Armen.

4.

THE ROBIN-REDBREAST.

Ein Rothkehlchen kam in der Strenge des Winters an das Fenster eines frommen Landmanns, als ob es gern hinein möchte. Da öffnete der Landmann sein Fenster und nahm das zutrauliche Thierchen freundlich in seine Wohnung. Nun pickte es die Brosamen und Körnchen auf, die von seinem Tische fielen, und die Kinder des Landmanns liebten das Vöglein sehr.

Aber als nun der Frühling wieder in das Land kam und die Gebüsche sich belaubten, da öffnete der Landmann sein Fenster, und der kleine Gast entfloh in das nahe Wäldchen, und baute sein Nest und sang ein fröhliches Liedchen.

Und siehe, als der Winter wiederkehrte, da kam das Rothkehlchen abermals in die Wohnung des Landmanns, und hatte sein Weibchen mitgebracht. Der Landmann aber und seine Kinder freuten sich sehr, als sie die beiden Thierchen sahen, die so zutraulich umherschauten. Und die Kinder sagten: Die Vögelchen sehen uns an, als ob sie uns etwas sagen wollten.

Da antwortete der Vater: Wenn sie reden könnten, so würden sie sagen: Zutrauen erweckt Zutrauen, und Liebe erzeugt Gegenliebe.

5.

THE VOICE OF JUSTICE

Ein reicher Mann, Namens Chryses, gebot seinen Knechten, eine arme Wittwe sammt ihren Kindern aus ihrer Wohnung zu vertreiben, weil sie den gewöhnlichen Zins nicht zu zahlen vermochte. Als die Diener kamen, sprach das Weib: Ach, verziehet ein wenig; vielleicht, daß euer Herr sich unser erbarme; ich will zu ihm gehen und ihn bitten.

Darauf ging die Wittwe zu dem reichen Mann mit ihren vier Kindern, eins lag krank darnieder, und alle flehten, sie nicht zu verstoßen. Chryses aber sprach: Meine Befehle kann ich nicht ändern, es sei denn, daß Ihr Euere Schuld sogleich bezahlet.

Da weinte die Mutter bitterlich und sagte: Ach, die Pflege eines kranken Kindes hat all meinen Verdienst verzehrt und meine Arbeit gehindert. Und die Kinder flehten mit der Mutter, sie nicht zu verstoßen.

Aber Chryses wandte sich weg von ihnen und ging in sein

Gartenhaus und legte sich auf das Polster, zu ruhen, wie er pflegte. Es war aber ein schwüler Tag, und dicht am Gartensaal floß ein Strom, der verbreitete Kühlung, und es war eine Stille, daß kein Lüftchen sich regte.

Da hörte Chryses das Gelispel des Schilfs am Ufer, aber es tönte ihm gleich dem Gewinsel der Kinder der armen Wittwe; und er ward unruhig auf seinem Polster.

Darnach horchte er auf das Rauschen des Stromes und es dünkte ihn, als ruht er an dem Gestade eines unendlichen Meeres, und er wälzte sich auf seinem Pfühle.

Als er nun wieder horchte, erscholl aus der Ferne der Donner eines Gewitters, und er glaubte die Stimme des Gerichts zu vernehmen.

Nun stand er plötzlich auf, eilte nach Hause und gebot seinen Knechten, der armen Wittwe das Haus zu öffnen. Aber sie war samut ihren Kindern in den Wald gezogen und nirgends zu finden. Unterdessen war das Gewitter hinaufgezogen, und es donnerte und fiel ein gewaltiger Regen. Chryses aber war voll Unmuth und wandelte umher.

Am andern Tage vernahm Chryses, das kranke Kind sei im Walde gestorben und die Mutter mit den anderen hinweggezogen. Da ward ihm sein Garten sammt dem Saal und Polster zuwider, und er genoß nicht mehr die Kühlung des rauschenden Stromes.

Bald nachher fiel Chryses in eine Krankheit, und immer in der Hitze des Fiebers vernahm er des Schilfes Gelispel und den rauschenden Strom und das dumpfe Tosen des Gewitters. Also verschied er.

6.
THE PEACHES.

Ein Landmann brachte aus der Stadt fünf Pfirsiche mit, die schönsten, die man sehen konnte. Seine Kinder aber sahen diese Frucht zum ersten Male; deshalb wunderten und freuten sie sich sehr über die schönen Aepfel mit den röthlichen Backen und dem zarten Flaum. Darauf vertheilte der Vater sie unter seine vier Knaben, und eine erhielt die Mutter.

Am Abend, als die Kinder in das Schlafkämmerlein gingen, fragte der Vater: Nun, wie haben euch die schönen Aepfel geschmeckt?

Herrlich, lieber Vater! sagte der Aelteste. Es ist eine schöne Frucht, so säuberlich und so sanft von Geschmack. Ich habe

9*

mir den Stein sorgsam verwahrt und will mir daraus einen Baum erziehen.

Brav! sagte der Vater. Das heißt haushälterisch für die Zukunft gesorgt, wie es dem Landmann geziemt.

Ich habe die meinige sogleich aufgegessen, rief der Jüngste, und den Stein fortgeworfen, und die Mutter hat mir die Hälfte von der ihrigen gegeben. O, das schmeckt so süß und zerschmilzt im Munde!

Nun, sagte der Vater, du hast zwar nicht sehr klug, aber doch natürlich und nach kindlicher Weise gehandelt. Für die Klugheit ist auch noch Raum genug im Leben.

Da begann der zweite Sohn: Ich habe den Stein, den der kleine Bruder fortwarf, gesammelt und aufgeklopft. Es war ein Kern darin, der schmeckte so süß wie eine Nuß. Aber meinen Pfirsich habe ich verkauft und soviel Geld dafür erhalten, daß ich, wenn ich nach der Stadt komme, wohl zwölf dafür kaufen kann.

Der Vater schüttelte den Kopf und sagte: Klug ist das zwar, aber kindlich und natürlich war es nicht. Bewahre dich der Himmel, daß du kein Kaufmann werdest!

Und du, Edmund? fragte der Vater. Unbefangen und offen antwortete Edmund: Ich habe meinen Pfirsich dem Sohne unsers Nachbars, dem kranken Georg, der das Fieber hat, gebracht. Er wollte ihn nicht nehmen, da hab' ich ihn ihm auf das Bett gelegt und bin hinweggegangen.

Nun, sagte der Vater, wer hat denn wohl den besten Gebrauch von seinem Pfirsich gemacht?

Da riefen sie alle drei: Das hat Bruder Edmund gethan! — Edmund aber schwieg still. Und die Mutter umarmte ihn mit einer Thrän' im Auge.

7.
THE DESERT ISLAND.

Ein reicher, gutthätiger Mann wollte einen seiner Sklaven glücklich machen: er schenkte ihm die Freiheit und ließ ihm ein Schiff mit vielen köstlichen Waaren ausrüsten. „Geh," sagte er, „und segle damit in ein fremdes Land; wuchere mit diesen Waaren, und aller Gewinn soll dein sein." — Der Sklave reiste ab; aber kaum war er einige Zeit auf der See, als sich ein heftiger Sturm erhob und das Schiff gegen eine Klippe warf, daß es scheiterte. Die köstlichen Waaren versanken im Meer, alle seine Gefährten kamen um, und er selbst erreichte mit genauer Noth das Ufer einer Insel. Hungrig, nackt und ohne Hülfe, ging er tiefer in's Land hinein, und weinte über sein Unglück, als er von fern eine große Stadt erblickte, aus der ihm eine Menge Einwohner mit großem Geschrei entgegen kam. „Heil unserm Könige!" riefen sie ihm zu, setzten ihn auf einen prächtigen Wagen und führten ihn in die Stadt. Er kam in den königlichen Palast, wo man ihm einen Purpurmantel anlegte, ein Diadem um seine Stirn band und ihn einen goldenen Thron besteigen ließ. Die Vornehmen traten um ihn her, fielen vor ihm nieder und schwuren im Namen des ganzen Volkes ihm den Eid der Treue.

Der neue König glaubte Anfangs, alle diese Herrlichkeit sei ein schöner Traum, bis die Fortdauer seines Glückes ihn nicht mehr zweifeln ließ, daß die wunderbare Begebenheit wirklich wahr sei. — „Ich begreife nicht," sprach er bei sich selbst, „was die Augen dieses wunderlichen Volkes bezaubert hat, einen nackten Fremdling zu seinem König zu machen. Sie wissen nicht, wer ich bin, fragen nicht, wo ich herkomme, und setzen mich auf ihren Thron! Was ist das für eine besondere Sitte in diesem Lande?"

8.
CONTINUATION.

So dachte er und wurde so neugierig, die Ursache seiner Erhebung zu wissen, daß er sich entschloß, einen von den Vornehmen an seinem Hofe, der ihm ein weiser Mann zu sein schien, um die Auflösung dieses Räthsels zu fragen. — „Vezier!" redete er ihn an, „warum habt ihr mich denn zu eurem Könige gemacht? Wie konntet ihr wissen, daß ich auf eurer Insel angekommen sei? Und was wird endlich mit mir werden?" — „Herr!" antwortete der Vezier, „diese Insel wird von Geistern bewohnt. Sie haben vor langen Zeiten den Allmächtigen gebeten, ihnen jährlich einen Sohn Adams zu senden, daß er sie regiere. Der Allmächtige hat ihre Bitte angenommen, und läßt alle Jahre, an dem nämlichen Tage, einen Menschen an ihrer Insel landen. Die Einwohner eilen ihm, wie du gesehen hast, freudig entgegen und erkennen ihn für ihren Oberherrn; aber seine Regierung dauert nicht länger als ein Jahr. Ist diese Zeit verflossen und der bestimmte Tag wieder erschienen, so wird er seiner Würde entsetzt; man beraubt ihn des königlichen Schmuckes und legt ihm schlechte Kleider an. Seine Bedienten tragen ihn mit Gewalt ans Ufer

und legen ihn in ein besonders dazu gebautes Schiff, das ihn
auf eine andere Insel bringt. Die Insel ist wüst und öde;
jener, der noch vor wenigen Tagen ein mächtiger König war,
kommt hier nackt an und findet weder Unterthanen noch
Freunde. Niemand nimmt an seinem Unglücke Theil, und er
muß in diesem wüsten Lande ein trauriges und kummervolles
Leben führen, wenn er sein Jahr nicht klug angewendet hat.
Nach der Verbannung des alten Königs geht das Volk dem
neuen, den ihm die Vorsehung des Allmächtigen jedes Jahr
ohne Ausnahme sendet, auf die gewöhnliche Weise entgegen
und nimmt ihn mit gleicher Freude, wie den vorigen, auf.
Dies, Herr! ist das ewige Gesetz dieses Reiches, das kein
König während seiner Regierung aufheben kann." — „Sind
denn auch meine Vorgänger," fragte der König weiter, „von
dieser kurzen Dauer ihrer Hoheit unterrichtet gewesen?" —
„Keinem von ihnen," antwortete der Vezier, „war dieses Gesetz
der Vergänglichkeit unbekannt: aber Einige ließen sich von
dem Glanze, der ihren Thron umgab, blenden; sie vergaßen
die traurige Zukunft, und verlebten ihr Jahr, ohne weise zu
sein. Andere berauschten sich in der Süßigkeit ihres Glückes;
sie getrauten sich nicht, an die wüste Insel zu denken, aus
Furcht, die Annehmlichkeit des gegenwärtigen Genusses zu
verbittern; und so taumelten sie, wie Trunkene, aus einer
Freude in die andere, bis ihre Zeit um war und sie in das
Schiff geworfen wurden. Wenn der unglückliche Tag kam,
so fingen Alle an, sich zu beklagen und ihre Verblendung zu
beseufzen; aber nun war es zu spät, und sie wurden ohne
Schonung dem Elende übergeben, das sie erwartete und dem
sie durch Weisheit nicht hatten vorbeugen wollen."

9.
CONTINUATION.

Diese Erzählung des Geistes erfüllte den König mit Furcht,
r schauderte vor dem Schicksal der vorigen Könige zurück und
wünschte, ihrem Unglücke zu entgehen. Er sah mit Schrecken,
daß schon einige Wochen von diesem kurzen Jahre verflossen
waren, und daß er eilen müßte, die übrigen Tage seiner Regierung desto besser zu nützen. „Weiser Vezier!" sprach er zu
dem Geiste, du hast mir mein künftiges Schicksal und die kurze
Dauer meiner königlichen Macht entdeckt; aber ich bitte dich,
sage mir auch, was ich thun muß, wenn ich das Elend mei-

ner Vorgänger vermeiden will." — „Erinnere dich, Herr!"
antwortete der Geist, „daß du nackt auf unfere Infel gekommen bift; denn eben fo wirft du wieder hinausgehen und nie-
mals zurückkehren. Es ift alfo nur ein einziges Mittel möglich, dem Mangel vorzubeugen, der in jenem Lande der Verbannung droht: wenn du es nämlich fruchtbar machft und mit
Einwohnern befetzeft. Dies ift nach unferen Gefetzen ver-
gönnt, und deine Unterthanen find dir fo vollkommen gehor-
fam, daß fie hingehen, wo du fie hinfendeft. Schicke alfo
eine Menge Arbeitsleute hinüber und laß die wüften Felder
in fruchtbare Aecker verwandeln; baue Städte und Vorraths-
häufer und verforge fie mit allen nothdürftigen Lebensmitteln.
Mit Einem Wort: bereite dir ein neues Reich, deffen Einwohner dich nach deiner Verbannung mit Freuden aufnehmen.
Aber eile, laß keinen Augenblick ungenützt vorüber gehen;
denn die Zeit ift kurz, und je mehr du zum Anbau deiner künftigen Wohnung thuft, defto glücklicher wird dein Aufenthalt
dort fein. Denke, dein Jahr ift morgen fchon um, und nütze
deine Freiheit wie ein kluger Flüchtling, der dem Verderben
entgehen will. Wenn du meinen Rath verachteft oder zau-
derft, fo bift du verloren, und langes Elend ift dein Loos."

Der König war ein kluger Mann, und die Rede des Gei-
ftes gab feiner Entfchließung und feiner Thätigkeit Flügel.
Er fandte fogleich eine Menge Unterthanen ab: fie gingen
mit Freuden und griffen das Werk mit Eifer an. Die Infel
fing an fich zu verfchönern, und ehe fechs Monden vergangen
waren, ftanden fchon Städte auf ihren blühenden Auen
Deffen ungeachtet ließ der König in feinem Eifer nicht nach:
er fandte immer mehr Einwohner hinüber; die folgenden
waren noch freudiger, als die erften, da fie in ein fo wohl
angebautes Land gingen, das ihre Freunde und Anverwandten
bewohnten.

10.
THE END.

Unterdeffen kam das Ende des Jahres immer näher. Die
vorigen Könige hatten vor diefem Augenblicke gezittert, diefer
fah ihm mit Sehnfucht entgegen; denn er ging in ein Land,
wo er fich durch feine kluge Thätigkeit eine dauernde Wohnung gebaut hatte. — Der beftimmte Tag erfchien endlich.
Der König wurde in feinem Palafte ergriffen, feines Diadems und feiner königlichen Kleidung beraubt und auf das

unvermeidliche Schiff gebracht, das ihn nach seinem Verban=
nungsorte führte. Kaum war er aber am Ufer der neuen
Insel gelandet, als ihm die Einwohner mit Freuden entgegen
eilten, ihn mit großer Ehre empfingen, und sein Haupt statt
jenes Diadems, dessen Herrlichkeit nur ein Jahr währte, mit
einem unverwelklichen Blumenkranze schmückten. Der All=
mächtige belohnte seine Weisheit: Er gab ihm die Unsterb=
lichkeit seiner Unterthanen und machte ihn zu ihrem ewigen
Könige.

* * *

Der reiche, wohlthätige Mann ist Gott; der Sklave, den
sein Herr fortsendet, ist der Mensch bei seiner Geburt; die
Insel, wo er anlandet, ist die Welt; die Einwohner, die ihm
freudig entgegen kommen, sind die Eltern, die für den nackten
Weinenden sorgen. Der Vezier, der ihn von dem traurigen
Schicksal, das ihm bevorsteht, unterrichtet, ist die Weisheit.
Das Jahr seiner Regierung ist das menschliche Leben, und
die wüste Insel, wohin er geführt wird, die künftige Welt.
Die Arbeitsleute, die er dahin sendet, sind die guten Werke,
die er während seines Lebens verrichtet. Die Könige aber,
welche vor ihm dahingegangen sind, ohne über das Unglück,
das ihnen drohte, nachzudenken, sind jene thörichten Menschen,
die sich blos mit irdischen Freuden beschäftigen, ohne an ihr
Leben nach dem Tode zu denken; sie werden mit ewigem
Elend bestraft, weil sie vor dem Throne des Allmächtigen mit
Händen erscheinen, die an guten Werken leer sind.

VOCABULARY.

1.

Schatzmeister, treasurer; Hirtenstab, shepherd's-staff; Amt, office; sich
emporschwingen, to rise; verklagen, to accuse; berauben, to rob; Schatz,
treasure; Kostbarkeiten, trinkets; verbergen, to hide; Gewölbe, vault;
versehen, to provide; besehen, to examine; erstaunt, surprised; ländlich,
rural; Strohsessel, chair of straw; Hirtenflöte, cane-flute; Hirtentasche,
shepherd's-bag; hüten, to look after; Schlaf, sleep; ziehen, to attract;
Hof, court; zubringen, to spend; der vorige Stand, the former state;
wiederholen, to repeat; Lied, song; Lob, praise; Schöpfer, Creator;
friedlich, peaceably; Heerde, flock; väterliche Fluren, native fields;
erzürnt, angry; verleumden, to slander; edel, excellent; umarmen, to
embrace.

2.

Räuber, robber; morden, to murder; plündern, to plunder, to rob; Kostbarkeiten, valuable things; Höhle, cavern; Lebensmittel, victuals; fort, gone; Bursche, fellow; tödten, to kill; unterwegs, on the road; Gefährte, companion; vergiften, to poison; behalten, to keep; Gift, poison; kaum, scarcely; treten, to enter; zuspringen, to rush upon; Dolch, dagger; durchbohren, to pierce; heftig, violent; Leichnam, corpse; aufhäufen, to accumulate.

3.

Spur, trace; verschwinden, to disappear; Ritter, knight; verwenden, to spend; verschönern, to adorn; Pilger, pilgrim; Nachtherberge, night's-lodging; abweisen, to refuse; trotzig, haughtily; Gasthof, inn; Frage, question; weiter gehen, to go on his way; zugeben, grant; bewohnen, to inhabit; Gast, guest; wirklich, indeed; lieber, rather; Himmel, heaven; ewig, eternal, everlasting; Wohnung, habitation; erlangen, to acquire; gewähren, to grant; für die Folge, afterwards; wohlthätig, charitable.

4.

Strenge, rigor; Winter, winter; fromm, good-natured; Landmann, peasant; als ob, as if; zutraulich, confidently; freundlich, friendly; Wohnung, house, dwelling; aufpicken, to pick up; Brosamen, Krümchen, crumbs; Frühling, spring; Land, country; Gebüsch, bushes; sich belauben, to leaf, to cover themselves with leaves; entfliegen, to fly away; bauen, to build; Nest, nest; fröhlich, joyful; wiederkehren, to return; abermals, again; mitbringen, to bring along with one; umherschauen, to look about; ansehen, to look at; Zutrauen, confidence; erwecken, to arouse; erzeugen, to produce.

5.

Gebieten, to order; Knecht, servant; Wittwe, widow; vertreiben, to expel; jährlich, annual; Zins, rent; verziehen, to tarry, stay; erbarmen, to have pity; krank darnieder liegen, to be ill; flehen, to implore; verstoßen, to expel; Befehl, order; ändern, to change; es sei denn, except; Schuld, debt; bitterlich, bitterly; Pflege, care, nursing; Verdienst, gain; verzehren, to consume; verhindern, to hinder; sich wegwenden, to turn away; Gartenhaus, summer-house; sich legen, to lie down; Polster, cushion; ruhen, to repose; pflegen, to use, to be in the habit; schwül, sultry, very hot; dicht, close by; fließen, to flow, to run; Strom, river; verbreiten, to spread; Kühlung, coolness; Stille, quiet; Luft, air; sich regen, to move; Gelispel, continual lisping; Schilf, reed; Ufer, bank; tönen gleich, to sound like, to resemble; Gewinsel, whining; unruhig, restless; darnach, then; horchen, to listen; Rauschen, rustling; däuchten, to seem; Gestade, shore; unendlich, endless; sich wälzen, to toss about; Donner, thunder; Gewitter, thunderstorm; Gericht, judgment; vernehmen, to hear; eilen, to hasten; nirgends, nowhere; unterdessen, in the mean time; hinaufziehen, to come up; gewaltig, violent; Unmuth, depressed spirits; umherwandeln, to walk to and fro; hinwegziehen, to pass away; zuwider werden, to be disgusted; genießen, to enjoy; rauschen, to rustle; Hitze, heat; Fieber, fever; dumpf, dull, hollow; Tosen, noise, verscheiden, to expire.

6.

Landmann, countryman; mitbringen, to bring along with one; Pfirsich, peach; röthlich, reddish; Backen, checks; zart, tender; Flaum, down; vertheilen, to divide; Schlafkämmerlein, little bedroom; schmecken, to taste, to like; säuberlich und sanft, delicious and sweet at the same time; Geschmack, taste; Stein, stone; sorgsam, carefully; verwahren, to keep; erziehen, to raise; haushälterisch, economical; Zukunft, future; sorgen, to take care; geziemen, to become; aufessen, to eat up; fortwerfen, to throw away; Hälfte, half; zerschmelzen, to melt; zwar, to be sure; flug, wise; nach kindlicher Weise, childlike; handeln, to act; Klugheit, prudence, wisdom; Raum, room; beginnen, to begin; sammeln, to gather, to pick up; aufklopfen, to open; Kern, kernel; schütteln, to shake; bewahren, preserve; unbefangen, unaffected; offen, frankly; Gebrauch, use; Thräne, tear.

7.

Gutthätig, kind, charitable; schenken, to give, to present; Schiff, ship; köstlich, precious; ausrüsten, to fit out, to equip; segeln, to sail; wuchern, to make profit; Gewinn, gain; kaum, scarcely; See, sea; heftig, violent; Sturm, storm; erheben, to rise; Klippe, cliff; scheitern, to wreck; versinken, to sink; Gefährte, companion; umkommen, to perish; erreichen, to reach; mit genauer Noth, narrowly; Ufer, shore; nackt, naked; Hülfe, help; tiefer hineingehen, to plunge into, to proceed farther; fern, far, distant; erblicken, to perceive; Menge, crowd; entgegen kommen, to come to meet; Heil, prosperity; blessings; Wagen, carriage; Mantel, cloak; besteigen, to ascend; die Vornehmen, the nobles; um ihn hertreten, to surround him; Eid, oath; anfangs, in the beginning; Herrlichkeit, splendor; Traum, dream; Fortdauer, continuation; wunderbar, wonderful; Begebenheit, event, adventure; wunderlich, strange; bezaubern, to enchant; Fremdling, stranger; besondere, singular; Sitte, custom.

8.

Neugierig, curious; Ursache, cause, reason; Erhebung, elevation; Auflösung, solution; Räthsel, riddle; was wird aus mir werden, what will become of me; Geist, spirit; bewohnen, to inhabit; allmächtig, almighty; landen, to disembark; entgegeneilen, to hasten towards; erkennen, to recognize, to acknowledge; Oberherr, sovereign; Regierung, government; dauern, to last; verfließen, to pass; wieder erscheinen, to reappear; Würde, dignity; entsetzen, to depose; berauben, to deprive; Schmuck, ornaments; wüst und öde, desert and desolate; mächtig, powerful; Unterthan, subject; Theil, part, interest; kummervoll, sorrowful; Verbannung, banishment; Vorsehung, providence; Ausnahme, exception; aufnehmen, to receive; vorig, preceding; Reich, kingdom; aufheben, abolish; Vorgänger, predecessor; Dauer, duration; Hoheit, sovereignty; Vergänglichkeit, transientness; Glanz, splendor; blenden, to blind; Zukunft, future; verleben, to pass, to spend; berauſchen, to intoxicate; Süßigfeit, sweetness; ſich getrauen, to dare; Annehmlichfeit, delight, sweetness; gegenwärtig, present; Genuß enjoyment; verbittern, to embitter; taumeln, to stagger, to pass; trun. fen, tipsy; um ſein, to be passed; Verblendung, blindness, fascination · ſeufzen, to sigh; Schonung, forbearance, mercy; Elend, misery; über geben, to deliver; vorbeugen, to prevent.

9.

Erzählung, recital, story; erfüllen, to fill; zurückſchaubern, to tremble. Schicfal, fate; entgehen, to escape; Schrecken, fright; die übrigen, the remaining; beſto beſſer, so much the better; nützen, to turn to profit; vermeiden, to avoid; ſich erinnern, to remember; Mittel, means; Mangel, want; drohen, to threaten; nämlich, namely; that is to say; fruchtbar machen, to fertilize; beſetzen, to fill; vergönnen, to permit; vollkommen, perfect; gehorſam, obedient; Arbeitsleute, workmen; Feld, field; Acter, field; bauen, to build; Vorrathshaus, magazine; verſorgen, to provide; nothbürftig, necessary; Lebensmittel, victuals; bereiten, to prepare; vorübergehen, to pass; ungenützt, without profit; Anbau, culture; Wohnung, habitation, dwelling; Aufenthalt, stay, residence; Ver= derben, ruin, destruction; verachten, to despise; Rath, advice; zaubern, to tarry; Loos, fate; Rede, discourse, speech; Entſchließung, resolu- tion; Thätigfeit, activity; Flügel, wing; das Werf angreifen, to set to work; Eifer, zeal; ſtehen, to be; blühend, blooming; Aue, pasture; deſſen ungeachtet, notwithstanding; nachlaſſen, to relent; angebaut, cultivated; Anverwandte, relations.

10.

Unterdeſſen, meanwhile; näher fommen, to approach; zittern, to tremble; Augenblick, moment; mit Sehnſucht entgegenſehen, to await with impatience; beſtimmt, fixed; erſcheinen, to appear; endlich, at last; ergreifen, to seize; berauben, to deprive; unvermeidlich, inevi- table; Verbannungsort, exile; Haupt, head; währen, to last; unver= welflich, never-fading; Blumenfranz, wreath of flowers; ſchmücken, to adorn; belohnen, to reward; Unſterblichfeit, immortality; ewig, eternal, everlasting; fortſenden, to send away; Geburt, birth; Welt, world; weinen, to weep; bevorſtehen, to await; unterrichten, to instruct; Werf, work; verrichten, to do; nachdenfen, to reflect; thöricht, foolish; irdiſch, worldly; beſchäftigen, to occupy; leer, empty

COLLECTION OF MUCH USED PHRASES.

1.

Thanks to God!	Gott sei Dank!
I owe it to you,	ich verdanke es dir;
God forbid!	bewahre Gott!
would to God!	wollte Gott!
very well, I agree to that,	gut, das laß ich gelten,
directly,	jetzt gleich;
presently, by and by,	sogleich;
this minute,	den Augenblick;
to-morrow, then!	auf morgen!
as quickly as possible,	so schnell als möglich;
as soon as possible,	auf's eheste;
at the latest,	spätestens;
at the most,	höchstens;
to have done,	fertig sein;
never mind,	das thut nichts;
come for it, send for it,	holen Sie es, lassen Sie es holen'
all in all,	Alles zusammen genommen;
by the by,	da fällt mir ein;
just in time,	zur rechten Zeit;
importunely,	zur Unzeit;
about nothing at all,	um nichts und wider nichts;
not by far,	bei weitem nicht;
have done with it!	höre auf damit!
by degrees, by little and little,	nach und nach;
by ourselves,	unter vier Augen;
heedlessly,	ohne Ueberlegung;
by turns,	wechselsweise, nach der Reihe;
it is my turn,	die Reihe ist an mir;
by snatches,	stückweise;
to my taste,	nach meinem Geschmacke;
methinks,	nach meinem Bedünken;
in my way,	nach meiner Art;

well-grounded,	grünblich;
among ourselves,	unter uns;
unwillingly,	ungern;
till I see you again,	auf Wiedersehen;
by one's self,	für sich allein;
to the right, to the left,	rechts, links;
purposely,	mit Fleiß, absichtlich;
delightful,	zum Entzücken;
as usual,	wie gewöhnlich;
for my part,	was mich betrifft;
joke apart,	Scherz bei Seite.

2.

Cheap,	wohlfeil;
pitiful,	zum Erbarmen;
against my inclination,	wider Willen;
unheard of,	unerhört;
not to be believed,	unglaublich;
with a loud voice,	mit lauter Stimme;
with a low voice,	mit leiser Stimme;
what is the use of that?	wozu das?
straight along,	gerade zu;
partly—partly,	theils—theils;
that is to say,	das heißt, nämlich;
that is yet to be seen,	das fragt sich,
to be, to do,	sich befinden;
at the end of a year,	nach Verlauf eines Jahres;
quite sure,	ganz gewiß;
in case of need,	im Nothfalle;
f the worst comes to the worst,	wenn's zum Aeußersten kommt;
repeatedly,	zu wiederholten Malen;
at random,	auf's Gerathewohl;
at break of day,	beim Anbruch des Tages,
at night-fall,	bei einbrechender Nacht;
in the heat of summer,	mitten im Sommer;
in the cold of winter,	im härtesten Winter;
sheltered from the rain, &c.	geschützt vor dem Regen 2c.;
at sunrise,	mit Sonnenaufgang.

3.

To believe him,	wenn man ihm glauben soll;
to hear him,	wenn man ihn so reden hört;
to speak candidly,	offenherzig gesagt;
to see him, you would take him for a common man,	wenn Sie ihn so sehen, so sollten Sie ihn für einen gemeinen Mann halten;
all but two dollars,	bis auf zwei Thaler;
he is fond of flowers,	er ist ein Freund von Blumen,
as far as you can see,	so weit, als das Gesicht reicht;
by dint of reading,	durch vieles Lesen;
without his parents' knowledge,	ohne Wissen seiner Eltern;
beginning from the first,	vom ersten an gerechnet;
from afar,	von Weitem;
by day, by night,	am Tage, des Nachts;
even and odd,	gleich und ungleich;
suppose,	gesetzt;
by force,	mit Gewalt;
thunderstruck,	wie vom Donner gerührt;
willingly,	gern;
pray,	ich bitte;
candidly,	aufrichtig;
in good humor,	guter Laune;
in bad humor,	übler Laune;
as well as one can,	so gut man kann;
more and more,	immer mehr.

4.

In all my life, ever,	in meinem Leben, von je her;
never to be forgotten,	unvergeßlich;
all at once,	auf einmal;
indeed?	wirklich? im Ernste?
so much the more,	um so mehr;
further,	ferner;
from the bottom,	von Grund aus;
by word of mouth,	mündlich;
with all my heart,	von ganzem Herzen;

what are you about?	was haben Sie vor?
what is the matter?	was gibt's? was ist los?
by name,	dem Namen nach;
by sight,	von Ansehen;
for want of money, of time,	aus Mangel an Geld, an Zeit,
you have no reason,	Sie haben nicht Ursache;
well, what are you talking about?	nun, wovon ist die Rede?
anew,	von Neuem;
every year, every day,	jährlich, täglich;
by writ, by rote,	schriftlich, auswendig;
(to be) on the point (to be) going,	im Begriff sein;
on the very spot,	an Ort und Stelle;
in the first place, in the second, in the last place,	zum Ersten, zum Zweiten, zum Letzten;
in the mean time,	unterdessen;
in some way,	einigermaßen;
on the way, on the road,	unterwegs;
in return,	dagegen, zum Ersatze;
in the open air,	in der freien Luft;
in broad day-light,	am hellen Tage;
in the open street,	auf freier Straße.

5.

The other day,	neulich;
excessively,	über alle Maßen;
topsy-turvy,	unterst zu oberst, kopfüber;
here enclosed,	beifolgend, inliegend;
sooner or later,	über kurz oder lang;
confusedly,	durcheinander;
whether you like or no.	man mag wollen oder nicht;
you have hurt me,	Sie haben mir weh gethan;
far from the point,	weit gefehlt;
on purpose	absichtlich;
not by far,	bei weitem nicht;
to be sure,	gewiß;
what is still worse,	was noch schlimmer ist;

nothing of consequence, somewhere, anywhere, nowhere, not anywhere, elsewhere, are we going anywhere? something hurts me, what is your pleasure? if you please, it is of no moment, what does it matter? done! in what do you amuse yourself? I amuse myself in reading, I like fruit very much, he likes wine better than beer, nor I neither,

nichts von Bedeutung; irgendwo; nirgends; anderswo; gehen wir irgendwo hin? es thut mir etwas weh; was beliebt? sein Sie so gut; es ist nicht von Bedeutung; was schadet es? topp! abgemacht! womit vertreiben Sie sich die Zeit? ich unterhalte mich mit Lesen; ich esse sehr gern Obst; er trinkt lieber Wein als Bier; ich auch nicht.

6.

Heaven be praised, to pass in a carriage, on horseback, that does well, that will not do, he is to come home, you are very much to be pitied, there are my scissors, some one rings the bell, he has done you no harm,

that is what he told me, thus did I answer him, that is just what you are, in this way we can arrange it, I am cold, warm, hungry, thirsty, what ails you? what is the matter with you?

Dem Himmel sei Dank; vorbei fahren, reiten; das geht gut; das geht nicht; er soll nach Hause kommen; Sie sind wohl recht zu beklagen; da ist meine Scheere; man klingelt; er hat Ihnen nichts zu Leide gethan; das sagte er mir; Folgendes antwortete ich ihm, so sind Sie; so können wir es machen; mich friert, mir ist warm, mich hungert, mich durstet; was fehlt Ihnen?

I am sick,	mir ist übel;
he has a competency,	er hat sein Auskommen;
I am much concerned about it,	es liegt mir am Herzen;
to have something on one's mind,	etwas auf dem Herzen haben;
you have but to speak,	Sie dürfen nur reden;
he needs but follow me,	er darf mir nur folgen;
you have but to come for me about six o'clock,	Sie dürfen mich nur gegen sechs Uhr abholen;
I cannot but praise him,	ich kann ihn nur loben;
you may depend upon it,	Sie können sich darauf verlassen.

7.

It is a pity,	es ist Schade;
I know nothing about it,	ich weiß nichts davon;
I never saw the like of it,	desgleichen habe ich nie gesehen;
there are eighteen of them,	es sind ihrer achtzehn;
there are three people, wanting to speak to you,	es verlangen drei Menschen, Sie zu sprechen;
what is the matter there?	was gibt es da?
three months ago, six months ago, fifteen months ago,	vor drei Monaten, einem halben Jahr, fünf Vierteljahren;
I have not seen you for such a long time,	ich habe Sie schon so lange nicht gesehen;
it will be crowded,	es wird voll werden;
there is nothing to say against it,	dagegen ist nichts zu sagen;
it is impossible to bear it, to make him bear reason,	es ist nicht möglich auszuhalten, ihn zur Vernunft zu bringen;
is there anything more beautiful than this garden?	gibt es etwas Schöneres als diesen Garten?
he is a man of his word.	er ist ein Mann von Wort;
my daughter got the fever yesterday,	meine Tochter bekam gestern das Fieber;
we shall certainly have a thunderstorm	wir bekommen gewiß ein Gewitter;

124

he has had one, and you shall have one likewise, — er hat eins bekommen und Sie sollen auch eins haben;

I have but glanced at it, — ich habe nur einen Blick darauf geworfen.

8.

They are already gone for it, — man besorgt es schon;

how far have you got? — wie weit sind Sie?

I do not know what I am about, — ich weiß nicht, woran ich bin;

you have hit at the right point, — Sie haben es getroffen;

that is too much, — das geht zu weit;

it is the same with all animals, — so ist es mit allen Thieren;

it will be of no use, — es wird nichts helfen;

I have said so all along, — ich habe es immer gesagt;

what is to be done? — was soll geschehen?

I do not know, which way to turn, — ich weiß nicht, wohin ich mich wenden soll;

come along? — komm mit!

what do you want, — was wollen Sie?

what is the name of that? — wie heißt das?

what is the meaning of that? — was heißt das?

to faint, — ohnmächtig werden

it is not to me, you must say **that**, — mir müssen Sie das nicht sagen;

it is, because I have been ill, — das macht, weil ich krank gewesen bin;

why, he did not know him, — er kannte ihn ja nicht.

9.

I am very glad of it, — es ist mir sehr lieb;

I am sorry for it, — es thut mir leid;

I am very comfortable, I feel very well, — es ist mir recht wohl;

I feel very ill, — mir ist's schlecht zu Muthe;

to be well off, — wohlhabend sein;

he has paid him a visit, — er hat ihm einen Besuch gemacht;

we have been to see Mr. N. who is ill,	wir haben Herrn N. besucht, der krank ist;
he is coming directly,	er wird gleich kommen;
it is going to strike twelve o'clock,	es wird gleich zwölf schlagen;
he has enlisted,	er ist Soldat geworden;
what things are these,	was für Sachen sind das?
he was just going out,	er wollte eben hinaus;
what shall become of you?	was soll aus Ihnen werden?
don't believe it,	glauben Sie es ja nicht;
have you finished the book?	haben Sie das Buch ausgelesen;
how do you do?	wie geht's?
how are you getting on?	wie geht's Ihnen?
it gets on well,	es geht gut;
that is a matter of course,	das versteht sich von selbst;
I am going to tell you,	ich will (muß) Ihnen sagen,
what are you about?	was fangen Sie an?
he does not succeed in it,	es gelingt ihm nicht?
my honor is at stake,	meine Ehre steht dabei auf dem Spiele;
I shall come to see you,	ich werde Sie besuchen;
does this suit you?	steht Ihnen das an?
this conduct does not become you,	dieses Betragen geziemt euch nicht;
go to meet somebody,	Jemandem entgegen gehen;
leave me alone,	geh' und laß mich zufrieden;
to be circumstantial,	etwas haarklein erzählen.

10

SIMONNÉ'S MANUAL OF

FRENCH VERBS. Comprising the formation of Persons, Tenses, and Moods of the Regular and Irregular Verbs; a Practical Method to trace the Infinitive of a Verb out of any of its Inflections; Models of Sentences in their different Forms; and a Series of the most useful Idiomatical Phrases. By T. SIMONNÉ. 12mo. 108 pages. Price, 75 cents.

The title of this volume, given in full above, shows its scope and character. The conjugation of the verbs, regular as well as irregular, is the great difficulty that the French student has to encounter; and, to aid him in surmounting it, M. Simonné has applied his long experience as a teacher of the language.

———◆———

SPIERS AND SURENNE'S

French-and-English and English-and-French Pronouncing Dictionary. Edited by G. P. Quackenbos, A. M. One large vol., 8vo, of 1,316 pp., neat type, and fine paper. Half Mor., $5.

The publishers claim for this work,

1. That it is a revision and combination of (Spiers's) the best defining and (Surenne's) the most accurate pronouncing dictionary extant.
2. That in this work the numerous errors in Spiers's dictionary have been carefully and faithfully corrected.
3. That some three thousand new definitions have been added.
4. That numerous definitions and constructions are elucidated by grammatical remarks and illustrative clauses and sentences.
5. That several thousand new phrases and idioms are embodied.
6. That upward of twelve hundred synonymous terms are explained, by pointing out their distinctive shades of meaning.
7. That the parts of all the irregular verbs are inserted in alphabetical order, so that one reference gives the mood, tense, person, and number.
8. That some four thousand new French words, connected with science, art, and literature, have been added.

9. That every French word is accompanied by as exact a pronunciation as can be represented by corresponding English sounds, and vice versa.
10. That it contains a full vocabulary of the names of persons and places, mythological and classical, ancient and modern.
11. That the arrangement is the most convenient for reference that can be adopted.
12. That it is the most complete, accurate, and reliable dictionary of these languages published.

———◆———

VOLTAIRE'S HISTORY OF

CHARLES XII. Carefully revised by GABRIEL SURENNE. 16mo. 262 pages. Price, 75 cents.

This is a neat edition of Voltaire's valuable and popular History of Charles XII., King of Sweden, published under the supervision of a distinguished scholar, and well adapted to the use of schools in this country.

———◆———

WINKELMAN'S FRENCH

SYNTAX; being a course of Exercises in all parts of French Syntax, methodically arranged after Poitevin's " Syntaxe Française; " to which are added Ten Appendices, designed for the use of Academies, Colleges, and Private Learners. By FREDERICK J. WINKELMAN, A. M., PH. D., Professor of Latin, French, and German, in the Packer Collegiate Institute. 12mo. 366 pages. $1.25.

This work is intended for students who already have a partial acquaintance with the French language, but wish to acquire a more thorough knowledge of its Syntax than can be obtained through the text-books in general use. It is arranged in the same manner as the practical part of Poitevin's " Syntaxe Française." The examples of Syntax are mainly translations of passages from the best French authors. The Appendices—of which there are ten—illustrate various difficult points in French grammar.

THE MASTERY SERIES FOR

Learning Languages on New Principles. By THOMAS PRENDERGAST, Author of "The Mastery of Languages, or the Art of Speaking Foreign Tongues Idiomatically." This method offers a solution of the problem, How to obtain facility in speaking foreign languages grammatically, without using the Grammar in the first stage. It adopts and systematizes that process by which many couriers and explorers have become expert practical linguists.

HAND-BOOK TO THE MASTERY SERIES, being an Introductory Treatise. Price, 50 cents.

THE MASTERY SERIES, GERMAN. Price, 50 cents.

———+———

German.

ADLER'S GERMAN-AND-

English, and English-and-German Pronouncing Dictionary. By G. J. ADLER, A. M., Professor of the German Language and Literature in the University of New York. One elegant large 8vo vol. 1,400 pages. Price, $6.

The aim of the distinguished author of this work has been to embody all the valuable results of the most recent investigations in a German Lexicon, which might become not only a reliable guide for the practical acquisition of the language, but one which would not forsake the student in the higher walks of his pursuits, to which its treasures would invite him.

In the preparation of the German and English Part, the basis adopted has been the work of Flügel, compiled in reality by Helmann, Feiling, and Oxenford. This was the most complete and judiciously-prepared manual of the kind in England.

The present work contains the accentuation of every German word, several hundred synonymes, together with a classification and alphabetical list of the irregular verbs, and a dictionary of German abbreviations.

The foreign words, likewise, which have not been completely Germanized, and which often differ in pronunciation and inflection from such as are purely native, have been designated by particular marks.

The vocabulary of foreign words, which now act so important a part, not only in scientific works, but in the best classics, reviews, journals, newspapers, and even in conversation, has been copiously supplied from the most complete and correct sources. It is believed that in the terminology of chemistry, mineralogy, the practical arts, commerce, navigation, rhetoric, grammar, mythology, philosophy, etc., scarcely a word will be found to be wanting.

The Second (or German-English) Part of this volume has been chiefly reprinted from the work of Flügel. The attention which has been paid in Germany to the preparation of English dictionaries for the German student has been such as to render these works very complete. The student, therefore, will scarcely find any thing deficient in this Second Part.

———+———

AN ABRIDGMENT OF THE

ABOVE. 12mo. 844 pages. Price, $2.50.

With a view of offering to the student of German such a portion of his larger work as would embody the most general and important lexicographical elements of the language in the smallest possible compass, the author has gone over the entire ground of the larger work—revising, condensing, or adding, as the case might require. All provincialisms, synonymes, and strictly scientific terms, have been excluded from these pages, and every thing that might prove unnecessary or embarrassing to beginners, or to travellers, and others for whom a smaller volume is better adapted.

From C. C. FELTON, *Prof. of Greek, Harvard Univ.*

"The careful manner in which Prof. Adler has investigated the language as employed by the great body of recent German writers, and the accuracy with which the best usage is explained in his definitions, make the work peculiarly valuable for English and American students."

ADLER'S HAND-BOOK OF GERMAN LITERATURE.

Containing Schiller's Maid of Orleans, Goethe's Iphigenia in Tauris, Tieck's Puss in Boots, The Xenia, by Goethe and Schiller. With Critical Introductions and Explanatory Notes; to which is added an Appendix of Specimens of German Prose, from the middle of the Sixteenth to the middle of the Nineteenth Century. By G. J. ADLER. 12mo. 550 pages. Price, $1.50.

For classes that have made some proficiency in the German language, and desire an acquaintance with specimens of its dramatic literature, no more charming selection than this can be found. Sufficient aid is given, in the form of introductions and notes, to enable the student to understand thoroughly what he reads. The progress of the language is graphically illustrated by specimens of the literature at different eras, collated in an Appendix.

———◆———

ADLER'S PROGRESSIVE GERMAN READER.

By G. J. ADLER, Professor of the German Language and Literature in the University of the City of New York. 12mo. 308 pages. Price, $1.50.

The plan of this German Reader is as follows:

1. The pieces are both prose and poetry, selected from the best authors, and present sufficient variety to keep alive the interest of the scholar.

2. It is progressive in its nature, the pieces being at first very short and easy, and increasing in difficulty and length as the learner advances.

3. At the bottom of the page constant references to the Grammar are made, the difficult passages are explained and rendered. To encourage the first attempt of the learner as much as possible, the twenty-one pieces of the first section are analyzed, and all the necessary words given at the bottom of the page. The notes, which at first are very abundant, diminish as the learner advances.

4. It contains *five* sections. The *first* contains easy pieces, chiefly in prose, with all the words necessary for translating them; the *second*, short pieces in prose and poetry alternately, with copious notes and renderings; the *third*, short popular tales of Grimm and others; the *fourth*, select ballads and other poems from Bürger, Goethe, Schiller, Uhland, Schwab, Chamisso, etc.; the *fifth*, prose extracts from the first classics.

5. At the end is added a vocabulary of all the words occurring in the book.

The pieces have been selected and the notes prepared with great taste and judgment, so much so as to render the book a general favorite with German teachers.

———◆———

A NEW, PRACTICAL, AND

Easy Method of Learning the German Language. By F. AHN, Doctor of Philosophy, and Professor of the College of Neuss. 12mo. Price, $1.

EICHHORN'S PRACTICAL GERMAN GRAMMAR.

By CHARLES EICHHORN. 12mo. 287 pages. Price, $1.50.

Those who have used Eichhorn's Grammar commend it in the highest terms for the excellence of its arrangement, the simplicity of its rules, and the tact with which abstruse points of grammar are illustrated by means of written exercises. It is the work of a practical teacher, who has learned by experience what the difficulties of the pupil are and how to remove them.

———◆———

ROEMER'S POLYGLOTT READER IN GERMAN.

Being a Translation of the English Selection. Translated by Dr. SOLGER. 12mo. $1.50.

WORMAN'S GERMAN GRAMMAR.

1 vol., 12mo. 500 pages. Price, $2.00.

The Elementary work by the same author has met with great success, having been introduced into a large number of schools and colleges.

OLLENDORFF'S NEW METHOD of Learning to Read, Write, and Speak the German Language. By GEORGE J. ADLER, A. M. 12mo. 510 pages. Price, $1.25.

KEY TO EXERCISES. Separate volume. Price, $1.

Few books have maintained their popularity in the schools for so long a period as the Ollendorff series. The verdict pronounced in their favor, on their first appearance in Europe, has been signally confirmed in America. The publishers have received the strongest testimonials in relation to their merits from the press, from State and county school officers, from principals of academics, and teachers of public and private schools in all sections of the United States.

Grammars for Teaching English to Germans.

OLLENDORFF'S NEW METHOD for Germans to Learn to Read, Write, and Speak the English Language. Arranged and Adapted to Schools and Private Academics. By P. GANDS. 12mo. 599 pages. Price, $1.50.

KEY TO THE EXERCISES. Separate volume. Price, $1.

BRYAN'S GRAMMAR FOR Germans to learn English. Edited by Professor SCHMIEDER. 12mo. 189 pages. Price, $1.25.

The publishers have got out these volumes in view of the great number of Germans residing in and constantly emigrating to the United States, with whom the speedy acquisition of English is a highly desirable object. To aid them in this, the services of competent and experienced teachers have been procured, and the admirable Grammars named above are the results of their labors.

The Ollendorff Grammar embraces a full and complete synopsis of English Grammar, applied at every step to practical exercises. It is constructed according to the "New Method" which has so generally approved itself to public favor. A month's study of this volume will supply the learner with such current idioms that he can comprehend ordinary conversation, and in turn make himself understood.

Bryan's Course is briefer, and better adapted for primary classes and those whose time of study is limited. It presents the cardinal principles of the language, well arranged and clearly illustrated. The anomalies of English syntax are handled in a masterly manner, and the general treatment of the subject such as to remove from it all difficulties by the way.

ELEMENTARY GERMAN READER. By Rev. L. W. HEYDENREICH, Professor of Languages at Bethlehem, Pa. Price, $1.00.

This is an excellent volume for beginners, combining the advantages of Grammar and Reader. It has received strong and cordial commendations from the best German scholars in the country; among whom are Prof. Schmidt, of Columbia College, N. Y.; William M. Reynolds, late Pres. of Capitol Univ., Columbus, Ohio; Edward H. Reichel, Principal of Nazareth Hall; W. D. Whitney, Prof. of Sanscrit and German in Yale College, etc., etc.

Italian.

MEADOWS'S ITALIAN-AND-ENGLISH DICTIONARY. In Two Parts. I. Italian-and-English; II. English-and-Italian. Comprehending, in the First Part, all the Old Words, Contractions, and Licences used by the ancient Italian Poets and Prose Writers; in the Second Part, all the various Meanings of English Verbs. With a new and concise Grammar, to render easy the acquirement of the Italian Language; exhibiting the Pronunciation by Corresponding Sounds, the Parts of Speech, Gender of Italian Nouns, New Conjugation of Regular and Irregular Verbs, Accent on Italian and English Words, List of usual Christian and Proper Names, Names of Countries and Nations. By F. C. MEADOWS, M. A. 1 vol., 16mo. $2.

ELEMENTARY GRAMMAR

OF THE ITALIAN LANGUAGE. Progressively Arranged for the use of Schools and Colleges. By G. B. FONTANA. 12mo. 236 pp. $1.50.

The object of this work is to present the language as spoken to-day, in its simplest garb, both theoretically and practically. The Grammar is divided into two parts, embracing Sixty Lessons and Sixty Exercises. The first part is exclusively given to rules indispensable to a general idea of the language; the second is framed for those who are desirous of having an insight into its theory, and consists of synonyms, maxims, idioms, and figurative expressions. The Exercises of both parts are very regularly progressive,—and those of the second part are of course the most difficult. Some of them contain extracts from celebrated poems translated into plain prose, so that the pupil may compare his Italian translation with the original, which has been inserted for that purpose at the end of the book. Others are biographical sketches of the most prominent among the Italian writers ; by which means the pupil, whilst acquiring the language, may become familiar with the life and works of some of the classic Italian authors, such as Manzoni, Alfieri, Tasso, Petrarch, and the father of Italian language and literature, Dante Alighieri.

FORESTI'S ITALIAN

READER : A Collection of Pieces in Italian Prose, designed as a Reading-Book for Students of the Italian Language. By E. FELIX FORESTI, LL. D. 12mo. 293 pages. Price, $1.50.

In making selections for this volume, Prof. Foresti has had recourse to the modern writers of Italy rather than to the old school of novelists, historians, and poets; his object being to present a picture of the Italian language as it is written and spoken at the present day. The literary taste of the compiler and his judgment as an instructor have been brought to bear with the happiest results in this valuable Reader.

From the Savannah Republican.

"The selections are from popular authors, such as Botta, Manzoni, Machiavelli, Villani, and others.

They are so made as not to constitute mere exercises, but contain distinct relations so complete as to gratify the reader and engage his attention while they instruct. This is a marked improvement on that old system which exacted much labor without enlisting the sympathies of the student. The idioms that occur in the selections are explained by a glossary appended to each. The Italian Reader can with confidence be recommended to students in the language as a safe and sure guide. After mastering it, the Italian poets and other classicists may be approached with confidence."

MILLHOUSE'S NEW ENG-

lish-and-Italian and Italian-and-English Dictionary. With the Pronunciation of the Italian. With many additions, by FERDINAND BRACCIFORTI. 2 vols., 8vo. Half bound, $6.00.

This Italian Dictionary is considered the best which has yet been published. It was prepared by the late John Millhouse, and is acknowledged, by those who have made themselves familiar with the Italian, to excel all that have yet appeared.

ROEMER'S POLYGLOTT

Reader, in the Italian Language; being a Translation of the English Book under that title. 1 vol., 12mo. $1.50.

Ollendorff's Italian Grammars.

PRIMARY LESSONS IN

Learning to Read, Write, and Speak the Italian Language. Introductory to the Larger Grammar. By G. W. GREENE. 18mo. 238 pages. Price, 75 cts.

OLLENDORFF'S NEW METH-

OD of Learning to Read, Write, and Speak the Italian Language. With Additions and Corrections. By E. FELIX FORESTI, LL. D. 12mo. 533 pages. Price, $1.50.

KEY. Separate volume. Price, $1.

In Ollendorff's grammars is for the first time presented a system by which the student can acquire a conversational knowledge of Italian. This will recommend them to practical students; while, at the same time, there is no lack of rules and principles for those who would pursue a systematic grammatical course with the view of translating and writing the language.

Prof. Greene's Introduction should be taken up by youthful classes, for whom it is specially designed, the more difficult parts of the course being left for the larger volume.

The advanced work has been carefully revised by Prof. Foresti, who has made such emendations and additions as the wants of the country required. In many sections the services of an Italian teacher cannot be obtained; the Ollendorff Course and Key will there supply the want of a master in the most satisfactory manner.

From the United States Gazette.

"The system of learning and teaching the living languages by Ollendorff is so superior to all other modes, that in England and on the Continent of Europe, scarcely any other is in use, in well-directed academies and other institutions of learning. To those who feel disposed to cultivate an acquaintance with Italian literature, this work will prove invaluable, abridging, by an immense deal, the period commonly employed in studying the language."

Spanish.

AHN'S SPANISH GRAMMAR; being a New, Practical, and Easy Method of Learning the Spanish Language; after the System of A. F. Ahn, Doctor of Philosophy, and Professor at the College of Neuss. First American edition, revised and enlarged. 12mo. 149 pages. $1.

KEY. 25 cents.

Prof. Ahn's method is one of peculiar excellence, and has met with great success. It has been happily described in his own words: "Learn a foreign language as you learned your mother tongue"—in the same simple manner, and with the same natural gradations. This

method of the distinguished German Doctor has been applied in the present instance to the Spanish Language, upon the basis of the excellent Grammars of Lespada and Martinez, and it is hoped that its simplicity and utility will procure for it the favor that its German, French, and Italian prototypes have already found in the Schools and Colleges of Europe.

(DE BELEM) THE SPANISH PHRASE-BOOK; or, Key to Spanish Conversation. Containing the chief Idioms of the Spanish Language, with the Conjugations of the Auxiliary and the Regular Verbs, on the plan of the late Abbé Bossut. By E. M. DE BELEM. 1 vol., 18mo. 17 cents.

DE VERE'S GRAMMAR OF THE SPANISH LANGUAGE. With a History of the Language and Practical Exercises. By M. SCHELE DE VERE. 12mo. 273 pages. Price, $1.50.

In this volume are embodied the results of many years' experience on the part of the author, as Professor of Spanish in the University of Virginia. It aims to impart a critical knowledge of the language by a systematic course of grammar, illustrated with appropriate exercises. The author has availed himself of the labors of recent grammarians and critics: and by condensing his rules and principles, and rejecting a burdensome superfluity of detail, he has brought the whole within a comparatively small compass. By pursuing this simple course, the language may be easily and quickly mastered, not only for conversational purposes, but for reading it fluently and writing it with elegance.

From the Philadelphia Daily News.

"No student of the Castilian dialect should be without this Grammar. It is at once concise and comprehensive—*multum in parvo*—containing nothing that is redundant, yet omitting nothing that is essential to the learner. The conjugations are so admirably arranged as no longer to present that stumbling-block which has frightened so many from the study of one of the richest and most majestic of languages."

BUTLER'S SPANISH TEACH-
er and Colloquial Phrase-Book: An Easy and Agreeable Method of Acquiring a Speaking Knowledge of the Spanish Language. By Professor BUTLER. 18mo. 233 pages. Price, 60 cts.

The object of the author is to make the Spanish language a living, speaking tongue to the learner; and the method he adopts is that of nature. He begins with the simplest elements, and progressively advances, applying all former acquisitions as he proceeds, until the learner has mastered one of the most perfect languages of modern times.

From the N. Y. Journal of Commerce.
"This is a good book, and well fitted for the purposes for which it is designed. The Spanish language is one of great simplicity, and more easily acquired than any other modern tongue. For a beginner, we recommend this little book, which is small, and designed to be carried in the pocket."

MEADOWS'S SPANISH-AND-
ENGLISH DICTIONARY. In Two Parts. I. Spanish-and-English; II. English - and - Spanish. The First Part comprehends all the Spanish Words, with their appropriate Accents, and every Noun with its Gender. The Second Part, with the addition of many new Words, contains all the various Meanings of English Verbs, in Alphabetical Order, all expressed by their correspondent Spanish, in a simple and definite sense. At the end of both Parts is affixed a list of usual Christian and Proper Names, Names of Countries, Nations, etc. By F. C. MEADOWS, M. A. 1 vol., 16mo. $2.

MERCANTILE DICTION-
ARY: A Complete Vocabulary of the Technicalities of Commercial Correspondence, Names of Articles of Trade, and Marine Terms in Eng-lish, Spanish, and French. With Geographical Names, Business Letters, and Tables of Abbreviations in Common Use in the three languages. By J. DE VIETELLE. 1 vol., 12mo. $2.

Ollendorff's Grammar for Teaching French to Spaniards.

GRAMATICA FRANCESA:
Un Método para Aprender á Leer, Escribir y Hablar el Frances, segun el Verdadero Sistema de Ollendorff. Ordenado en Lecciones Progresivas, consistiendo de Ejercicios Orales y Escritos; enriquecido de la Pronunciacion Figurada como se estila en la Conversacion; y de un Apendice, abrazando las Reglas de la Sintaxis, la Formacion de los Verbos Regulares, y la Conjugacion de los Irregulares. Por TEODORO SIMONNE. 12mo. 341 pages. Price, $2.

KEY TO EXERCISES. Sepa-
rate volume. Price, $1.

M. Simonne has done a good work in bringing the French language within the reach of Spaniards by this application of the Ollendorff system. A few weeks' study of his "Gramática Francesa" will impart a knowledge of the more common conversational idioms, and a thorough mastery of it will insure as perfect an acquaintance with French as can be desired. With the aid of the KEY the study can be pursued without a master; for the illustrative exercises at once show whether the grammatical rules and principles successively laid down are properly understood.

ROEMER'S POLYGLOTT
READER (IN SPANISH). Translated by SIMON CAMACHO. 1 vol., 12mo. Half bound, $1.50.

KEY TO SAME (IN ENGLISH).
1 vol., 12mo. $1.50.

MORALES'S PROGRESSIVE

SPANISH READER. With an Analytical Study of the Spanish Language. By AGUSTIN JOSÉ MORALES, A. M., H. M., Professor of the Spanish Language and Literature in the New York Free Academy. 12mo. 336 pages. Price, $1.50.

The prose extracts in this volume are preceded by an historical account of the origin and progress of the Spanish Language, and a condensed, scholarlike treatise on its grammar; the poetical selections are introduced with an essay on Spanish versification. Prepared in either case by the preliminary matter thus furnished, bearing directly on his work, the pupil enters intelligently on his task of translating. The extracts are brief, spirited, and entertaining; drawn mainly from writers of the present day, they are a faithful representation of the language as it is now written and spoken. The arrangement is progressive, specimens of a more difficult character being presented as the student becomes able to cope with them.

NEW SPANISH READER.

Consisting of Extracts from the Works of the most approved Authors in Prose and Verse, arranged in Progressive Order. With Notes explanatory of the Idioms and most difficult constructions, and a copious Vocabulary. By M. VELAZQUEZ DE LA CADENA. 12mo. 351 pages. Price, $1.50.

This book, being particularly intended for the use of beginners, has been prepared with three objects in view: first, to furnish learners with pleasing and easy lessons, progressively developing the beauties and difficulties of the Spanish language; secondly, to enrich their minds with valuable knowledge; and thirdly, to form their character, by instilling correct principles into their hearts. In order, therefore, to obtain the desired effects, the extracts have been carefully selected from those classic Spanish writers, both ancient and modern, whose style is generally admitted to be a pattern of elegance, combined with idiomatic purity and sound morality.

OLLENDORFF'S SPANISH

GRAMMAR; A New Method of Learning to Read, Write, and Speak the Spanish Language. With Practical Rules for Spanish Pronunciation, and Models of Social and Commercial Correspondence. By M. VELAZQUEZ and T. SIMONNE. 12mo. 560 pages. Price, $1.50.

KEY TO THE SAME. Separate volume. Price, $1.

The admirable system introduced by Ollendorff is applied in this volume to the Spanish language. Having received, from the two distinguished editors to whom its supervision was intrusted, corrections, emendations, and additions, which specially adapt it to the youth of this country, it is believed to embrace every possible advantage for imparting a thorough and practical knowledge of Spanish. A course of systematic grammar underlies the whole; but its development is so gradual and inductive as not to weary the learner. Numerous examples of regular and irregular verbs are presented; and nothing that can expedite the pupil's progress, in the way of explanation and illustration, is omitted.

From the Republic.

"It contains the best rules we have ever yet seen for learning a living language. It leads the student on, by almost imperceptible steps, from the simplest principles to the most recondite and complex combinations of grammatical constructions; and the parts are so arranged as to render every thing subservient to that which should be the chief point of view, the great object of ambition, viz., use, speech, conversation. Every part of speech, every simple and compound sentence, is so analyzed, so illustrated by explanatory dialogues, that it is impossible to open the book at any page without acquiring some valuable information capable of advancing the student in his progress as a linguist."

From the N. Y. Courier and Enquirer.

"The editors of this work are widely known as accomplished scholars and distinguished teachers, and the book derives still higher authority from their connection with it. We commend it with great confidence to all who desire to become acquainted with the Castilian tongue."

AN EASY INTRODUCTION
TO SPANISH CONVERSATION.
By M. VELAZQUEZ DE LA CADENA.
18mo. 100 pages. Price, 50 cents.

This little work contains all that is necessary for making rapid progress in Spanish conversation. It is well adapted for schools, and for persons who have little time to study, or are their own instructors.

ELEMENTARY SPANISH
READER. By M. F. TOLON. 12mo. 156 pages. · Price, $1.

This is one of the best elementary Spanish Readers, not only for the purposes of self-instruction, but also as a class-book for schools, that has ever been published. The contents are varied in style, including didactic, descriptive, colloquial, historical, and poetical extracts, drawn from the purest and most meritorious writers. The orthography conforms to that established by the Royal Academy. A full Vocabulary of all the words employed is appended, rendering a larger dictionary unnecessary.

STANDARD PRONOUNCING
SPANISH DICTIONARY: An Abridgment of Velazquez's Large Dictionary, intended for Schools, Colleges, and Travellers. In Two Parts. I. Spanish-English ; II. English - Spanish. By MARIANO VELAZQUEZ DE LA CADENA. 12mo. 883 pages. Price, $2.50.

In making this abridgment from the octavo edition, the author has constantly kept in view the wants of classes beginning the study of Spanish. By rejecting all obsolete words, unusual phrases, and exclusively scientific terms, as well as other superfluous matter, he has found room for everything likely to be needed by the ordinary pupil or the traveller, who would find it inconvenient to use the larger work. The fine typography, scholarly arrangement, and remarkable correctness of this Abridgment, have made it the acknowledged standard school dictionary of the Spanish language.

SEOANE'S NEUMAN AND
BARETTI'S Spanish-and-English, and English-and-Spanish Pronouncing Dictionary. By MARIANO VELAZQUEZ DE LA CADENA, Professor of the Spanish Language and Literature in Columbia College, N. Y., and Corresponding Member of the National Institute, Washington. Large 8vo. 1,300 pages. Neat type, fine paper, and strong binding. Price, $6.

The pronunciation of the Castilian language is so clearly set forth in this Dictionary, as to render it well-nigh impossible for any person who can read English readily to fail in obtaining the true sounds of the Spanish words at sight.

In the revision of the work, more than eight thousand words, idioms, and familiar phrases have been added.

It gives in both languages the exact equivalents of the words in general use, both in their literal and metaphorical acceptations.

Also, the technical terms most frequently used in the arts, in chemistry, botany, medicine, and natural history, as well as nautical and mercantile terms and phrases—most of which are not found in other Dictionaries.

Also many Spanish words used only in American countries which were formerly dependencies of Spain.

The names of many important articles of commerce, gleaned from the prices-current of Spanish and South American cities, are inserted for the benefit of the merchant, who will here find all that he needs for carrying on a business correspondence.

The parts of the irregular verbs in Spanish and English are here, for the first time, given in full, in their alphabetical order.

The work likewise contains a grammatical synopsis of both languages, arranged for ready and convenient reference.

The new and improved orthography sanctioned · by the latest edition of the Dictionary of the Academy—now universally adopted by the press—is here given for the first time in a Spanish-and-English Dictionary.

Ollendorff's Grammar for Teaching English to Spaniards.

GRAMATICA INGLESA : Un

Método para Aprender á Leer, Escribir y Hablar el Inglés, segun el Sistema de Ollendorff. Acompañado de un Apéndice que comprende en Compendio las Reglas contenidas en el cuerpo principal de la obra; un Tratado Sobre la Pronunciacion, Division y Formacion de las Palabras Inglesas; una Lista de los Verbos Regulares ó Irregulares, con sus Conjugaciones y las distantas Preposiciones que Rigen; Modelos de Correspondencia, etc., todo al alcance de la capacidad mas mediana. Por RAMON PALENZUELA y JUAN DE LA C. CARREÑO. 12mo. 457 pages. Price, $1.50.

KEY TO EXERCISES. Separate volume. Price, $1.

Spaniards desirous of learning English will find in this volume all that is needed for its speedy and thorough acquisition. The system adopted is clear, simple, philosophical and practical. It is essentially the system of the popular Ollendorff series ; accompanied with a full grammatical course, a treatise on English pronunciation, a list of the irregular verbs, models of correspondence, and other matters which, as the experience of Señores Palenzuela and Carreño has shown them, aid in removing the difficulties that have heretofore impeded and discouraged the Spanish learner.

TORNOS'S COMBINED

SPANISH METHOD: A New, Practical, and Theoretical System of Learning the Castilian Language, embracing the most advantageous features of the best-known Methods. With a Pronouncing Vocabulary, containing all the Words used in the course of the Work ; and References to the Lessons, in which each one is explained, thus enabling any one to be his own Instructor. By ALBERTO DE TORNOS, A. M., former-

ly Director of Normal Schools in Spain. 1 vol., 12mo. 470 pages. Price, $1.75.

"This volume is the result of the experience of twenty years as a teacher of the Spanish tongue. All the good features of the various methods which have been published within the last 100 years have been studiously examined, with the view of presenting to the public a theoretical and practical grammar, which the author now presents under the title of the COMBINED SPANISH METHOD."

D. Appleton & Co. also publish :—

BELLO (D. ANDRES). Compendio de la Gramática Castellana. 1 vol., 18mo. Price, 50 cents.

CERVANTES. El Ingenioso Hidalgo Don Quijote de la Mancha, segun el texto corregido y anotado por el Sr. Ochoa. 1 vol. 605 pages. 12mo. Price, $1.50.

DE MARCHENA (A. R.) Compendio de la Historia Antigua. 1 vol., 18mo. Price, 75 cts.

ELEMENTOS DE QUÍMICA ; Para uso de los Colegios y Escuelas. Por Eduardo I. Youmans, D. M. Traducido de la última edicion Inglesa, por Marco A. Rojas, D. M. 1 vol., 12mo. Price, $2.

ELEMENTOS DE HISTORIA UNIVERSAL, para uso de las Escuelas Suramericanas. 1 vol., 8vo. Cloth. Price, $3.

NUEVA BIBLIOTECA DE LA RISA, por una Sociedad de Literatos de Buen Humor. 1 vol., 12mo. Cloth. Price, $1.50. •

Portuguese.

A NEW METHOD OF LEARNING THE PORTUGUESE LANGUAGE. By E. J. Chaubert. 12mo. $1.50.